Tattoo of Crimson

Copyright © 2022 by Sarah Chislon

Cover design by Lena Yang

All rights reserved. No part of this book may be reproduced in any form or by any electronic or mechanical means, including information storage and retrieval systems, without written permission from the author, except for the use of brief quotations in a book review.

This is a work of fiction. Names, characters, places, and incidents either are the product of the author's imagination or are used fictitiously. Any resemblance to actual persons, living or dead, events, or locales is entirely coincidental.

www.sarahchislon.com

For CJ—my beloved husband.

You're a man of integrity—wise, kind, and steadfast. We've celebrated numerous blessings and delights and weathered many storms together. Through it all, I count it a privilege to do life with you. I love you, now and always.

SERIES READING ORDER

For the optimal reading experience, the *Blood of the Fae* series should be read in sequential order, starting with *Whispers in the Waters*—although you can begin with *Tattoo of Crimson*, if desired.

Series order:
   Whispers in the Waters (prequel)
   Tattoo of Crimson
   Ruins of Bone (coming October 2023)

Reader bonuses (available free to newsletter subscribers):
   Jewel of Blood: A *Blood of the Fae* short story
   Whispers in the Waters bonus scene
   Tattoo of Crimson bonus scene

https://go.sarahchislon.com/botf-series

CHAPTER 1

Never bargain with the fae, lest you condemn yourself to an unpleasant death—or a fate far worse. Mothers and fathers repeated this and similar cautions to their children; nannies, governesses, and tutors echoed the refrain until these warnings imprinted themselves on the souls of every child in the kingdom of Byren.

Even the smallest lisping infant knew the threat posed by the Otherworld. Yet some foolhardy individuals still ventured beyond its borders, either driven by a desire for wealth and conquest, compelled by desperate circumstances, or snared by some Otherworldly lure. Regardless of the cause, the outcome was always the same—disaster.

A disaster I'd no desire to invite into my life, yet one determined to find me, wherever I went. Enderly Park should have been safe, a stroll through its meandering paths an excursion suitable for ladies and gentlemen alike.

Yet when our carriage crossed through the iron gate marking the entrance to Enderly, pressure built at my temples, and my skin prickled with the uncanny sensation of *Other*. Never mind the claims of a recent spectre sighting within its bounds, since Enderly Park belonged to the city of Avons, any encroachment of the Otherworld should have been an impossibility. The Vigil prided itself on keeping the seat of the king well-warded from any possible fae incursion. No denizen of the Otherworld would dare tread here, at least according to those who guarded Avons.

Yet this tingle, as discomfiting as the rush of blood through numbed limbs, matched the sudden surge I'd first experienced weeks before in Milburn. Perhaps I could have excused it then, in an edgetown situated near a fae Crossing, but not here, not now.

It should not be.

Nor should I be fae-touched, when I'd never ventured into the Otherworld, when neither my mother nor my father had engaged with its inhabitants. Though I possessed no explanation, the affliction had strengthened, a taint I could no longer deny, one which altered my senses and tugged me down a path toward madness. Unwilling to be constrained, it battered against the cage of thorned vines I'd constructed within my mind to contain it.

Unless I wished to betray myself to my sisters, who occupied the bench opposite, I must hide these sensations, at least until I gained the knowledge to master them—or they overpowered me and deprived me of reason . . .

No, I could not allow myself to envision such a fate.

I leaned into the leather seat behind me, solid and cool despite the warm morning, and rubbed my temples. The safeguards I'd devised early in life—the exercise of strict control over my emotions and the cultivation of the cage within—had proven sufficient to prevent the fae-touch from consuming my mind in years past. After my encounter with water sprites in

Milburn, which strengthened it, I'd struggled to lock it away, and now Enderly exposed it once more.

More concerning, some part of me didn't *wish* to make the attempt, but quickened with longing for the connection I sought to sever.

Jade, my enormous black cat, clambered into my lap, and her throaty purr distracted me from the turmoil within. I turned my attention to the cheerful chatter of my sisters before they could notice anything amiss.

Across from me, Ainslie moved to the edge of her seat to better peer out the window between us. "What do you think, Jessa? Is Enderly everything you hoped?"

Beyond the glass, tall lilacs waved blossoming branches, and columbine, sweet briar, and forget-me-nots clustered beneath their boughs. The lavish beds flourished and expanded with wild abandon, a sharp contrast to the well-ordered and rigidly maintained parks closer to the center of Avons. Beyond these cultivated areas along the road stretched rolling hills of tall, waving grasses and wildflowers of every hue, and in the distance, a dark tree line marked the boundary between the park proper and the forest beyond.

"It . . . exceeds my expectations." In other circumstances, I'd linger to inspect and sketch as many of the blossoms as possible, seeking new additions for the herbalism guide that occupied much of my spare time. "It certainly deserves its reputation as the most magnificent park in Avons."

"As long as that's the only way it lives up to its reputation, all will be well." Ada tugged Ainslie back into a more proper position. "You'll tumble onto the floor if you don't take a care."

"It scarcely matters—there's no one here to witness if I do make a spectacle of myself, and I can endure a few bruises." Despite her protest, Ainslie folded her hands in a demure fashion and sat upright. Only the slight dimpling of her cheeks hinted that she humored Ada with her cooperation.

We continued toward the center of Enderly, lurching at intervals over ruts in the road. In search of further distraction, I sought my sketchbook, easing Jade to the bench beside me so I might have space to work. Though I'd captured my sisters' features countless times before, they still inspired me: lively Ainslie, the queen's glory rose, her striking beauty and vivid coloring attracting attention wherever she went; and sweet Ada, the soft ivory-and-pink ranunculus blooming alongside the rose, her lovely, engaging charm a perfect complement to her twin.

Sometimes I imagined I caught a glimpse of Mother in their faces. While living, she'd refused to have her portrait taken—she'd said only the vain indulged in the practice of placing their likenesses in prominent locations for all to admire—so I had to rely on my childhood memories to recreate her appearance. Had she shared the gentle curve of Ada's cheek? Or the sparkling smile with which Ainslie beguiled the world? Perhaps her eyes had been the deep brown of the twins' or maybe even the dark sapphire of my own . . . perhaps if she were here, she would understand what they did not.

My pencil had stilled, and I forced it into motion again. There was no sense reflecting on what was past, not with so many troubles in the present.

Ada and Ainslie fell silent, leaving only the clatter of carriage wheels over cobbled stone and the sweep of pencil over parchment to fill the void. I attended fully to my sketch, rather than the glorious view outside our windows, since the attempt restrained the pervasive sense of Other seeking to influence my thoughts.

After our driver halted the carriage, our footman, Ives

opened the door and offered his assistance down the steps. I waited with Jade, allowing Ada and Ainslie to disembark first.

Aunt Caris had insisted we needed Ives's accompaniment for protection against the recent threat of the Crimson Tattoo Killer. Though the Magistry assured all of Avons that the killer wouldn't strike in daylight nor in public view, Aunt Caris still maintained we must exercise every caution.

I couldn't fault her fears, not when most of Avons shared them. Never before had the city faced a series of murders, and certainly not any so unnerving, with the victims marked by a crimson tattoo they could not recall receiving shortly before their deaths. More than once I'd caught myself speculating on the unpleasant ways such a mark could be left—perhaps with the use of sedative herbs, or worse, alchemical devices. Regardless, the Magistry proclaimed their increased presence on the streets would keep us safe, and the king himself insisted we must live our lives with as much normalcy as possible, despite the looming threat. Aunt Caris would never gainsay the dictates of society, despite her own concerns, so here we were.

When Ives helped me down from the carriage, Jade rumbled low in her chest and glared at him. Through no fault of his own, he did not meet with her approval—very few did, and she shared her affections with none besides me.

Once I'd emerged from the confines of the carriage, the shock of life within Enderly rushed over me—the exuberant riot of creamy hawthorn blossoms, come early this spring; the shy carpet of violets beneath, murmuring their intent to ease hearts and calm minds; and the graceful sweep of beech branches above, celebrating the arrival of spring with a sap-quickening song . . . no.

I must not attend to their voices. The fae-touch sought to bend my senses and make me hear what I should not, but I refused to surrender. I wrapped my fingers around my ward-pendant, its etched stone cool to the touch, and concentrated on weaving the cage of thorns tight enough to choke out every aberration.

I could maintain control; I must.

After all, I was here for Ibbie. Given the many kindnesses my mentor had extended, including her support for my unladylike pursuit of publishing my herbalism guide, I'd take more than this slight risk on her behalf. I forced myself to move away from the haven of the carriage toward the fountain that rested at the heart of Enderly.

Numerous smaller paths wended away from the stone-cobbled center and the rushing fountain, time-worn trails etched into the earth. Unaware of my fears, Ada and Ainslie strolled down the nearest path, arm in arm, the dark curls Mother had bequeathed to all of us peeping from beneath their hats.

Something twisted within my chest. They always appeared to understand one another without words. If I shared whatever connected them as twins, might they perceive my struggle and extend that understanding to me?

As if she sensed the ache within, Jade nudged my ankle. I lifted her, and she scrambled into her favorite position, draped like a stole around my neck. Comforting warmth radiated through her thick fur. In both size and constancy of nature, she resembled a dog more than a cat. Since the day I'd found her grievously injured in our glasshouse and offered her a home, she'd become the companion I didn't know I'd longed for.

Despite her added weight, I hurried after my sisters, and Ives fell in behind me, while our driver remained at his post with the carriage. However indecorous, my pace allowed me to swiftly overtake Ada and Ainslie.

"I simply cannot believe spectres haunt Enderly. It's far too quiet and lovely," Ainslie said.

"Yet Lord Hemston gave a creditable account of his experience, and he's not known as a sensationalist, though I suppose he could have been mistaken or taken in by a prank." Ada glided down the uneven path with her usual grace, as though the irregular terrain were a well-polished ballroom floor. "I'll grant it's beautiful, though it's not as if beauty repels spectres."

Ainslie's dark brown eyes sparkled, and her lips curved upward. "More's the pity. If that were true, we'd all be safe for certain, according to Lord Fielding."

Ada laughed softly. "You can only give so much credence to a gentleman determined to claim one more dance than is proper."

Which was to say, none at all. I couldn't restrain a smile, despite my growing disquiet. Enderly should have offered a welcome haven, a respite from the bustle of Avons. Yet who could find refuge in a habitat that pulsed with life not altogether of this world? I shifted my collecting basket from one arm to the other. "It may be peaceful now, but I'm inclined to think if there were any place in Avons a spectre could strengthen enough to appear, it would be here."

Spectres didn't follow the normal pattern of Otherworldly beings, who were constrained to enter our world at Crossings. Instead, they could force a shadow of their form to move between worlds. Then they fed on the fear their uncanny appearance sparked, drawing strength from the terror they inflicted until they could appear as corporeal entities in our world.

"Well, I can't imagine the Vigil would allow anyone to venture into Enderly if they believed the rumors true." Ainslie nudged the brim of her hat back slightly and surveyed our surroundings as we trudged up a small hill. "Regardless, we must steel ourselves not to fear, no matter what we see, and sally forth—or admit ourselves bested by gossipmongers and sensationalists."

"There's no reason to—oh." At the top of the hill, I halted. To our right stretched a bedewed field shrouded with hundreds of spiderwebs, their gossamer threads shimmering in the early morning light. They even draped across the lower limbs of the nearest trees.

Ada tilted her head. "Perhaps you spoke too soon, Ainslie. That display rather mars the scenery."

It more than marred the view—the meadow appeared swathed in winding sheets and ready for burial. I gripped my collecting basket tighter. "Spiders, of all things. What would make them cluster so?"

"I'm not sure, but perhaps their presence—and this unnatural display—gave rise to the rumors of spectres," Ada said.

I lowered my gaze to the earthen path. Though it was illogical for one who favored time spent out-of-doors, I loathed spiders: their dark clustered eyes, their bulbous bellies filled with the blood of the living, their wisp-wire legs weaving nets to ensnare helpless prey.

If needs must, I could dispatch a venomous snake or snare a mouse and remove it from my bedchamber, but spiders . . . my toes curled within my leather walking boots.

Before I could propose taking an alternate, spider-free path, a jubilant melody impressed itself upon my soul, a call so insistent that it compelled me onward. I looked beyond the crystalline webs to where the meadow joined the forest. On this border, brilliant blossoms swayed in the breeze. Their fragrance, sweet as summer honey, drifted toward us, carrying a gentle offer to lighten the heart and lift the spirits—just what I sought for Ibbie. One of her periodic melancholies had fallen upon her, but this time it ran darker and deeper than usual, a megrim that refused to release its hold, one tinged with uncommon fear.

Not that the whole of Avons wasn't beset with fear, given the recent murders, but something more appeared to be at work within Ibbie. No matter the cause of her distress, I must find a way to lift her spirits . . . and after all she'd done to support my endeavors, I would venture into terrain far more unpleasant than this on her behalf. So, with a slight shudder, I approached the edge of the path and lifted the hem of my gown.

"Wait, Jessa. Surely you don't mean to cross *that*?" Ainslie wrinkled her nose.

"I see no other way to reach the tree line."

Ada reached out and caught my wrist. "Oh, Jessa. Your dress will be all over mud and damp. And who knows what creatures lurk in the undergrowth?"

"Spiders for a fact, and there may well be snakes, besides the rumored spectre." Ainslie brushed a curl away from her face, and the sun glimmered on the silvery-gray scar marking her upper arm. "Why must you reach the woods? There's ample opportunity to explore without venturing from the path."

"For that matter, you never explained why this expedition to Enderly is so important to you." Ada fixed me with a steady gaze, as though in so doing, she might compel me to speak truth. "I cannot believe you wish to add your name to the list of sensation seekers who have come here in recent weeks. We could have gone to any of the other charming parks Avons has to offer and not risked an Otherworldly encounter."

At least she credited me with more sense than those who sought spectres, goblins, or other low fae, in order to pass on lurid stories of their encounters, most likely figments of imagination, since the adventurers returned unscathed. While I weighed my words, Jade launched herself from my shoulders to stick her nose into the damp grass. She promptly sneezed and shook droplets of dew from her whiskers.

I gently pulled free from Ada's grasp. "When I mentioned to a local herbalist that I sought something to lift Ibbie's spirits, she told me Enderly is known for its rare plants." She'd added a caution about the peculiarity of the place, but I saw no need to share that. "I also thought I might find something I could use to formulate a new balm for Ainslie's scar."

Though Ainslie didn't possess a scrap of vanity, the peculiar scar on her upper arm troubled her more than she'd confess. She often rubbed at it or attempted to artfully arrange her sleeves or shawl to conceal the pattern of fine lines. Over the past several months, I'd crafted countless healing balms and salves, combining and recombining herbs and oils in an attempt to smooth the lines and soothe the residual discomfort. Yet nothing faded the symmetrical mark in the slightest, not even the salve that had healed our cook of a severe burn, crafted from the amelior I'd brought home from my travels.

It defied reason. But I delighted in a good puzzle, and I'd not yet given up.

"I've begun to think it's here to stay." A furrow creased Ainslie's brow, but she attempted a casual lift of her slim shoulders. "Perhaps if anyone takes note, I shall simply claim it came from an attack by highwaymen from which I scarcely escaped with my life. It would keep them so busy discussing my harrowing tale that they'd soon forget the scar altogether."

Yet Ainslie herself could not, though she claimed she couldn't remember how she'd come by the injury that caused it, a peculiarity I found troubling. But if she wished to keep her own counsel, I was in no position to cast blame, not when my own secrets wove an ever-tightening web about me.

Ada unfurled her lace-edged parasol to block the strengthening sun. "As for Lady Dromley, I'm sure she'd be pleased to receive any of the lovely blooms you've grown in our gardens. Or if you mean to make her a decoction, why not the one you gave Aunt Caris?"

"They don't share the same ills." It was true enough. The simple myrobalan syrup that brought Aunt Caris relief from nightmares of the killer and eased her daytime fears would never suit the deeper melancholy that rested on Ibbie, yet I left out the more dangerous explanation—that I came to Enderly because none of the plants growing within our gardens or among the other Avons parks and lanes whispered assurance of bringing Ibbie relief.

If my sisters knew the way plants called to me, how they revealed their natures with such vigor that I was hard-pressed to block them out, it would endanger them as much as me. Unless they chose to turn me over to the Vigil for confinement in an Institution, they could receive accusation themselves—and would certainly bear the shame of my taint, should the truth become known. Even if it were not revealed in public, could I bear the look in their eyes if they understood my disgrace?

My throat tightened, but I forced a smile. "Besides, you know Ibbie appreciates the rare and unusual."

Ada adjusted the angle of her parasol. "Perhaps you could choose something closer to the path?"

"Nothing that would compare to those." I gestured to the profusion of white-gold blooms skirting the forest, a stark contrast to the deep greens and browns beyond. "They're just what she needs."

"I don't know how you can tell from this distance—"

Before Ada could seek to sway me further, I plunged into the field, a large stick held before me to clear away the webs. The tall grasses and wildflowers brushed my skirt, and I endeavored to block visions of spindly limbs crawling upward and scrabbling against my skin.

I quickened my pace, and Jade kept stride, gingerly picking her way across the wet grass. Together we forged a dark trail across the dewy meadow, though when I glanced back some trick of light made it appear as if fog swirled through our footsteps.

The sensation of crawling legs crept over my skin once more, but I ignored it, attending instead to the flowers lining the woods. They swayed gently, bobbing in the breeze, their unfamiliar forms beckoning me onward.

The glorious white blossoms waved above glossy black-green leaves, their pale petals forming a star around centers of darkest gold. From the central star, tiny tendrils feathered out around each petal, giving the bloom an ethereal appearance. I knelt in the grass before them and skimmed the silken blooms with my fingertips. The tension ebbed from my shoulders, and the spider-scratching sensation vanished. I inhaled their sweet-spice scent, and peace seeped into my soul.

They were perfect for Ibbie.

Most herbalists and scholars agreed that the strongest herbs in our world grew near Crossings, though of course, those failed to compare to the strength of Otherworldly materials, used by alchemists to create powerful devices and compounds. The potency of these blossoms lent credence to my sense of Other within Enderly. But no Crossing intersected Enderly, nor anywhere near Avons, so what influence held sway here?

It was a conundrum for another day, perhaps one that might be solved by time within the library stacks, but only after I'd dealt with the more pressing problem—unearthing whatever I could about how fae-touch might be constrained, were such a thing possible.

For now, I loosened three of the plants—which I dubbed goldhearts—from the soil, preserving their roots. They freed themselves willingly, and I tucked them into the nest of my earth-filled basket, their spiced-honey fragrance permeating my surroundings.

As I worked, a low keening sound emanated from the forest. A prickle started at the base of my spine and tingled up toward my neck. When I lifted my head to seek the source of the moan, a fluttering of palest gray caught my eye, shimmering between the evergreen hemlock boughs deeper in the forest. A bird, perhaps?

Jade stalked forward, her green eyes glinting in the sunlight, her pupils narrowed.

The flutter of gray broke through the branches again, still nebulous, but far too large to be a bird of any sort. The prickle strengthened. I fumbled in my reticule for the small penknife I used to sharpen my sketching pencils, though it would do little against an Otherworldly intruder. Then I edged closer to the forest.

Ada called out, "Where are you going, Jessa?"

"I think I see something in the woods." And I wasn't about to allow it near my sisters.

"Whatever it is, you should stay out of the forest—it's beyond the bounds of Enderly." A note of urgency threaded Ainslie's voice. "Oh, Ives, fetch her back."

"There's no need," I called over my shoulder. If this were a spectre, and I displayed fear by turning and fleeing toward safety, it might well materialize in full and take up the pursuit, endangering my sisters. I'd driven away the sprites in Milburn; surely I could find a way to keep a spectre from my sisters within the far-more-civilized bounds of Avons. I must show it I did not fear, then perhaps it would leave us alone.

I unfolded the penknife to expose the blade and strained to perceive what lurked within the depths of the forest without freeing the sensations born of my fae-touch. It might allow me to discern more, but at what cost? I'd scarcely maintained control after I allowed it liberty in Milburn.

I couldn't risk it again.

So I must rely on whatever information my mortal senses could provide. I stepped nearer once more. The mists swirling around the trees—mists which had not existed moments before—obscured my vision. Through the wafting white, a shape of darkening gray coalesced, closer now.

The form moved with a peculiar gait, flicking between trees, in and out of view, growing darker as it approached. Like the mournful call of a dusk-owl, a desolate, aching cry ripped from its throat.

I closed my eyes and inhaled the fragrance of the goldhearts. Their white-and-gold joy blazed through me, strengthening my resolve. If I truly witnessed a spectre, and not merely a young blade intending to play a prank on those who sought a thrill, I'd not permit it the chance to prey on my sisters.

When I allowed my eyes to open, the mist-shrouded form appeared between the boles of two tremendous elms, only a few ells away, close enough to reveal a splash of crimson amid the shades of smoke and ash—and to intensify the sensation of Other prickling down my spine.

No doubt remained.

A bitter chill stole through my limbs, and I wrapped my arms around myself. I'd spent my entire life working to exert control over my emotions, and I refused to fail now. I would not fear, would not strengthen this apparition. But how might I repel it? Could it be as simple as rejecting any claim it might have over my emotions? Fae often sought to entertain themselves at mortal expense, and if I offered no such promise . . .

"I'm not afraid of you." I lifted my blade, and the wind carried my words into the woods. "It's time you were gone."

The misty form wavered, then vanished behind the trunk of an elm—and I could breathe once more.

"What do you see, Jessa?" Ada asked.

I lifted my basket but did not release my hold on the penknife. "It's nothing. I was mistaken."

I turned my back on the forest.

CHAPTER 2

When I rejoined my sisters, they insisted we depart Enderly at once, despite the reassurances I offered. I didn't protest, since I shared their sentiments. My shoulders tingled as if at any moment the spectre might hook its clawed fingers across them and pull me into the Otherworld, from which there would be no escape. No, it was past time to take our leave, even if I hadn't yet found an herb to aid Ainslie.

In my haste to flee the shrouded meadow, I stumbled over a stone. Ives murmured, "Careful, miss," but I paid him no heed, attending only to strengthening the wards within.

The meandering path seemed to stretch interminably, but at last we reached our carriage. When we traveled through the iron gate bounded by tall white stones that marked the border of Enderly, the prickling sense of Other subsided, and some of the pressure in my chest eased.

Yet I couldn't blot out the image of the spectral form in the trees, a splash of charcoal and crimson lurking amid the dark hemlocks and pallid mists. Though we'd left Enderly behind, whispers still threaded past the fraying seams of my cage of thorns, perhaps strengthened by my elevated emotions.

The few days since our return from Milburn had offered me no opportunity to unearth answers on how to prevent my fae-touch from consuming me. One way or another, I had to regain control—and buy myself time to find the information I needed.

Within my mind, I rehearsed familiar passages from the Script, first the proper way, then in reverse, word by word. The rigid structure of the exercise forced my thoughts into order and pushed the errant sensations beneath the surface.

The strike of hooves against stone mingled with the clatter of the carriage, and all the while, Ada and Ainslie debated whether we'd come near the rumored spectre or if I'd caught a glimpse of some innocuous forest creature, as I'd suggested earlier. Beyond the windows, sunlight sparkled off the polished globes of the gas lamps lining the streets, radiating good cheer that did not suit my mood.

An ache pulsed at the sides of my head.

The moment we reached our townhome, I fled the discussion of what I wished to forget. When our butler Holden opened the door, I paused in the arched opening long enough to murmur my thanks before I passed into the entry. While the cool greens and ivories of the floral paper-hangings and the relative silence of the interior soothed, I craved solitude. I hastened down the long corridor and out the back door to the gardens.

From its corner against our back wall, the glasshouse beckoned, promising peace, if only I could ignore the murmurs of the plants within and without. But no sooner had I entered its embrace, the scents of earth and loam and greenery wafting about me, than Ainslie appeared.

She surged into the glasshouse like a tempestuous autumn wind and perched on an overturned crate. "Why were you so quiet on the way home? You always want answers, even to the most mundane of questions, so I cannot credit your disinterest in what you saw."

"I wasn't disinterested, only sobered by the reflection that I could have put you in danger by pressing for a visit to Enderly." I placed the collecting basket on the ground beside the door, and Jade curled herself around it, purring.

"You're certain there's nothing more?" She leaned forward on her precarious perch, and the aged crate creaked beneath her. "Since your travels with Aunt Caris, you've seemed troubled at times, and so has she. We—Ada and I—just wondered if something went amiss on your journey."

Only an indisputable confirmation of my fae-touch, a bargain with sprites, and a secret Aunt Caris refused to disclose. I bent to fetch a rich blue pot from the shelf tucked beneath the nearest table and so hid my face. "Did Ada dispatch you to make inquiries?"

"You know her well." She dimpled. "She's asked perhaps a dozen times since your return if I believed you *quite* all right, and when I told her this morning to cease her mother-henning, she insisted she couldn't until her mind was set at ease. So here I am to unearth the truth."

Blight and rot, I thought I'd done a better job concealing my struggles these past few days. "I'll grant I've been more . . . weary since our travels. I didn't anticipate what staying in an edgetown would be like, and of course, Aunt Caris's friend was struggling. But truly, there's no need for concern."

She lifted a perfectly arched brow, her skepticism evident. "Then you'll agree to pay calls with us later this week? You've scarcely ventured out since your return from Milburn, except to the library and to visit Lady Dromley."

If that was the price I must pay to alleviate their concerns, then so be it. "If you wish—"

Ainslie leapt up from the crate. "Wonderful! It will be lovely, all three of us together again. There's a family newly come to Avons, whom we just met at Lady Haverstock's dance, and their daughter is of an age with you and perfectly charming—"

A faint swirl of gray at the edge of my vision distracted me from Ainslie's rambles. My breath caught, and I whirled to face the south corner full-on, but found nothing amiss, only the cluster of sweet orange trees spreading branches above the assorted blossoms below.

I gripped the pot with whitening fingers. To imagine the spectre had followed me here . . . it was absurd. Evidently, I'd not done as well at suppressing the fae-touch as I believed—or madness had already begun to sway my senses.

I turned my back to the south corner and knelt to place the goldhearts in their new home. Ainslie continued to chatter, and I murmured some vague affirmation as I tucked the flowers in. I'd plant two within the pot for Ibbie and save one to nest beneath the oak in our garden so I might fully study its properties in the future.

"That's settled then." Ainslie brushed the detritus of the crate from her skirt, pressed a kiss to my forehead, and glided from the glasshouse.

Wait, what had I agreed to unaware? I knew better than to allow these peculiar sensations to distract me—it was far too dangerous. I bowed my head until it brushed the soft petals of the goldheart, and they caressed my cheek, their gentle touch and sweet fragrance reassuring. Never mind the events of the morning, I still had time before Father expected my assistance with his correspondence. Surely I could collect myself before then.

I withdrew my sketchbook to draw the goldhearts. Later, I'd capture them again in watercolor, or perhaps in oil, a better fit for their vibrant tones. They'd be a worthy addition to my manuscript on plants and herbs, which currently made its rounds to the publishers in Avons and beyond, seeking one which would see its worth and accept it.

Before I sent it out again, perhaps I could add a section that addressed issues of melancholy and other afflictions of spirit, not only physical maladies. How many people could that aid? Though Father refused to speak of it, Mother had suffered from low spirits at times, particularly in the weeks before we lost her, a fact which led some to speculate after her passing as to the true cause of her death . . .

My pencil scratched across the page, a line too harsh and dark to suit the blossoms, and I removed it with my rubber. Best not reflect too long on such matters, but rather attend to what I might do to help others so afflicted.

Would my ideas find welcome or scorn? I supposed it mattered little, since none would hear of them, unless I convinced a publisher to take a risk on my manuscript. Ibbie—the only one who knew of my hopes—championed it with zeal, but so far, even she had met with unyielding resistance.

Jade curled up on my feet, and I lost myself in the process of creation until familiar footfalls crunched along the crushed-stone path. Aunt Caris approached, but instead of entering the glasshouse, she veered toward the sheltered bench at the heart of the small garden.

A few moments later, brisk steps followed, announcing a far less welcome visitor.

"There you are, Caris." Aunt Melisina marched up to her. "We have matters to discuss."

Aunt Caris sighed. Perhaps she'd sought the gardens for a

brief respite from responsibility—or simply to avoid Aunt Melisina—but whatever her purpose, there'd be no escape now.

Instinctively, I withdrew deeper into the glasshouse. My last encounter with Aunt Melisina had left me feeling like an awkward, ill-bred child. If she found me in the gardens once more, with dirt-stained hands and missing hat, she'd not hesitate to make her disapproval known. I had an abundance of aunts and uncles, some scattered far beyond Avons, but none so . . . trying as Aunt Melisina. I attempted to immerse myself in my sketchbook but failed to block out her strident voice.

"I heard from Ada that the girls visited Enderly today," Aunt Melisina said. "Whatever were you thinking, allowing them on such an unorthodox expedition? They may be accustomed to romping about the countryside near Caldwell House, but they're in town now and must behave like proper young ladies."

"I was given to understand a trip to the park was an acceptable excursion." Aunt Caris spoke softly.

"Perhaps Calcot Park or even Benhem, places where one might stroll and be *seen*. But the wilds of Enderly? It's scarcely within the bounds of Avons, and its reputation?" She rapped the handle of her furled parasol against the bench where Aunt Caris sat. "It will never do."

Aunt Caris murmured something conciliatory, but Aunt Melisina cut her off. "Ada and Ainslie appear to understand what's necessary to move in society, even if Alden has permitted them to refuse several excellent matches, but since he decided to bring you and Jessa from Caldwell House to take up residence in Avons, they've been led astray. I must conclude the fault lies with you. When the twins were in my home this past season, they certainly indulged in no such nonsense. You must exert yourself to govern all the girls with a stronger hand, but particularly Jessa."

"Now, Melisina, she's done no harm."

"No harm? If she persists in keeping company with Lady Dromley and entertaining all her ridiculous notions of women in academia, she'll gain a reputation as a bluestocking."

"Surely not—"

"And those callouses on her hands are appalling. To take interest in the design of one's garden won't raise brows, but when one stoops to muck about in the dirt like a gardener—well, it won't be viewed with favor."

Heat swept up my cheeks, and I clutched the sketchbook to my chest. I shouldn't be here, listening. I should have revealed myself as soon as Aunt Melisina arrived—it was my duty as a niece—and then I would not have overheard the condemnation she heaped upon me.

Aunt Caris sighed again. "But it brings her such pleasure."

"All well and good, but you can't pretend it won't hurt her chances. I would never consider such a girl for my own Lovell. No, if she's to make a good match, she must conceal her peculiarities in order to appear to best advantage. Her looks will stand her in good stead as they have her sisters, but given their dowries are less than impressive, we must be prudent. Besides, you can't say you believe her interests well-suited to a lady."

"Perhaps the drawing, but . . . otherwise, not particularly." The words emerged slow and reluctant.

"There you have it." Aunt Melisina's voice echoed with triumph.

Jade clambered onto my lap, and I pulled her close. I knew I didn't belong, could never quite *fit* with those I loved, despite my best efforts, but to hear it expressed so plainly that my natural inclinations must be set aside, that I must conceal my true interests so I might find a favorable match and thus avoid becoming a burden to my family . . . oh, it was impossible.

Yet the alternatives to an arranged marriage presented equal difficulties. To wed for love, as Mother had done, would be a privilege denied me. Keeping my secret from my family was difficult enough, but concealing it from a man I vowed to love? A breeze pulled the sharp scent of wormwood from the gardens, and it swirled unpleasantly around me.

No, if I shared any sort of true intimacy, it would surely expose the truth of my fae-touch in time. Then the man in question would face the impossible choice I'd fought to keep from my family—report me to the Vigil, so I might be Institutionalized to protect those around me from the believed-to-be-inevitable madness brought on by fae-touch, or suffer the consequences of flouting the law.

Aunt Melisina and Aunt Caris had fallen silent, perhaps contemplating the magnitude of the task before them, even as I considered my choices.

If I did not wed, then what? Mother had left a small legacy to my sisters and me that would come to us upon our majority, but would it provide sufficient support for a simple life? Or would I become dependent on whichever relation would take me in? If I followed my own inclinations and sought some sort of position to assist others as I had Ibbie, it would ruin my family.

I bent over and buried my face in Jade's fur, and my stays dug into tender flesh, a rebuke against poor posture.

At last, Aunt Caris spoke. "What do you propose, sister?"

"Jessa must begin to appear in society," Aunt Melisina said. "It's too late in the year for any sort of formal presentation at court, but she can begin to mingle in more intimate gatherings —dinner parties, small dances, musicales. It's become common in Avons for younger daughters to move about in such a way even before their elder sisters are wed. Certainly, with the three girls so close in age, no one would look askance upon it. At twenty, she should have already been full out."

"She has no interest in—"

"It doesn't matter." Another rap of the parasol. "Don't you want to see her well-situated?"

"Of course." This time, Aunt Caris's voice trembled.

My heart squeezed at the sound. All Aunt Caris had ever cared about was our well-being, so such a barb must have sunk deep. Would it move her to redouble her efforts to see us wed? I shifted against the slats of the bench. Surely I needn't worry overmuch now, not while they had Ada and Ainslie to consider. But once my sisters married . . .

Jade squirmed in my arms, and I loosened my hold on her. Marriage—or lack thereof—would be a trouble for another day. She nudged my chin, a gentle demand for me to stroke her favorite spot, the starflower patch of white fur on her chest.

As I attended Jade, they discussed plans for my future, Aunt Caris acceding to Aunt Melisina's wishes as always. After all, Aunt Melisina was the successful sister, wed to Lord Stanford, with a fortune and a prominent position, while Aunt Caris was a spinster living in the household of her brother, doomed to a life of obscurity—if society were to be believed.

Yet Aunt Caris enjoyed rich connection with her family that Aunt Melisina utterly lacked, and she possessed the ability to give and receive love in a way that mattered. She'd sacrificed so much to raise us after Mother passed, her own opportunities for a husband and family, her future and whatever desires and dreams she might once have possessed. If I must move into society to avoid causing her distress and to make peace between her and Aunt Melisina, then so be it.

Only, what else would they demand? I stared at my partially

completed drawing, and the leaded lines blurred beneath my gaze.

∼

I*n the deepest night*, Mother walked through the gardens of Caldwell House, her hair unbound and tumbling down her back, glossy in the moonlight. Mist wafted around her.

I called to her, but she could not hear.

She moved farther down the path toward the fountain, its waters shimmering silver like a beacon in the night.

I hurried after her.

Around the fountain, something stirred—what? Vines. They writhed past its borders, sinuous as snakes, coiled around her ankles, pulled her off her feet.

She fought for a hold, but the pebbled path offered no purchase.

"Mother!"

She lifted her head, whispered my name.

And then they dragged her away.

I extended a hand toward the vines, willing them to release, willing them to return her to me . . . but they ignored my plea, and she vanished into the misty night.

The scritch and scrabble of dark vines against unyielding ground drifted back to me as I ran after Mother, the only remnant of her passing . . .

Scritch, scratch, scritch.

I woke with a gasp, the bedcovers twined round my limbs, my body damp with perspiration. It was only a dream—yet the rasping of vines refused to fade.

Scratch, scritch.

The sound issued from the south window, faint enough I could *almost* dismiss it. Instead, I disentangled myself from the covers and crept to the window, where I drew back the curtains. Thick swaths of ivy crisscrossed the glass panes, ivy that hadn't been there when I'd retired the night before, the weight of my aunts' disapproval still a heavy burden.

I recoiled, stumbling over the edge of the rug behind me in my haste to distance myself from the sight.

The ivy murmured low and mournful, and I shrank back further still. It should not, could not be here. Ivy might grow quickly, but not overnight. What would Aunt Caris say if she noticed? How could I explain the inexplicable?

Somehow I must remove it before anyone took note. I drew a deep breath and forced myself to lift the lower sash, which groaned as I wrenched it upward. The ivy hung in the void it left, swaying ever so slightly.

I reached for the stiff leaves, and when I touched their glossy surface, they trembled. I couldn't get leverage to detach the aerial rootlets that anchored all the way down the side of the house, but they must go. Perhaps it was early enough that I might fetch a ladder without attracting attention . . . but then the vines quailed. One tendril after another, they loosened themselves and tumbled back down to the trellis below.

A wave of dizziness swept over me, and I gripped the window frame to keep from tumbling after them. Jade leapt upon the sill and peered down, chattering in a peculiar way.

"I know. I don't like it either."

Dislike was an understatement, for a number of horrifying possibilities worked through my mind, putting down roots and spreading as fast as knotweed. What did it portend? Was it another sign that the taint of my fae-touch was spreading?

I nudged Jade from the sill and firmly closed the sash, then crossed to the washbasin and scrubbed my hands twice to rid myself of any residue left by the ivy.

It was early yet, and only Father awaited at the well-appointed breakfast table, already immersed in a stack of gazettes. He mumbled a greeting, but experience taught me he would offer little conversation to distract from the memory of climbing vines . . . and of Mother.

He'd discarded the society section of the *Morning Chronicle*, and it rested on the surface across from my chair. One of the headlines featured Aunt Melisina's latest dinner party. The article went on to detail the many courses, the perfect décor, her own magnificent gown, and the dashing appearance of her son Lovell. The reminder of her plans for me within society stole what little appetite remained after the ivy incident.

I took my seat and nudged the article away.

Jade leapt into the chair beside mine and watched me expectantly, black pupils wide in her green eyes. When I passed her choice bits of sausage and cured ham, she nudged my hand in appreciation before settling down to enjoy her meal.

Before I could think better of it, I asked, "Father, what did Mother want for us?"

"Your mother?" He looked up, blinking. "What do you mean?"

"What did she hope for our futures?"

He cleared his throat. "She wanted your happiness, always."

"But what did that mean to her?" Would she have urged me to countermand my own inclinations and make a suitable match, regardless of whether my affections were engaged? Or would she have encouraged me to seek a bond with my husband like the one she'd shared with Father? Could I have confided in her, could she have advised me on the impossibility of my situation?

"She had her own ideas." His voice dropped low. "I can't speak for her. Would that you could ask her yourself."

I unfolded my napkin onto my lap, tracing the embroidered edge with one finger. Talking of Mother always pained Father, but it was safer than making the more important inquiry—how did *he* define our happiness? If I dared ask outright, he might take the opportunity to lend support to Aunt Melisina's plans. Unlike her, he had the authority to enforce them. It wasn't his way to impose his will on his daughters, but still, it was better to keep this all in the realm of theory. I stirred sugar into my tea. "Would she have kept us in Avons, seeking suitors?"

He returned one of the gazettes to the stack beside his plate and rummaged for another. "I can't imagine it. She wasn't fond of Avons society."

"I didn't realize."

"It's why we spent most of our time at Caldwell House. Why she insisted on taking those trips to Thornhaven, despite its proximity to Aelfgard Crossing. She said it cleared her mind."

Mother had come of age and into a familial inheritance before she wed Father, some of which she'd used to purchase Thornhaven, while much of it later went into the Caldwell coffers to bolster the estate. I'd known she'd loved Thornhaven—and Caldwell House—yet it never occurred to me that with all her poise, she might have preferred to avoid society.

"We can't dwell on the past. You know that, Jessa. Your aunts will look after you and see you have a bright future. You've no need for concern."

On the contrary, if that were the case, I'd *every* reason for concern. Father lifted the gazette to hide his face, ending the conversation. I studied the carved mantel across from me, the portrait of Grandmother and Grandfather looming large above it. If Father meant to leave my future in the hands of my aunts . . .

No, I refused to borrow future trouble, for problems enough

plagued me already. They had Ada and Ainslie to seek matches for before they'd turn their full attention to my own matrimonial prospects.

I attempted to focus on the slim book of conundrums I'd brought in case of a quiet meal, an attempt to distract myself with figurative problems. Yet finding the solutions brought less satisfaction than usual, and before long, I only stared blankly at the words. The patterns of ivy seemed to crisscross the page before me, and the buttery scone turned dry in my mouth. What was I to do if my fae-touch continued to strengthen?

On our travels home from Milburn, I'd had time to work out a plan for how I could investigate my fae-touch without drawing undue attention. One might imagine gathering such information would be a simple matter—yet fears and rumors abounded, and a cursory search had confirmed that the capacious libraries of Avons held little accessible information. It would take time to dig deeper into adjacent subjects, in hopes of gleaning some kernels of truth.

If one wished to know about fae-touch, the most logical associated topic was the Vigil. They guarded their knowledge as fiercely as a dragon its hoard, justifying their secrecy as necessary to protect the kingdom from the Otherworld. Yet if I could manage to learn more about them, I might gain insight.

None of the libraries kept records of the Vigil, so I'd turned to Ibbie, asking her if she could obtain an obscure tome on their history. Bless her, for she'd not looked askance at my request nor required my reasons, only ordered it from one of the many book vendors she patronized throughout Byren. She generously suggested I keep it as long as I desired before returning it to her collection—and she'd sent word last night that it had arrived.

I snapped my book shut and rose. Despite the early hour, I

would call upon Ibbie, then venture to Spenser's Repository for deeper exploration into the world of fae and mortal encounters.

I collected my hat and gloves and escaped to the garden. The ivy-covered trellis loomed dark and formidable against the honey-colored stone of the house. I shivered slightly and turned away.

Never mind that now; Ibbie awaited. Aunt Caris always said the best way to forget one's troubles was to offer aid to someone else, and I'd found her advice true on more than one occasion. I gathered the potted goldhearts, placing them within a covered basket for easier transport, and then attempted to coax Jade into a particularly brilliant patch of sunlight.

She would have none of it; she persisted in bobbing and weaving between my ankles.

"You can't come with me today. You know Ibbie dislikes cats, and I wish to lighten her spirits, not trouble her further."

A low rumble emerged from Jade.

"I'd prefer to leave you here to watch over the glasshouse, but if I must, I'll take you to my bedchamber."

She fixed me with a gleaming green glare.

"You know I'd take you if I could. Perhaps later we'll walk in the park. But for now, what's it to be?"

After a moment, she stalked over to the patch of light and stretched out in its warmth as if it had been her idea all along. Only a slight twitch of her tail hinted at her displeasure.

I lifted the latch on the iron gate, the chill metal biting against my fingers, and slipped from the gardens into the stone footwalk that ran alongside the cobbled streets of Avons. As I strolled down the winding ways, my spirits lightened. The gentle thrum of activity at this hour was invigorating, not overwhelming like the later crush would be, and the sun had yet to draw out some of the more unpleasant city scents.

After Aunt Melisina's criticisms the day before, if Aunt Caris had been present at my departure, she may well have insisted I take our lady's maid along rather than roam Avons unchaperoned. Yet as she remained abed, I could enjoy solitude on this brilliant morning. If that changed, if every move within Avons must be attended by watchful eyes lest the very act of strolling through the city give rise to scandal, as Aunt Melisina appeared to believe, our stay in the city would swiftly become untenable.

A silverwing fluttered down to land on an iron lamppost and chirred a pleasing song before soaring up between the towering rows of townhomes. Their tall, narrow frames, fashioned of sovstone, and their capped roofs of deep blue slate—a shade said to repel aerial fae—presented a tidy, rather pleasing appearance. Yet not for the first time, I yearned for the sprawling expanse of hill and forest at Caldwell House and the bountiful beauty out-of-doors there that Avons could not begin to match.

By the time I arrived at Wyncourt, the day had warmed considerably. The house loomed above me, its windows peering out at the street like dark eyes in the face of a giant. Unlike the rowhouse in which we lived, Wyncourt sprawled in an asymmetrical expanse that always gave me a slightly out-of-kilter feeling. I preferred not to attend it too long.

I lifted the stately brass knocker and gave a gentle rap, awaiting Danvers, Ibbie's butler.

Instead of Danvers, a new, unfamiliar servant greeted me at the door. The tall, narrow-faced man offered a slight nod, followed by a close examination. "Lady Dromley is not at home."

A polite dismissal, for where else would she be at this hour? If he held doubts about my suitability to call on Lady Dromley, he should have extended a polite invitation to wait in the entry while he ascertained if his lady was at home. Perhaps he was untrained, but Ibbie tolerated no incompetence in her staff—and this man didn't hold himself as a servant would. The basket handles dug into my arm, and I shifted uncomfortably. "Are you certain she's not at home? She requested I call this morning."

"So you say." His eyes narrowed further.

How was it that a servant dared interrogate a guest? And where was Danvers? He never failed to answer the door and offer a warm greeting, no matter the hour of my call. I edged forward. "It's important that I see Ibb—Lady Dromley. As I said, I'm here at her request."

His gaze lingered a moment on the large basket I held, but at last he gave a slight bow. "I'll ask Lady Dromley if she's receiving."

He stepped back to allow me into the entrance hall. While I waited, several soft creaks and groans came from within Wyncourt, as if it disapproved of the peculiar goings-on within its walls.

A moment later, Ibbie swept into the entryway in a flurry of dark gray silk, a shade she favored for its stain-concealing properties. She brushed a kiss across my cheek, and her damask rose perfume swirled around me. "Forgive the lack of welcome. I've been so distracted this morning that I entirely forgot to tell Robart you were expected—but come, come!"

Skirt rustling, she bustled down the corridor to her study, and I followed in her wake. In the confines of the study, at least, nothing had changed. Papers lay scattered across an enormous mahogany desk, an uncapped ink bottle had flaked specks of dried pigment around its rim, and books towered in precarious stacks all over the room, some having already toppled from their lofty heights. Only the antiquities had been meticulously catalogued and organized, then encased in glass where no harm might come to them.

Ibbie left the door slightly ajar, and Robart lurked in the corridor, his attention locked upon us. I angled my body away from him and surreptitiously studied Ibbie. She wore a mask of determined good cheer, which, along with ceaseless activity, were her favored methods of concealing any hint of melancholy from the world. For all her efforts, she couldn't hide the deep shadows pooled beneath her eyes, nor the muting of their bright blue into a murky-sea gray.

Before I could make my offering, she lifted a paper-wrapped parcel. "I'm glad you came yourself to fetch this, for I have some news to share. Ill news, I'm afraid."

I accepted with murmured thanks and waited.

Ibbie squared her shoulders. "Fancourt Press declined your herbalism guide."

"Well, I can't say it's unexpected." Still, something twisted in my chest. On pretense of making space for my basket on the nearest worktable, I turned aside. "I appreciate all you've done, but if he has declined along with the others, then perhaps there's some fault in the manuscript I cannot see."

"Nonsense." She rounded her desk. "You know I don't believe in mincing words. If it was about a lack of merit in your work, I'd recommend you reconsider your path, but that's not the case. I've known Mr. Fancourt since he was in small pants, so I demanded an answer as to why he declined. He danced around the matter, of course, but in the end, it's simple as this: none of them want the risk of putting a woman's name on what would be an authoritative work in the field. They think it won't garner the necessary respect, won't be worth the risk in printing."

And it would be no small risk, given the cost of the countless illustrations meant to aid in proper plant identification. I sank into a chair, the stacked papers crackling beneath me. "I see."

"It's absurd." Ibbie paced the room. Sunlight poured through the nearest window, glinting across the white strands woven into her cinnamon-brown hair and emphasizing a new gauntness in her usually full features. "I mean to take matters into my own hands and invest in printing equipment myself."

"No, Ibbie. You've done so much already—"

"It's high time I took action. Life's too short to wait for others to accomplish what one can do for oneself."

"But, Ibbie—"

"It will serve me as well, since I want to publish the results of the antiquarian expedition Mr. Tibbons carried out on my behalf in Bervale." She rummaged through a drawer and procured several pamphlets—perhaps printing samples? "I owe it to you that I've returned to what I love. Your passion for your work gave me the courage to pursue my own once more. Why shouldn't I return the favor?"

"There are no debts between friends." A faint shuffling sound in the corridor reminded me of Robart's presence. Never mind him, I must speak. "I'm deeply grateful, but what Mr. Fancourt and the others have said is true. The risks and expenses are considerable. If you do this, and I fail . . . I don't want to let you down."

"Who else should I spend my resources on?" She closed the drawer with more force than necessary and set the pamphlets on the desk. "I have no children, and my husband is gone. I'd rather use what I have on your behalf than that of some distant relation. I'm doing as *I* wish for once. Why shouldn't I suit myself while I still can?"

While she still could? The back of my neck tingled as though wisps of cobweb brushed my skin. "There's something more. Something wrong."

With ink-stained fingers, Ibbie plucked at the ruby brooch holding her shawl in place. "I merely intend to see matters handled properly, rather than wait around for others to accomplish what I can better manage myself. I wasted so many years, burying my dreams and desires, feeling nothing after Edward left—attempting to find consolation in becoming a patroness to those carrying out the work I longed to do myself. Now there's no time to waste, and—"

"Ibbie."

"What is it?"

"Please don't shut me out." I trusted her enough to not mince my words nor conceal my true feelings beneath polite niceties.

"What do you mean?" she whispered.

"I can tell something's troubling you." I crossed the room to stand by her side. "Will you let me help?"

For what felt an age, she stood silent, her features as still and colorless as if they were fashioned from alabaster. At last, slowly, she reached for her brooch, unfastened the clasp. The silk shawl tumbled away from her neck, revealing the truth: against the fair skin below her jaw, vivid lines of crimson blazed, a labyrinthine tattoo.

She was marked.

Marked for death.

My chest tightened as though the vines from my dream had returned to coil around me, their barbs pressing into soft flesh. If I could breathe, perhaps I could speak, could offer some reassurance, but the coils wrapped tighter still, driving the air from my lungs.

At once, the fragrance of the goldhearts flooded the room, bright and triumphant. It drove back the constricting fear long enough that I managed to offer Ibbie my hand.

She gripped it tight, as though it were a navstone to guide her safely home.

"I didn't want you to know, in case it would put you in danger. Maybe I shouldn't have told you." Her voice dropped to a whisper. "But I don't want to endure it alone, no matter what the Magistry says."

"Nor should you." I wrapped my arm around her, pulling her close. As though she were a child seeking comfort, she rested her head on my shoulder. I tightened my hold. "What do you recall?"

"Nothing. Just like the rest. Last Friday when Hazel dressed me for the day, she discovered it. I forbade her to speak of it to anyone. I suppose I felt if I ignored it, it would vanish—but it did not." She brushed her fingers across the tattoo. "When I read the news articles these past months, I imagined the other victims intoxicated or feeble-minded . . . for else how could you receive a tattoo and have no recollection of it? But now I share their fate."

What could I possibly say to comfort her? I'd thought her claimed by a megrim, not marked by a murderer. How could I have been so blind? My vision blurred, and I blinked rapidly to clear it. "But you did speak to the Magistry?"

"Yesterday. It was why I asked you to forgo our usual visit and come this morning instead. I summoned the Magistry, as I should have done from the first." She pulled away and stood upright, her words becoming crisp and even once more. "They replaced my butler with Robart, a stratesman. And they have additional men commissioned to watch for the killer. They've stationed themselves along the streets, front and back, and they wear no insignia, so they might escape notice. The Magister assures me they'll keep me safe, even at the cost of their own lives."

But how, when they'd failed to protect the victims so many times before? Unless they kept knowledge concealed from the public, they'd no notion of his appearance or nature. One who took the lives of others should appear *different*, should display their inner malice—or madness—in some outward way. Yet it was more likely that the murderer would appear in an innocuous guise, like a Brother of Fidelity on an errand of mercy, a charming dandy out for a stroll, or a nondescript charwoman about her daily duties. How could they hope to perceive the truth before it was too late?

I clasped my arms around my middle. "Are they taking any other precautions?"

"They won't permit any visitors, except those I know and approve, and they won't so much as allow me to enter a room without inspecting and securing it." She passed her hand across her eyes. "They're taking what care they can, but they have no new information, at least none they'll share with me."

And already several days had passed since Ibbie had received the mark. As far as I recalled from the reports in the newspapers, the longest stretch between a victim receiving the mark and their —end—was a fortnight. The coiling-vine sensation returned. I rubbed my breastbone—now wasn't the time for distraction. "What can I do?"

She gave me a sharp look. "I suppose you won't listen if I tell you to keep out of the matter?"

"Would you, if our roles were reversed?"

"Indeed not." A small smile crossed her lips for the first time since my arrival. "As a matter of fact, there is something you can do, from the safety of your home, mind you. I'll not have you taking risks on my account."

I nodded.

"I intend to request the case notes from the Magistry."

For most, such a request would be firmly declined, but someone of Ibbie's stature *might* succeed.

"You have a bright, inquiring mind. You see connections where others don't and view the world differently."

If she knew how differently, she might not have asked for my help. Even now, the goldhearts murmured softly from their basket, attempting to comfort, and only with effort could I close my ears to their chiming tones. I turned away from them and gave my full attention to Ibbie.

"Once I have the notes, I'd like you to review them and see if you notice any patterns, anything the stratesmen may have missed."

"Of course."

"Very well, then." She brushed her hands together briskly. "In the meantime, about your manuscript—"

"Never mind my manuscript." How could she consider it at a time like this? I rubbed my temples, which throbbed from the effort of keeping emotion in and fae-sensation *out*. "All our energies must go toward your safety."

"What can we do that the Magistry has not?" She toyed with the fringe edging her indigo shawl. "If I allow my thoughts to dwell on it, I'll go mad. You review the case notes when they arrive, and I'll occupy myself with the printing arrangements. I need the distraction."

She might require distraction, but I wanted to concentrate on what mattered most—her safety. The Magistry might intend to protect the citizens of Byren, but their interest was impersonal, while mine was that of a friend. If I lost Ibbie, it would be unbearable.

Dismissing the argument as won, she turned toward the basket on the table. "What have you brought today?"

In light of her true situation, the gift felt like a feeble offering. The goldhearts might help to lift melancholy, but they offered no protection from a deranged killer. Nevertheless, I withdrew them from their basket, and their sweet aroma permeated the air. "Just something I thought you might enjoy."

The lines around her eyes smoothed out as she accepted the flowers, and the smile she offered no longer appeared a pale imitation of its usual form. "Thank you, Jessa. They're quite remarkable. I think I'll keep them in here to remind me of all that's still beautiful within the world."

She placed them on the mantel, where they stood like ethereal guardians over the room, but my gaze kept drifting back to the tattoo of crimson. Surely I could do something to see to her protection, beyond waiting on case files that might never arrive. But what?

CHAPTER 3

After I departed Wyncourt, I fled to the haven offered by Spenser's Repository, the largest circulating library in Avons. Even when residing in the country, Father had maintained a subscription to Spenser's, and I'd never felt more thankful for it. While known for their large collection of books and old manuscripts, they also maintained a broad assortment of academic papers and popular gazettes, which they stored in the archive.

Though this morning I'd hoped that Spenser's archive would offer further insight about my fae-touch, the chilling threat to Ibbie's life replaced my fears of Otherworldly influence. Nothing else mattered now but to see her kept safe.

Since news of the murders had been hidden until after Aunt Caris and I had departed for Milburn, I'd seen nothing of the earliest reports. If I wanted to better understand the threat Ibbie faced—and what might be done to keep her from falling prey to this killer—then the sensible place to start was the information available to the public.

Like most of the older buildings in Avons, the library was

constructed with traditional protective measures against fae, and the iron-strap hinges and studs intended to repel Otherkind provided a sharp contrast to the brilliant white paint used on the double doors at the entrance.

When I slipped through them, the quiet thrum of lowered voices and the soft sigh of turned pages enveloped me. Deep blue walls and white crown-and-vine trim framed shelf after shelf of books. I inhaled the scents of leather and ink and the beeswax polish used on the shelves, attempting to force my riotous emotions to quiet.

Even the comforting familiarity of my surroundings couldn't alleviate the ache in my chest, but if I allowed my mind to remain clouded by my fears for Ibbie, then I'd have nothing to offer her. When I'd lost Mother, I was only a child and powerless to help, but this time, I could act, even were it only in a small way. Ibbie had forbidden me to take any risks, but accessing the archive for additional information could cause no trouble.

I crossed the polished marble floor and crept past the central circular desk toward the archive, a spacious chamber accessed through glass-paned doors. While ladies frequented the other areas of the library and often enjoyed lighthearted conversations therein, men dominated the archive with its academic works and Assemblage records. Women weren't denied access, yet they rarely entered. Perhaps they dreaded being dubbed bluestockings, as Aunt Melisina suggested. Regardless, I'd found if I kept quiet and timed my visits properly, I could avoid drawing undue attention as I went about my work.

I collected the papers and gazettes I desired, then walked to my favorite table, one almost hidden in a shadowed alcove at the back of the archive. Once situated, I located the earliest gazette report containing news of the killings. It bore the blazing headline *Murderer at Large!*

Beyond that, I found my vision blurred. I swiped at my eyes and blinked the words into focus. Perhaps if I forced myself to think of the situation as a purely theoretical one, like a conundrum in a book, I could gain the clarity of mind I required. With effort, I pushed Ibbie from my thoughts and attended strictly to the written record of the murders. Some articles were lurid and sensational, others staid and matter-of-fact. Often the writers repeated and sensationalized the scant details available, perhaps to conceal their lack of knowledge. But one—P. Smith—appeared more astute than the others. He raised thoughtful questions, and he further commented on the refusal of the Magistry to disclose any tangible information that might help the citizens of Avons better protect themselves. Perhaps I could find some way to contact him and inquire about what he'd learned.

For now, I noted the victims in my sketchbook:

A sailor on the Eventide, seasoned and advanced in years.
A lady of the night, beautiful and much-abused.
An elderly solicitor, distinguished and retired from his practice.
A newsboy, young and poor.
A housekeeper, upright and faithful in service.
A merchant's wife, protected and sheltered.
A baron's son, wealthy and well-liked among his peers.

All dead.

Seven lives stolen in a few short months. Not a single action taken by the Magistry had served to protect the victims; not a single clue had emerged to direct the authorities toward the culprit. Every report contained speculation—perhaps the killer was a fae-touched individual who no longer retained control of his faculties, or a depraved soul with a seared conscience and wealth enough to conceal his misdeeds, or a malingering crew of evildoers advancing some dread scheme. But none supported their theories with facts.

Early on, some speculated that the tattoos were linked to arcane activities that eventually led the victims to claim their own lives—but the Magistry refuted this statement in the strongest terms, declaring the deaths to be murders. However, they refused to explain the reason for their confidence, nor did they divulge anything about the method by which the victims were killed. Whatever the mechanism of death, it must be one that the victims could not reasonably have accomplished themselves—but what?

If I had knowledge of the sort of death the victims suffered, perhaps I could suggest to Ibbie some means of defense . . . but for now, it was only idle speculation.

I folded the gazette and set it to the side.

Unless they withheld it from the public, the stratesmen had uncovered no connection between the individuals chosen by the killer, a fact which served to heighten both fear and conjecture. After all, with such a varied lot of victims, anyone could be next. Could they have something in common, something hidden?

If Ibbie could sever that connection—whatever it was—might her life be spared? I tapped my pencil against my lips.

At once, a vision of Ibbie with the stark crimson web spread over her neck flashed through my mind. I stroked its contours across the page of my sketchbook, vivid spiraling lines pouring from my pencil. Often, the release of images onto the page brought relief—but not now.

I turned to a clean page and then reached for another gazette. As I worked my way back through the articles, I noted the names of the families involved and those who found the victims, along with anything else that stood out to me, marring my sketchbook further with stark words on death.

The last two marked individuals had been murdered despite the watch set by the Magistry. Their best men had witnessed nothing. I straightened, stretching the tight muscles in my back. Given that, the sensible explanation was that the murderer used some sort of alchemical device, something to confuse the senses of those standing guard or conceal his person so he might act undetected.

Granted, no known alchemical device could accomplish such a feat. But what might alchemists have achieved in private? They held their secrets close, divulging bits here and there to those wealthy or powerful enough to procure their more sophisticated devices, and it was well known they kept their most powerful artifacts from public knowledge. Alchemy appeared a more likely explanation than the Magistry suddenly developing a case of complete incompetence, yet most articles dismissed the notion.

Why?

I stared unseeing at the folios on the shelf across from me. Given their desire to avoid all regulation, the Alchemists' Guild would have every reason to suppress rumors of their devices being involved with these crimes. King Everill had long sought a reason to bring them more under his control. If their devices were being used to carry out these murders, he could justify such an act.

From Father's correspondence with Alchemist Tarquin, I knew they jealously guarded their secrets and the power they afforded the Guild. Unlike most of his colleagues, Tarquin's thirst for knowledge drove him to admit what he did not understand and consult with Father about his areas of expertise, which had allowed a relationship to spring up between them. He'd unbent enough to confide in Father about the race among his fellow alchemists to achieve the ultimate pinnacle of their craft—invisibility of the sort fae practiced naturally through glamour.

I traced one of the bold headlines with my finger. If Avons weren't so heavily warded against fae, I might almost think . . . no, surely it was an impossibility.

I exhaled.

It was far more logical to theorize that the alchemists had at last succeeded in their aims than that hundreds of years of vigilant protection of Avons from Otherworldly incursions had failed.

Surely the Magistry had already attempted to delve into the matter, but I couldn't imagine them gaining much ground with the Guild. Though stratesmen—backed by the Magister and ultimately King Everill—held authority to question any they chose, the alchemists possessed sufficient clout to resist offering straightforward answers. Or if they wished to appear cooperative, they could easily babble misleading nonsense that none but another alchemist could prove false.

If the Guild chose to act the part of a will-o'-the-wisp and lead the stratesmen astray, what recourse did the Magistry have? Without facts to base their suspicions on, they'd travel the wisp-path given.

Unless . . . I went to the Magistry and shared what little I knew about the quest to mimic glamour through alchemy. If I made a report citing evidence of such from an alchemist, would it allow the stratesmen to press the Guild further?

I snapped my sketchbook shut. In truth, I'd rather crawl through a patch of thistles, but what choice did I have? If I kept back any bit of information, however small, and it later proved important, I'd never be able to reconcile with myself. Indeed, the

Magistry had requested that all citizens with information divulge it at once. If an alchemist *was* responsible, surely knowledge of the devices used would enable the Magistry to find countermeasures to protect Ibbie.

It must.

I gathered up my materials, tucked the papers back into their proper places, and then glanced at the nearest bracket clock. Half past three—I'd lost hours.

I quickened my steps as I passed into the central chamber of the library. I'd have to hurry or else disappoint Aunt Caris. After dinner last night, she'd requested that I join her at the Harper musicale later this afternoon. Given what I'd overheard between her and Aunt Melisina, I'd dared not protest—indeed, were it only a musical performance rather than an event designed to foster proper social connections, I'd even enjoy it.

But if I joined them, I wouldn't have an opportunity to speak with the stratesmen today. It might be a fool's errand, in which I informed the Magistry of what they already knew, but if I refrained and Ibbie was lost . . . no, I refused to consider it.

I'd simply have to return home and make my excuses—and hope that Aunt Caris would understand.

Upon my arrival, Holden opened the door, and when I inquired about Aunt Caris, he directed me to the morning room. The sound of the fountain murmuring within greeted me as I approached, a cheery, carefree burble unbefitting the dire news I carried. Though I supposed it would be more cause for concern if it had fallen quiet and failed in its purpose of appeasing nisi—never mind that none of the household fae had appeared in decades, and certainly never within Avons.

When I crossed the threshold, I found Aunt Caris seated in her favorite chair, bent over her embroidery.

"Oh, there you are, dear. Lady Dromley kept you a great

deal longer than usual. I was just about to send Ives to fetch you, and truth be told, you should have taken him with you from the first. In times like these—"

"Aunt Caris." I couldn't bear to let her continue. "It's Ibbie."

Even to my own ears, I sounded stilted and unnatural. Aunt Caris looked up, her brows drawing together. "What happened?"

"The killer . . . he . . . he left his mark."

"Not Lady Dromley?" Aunt Caris leapt up, her embroidery tumbling to the floor.

I nodded. "She told me this morning."

"Oh, my dear." She hastened across the room and clasped my arm, examining me closely. "But you're well? You weren't hurt?"

"I'm unharmed, but Ibbie . . . she's already had the mark for several days." I clutched my sketchbook to my chest. "I must beg off the musicale, so I can visit the Magistry this afternoon."

Aunt Caris staggered back. "The Magistry? Whatever for?"

I should have held my tongue, would have, if my emotions hadn't clouded my judgment. How could I make this acceptable to Aunt Caris?

She hurried on. "Of course you want to assist Lady Dromley, but my dear, there's nothing you can do. The stratesmen will look after her, and you simply can't gallivant around Avons. Such things aren't done here. It's one thing for you to call on Lady Dromley alone, but to visit the Magistry—it's no place for ladies, accompanied or not. Send them a note if it will ease your mind, and perhaps they'll call tomorrow."

"Tomorrow may be too late." I couldn't bear to simply sit at home—or worse, attempt to make small talk at the musicale—unaware of what the Magistry intended or how they planned to protect Ibbie, all the while waiting for the murderer to strike. Unable to remain still, I crossed to the window. Scarlet bleeding hearts danced amid white hellebore in the garden bed below, and their steady pulse bolstered my own.

I turned back to Aunt Caris, and words escaped me in a rush. "What if the Magistry fails her? They're doing their best, but they couldn't protect the others."

"Even so, what can you hope to do?"

"Perhaps not much, but after I talked to Ibbie, it occurred to me alchemical devices are likely involved in the deaths. Alchemist Tarquin made some confidences in Father that I'm not certain the Magistry knows, and they could well have bearing on the case. Perhaps if I share the knowledge, they'll better protect Ibbie. I want to be sure they've taken it into account—that they'll provide her with alchemical protections as well as practical ones and that they can seek the Guild for answers if needed."

Aunt Caris clucked softly. "I know you're distressed, but consider—"

Ainslie flitted into the room, her gauzy white gown swirling around her ankles. "Who's distressed?"

"Jessa," Aunt Caris said. "There's been dreadful news. It seems Lady Dromley has received the tattoo."

Ainslie gasped. "Oh, Jessa. Surely not!"

"I wish I could say there's a mistake, but I saw it myself, and . . ." My voice faltered. "They've set a watch on her, but she's afraid. And I'm afraid for her."

"I'm certain the Magistry will do everything in its power to protect her." Ainslie hurried to my side and pulled me into a fierce hug, her wild-rose scent swirling around me.

I leaned into the comfort she offered until I remembered Ibbie, alone, with no one to ease her fears. I pulled back. "I'm certain they'll try, but I can't rest until I know she's safe."

Aunt Caris shook her head, and flyaway copper curls bobbed

with the motion. "It's not your responsibility, my dear. It's only natural that you want to help, but I can't have you putting yourself at risk nor getting involved where you have no place." A furrow creased her brow. "Besides, Melisina expects us at the musicale, and I hate to disappoint her."

"I can't possibly go. Please, Aunt Caris." I pressed my lips tight, attempting to hold my emotions in check.

She stroked my cheek, the furrow in her brow deepening. "You don't look well."

"I don't feel well." Indeed, a relentless, pounding pulse drummed in my head, and the room darkened at the edges.

"Stay and rest then, dear. I can't imagine you thought to eat, so I'll have Gaile bring you up a pot of chamomile tea and some luncheon, and I'm sure you'll start to feel more yourself."

I murmured assent. I couldn't bear to argue further, but I must do what I believed right. I'd rest until they left the house, as I assured Aunt Caris, then I would seek the Magistry. Otherwise, I'd have no peace.

Aunt Caris escorted me upstairs and hovered on the threshold of my bedchamber. "Perhaps I should stay. I know how much Lady Dromley means to you, and I don't want you alone with your fears."

I drew back. "That's kind of you, but there's no sense in everyone staying home. I'll be here when you return."

"Well, if you're certain . . ." She hesitated a moment longer, but after further reassurances, she slipped away to prepare for the musicale.

In the quiet of my bedchamber, I paced the floor as if it were a cage. Jade wove between my ankles. When I didn't stop to give her attention, she sat on my feet, effectively halting me. I scooped her up and settled onto the edge of my bed, and she clambered atop my shoulders into her favorite position, where she remained as I dutifully sipped the tea Gaile provided and nibbled on some biscuits. Despite the deft hand of our cook, they tasted dry as dust to me, and I soon abandoned the attempt to eat.

When the family carriage rattled away with Aunt Caris, Ada, and Ainslie tucked inside, I ventured downstairs. The door to Father's study remained closed, and all the servants were occupied elsewhere. I slipped from the house and hired a hack to take me to the business district.

Whatever the possible improprieties, I must go to the Magistry.

~

THE MAGISTRY SHOULD HAVE BEEN a magnificent, imposing building, one that towered above its companions and signaled the authority it carried by grant of the king. Instead, the dull, nondescript building offered nothing noteworthy or commendable. It squatted on the street corner, a dour and unembellished construct.

Perhaps the Magister preferred to maintain an unobtrusive appearance so his men might keep watch over the city from the shadows. A chill skittered down my spine, and I clutched my wrap tighter, the warm indigo-and-ivory paisley a comfort.

After I climbed from the hack, I hesitated on the corner. What would I discover when I ventured inside? No sense wondering when I could find out. I straightened to my full, rather unimpressive height and marched toward the Magistry.

I passed through the oak door into the entrance hall, a narrow slice of a chamber with pale gray walls and dark slate floors. Perhaps they intended its doom-and-gloom appearance to deter wrongdoers from the path of destruction. Not a single woman was in sight, and the few stratesmen I passed stared as I walked by.

Their gazes burned into me, and I lowered my own to the floor. However uncomfortable, their censure could do me no harm. It wasn't as if I was known in society, with a name that might be touted about gazettes and spread in scandal. I might be a gentlewoman, but I held no title, nor any great wealth. With good fortune, I might remain unrecognized and return to obscurity once I'd completed my errand.

At the end of the entrance hall, a long oak table barred further progression into the building, and a lean, iron-haired man scribed in an immense logbook behind it.

I crept forward until I stood before him. He gave no sign of noticing my presence, so at last I said, "Excuse me, sir?"

Still no response, aside from the scratch of quill on parchment.

"Excuse me?"

"What's that?" Deliberately, he placed the quill across the logbook and glowered at me from beneath bristling brows. "Speak up, girl."

Perhaps he was hard of hearing—or perhaps he simply wished to give me a difficult time. Either way, I pitched my voice louder. "I'm looking for someone to speak with about the Crimson Tattoo Killer."

"You and half the city. Nuisances, the lot of you, all looking for what fame or fortune a report might give you, though it's a first that a lady has misadventured here. Or mayhap you're not such a lady after all?" One corner of his mouth curled up.

"It's not like that." I stepped back, putting distance between us. "I'm a friend of Lady Dromley and—"

"So you say. Give me some proof you're not here to waste our time. We're stretched mighty thin, and I'm not inclined to give you the benefit of the doubt." He looked me up and down, and a discomfiting gleam appeared in his eyes. "Unless you're willing to . . . persuade me."

I crossed my arms over my chest, wishing I could hide within the folds of my wrap. Oh, why hadn't I listened to Aunt Caris? I'd imagined I might encounter disreputable members of society—not be treated as one myself. But what did it matter? I'd come for Ibbie, and it would take more than a lascivious clerk to turn me away. I lifted my chin, assuming a confidence I did not feel. "I'd not heard it was the practice of the Magistry to harass civilians. I'd like to speak to someone with authority in this matter."

He pushed up from his chair. "Look here, I—"

"That's enough, Tavers." A well-built man with angular features and dark hair detached himself from a shadowed alcove in the chamber and rounded the table to stand before me. His clothing resembled that of a gentleman, impeccable in style and order. No stratesman's insignia marked his shoulder, yet Mr. Tavers bowed and withdrew.

Then the newcomer addressed me. "If you'll come this way, Miss—"

"Jessa Caldwell." I let my arms drop to my side.

"Miss Caldwell." He gave a nod. "I'm Mr. Burke, one of the stratesmen overseeing this case. Follow me, please."

We walked deeper into the corridor, through a long, narrow stretch where little sunlight reached and into a small, rather barren room, kept from resembling a cell only by tall windows set at intervals into the far wall. Diagonal iron muntins divided them into diamond-shaped panes, so even if one were minded to break a panel, the small hole would afford no escape. The only furnishings were simple hardback chairs set around a low table, and the stone walls were left unadorned, as were the windows—an altogether unwelcoming place.

Stratesman Burke motioned to the seats. "Please sit, Miss Caldwell."

I perched on the edge of the nearest chair, and he settled in one across from me.

"How may I assist you?" He surveyed me with steel-gray eyes, intent as a kestrel seeking prey.

Had he brought me to this out-of-the-way chamber to attempt some sort of interrogation? I shifted, and the slats of the chair dug into my spine. "Stratesman Burke—"

"Mr. Burke will do."

I considered him once more. His attire and diction suggested he came from among the gentry, yet he'd chosen this profession. Perhaps he was a younger son, with no prospects otherwise. "Mr. Burke. As I attempted to express to Mr. Tavers, I'm concerned for the safety of Lady Dromley."

"I'm sure your concern does you credit, but this affair is no place for a lady—nor is the Magistry."

His censure brought heat to my cheeks, but I maintained a mild tone. "Yet a lady is involved, through no fault of her own, and her very life at risk."

"The Magister himself oversees the details of her protection." The edge to his voice kept his words from offering reassurance. "So be at ease. She has the best of care. If that is all, I'll see you out."

I clasped my hands in my lap. "Have you spoken with the Alchemists' Guild?"

The kestrel-sharp look returned. "Why do you ask?"

"Because no one has seen the killer or found evidence of his movements."

"And?"

"And for some time, alchemists have sought to create a device that would permit its bearer to pass unseen, as the fae do with glamour."

His eyes narrowed further. "Who told you that?"

"My father."

"And he's an alchemist?"

"No, he studies astronomy and mathematics."

"A gentleman scholar, then." Was that a hint of disdain in his tone? For scholars? Gentlemen? The intersection between the two? It didn't matter, as long as he protected Ibbie. "How is your father privy to such information?"

"He's developed a friendship with an alchemist, as they've corresponded on academic matters."

"I see. And you've made a spectacle of yourself simply to present this theory? I find that difficult to believe." He tented his fingers. "Why are you truly here, Miss Caldwell? Have you come to join the attention-seekers? Do you intend to gather information to sell to the gazettes? You would not be the first, but I must tell you we deal with such individuals severely."

"The Magistry *did* put out a call for information, and I've come in response to it—and out of concern. I would never consider disrupting your work to try to profit from it." I drew in a shuddering breath. "Have you ever lost someone you loved?"

A muscle near his jaw twitched, but he remained silent.

"If you had, you'd understand. It's worth any amount of effort to prevent another such loss." I looked out the diamond-paned windows but could catch no glimpse of green, no leaf or bloom to soften the grim surroundings or provide comfort. "Given the tension between the Alchemists' Guild and King Everill, I thought it possible that the Magistry remained unaware of their endeavors."

All expression vanished from his face, leaving it blank as stone.

Blight and rot. I rattled on to fill the ominous silence. "I imagined if you knew, you might approach the details of her protection differently or you might use the information to press the Guild for answers. Perhaps I was mistaken, but I felt it my duty to tell you and to offer assistance corresponding with Alchemist Tarquin on the matter, if you wish."

"We need no assistance." His eyes darkened to a storm-gray. "If you have any actual evidence to report, we'll gladly receive it. Otherwise, leave the investigation with the Magistry, where it belongs."

"Will you at least consider—"

"Enough, Miss Caldwell." His hand cut downward. "Since you evidently lack a watchful guardian, I'll offer you this counsel: cease meddling in the affair. I don't want to find your body alongside hers."

"And I don't want any bodies found at all." I spoke softly, though I'd rather have shouted, however unladylike the act. Why wouldn't he listen?

"Then we are in accord." He rose, a clear act of dismissal.

Aunt Caris had been right about my reception here—I'd done no good, and I'd risked bringing distress to my family if word somehow returned to them. I stood and offered a polite smile, a wan imitation of the one Aunt Caris donned for unwelcome guests. "Thank you for your time, Mr. Burke."

He gave a clipped nod. "Have a care, Miss Caldwell. And don't let me see you here again."

CHAPTER 4

I awoke the next morning to Jade batting my face with a velvet paw. When I cracked my eyes open, she gave a pitiful mew, and then crawled onto my chest, her weight stealing my breath.

I nudged her aside. "I know you expect breakfast promptly, but would it hurt you to wait an extra hour?"

Mrow.

Evidently, she believed it would. I pressed upright. Loose papers tumbled to the bed around me. I'd fallen asleep in the small hours of the night while poring over my notes and creating theories. It was a fruitless endeavor. I didn't possess enough information to make speculation worthwhile, nor could I gather it without overstepping the bounds of propriety. Yet I couldn't restrain myself from theorizing.

I climbed from bed and rummaged for the tin of dried fish I kept in the lower drawer of my bedside table. The book from Ibbie, in which I'd hoped to find answers about my fae-touch, remained unopened atop it. When I opened the tin, a pungent odor invaded the room, drawing a purr from Jade.

This offering should satisfy her until we reached the breakfast table.

I brushed a few flakes of fish from my hands and went to fetch a clean gown. My sisters and I shared one lady's maid between us, but even had we not, I preferred to handle my morning preparations on my own.

Sometime after midnight, it had occurred to me that while seeking information on the killer might be an act beyond the pale, surely I couldn't be faulted for seeking a way Ibbie might better protect herself. Well, perhaps I could, but it was an easier act to justify—and I couldn't bear to do nothing.

If I was to seek information without giving Aunt Caris cause for concern, I needed to look to our connections within proper society. The last victim was the son of Baron Tarleton, and Aunt Melisina was almost certainly acquainted with the family. If I could speak to them and learn what the Magistry had done on their behalf, learn if they had engaged any means of protection themselves, I might discover where they went wrong. At the very least, I wouldn't waste time suggesting to Ibbie what had already failed.

A conversation with Lady Tarleton could lend valuable insight, yet I couldn't speak to her without an introduction, which I must somehow persuade Aunt Melisina to provide. I hesitated in front of the open clothes press. At last, I selected my newest gown, fashioned from a rich sapphire-colored material. Aunt Melisina insisted I wear deep blues as often as possible, whether in attire or accent. According to her, I must make the most of my striking blue eyes, for I needed all the help I could get.

Once attired, I pulled back the curtains and glanced out at the lowering clouds. A fine mizzle dusted the windows, and in the gardens below, thirsty plants drank in the damp. Never mind the inauspicious weather; I'd take the carriage today, if Aunt Caris assented, and call upon Aunt Melisina after Ibbie.

When I broached the matter with Aunt Caris, she hesitated, but my proposed visit to Aunt Melisina decided the matter in my favor. She gave reluctant consent to my excursion, as long as I remained protected by Ives and our driver.

But when I tried to depart, Jade wove her claws into the fabric of my dress. Every attempt to detach her resulted in chilling yowls.

At last, I gave up. "Very well, you may come, but you'll have to wait in the carriage at Wyncourt. I don't want Ibbie bothered."

Once at Wyncourt, I braced myself for possible battle with Robart, but evidently Ibbie had issued orders concerning my visits, for this time he didn't turn me away.

Yet the air within held a chill, and Ibbie greeted me with brittle good cheer and a smile that wavered at the edges. After only a quarter of an hour, she shooed me away, saying she'd no need of company—she had business to attend to.

She overruled my protest and insisted I must go, but when I stopped in the corridor and glanced back, she had sunk onto the divan and buried her face in her hands.

I moved toward her, but Robart blocked the way.

"Best leave, miss."

"But I—"

"Magister's orders. Lady Dromley must be kept safe, and visitors only hinder."

So he'd permitted me in that I might receive orders from Ibbie herself. My eyes prickled, but I refused to give way to tears. It would only create a scene and distress Ibbie further. I offered a small nod to Robart and swept from the house, fear my only companion until I climbed into the carriage where Jade awaited.

I curled my arms around her warm bulk. She nudged my chin with her nose, and her steady purr calmed my agitation—at least until our carriage halted in front of Aunt Melisina's townhome.

The double-width row house towered up five stories, impeccable in detail and design. In keeping with the more recent trends of architecture—trends ushered in by the design of Wyncourt—it eschewed black ironwork accents in favor of white granite brought from the mountains to frame doors and windows. The intricate patterns carved into the frames further softened the honey-colored sovstone used for most dwellings in Avons, creating a pleasing palette for the eye. While eliminating the iron traditionally used to ward against fae might not be prudent, it was easy to justify, given no one had witnessed high fae in Avons since the time of King Aldred—let alone experienced an Otherworldly invasion.

On Aunt Melisina's doorstep, I examined my clothing for any dishevelment, brushing my skirts to remove stray strands of fur left by Jade and checking my hat and gloves. A dragon perched atop its hoard would be less intimidating than Aunt Melisina in her domain—and she parted with favors less willingly than a karzel its gold. After one last adjustment to the angle of my hat, I rapped on the door.

Aunt Melisina's butler, Oversby, offered a welcome and escorted me into the morning room, where Aunt Melisina labored over her correspondence, looking for all the world like a dahlia, her stiff, formal beauty encased in a confection of deep purple.

When I entered, she set aside her pen. "Jessa. To what do I owe this unexpected visit? I scarcely hope you've come to your senses and decided to heed my advice about moving into society."

"Yes, I mean no." I shifted from one foot to the other. "That's not why I've come."

"Then why?"

Jade chose that moment to stroll from behind my skirt and sniff at one of the many tasseled pillows.

Aunt Melisina frowned. "Must you drag that beast around town? It may be all the rage to take one's pets about, but most have the sense to confine themselves to small, well-groomed animals that will enhance their appearance, rather than wild creatures that appear to have escaped from the Otherworld."

A quiet growl emanated from Jade, and I exhaled slowly. "If you prefer, I can return her to the carriage."

"I prefer you avoid any further waste of my time."

For what could I be to her, besides a waste of time? Certainly, I'd never satisfied her expectations for a niece. I adjusted my gloves once more. "May I sit?"

She waved dismissively to the nearest chair. "What do you want?"

A large jasmine plant towered behind me, and its uplifting aroma cleared my mind. Careful to conceal all emotion, I offered the barest facts about Ibbie and her mark.

Aunt Melisina surveyed me coolly. "The morning papers carried the news about Lady Dromley, but I fail to see why it has prompted your call."

"Are you acquainted with Baron Tarleton and his wife?"

"Of course." Her ebony eyes glittered. "I hope you don't intend to join the ranks of Avons gossips and hound them for information or a sighting of the crime scene. They've suffered quite enough without visitors intruding."

"I have no wish to intrude on their grief nor to gossip about their suffering. I only hoped to find out if they knew something that might help protect Ibbie."

"Word has it that the Magister himself spoke with them after the . . . incident." She straightened the pile of invitations before her, the parchments rasping together. "What can *you* possibly hope to find?"

How could I confess to Aunt Melisina my fears, my need to act in some way, however small? She'd find fault with whatever I said and use it as a reason to deny my request.

At that moment, Lovell bounded through the open door. "Mother, I—"

He caught sight of me and changed directions to drop a kiss on my cheek. "Heard about Lady Dromley, Jess. How are you taking it?"

Throughout our childhoods, Lovell had spent nearly as much time in our home as his own, and he'd always acted more like a brother than a cousin, so he knew how much Ibbie meant to me. His kindness threatened to undo my fragile control, and I struggled to steady my voice. "I . . . I want to help her, if I can. Which is why I hoped Aunt Melisina might introduce me to Lady Tarleton."

"What do you say, Lady Mother?" Lovell flashed a smile at her, livening his already expressive features. His natural charm had caused many a feminine heart to flutter, and his mother was no exception.

The stern lines of her face softened when she gazed at him, but she held firm. "I can't possibly approve of Jessa involving herself in such a sordid affair."

"But Lady Tarleton is the sort you wish Jess to meet, right? It can only help her get known around town. Besides, paying a call could hardly be considered sordid."

"It could if one probes into personal matters." She rapped the stack of invitations on the tabletop, causing them to fall into perfect alignment. "Lady Tarleton remains in mourning, after all, and Jessa is a stranger to them."

"But now that they're outside their first month of mourning, they can receive calls, even if they cannot pay them to others." Lovell dropped himself in the chair across from her and flashed an even brighter smile. "Might lift Lady Tarleton's spirits to have a change of pace. It's not as though Jess is a rabble-rouser—her company is quite restful."

"If one can overlook her general bent toward intellectualism and difficulty mastering even the most basic of social conventions."

A low rumble emanated from Jade, and I murmured a shushing sound. Though it was discomfiting to be discussed as if I was not in the room, Lovell had far greater chances of persuading Aunt Melisina than I did, and he knew what he was about.

Lovell gripped his ivory-handled walking stick. When he finally spoke, the words emerged with careful restraint. "Were that true, perhaps practice would refine those skills. Come, Mother, give it a chance."

"Very well." Aunt Melisina opened the table drawer and drew out a fresh stack of paper before returning her attention to me. "I suppose I can offer an introduction—provided you conduct yourself with *great* propriety and discretion. But I expect something in return, Jessa."

My stomach tightened.

"There's an upcoming garden soiree, and I want you to attend with me. You'll allow me to purchase the proper attire and introduce you to the proper individuals without complaint. In all matters, you're to do just as I say. You will not discuss your plants nor your work with Lady Dromley, and on no account will you make mention of your recent edgetown excursion."

"Yes, Aunt Melisina."

"That's settled then." Her lips tightened slightly. "I know you'd rather not move about in society, but I have a duty to my brother to see you suitably wed and established. It's for your good as well as his."

"I understand." In one sense, I did. Aunt Melisina meant well—only her views on marriage and family in no way aligned with my own.

"Now, it's hardly proper calling hours yet—"

A pointed reminder that though I was family, I should have observed the proprieties.

"But you may occupy yourself in the music room or gardens as you like for the next hour, then we will depart."

Lovell glanced between the two of us. "Aren't you supposed to take tea with Lady Cramer this afternoon? Why don't I take Jess?"

She permitted herself a slight smile at her darling boy. "You're always so thoughtful. I suppose that would do."

Then she turned to me. "I expect you to set aside the entire afternoon tomorrow to visit the dressmaker. If we're to have you suitably attired for the soiree, we must get to work at once."

"Then it's settled." Lovell stood and offered his arm. "Shall we go? We can stroll Calcot Park until it's time."

I gratefully accepted the avenue of escape. Lovell dismissed my carriage and drove us to the park in his phaeton. Calcot was far more formal than Enderly, immaculately maintained and bustling with ladies and gentlemen alike, all dressed to perfection, their curricles and gigs polished and gleaming. Yet the profusion of growth, however well-manicured, pressed against my senses, and as we passed deeper into the park, blossom and bough alike sought to establish their hold.

I picked up the pace, Jade keeping stride.

Lovell, who preferred to proceed through life in a languid, carefree way, stopped short. "What's the hurry?"

"There's no particular hurry, only . . ."

Only how could I begin to express the emotions that roiled inside without betraying far more than was safe? I could scarcely confess that fae-touch encroached once more, wakening a stomach-churning fear that I'd be unable to stave off madness and a desperation to hold on until I knew Ibbie was safe.

Lovell patted my arm. "It'll be all right, you know."

"No one can promise that."

"I suppose that's true, but fretting won't solve it either."

I pasted on a smile. "You're right, of course."

He kept up a steady stream of affable conversation as we crossed from one end of Calcot to the other, interrupted every so often by a friend or acquaintance of his, each of whom he engaged in easy discourse. Lovell moved with ease in this refined crowd, everything from his perfectly styled hair and dark sideburns to his ivory-and-blackwood walking stick and polished boots marking him as one of their own.

Though I allowed him to carry the conversation, by the third introduction, I was ready to flee the park. He guided me on with a steady arm until the bells from the various oratories of Avons tolled three times in harmony. Then he ushered me from Calcot to call upon Lady Tarleton.

As we traversed the streets of Avons, I struggled to calm my burgeoning nerves. At least I would face her with Lovell at my side.

Once we were admitted by the butler and ensconced within Lady Tarleton's sitting room, Lovell performed the introductions between us, his natural charisma easing any strain. He then offered condolences, which I echoed.

"Thank you." Lady Tarleton dabbed at her eyes with a lace-edged kerchief. "It still doesn't seem possible that Reynold is gone."

Her sorrow stabbed through me. Could I bear to intrude further on her grief? Yet pain akin to the one she lived with would become my own—unless Ibbie could be spared. I forced a reply. "I know you must miss him more than words can express."

"Yes, and—no one wants to talk of *him*, apart from the dreadful circumstances of his death. They wouldn't even allow me to see his body after his valet discovered him, not once. They said it would be too distressing, as if it's not far worse to have him erased from our lives." Lady Tarleton crumpled her handkerchief. "We don't even have a likeness of him, full-grown, for he kept too busy to sit for one. Our only painting was of him as a boy. If I could just look upon his face again . . ."

The ache in my chest increased. I'd always yearned for a picture of Mother, but her steadfast refusal of a portrait had denied me that privilege. If I could provide for Lady Tarleton the comfort I'd lacked . . . I leaned forward. "I have no great skill, but I enjoy painting and sketching. Perhaps, if you let me see his boyhood portrait and described him to me as a man, I could try to create a likeness."

The moment the words left my mouth, I regretted them. Who was I to undertake such a task?

But a bit of light kindled in her eyes, breaking through the shadows. "If you'd try, you'd have my eternal gratitude."

"I can give no promise as to the results, but I'm happy to make an attempt."

She beamed upon me.

Lovell braced his hands on his legs. "While you sketch, I'll go find Farley. When I saw him at Riverton, he promised to show me his firearm collection, and I intend to take him up on his offer."

"He'd enjoy the distraction," Lady Tarleton said. "Since the loss of his brother, he's not himself. None of us are."

Lovell strode from the room, and Lady Tarleton sent a servant to fetch the portrait of young Reynold. While I studied it, she reminisced about him. As I listened to her effusive descriptions of her son—the small ways his face changed as he grew, the broad lines of his shoulders and neck, the shape of his smile and the way it lifted one corner before spreading to overtake his face, all the little details only a mother would notice—the sunlight pouring over his likeness seemed to brighten, drawing forth vivid colors, and an image fashioned itself in my mind of the lad transformed into a young man.

The sensation left me feeling as though I were a top spun round one time too many. When I blinked, the dizziness receded, but the image remained, and my fingers ached to pour it forth onto the page. I accepted the ladies' sketching kit she offered—and as soon as pencil met paper, the vision poured forth.

Lady Tarleton worked her embroidery while continuing to speak of Reynold. Apparently, she required little response, only a willing listener. She shared of his kindness to his sisters, of his exemplary manners, of his habits and hobbies, and finally, of the days leading to his death. "Many were kind, dear friends of our family like Lord and Lady Aftwell, and even those we didn't know well but had great sympathy for our plight. Lord Blackburn was most assiduous in his attentions after Reynold received the mark, and even more so after his death. He understands what it is to lose a child, you see, and so had sympathy for us despite no great acquaintance. But then there were the curious, the gossips and sensation seekers—oh, it was abominable."

"That sounds difficult."

"We didn't get a moment's peace until the stratesmen put an

end to it, for Reynold's safety." Lady Tarleton rethreaded her needle. "Then it was so dreadfully quiet. We could do nothing but wait. And even till the end, everything seemed so perfectly ordinary. I cannot fathom it."

"There was nothing unusual at all?"

"After . . . after he received the mark, he slept little, but who could blame him?" Lady Tarleton drew a scarlet thread through the pale fabric stretched over the embroidery hoop. "He spoke of dreaming a great deal, all nonsense, nightmares of spiders and voices and monsters. He wasn't prone to flights of fancy, so I suppose fear of what might come disturbed his rest."

She blinked rapidly, as though seeking to govern emotion. "Forgive me. Perhaps you'd rather not hear this."

"So long as it doesn't distress you, I'm happy to hear whatever you wish to share." With that, our roles were sealed. I kept sketching, and she kept speaking of her son. The image I drew wasn't refined and polished like that a professional would craft, but rather raw with the emotion that bled from my soul as I absorbed her stories.

One final stroke along his jawline, and I lifted my pencil. The strange shimmer of color tinting the edges of the morning room faded, leaving an empty hollow in my stomach.

What had I done?

Were these unfamiliar sensations another manifestation of the fae-touch, seeking a new part of my mind to claim? I dropped the pencil into my lap as though it scalded me.

Lady Tarleton set aside her embroidery and reached for the drawing. "May I see?"

"Please don't expect too much." Hesitantly, I tilted the paper toward her.

"Oh . . . oh my! It's his very likeness. Not stiff and formal as he loathed, but *him* somehow." She traced his face with her fingertips, tears gathering at the corners of her eyes. "How can I thank you?"

"No thanks are needed." I gathered the rubber and various shading pencils and tucked each back into its proper place, attempting to gather my courage. "But, if you'll forgive the impertinence, I'd wondered if I could inquire what protections the Magistry set in place for Reynold and what precautions you took. I know it's a peculiar request, but Lady Dromley has received the mark. She's a dear friend of mine, and I thought . . . if I knew more, I might help her find some means of protection against the killer."

Each time I spoke it, the notion sounded less plausible.

"Heavens." She rested the portrait in her lap. "I can't imagine it would help, but if it eases your mind as you've eased mine, I'll tell you what I know."

"Thank you."

Lady Tarleton straightened, as though she braced herself for the recounting. "The Magistry was remarkably tight-lipped about the whole affair. Anyone would grant we had a right to know everything—it was our son in danger. Yet they refused to tell us any details. They only offered vague reassurances, and of course, they kept their men posted with Reynold at all times. No one came or went in those days. It should have been impossible for the killer . . ."

A faint sound caught my ear from the far side of the room. I looked toward the doorway, where a young girl had tucked herself behind one of the immense wing chairs flanking the entrance. How long had she hidden there?

Her glossy nutmeg-colored hair resembled that of Lady Tarleton, and she wore the unrelieved black of deepest mourning. But if she were Lady Tarleton's daughter, why would she skulk behind the furniture? She should be in the care of a governess when not in company with her mother. But then, who was I to judge what was proper? If she wished to conceal herself, I'd not betray her presence.

I turned my attention back to Lady Tarleton. "I'm certain they did all they could."

"Perhaps." She lifted a shoulder. "Those days felt like an eternity. We put our trust in the Magistry fully, and I regret it more than I can say. For though they promised his safety, they failed. Perhaps if we'd done as you said, if we'd availed ourselves of hired protection or sought the alchemists or done *something* . . . he'd still live."

She blinked rapidly and dabbed at her eyes again.

I reached for her hand and clasped it gently. "You cannot blame yourself."

"So they say." She drooped in her chair.

"You're weary, and I've troubled you long enough." I released her hand. "I don't wish to overstay."

She forced a smile, though its edges quavered. "I'm grateful you called, and I thank you for your kindness in creating Reynold's portrait."

At her summons, a maid arrived to escort me out. The girl detached herself from the nook behind the chair and followed us from a distance.

When we reached the stairwell, she rushed forward to address the maid. "That will be all."

Though she couldn't be more than twelve years of age, she spoke with assurance. What was her purpose in dismissing the maid? I studied her more closely. "Are you Reynold's sister?"

"Yes, I'm Levina. I heard you asking Mama about Reynold." Her voice emerged a brittle whisper. "Do you want to know what I saw?"

What she saw? A little tingle raced down my back. Had she witnessed a sign of the killer? I stepped toward her. "I do."

"Then come with me." She clasped my hand and drew me up the stairs. Her dress hung on her slender frame, suggesting she'd lost weight since the death of her brother, yet her steps were sure.

I allowed her to tug me up the stairs and down the corridor toward what must surely be family quarters. Midway down the hall, I hesitated. "Levina, perhaps . . ."

"Shh, not yet!" She swung open a door to reveal a distinctly masculine bedchamber, with heavy mahogany furniture, dark blue curtains, and rich oil paintings on the walls. Had it been Reynold's?

Regardless, I should not be here. It was the height of impropriety, and yet I could not deny Levina, not when she turned her dark, beseeching eyes toward me.

"You'll believe me, won't you?"

"I believe you have something of importance to say. What did you wish to tell me?"

Her shoulders slumped. "This is where he died, you know."

The drapes and bedcovers bore neat creases and orderly lines, and not the slightest trace of dust had accumulated on any surface, despite the room lacking an occupant. Lady Tarleton must still require minute attention to her son's room. If there'd ever been signs of what had transpired, the attention of the maids had likely obliterated them.

"If only I'd stayed awake, I could have called for the stratesman. I could have stopped him," she said.

"You were here the night the killer came?"

"I was waiting for Reynold. He wanted to see my watercolor once I completed it. He said he'd hang it on his wall, the better to admire it. I planned to surprise him, so I snuck into his bedchamber, but he took a long time coming, and I fell asleep in his chair." She rubbed her hand against her thin collarbone. "When I heard a creak on the floor, I woke. I thought it was Reynold, so I leapt up to surprise him."

The room seemed to dim about us. "What did you see?"

"There was a man. I couldn't see him very well, because the lamps weren't lit, and the moon was only shining in a bit, and the room was all dark, and his face was like a shadow. I couldn't move, and he laughed, and it was a horrible laugh, all dry and creaky. Then he touched me and it stung, and there was a smell that burned my nose." Her voice quivered, even as the words tumbled one over the other. "Everything got all wobbly, and I don't remember anything else. When I woke up, I was in my bed, and Mother was crying, and the stratesmen were running about, and Reynold was—he was . . . dead."

She tugged at the unadorned sleeves of her mourning gown, and her pain burned in my chest. What could I say to such grief?

She'd thought I wouldn't believe her, but sincerity echoed in her voice. Yet since she'd seen him, why had the killer not claimed Levina along with her brother? What had she seen, truly? Nothing that would lend to his identification. It sounded as though he'd used some sort of sedative as well—perhaps he counted on it muddling her thoughts and driving away recall. Besides, every killing thus far followed a prescribed order: the mark and then death, days to weeks later. Perhaps he refused to kill otherwise?

Still, I cast an uneasy glance over my shoulder. "Did you tell the stratesmen?"

She dipped her head down. "I tried to talk to Mother, but she said I'd only had a nightmare, and no wonder, and then she started to cry. Father was there, and he said I was never to speak of that night again, because I was upsetting Mother."

"But you've told me?"

"I heard you say you wanted to keep your friend safe. I wanted you to know. I want her to be safe." Her stark black gown overshadowed her delicate features, emphasizing the circles beneath her eyes, which were so deep they appeared like bruises. "And . . . I needed to tell someone who would believe me . . . in case he comes back."

"I do believe you, and I'm sorry you've suffered so." Oh, how I wanted to promise the killer would never touch her again. But I could not make such a claim with confidence. I closed the gap between us. "I cannot think he'd return to the same household—he never has before—but the stratesmen must hear your account, so they can look after you."

She shrank into herself further. "Father said I'm not to speak of it. He'll be so angry."

"Not when he understands."

"He won't understand! He never does." She marched to the window, her back ramrod straight, and stared out into the street.

I moved toward her, and something beneath the chest of drawers caught my eye—the slightest pale sheen within the shadowed space.

A scrap of gray-green was caught on a cobweb.

I bent to pick it up. It was a small feathery leaf, long since dried up and curled inward, its velvety texture and curved form unfamiliar and—oh, even in its dead state, an echo of longing passed through it, an ache for home, for its companions.

No, not now.

I envisioned the cage of thorns within my mind, coaxing the vines to weave more closely, to form a dense net through which nothing could pass. I'd indulged in too much emotion today. While Father had been wrong about emotions birthing the aberrations I experienced, he was right that when they heightened, my control over the cage within diminished, and the fae-touch surged to the surface, clamoring for its freedom. If I allowed it, I could do Ibbie no further good. I must rein it in and buy myself more time.

I closed my hand around the leaf.

It meant nothing. If Lady Tarleton's son were an outdoorsman, he could have easily carried the leaf home in the crease of his boot or clinging to his breeches. It might have drifted below the chest of drawers and caught on the web, where it remained unseen. Naturally, the maids would have concentrated their efforts at eye level, perhaps they'd even been reluctant to touch the floor where he lay . . .

It was of no consequence, not when a living and very distressed girl required comfort. Only what could I say?

Brisk footsteps clicked along the polished wood floor in the hallway, interrupting my thoughts. Then a portly, red-faced man barreled into the room. "What is the meaning of this?"

Levina shrank against the window, while I froze in place.

Before either of us could answer, he fixed his glare upon me. "I don't know who you are or what you think you're doing, but no one is permitted in my son's room. You should be ashamed of yourself—taking advantage of a child in her grief to satisfy your morbid curiosity."

"I . . . I'm sorry."

Her pale face set, Levina scurried past me.

If I accepted the blame for this excursion, perhaps she wouldn't face her father's wrath. "I should not have come, but I—"

"You'll leave at once," he snapped.

I backed away, stumbling over the rug. The corner of the carpet lifted, revealing dark concentric lines burnished into the maple floor. I dared not take the time to look more closely, but hurried from the bedchamber into the hall, murmuring further apologies that did nothing to ease Lord Tarleton's ire.

He stabbed his finger toward a maid dusting at the end of the corridor. "You. See her out."

The maid hurried toward me. And for one unguarded moment, Lord Tarleton's anger faded enough to reveal something else flickering in his eyes—fear? A pallor lurked beneath the flush on his cheeks, and he looked both ways before he slammed the door shut.

What did he conceal? And why such fear, after the worst had already befallen his family? Unless he guessed what Levina had confided in me and worried it would cause trouble?

In silence, I trailed the maid down the stairs. Despite the insights I'd gained, I'd done as Aunt Melisina feared. I'd inflicted further pain on a family who'd already suffered enough—and perhaps risked shaming my own, if Lord Tarleton chose to make my deeds public.

Gaze lowered to the floor, I allowed the maid to escort me to the library, where Lovell examined a revolving pistol, his head bent close to study the interior mechanisms.

I hesitated on the threshold. "I'm afraid we must go, Lovell."

He took one look at my face and returned the pistol to Farley. In silence, we departed.

Once in the carriage, Lovell lifted the reins. "What happened? Did speaking with Lady Tarleton help?"

"Perhaps." I shook my head. "But I think I made matters worse in other ways."

"Don't take it to heart, Jess," Lovell said. "I know you want to help Lady Dromley, but let the Magistry handle the matter. They'll take it in hand, no need to worry."

Everyone agreed I should leave the whole affair to the authorities. Did that mean my desire to offer Ibbie aid was foolish? She *had* asked for my assistance, but she'd also lectured me on staying out of danger and keeping my endeavors to research and analysis. Yet it felt so feeble, even more so in the face of the Tarleton family's oppressive grief.

I stared unseeing at the passing rows of houses. I didn't see a way to satisfy my own conscience and the expectations placed upon me. Why was it so difficult to do both?

I opened my hand and examined the leaf, somehow uncrushed despite its confinement in my glove. Where had it come from? I sighed softly. Its unusual form was only one small peculiarity among a dozen, none of which were mine to figure out, however much I might desire to do so.

CHAPTER 5

After breaking the fast with Father the next morning, I rifled through the post in hopes of finding a reply to the note I'd sent to Ibbie yesterday after my return from calling on Lady Tarleton. I soon found the object of my quest—an ivory envelope bearing Ibbie's energetic scrawl tucked amid an assortment of invitations.

I withdrew it from the pile and broke the seal.

My dearest Jessa,

The Magister has refused access to the case accounts, but I'm not to be deterred. I'm confident I can bend him to my views and certainly intend to give him no peace until he relents. In the meantime, he advises me to keep all visitors from Wyncourt, for their safety and my own. I've agreed for now, however, I mean to call on you once I have the files for review. I'll not be held prisoner, nor give up living just yet.

And I will not have you worry on my account. Put your mind at ease. I've considered what you shared about alchem-

ical involvement in the murders, and with the aid of Alchemist Lyons, I've taken some precautions of my own. Just let the murderer try, and he'll meet with some unpleasant surprises.

In the meantime, I've much to do to see to our printing press. We shall take Avons by storm with your work.

Until later,
Ibbie

I folded the letter and tucked it into the secretary. Determined cheer bled through her words, yet her demeanor the previous day did not bear it out. Still, at least she'd acted swiftly to add alchemical defenses to the resources the Magister provided.

I penned a reply to Ibbie and included a lighthearted sketch of prominent society members embodied as garden flowers that I hoped would provide some entertainment. Then I withdrew a fresh sheet of paper to write to P. Smith in care of his editor, asking if his research had provided any insight on how we might defend ourselves against the killer. I hoped he'd attribute my questions to the natural fears the inhabitants of Avons shared, rather than any particular interest in the case.

After some hesitation, I jotted a message to Mr. Burke as well, recounting the story Levina had shared with me. Would he even give it consideration, when her own parents dismissed the encounter as a nightmare? Yet if I withheld her confidence and something happened to her . . . it did not bear considering. I only hoped he'd be discreet in handling the matter, as I'd pleaded in the missive.

My correspondence complete, I attempted some pen-and-ink work, but all that would emerge onto the page were variants of the tattoo Ibbie bore, over and over, the stark black and white lines mocking my endeavors.

Ainslie entered the room, a small stack of letters in her hand. "I'll take yours to Holden as well, if you wish."

"Thank you."

When she scooped up my messages to add to her own, she fumbled, nearly dropping them. "What's this? You're writing to the papers now? What do you want from this Smith fellow?"

"I found his articles about the Crimson Tattoo Killer insightful." I stared at the sketches on the paper before me. "I thought he might have theories Ibbie could address with the stratesmen, perhaps an idea of what she could use to protect herself."

A little gust of breath escaped her. "I'm sure you know what you're about, but Jessa—"

"I know. I'm to stay out of it."

"That's not what I was going to say." She tucked my letters beneath her own. "Just don't let Aunt Caris know you're corresponding with anyone so . . . common."

I nodded, and she swept from the room.

I couldn't bear to look at the sketched tattoos any longer, so I crumpled my drawings and tossed them into the wastebasket. The wood-paneled walls seemed to close around me. If I remained withindoors, thinking of Ibbie and waiting for my impending excursion with Aunt Melisina, I'd succumb to all sorts of nervous fancies, so I slipped from the house and busied myself in the gardens. I selected choice blossoms to rebuild the bouquets for the household, as they'd all begun to look a bit wilted.

I started with belowstairs. Our cook Estine particularly benefited from the calming influence of sweet jeslyn and lavender, and the soft white and varied shades of purple blended nicely. I bound the blossoms together and set them in the bottom of my wide-rimmed basket. Before I left with Aunt Melisina, I'd place them into the simple pottery vase that occupied the center table of the kitchen.

Bit by bit, I assembled bouquets for each area of the house, in keeping with the desires and preferences of the primary occupants of each room. The warm sun strengthened the gentle floral fragrances, an aroma that usually brought a sense of peace—but this time, it did not. Nor did the familiar motions of building the arrangements soothe as they ought, not when the threat of the killer loomed large.

I should be *doing* something, only Aunt Caris constrained me to remain at home today, until my outing with Aunt Melisina. The hours trickled by without restoring any sense of equilibrium, and far sooner than I wished, Aunt Melisina bustled into the glasshouse.

"By the Crossings, Jessa! You're all over grime. And what have you done with your hat?"

"I forgot to put one on." Between the battering of branch and bloom against my senses and the relentless whispers of fear for Ibbie, few other thoughts had room to take root.

"You may have an excellent complexion, but if you don't take care to preserve it, you'll find yourself looking as brown and worn as any common farmer's wife. And then where will you be? Goodness knows your behavior offers no attraction for a suitable husband." Aunt Melisina tilted her parasol to better block the sun. "Now, hurry along and change into proper attire."

"Yes, Aunt Melisina."

Jade stopped batting at the nearest catnip plant and glared at Aunt Melisina. In turn, she peered at Jade as though she'd spotted a rat in her bedchamber. "I expect you to leave that creature here."

I nodded, but Jade growled a protest. Before she could consider baring her teeth at Aunt Melisina, I lifted her and whisked her away. Conventional wisdom held animals sensed those who disliked them, and Jade, being rather aggressive in nature, was more likely to retaliate than accept a slight.

Upstairs, in a whirl of activity, I changed into one of my nicest gowns and selected hat and gloves to match—all the while soothing Jade the best I could manage.

On the way downstairs, I sought Ainslie and pleaded with her to accompany us. She and Ada rarely parted, but a new parcel of sheet music had been delivered today, and Ada had already lost herself in playing the pianoforte, so Ainslie readily gave assent.

We rode in Aunt Melisina's well-furbished carriage to the Uptown Market District, where the finest merchants, modistes, and haberdashers displayed their wares. Aunt Melisina maintained a steady stream of instruction on the proprieties to observe when moving in society, interspersed with information on the likely attendees to the upcoming soiree. Before long, my temples throbbed.

But I'd given my word, so I did my best to absorb all she shared and nod in all the right places. When we blessedly arrived at our destination, her footman assisted us from the carriage.

At the nearest street corner, an old woman lifted a fistful of simple necklaces, leather thongs wrapped around blue-marbled stones. "Keep the fae from stealing yer souls! Keep them from taking yer babes!"

I paused to study her. Cotton-white wisps of hair framed deeply wrinkled features, creased further by earnest supplication. What would a soul look like, if pulled from a mortal frame? And were such a thing possible, what could the fae possibly want with one? While some legends indicated blue irstone, such as the old woman sold, deterred fae, there was nothing to prove it true. Yet still she peddled, and many bought, especially now.

"Don't dawdle, Jessa." Aunt Melisina's face pinched. "I cannot fathom why the Magistry allows such unseemly displays in the Market District."

"People are afraid." I spoke quietly. "They'll take anything that will make them feel safe."

Aunt Melisina sniffed. "As if such baubles could offer protection."

Ainslie shot me a sympathetic glance. "Oh, look, Aunt Melisina. Is that Lady Stanforth? What a remarkable hat she's wearing."

Aunt Melisina thawed slightly. "It's the newest mode, and it would suit you nicely. Perhaps we should select one for you while we're out."

"That would be delightful," Ainslie said.

I breathed silent thanks that she'd chosen to come along and deflect Aunt Melisina's disapproval. Ainslie linked her arm through mine, and together, we swept after Aunt Melisina into the dressmaker's shop.

Though I might protest Aunt Melisina's methods, her taste was impeccable. Lavish fabrics, delicate lacework, and ribbons of rich and varied hues made this a beautiful bower, and I spun slowly, absorbing the pleasing arrangements.

Under other circumstances, the beauty around me might have made the outing more bearable, yet my thoughts continually drifted to Ibbie. She was far more social than I . . . how was she enduring the solitude with her fears? And more pressing, was she safe?

"Jessa!" Aunt Melisina broke into my thoughts. "Have you heard a single word I've said?"

"Forgive me, aunt." I glanced down at the rich blue she'd draped me in. "This is lovely."

With that encouragement, Aunt Melisina continued to instruct the seamstress on the design of the gown. As the moments ticked by, the shop started to feel like a cage, one that kept me from doing as I ought. I wished Ibbie hadn't banished me. Should I ignore her instruction and go to keep her company?

If I did, Robart would surely deny me entrance. And then what? Round and round, the scant facts about the killer swirled through my mind as the dressmaker took my measurements, clucking and cooing over what a pleasure it would be to craft a dress to suit so lovely a form.

Aunt Melisina requested a beaded reticule to match, and I ventured to request the seamstress line it inside with waxed canvas. I'd taken to reinforcing all my reticules in such fashion, so if I collected some botanical specimen while exploring, it wouldn't stain the outside. But both the seamstress and Aunt Melisina stared at me as if I were an apple tree that had suddenly begun to produce figs instead of the expected crop.

"Why in the Crossings should she do such a thing?" Aunt Melisina asked tartly.

"I only thought . . . it's of no matter." I subsided into silence until the seamstress completed my fitting.

Afterward, I followed Aunt Melisina to Afton Millinery and murmured my appreciation for her selections while Ainslie carried on lighthearted conversation with everyone we encountered.

When we left the millinery, an unexpected gust of wind tugged at my bonnet, fluttering the ribbons and swirling my skirts. I glanced up and found a dark knot of clouds coiled to the north.

"It looks like it may storm, Aunt Melisina. Perhaps we should finish another day."

"Never put off till tomorrow what can be accomplished today." She frowned at the unruly sky. "We've only one more stop, surely the rain will hold until then."

She spoke as if she expected the weather to heed her command. And perhaps it would, rather than face her wrath. We meekly continued to the haberdashery to purchase what she dubbed the finishing touches, and then back to the carriage—just in time, for the dark clouds massed across the sky released their burden at last, bursting upon us with a torrent of rain.

Once home, Ainslie and I dashed through the downpour, soaked in an instant despite our efforts. I almost welcomed the shock of cold water, as it drummed away my fears.

But they flooded back the moment we entered the drawing room, where Ada and Aunt Caris huddled together on the chaise, drawn near as if for comfort.

When we entered, Aunt Caris lifted her head. An unusual pallor rested on her features, and the brightness of her eyes had dimmed. "Oh, thank heavens, you've returned—and you're safe."

Heart drumming in my ears, I halted on the threshold. At once, I wanted to flee to the gardens, to hide from whatever had shaken Aunt Caris so. Yet I took a tremulous step forward. "What's happened?"

Aunt Caris fluttered toward me. "Perhaps you should sit down."

My limbs went numb, my feet leaden. I could no more move toward her than leap across the room in a single bound. "Please, just tell me—whatever it is."

Ada looked up, and tears stained her cheeks. "It's . . . it's Lady Dromley."

I took one step back, then two, shaking my head.

"Her housekeeper sent word shortly after you left. She was found in her study," Aunt Caris said.

"Found?"

Aunt Caris started to reach for me, then stopped. "I'm afraid she's gone, my dear."

My body burned first hot, then unbearably cold, as though I'd plunged through ice into a frigid lake beneath. They were wrong, they must be wrong. Just this morning, she'd told me she'd purchased further protection. She was warded against alchemy, the stratesmen ever-present, and she *must* be safe.

If not, if I'd allowed myself to waste time purchasing frivolities while the killer claimed Ibbie's life . . . I clenched my hands so tightly that my fingers numbed. "It can't be. She was protected."

"I'm afraid there's no mistake, my dear. Mrs. Peters wanted you to know right away because she knew how you cared—"

"Please, stop." What did my concern for Ibbie matter now? I'd deceived myself, thinking I could keep her safe if I tried hard enough, and now . . . my throat tightened around tears I refused to shed.

"Oh, Jessa." Ada wrapped me in a hug, but I pulled away from the tender sympathy she offered.

I did not deserve it.

Heedless of the downpour, I dashed from the house and roused Ives with a sharp order for the carriage. Startled, he leapt into action, and our driver brought the carriage around in record time. "Where to, Miss Jessa?"

"Wyncourt. Quickly."

Rain lashed against the windows as he drove at a rapid clip. The relentless drumming echoed in my chest. Ibbie wasn't dead.

She couldn't be.

But why would they lie? We clattered down the cobbled streets, and each strike of hoof against stone fell like a blow.

Dead.

Dead.

Dead.

No, not dead—murdered.

She'd told me not to worry, to stay safely away, then she let the grave claim her . . . like Mother had. The two women who understood me best had both left me.

A sob broke free, first one, then another, as unstoppable as the tide. I couldn't breathe, couldn't think, could only feel a flood of loss, a gaping wound rent through my soul. Everything faded to a pale gray.

At last, the carriage halted before Wyncourt. The familiar lines of the house blurred in the downpour. I stumbled down the carriage steps, ignoring Ives's proffered hand and the cold drops soaking through my flimsy gown to chill my skin. I'd forgotten a wrap, but it did not matter. I clambered up the stairs of Wyncourt, stumbling and scraping my shin. At the peak, I pounded on the door.

A portly stratesman pulled it open and permitted me entrance. His mouth dropped slightly as he took in my disheveled state. "Are you well, miss?"

"Well? No, I'm not well, not at all. My dearest friend has been murdered." My voice wobbled. "Unless . . . unless it's not true?"

He shuffled as if discomfited by my emotions. "Sorry, miss, but it is."

"Was it the killer?" My gown dripped onto the polished walnut floor below. What kind of question had my shocked senses spun? Of course it was the killer. Ibbie had been in prime health, and reaching mid-age hadn't diminished her vigor in the least. Besides, she'd been marked. "How did he get to her?"

"I can't discuss the case, miss." He crossed his arms across his chest, the white insignia prominent on his shoulder. "Not while we're investigating."

Heat rose in my chest, displacing the ice of grief. They'd failed Ibbie, but I'd not let her death go unaccounted for. If he wouldn't tell the truth, then I'd find it for myself. I swept through the entrance hall. "I want to see her."

"We're not allowing anyone to view the body, miss." He moved to check my advance, his stolid face set. "It's not what you'll want to remember, if you were fond of her. Not suited for a lady, not at all."

My hands tightened into fists; my voice lifted. "That's not for you to say, nor for you to dictate how her loved ones grieve."

He scrubbed at his face with an ungainly hand, appearing taken aback. And so was I.

I'd never forgotten propriety so thoroughly before, never so completely cast aside the expectations set for a lady—demure, gentle, quiet. It all fell away, as I considered Ibbie. I stepped forward. "Please move aside."

"What's all this?" A smooth voice issued from the corridor, followed by the form of Mr. Burke, calm in demeanor and immaculate in attire, as though neither mayhem nor murder had the power to ruffle his sensibilities.

"I must see Ibbie . . . Lady Dromley." I choked out the words.

"Come, Miss Caldwell." He took my arm and gently ushered me into an antechamber. "I'm afraid that won't be possible."

"Why not?" I shook free of his grasp.

"I'm deeply sorry for the loss of your friend, but the Magister had the body removed. It's already gone."

The body.

No longer Ibbie, but a frail mortal shell left behind.

The Brothers and Sisters—indeed, even the Script itself—assured us we would reunite with those we loved one day, in the world beyond all others, the Final Haven prepared by the Infinite for the souls of his followers once their bodies failed.

But for now, I was left alone.

The inner fire receded, leaving me cold once more, my legs weak and trembling. Yet a task remained before me, if I could summon the strength. I sank into the nearest chair, ignoring the damp soaking from my dress into the cushion. "Then I will go to her."

Mr. Burke stood strong and straight as an iron balustrade, blocking the doorway. "Only those investigating the murder will have access—and it's nothing a lady would wish to witness. You must put it from your mind. We'll handle the matter."

"As you did her protection? You promised you'd keep her safe—and now she's dead. Forgive me if I have no trust in your investigation." I clutched my arms around my chest, attempting to hold myself together. What had come over me, to make so free with my words?

The gaslights on the wall flickered, casting shadows across Mr. Burke's face. "You're overwrought, Miss Caldwell. Who can I summon on your behalf? You shouldn't be alone in such a state."

I looked away, unable to bear any hint of pity in his gaze—or worse, condemnation for my lack of control. On the table across the room lay my last letter to Ibbie. The sketch I'd penned to cheer her rested lifeless atop the envelope. At once, I could no longer breathe.

Perhaps they'd failed Ibbie, but so had I, writing her lighthearted letters and abandoning her to her fate. How could I have left her alone?

She'd sent me away, and somehow, despite those stationed for her protection, the killer had found her vulnerable. How much had she suffered when he claimed her life? Had she called for help, with none able to hear? I should have been with her, should never have let her cast me out.

I shivered uncontrollably, frigid in my soaked gown. And the pain rose to swallow me, blotting out my surroundings. No stratesmen existed here, no Wyncourt, no order or shape or form, only an enormous dark gulf of grief with no shore or boundary to hem it in.

The rain lashed against the windows, blurring the world outside to streaks of black and gray, and beyond, in the window boxes, a hint of crimson showed itself where bleeding hearts bloomed. The blossoms mocked me, their song still jubilant even in the face of suffering and violence and death.

I could not drown it out, the melody that brought such pain, could not strengthen my cage enough to regain control.

Warm wool dropped about my shoulders, and a firm hand tugged it close about me. Low voices spoke in the background, but my mind made no sense of their words.

Oh, Ibbie, I'm sorry, so sorry.

But she was gone and would never again hear my voice, nor I hers.

CHAPTER 6

My head muzzy with the peculiar sensation of half-waking, I blinked once, twice, chasing away the scarlet blossoms that consumed my vision, a remnant from the world of dreams. In that nightmarish reality, the flowers had turned to blood and become a rising tide that sought to drown me, while in the shadows a mist-shrouded figure with a rasping laugh mocked my efforts to escape.

I drew the bedcovers up to my chin, and Jade nuzzled my cheek, her green eyes glowing in the gaslight. Someone—Aunt Caris, perhaps—had left the wall lamp burning low.

Not even the slightest sliver of light peeped round the drawn curtains. The mantel clock read a quarter past three in the morning. What had happened in the missing hours? I strove to recall hazy events. Aunt Caris and my sisters had removed me from Wyncourt, fetched me home, forced me to bed. I reached for a glass of water left on the bedside table. The bitter taste of sleeping powders still coated my mouth.

Aunt Caris must have brewed them with the tea. In my grief, I'd downed them without recognition.

The rapid pulse of my heart burned away the remnants of the powders but did nothing to warm my body. I stumbled across the room and withdrew a heavy quilt from the bottom of my clothes press. Though I wound it tight around myself, it made no difference.

Jade curled herself next to me, and I clasped her close. She let my tears soak into her fur without protest, nudging me with her nose from time to time, a reassuring reminder that she would never leave.

Not like Ibbie.

Oh, how I ached for her.

I pushed upright and reached for my sketchbook and tin of charcoals. In varied shades of gray, I shaped Ibbie's face. I filled page after page with living memories. I captured the abstracted expression she wore when she considered matters of antiquity, the glow of delight sparked by examining a new-to-her artifact, the gleam of pride evident when she reviewed my work—and even the melancholies that plagued her at intervals.

But I avoided what should have been the final sketch—Ibbie bearing the mark, Ibbie devoid of life. What had she suffered alone?

I stared at the succession of images. Ibbie had been family, bound by love if not by blood. And now she was gone. If I'd pursued information about the killer directly, if I'd sought the truth without fear of the consequences . . . would she still live? The Magistry had kept order for countless years, yet in certain ways I held an advantage. I could freely seek the alchemists with inquiries, and—in theory at least—I could move about society and address its members without raising suspicion.

What a lady would reveal to another of her gender and station, what she might recall in a situation of familiarity and comfort, would be markedly different from what she'd divulge to a stratesman. Particularly if the blunt, unyielding Mr. Burke represented their force. I couldn't imagine anyone offering up thoughts, insights, or intuitions to a man who insisted on facts alone.

Lady Tarleton had poured out a great deal to me, though I'd not pressed her for information beyond inquiring about the safeguards she'd used for her son. What more might she have shared, if only I'd asked? Who else might have knowledge to impart?

If I'd only acted sooner, could I have uncovered something to make a difference?

I closed my eyes, blotting out Ibbie's likeness. Perhaps the outcome would have been the same, but if I'd acted, I would at least have the small comfort of knowing I'd done all I could.

And what of the future? Next week, next month, or next year, the killer could steal another member of my family. The thought tore at my mind like the claws of a dragon, cold and rending. Unless something changed, the killer would mark and claim whomever he desired. No one could predict when he would strike next, nor whom he would choose. The Magistry appeared helpless to stop his ravages. If they couldn't find him, all that remained was suffering and loss.

I refused to accept that.

I set aside the sketchbook and moved to the window to draw back the curtains. A thick fog hung over the garden, and a slender crescent moon tinted the mists the pale silver of a funerary shroud. I leaned my forehead against the cool glass of the window. Though I didn't wish to see Ibbie devoid of life, something troubled me about the Magistry's refusal to allow any outside their ranks to view the body.

What had the killer done to her that the Magistry sought to hide? Could the method of her death give insight about the nature of the murderer?

An errant wind swept the garden, and the fog stirred, coils and tendrils wrapping themselves around branch and trunk below. Nothing in the eerie scene resembled my comforting, familiar garden.

Perhaps it was fitting, for why should my beloved garden remain untouched, when all of Avons had been shaken? My skin pebbled with the cold, but still I stood vigil.

Ibbie had asked for my help with the files of the victims, but if she'd not been able to force them from the Magistry, then I had no hope of succeeding.

Yet somehow, I must act.

I had let her down in life, but I would honor her in death. To pursue the truth about the killer meant risk. It meant going against what everyone expected of me. But why should my life continue as it had before, as though Ibbie's death meant nothing? If the Magistry found the murderer before me, so much the better, but I couldn't trust their efforts alone, not with the cost of failure unbearably high. No, I would work to identify the murderer before he could claim another precious life.

The cloud encroaching on the moon engulfed it, plunging the gardens into full dark. I turned from the window and fetched my sketchbook once more.

Tomorrow, I would begin.

～

WHEN MORNING DAWNED, I had no opportunity to act on my resolve. As soon as I ventured downstairs, Aunt Caris fussed about me like an overzealous hen with only one chick. She refused to allow me from her sight and kept up a steady patter of words she intended for comfort until I wanted to flee to my bedchamber and bury myself beneath the covers once more. At least the confinement withindoors held the fae-touch at bay, for now.

But the pressure of containing my emotions to keep her from worry formed a tremendous knot in my chest. I forced myself to maintain a rigid smile, to nod in receipt of her reassurances as though my world had not been upended. For if I could convince her that I was well, she'd cease to fuss, and I could escape to carry on with fact-gathering. As far as I could see, the place to begin was with the servants at Wyncourt, with whom I was already familiar. They at least would welcome me.

After a late breakfast, Aunt Caris coaxed me into the morning room, where she plied me with honeyed tea before settling down with her embroidery. I perched on the edge of a chair, gripping a puzzle book to give myself an excuse to withdraw from conversation. But I couldn't manage to read a single word. My mind kept turning over the list of victims, seeking some sort of link or commonality between them, and coming up dry.

But perhaps . . . perhaps something of note would occur at her funeral. The killer liked to taunt his prey, else why the tattoos? Would he dare show his face there? I lifted my head. "I'd like to attend Ibbie's burial."

Aunt Caris snipped a loose thread. "My dear, it's out of the question. It won't be an ordinary occasion, not with the Magistry there in force and who-knows-what sort of riffraff attracted to the event by virtue of its connection with the killer. I cannot think any of the ladies of her acquaintance will attend, not given the possible dangers."

"But it's the only opportunity to honor her memory, since the Magistry won't permit her body to be held in state at Wyncourt."

"I wish you could observe the usual rites of mourning, but

given the circumstances, it changes nothing. I know you're grieving, but your father and I discussed it, and we're quite decided."

It was rare for Aunt Caris to speak with such finality. Worry gave her words a sharper edge than usual, and each one pierced the raw wound left by Ibbie's death. I lowered my gaze back to the page, and the words blurred before me.

Aunt Caris continued. "I understand your pain, my dear. I've not forgotten how I struggled when I lost my sister, all the more for it coming so soon after your mother. I don't wish you to think me unsympathetic, but—"

Holden appeared, cutting short whatever she intended to say. "Miss Caldwell, a Mr. Ludne and Mr. Burke from the Magistry have come to speak with Miss Jessa."

Aunt Caris tugged her needle with such force that she snapped her thread. "Send them away, Holden. Tell them we're not at home, whatever you must."

While I didn't want to see Mr. Burke after my humiliating display of emotion the day before, it would be far better than spending the rest of the morning wondering about his aims. Had he called about the letter I'd sent, or did he have another purpose? I set a ribbon in my book and snapped it shut. "Aunt Caris, it would ease my mind to speak with them."

She examined me, her brow creasing. "If you feel you must, I'll allow it. But I'll end the conversation promptly if they overstep. They must know how distressing this whole affair has been."

"I don't believe stratesmen concern themselves with anyone's feelings. Their job is justice, not mercy."

"Well, they'll mind themselves today." She jabbed her needle into her embroidery and sought her spool of thread. "I won't have you upset further."

I would protest that I wasn't as fragile as she believed, but my lack of self-governance yesterday suggested otherwise. I hadn't allowed my emotions to escape in such a fashion since I was a young girl, and for good reason—the display left me vulnerable, not only to the perception of others, but also against the influence of the fae-touch. And I needed all the protection I could obtain. So I lowered my head in assent.

"We'll receive them in the drawing room, Holden," said Aunt Caris.

"Very well." He gave a slight bow and left.

I rose to follow, but Aunt Caris checked me. "A moment, my dear. It will do them no harm to wait for us. They needn't think they can summon us at will."

When at last Aunt Caris deemed it time, she swept down the hall and into the drawing room, leaving me to follow in her wake.

Mr. Burke and an unfamiliar gentleman rose to greet us. Mr. Burke bore a statesman's insignia on his shoulder today, but the other man, one of dark complexion and tightly drawn features, did not. A strong scent emanated from the stranger, something sharp, almost repellent, and my head began to ache dully, as it sometimes did with too heavy a cologne.

Mr. Burke introduced him as Mr. Ludne, with no further explanation. So who was he?

After we exchanged polite greetings, Mr. Burke settled back into his chair. "I trust you've recovered, Miss Jessa."

"I have indeed." I folded my hands in my lap, determined to project calm. "Thank you."

Aunt Caris shook her head, and the copper curls wisping about her cap shivered with the motion. "Yet I must insist you keep your visit short. Jessa isn't one to complain, but she's greatly wearied after the events of yesterday."

"Is she?" As when we first met, Mr. Burke pinned me with his kestrel-like gaze, and I shifted uncomfortably.

Mr. Ludne set his walking stick across his legs, and the iron raven-head handle seemed to glare at me with its fixed black eyes. He neatly interposed himself into the conversation. "Then we shall be direct. I understand you spent considerable time with Lady Dromley, and the two of you shared a close connection."

"That's correct."

"Excellent. We're hoping you can shed some light on a few matters."

"When you say we, do you mean the Magistry? Or do you represent someone else's interests?" I worked to maintain a placid smile, as if the question were inconsequential and represented no deeper thought.

Mr. Ludne raised a neatly trimmed brow. "Does it matter?"

"I prefer to know to whom I speak."

Aunt Caris wore a pinched look, but offered no protest. No doubt she made allowances for my grief—or else I would receive a reminder on ladylike behavior later, in private.

Mr. Ludne tapped long, thin fingers against his walking stick, appearing to weigh his words. "I represent the Vigil."

If he'd struck me with his walking stick, the shock would have been less. For a moment, rational thought fled. A Vigilist, here? An unwelcome heat surged up my chest, and oh, I hoped it did not color my cheeks nor serve to betray my discomfort. I forced a light tone. "How very fascinating. And what interest does the Vigil have in this case?"

Mr. Burke cleared his throat. "We're losing sight of the purpose here. These murders have stretched our resources to the limit, and the Vigil has offered temporary support to bolster our efforts. I'm certain you appreciate the added protection, as does all Avons."

"Of course, but—"

Mr. Burke continued as smoothly as if I'd never spoken. "We found several alchemical devices at Wyncourt. Do you know anything about their presence?"

Though every sinew ached to flee from Mr. Ludne and the threat he represented, I maintained my position and attended to Mr. Burke. "Lady Dromley told me she enlisted the aid of an alchemist to provide additional protection."

"Which alchemist?" Mr. Ludne leaned forward, and the chair groaned beneath him. His bothersome scent intensified, filling the air between us.

I wished for a fan to wave it away, but settled for shifting back in my chair. "Alchemist Lyons. I believe he belongs to the Avons Sect."

Surely they must know this; their men must have seen him coming and going. So why the questions?

"When did she speak with you about this?" Mr. Burke asked.

"We didn't discuss it—she sent a letter."

"I'd like to see it, if you will." On the surface, it was a request, one I'd rather deny. But unmistakable command laced his words.

I slipped from the room to fetch the letter, taking advantage of the momentary lull to gather my thoughts. Perhaps I could still gain something of value from the conversation. I didn't fully believe Mr. Burke's explanation about the involvement of the Vigil. Assuming Mr. Ludne didn't somehow suspect my fae-touch, he could have only one other purpose. And this was my chance to find out the truth. I hurried back to the drawing room, determined to have the unpleasantness over with as quickly as possible.

When I offered the letter to Mr. Burke, he accepted without comment and surveyed the scant contents, his face unreadable.

While he reviewed the letter, I turned to Mr. Ludne—and I did not have to feign the fear prompting me to ask, "Do you suspect Otherworldly involvement in the matter of these murders?"

Aunt Caris gave a soft gasp.

But Mr. Ludne simply studied me through pale gray eyes, the exact shade of frost-touched winterberry. I suspected his person was as astringent as the aforementioned berry.

"Do you, Miss Jessa?"

"It's not impossible." Even as I spoke, disquiet stirred. For it *was* possible, no matter that Vigilists and alchemists alike proclaimed Avons protected from Otherworldly influence. On this one matter alone, they agreed. Avons was the safest city in Byren, untouchable by any malevolent fae force. But how could any mortal be certain when it came to Otherkind?

"Nor is it impossible that the rivers could rise and flood the whole city, given the proper circumstances—and yet, no such circumstance has ever occurred. Why should this be different?" Again, the relentless rapping of his fingers against his walking stick, but this time, the rhythm faltered on occasion, betraying . . . what? "No, we seek a mortal murderer, blighted by madness or fae-touch, not that there's much difference between the two in the end."

How that stung. Before I could collect myself for another line of approach, Mr. Ludne took the offensive.

"Do you know anyone in Lady Dromley's life who might fit that description?"

My stomach lurched. How much could the Vigil perceive?

Was he toying with me? Could he tell that *I* fit that description? That I bore the taint of the fae pulsing through me and shaping my every interaction with the world no matter how I tried to lock it away? I smoothed a minute wrinkle from my skirt. "I'm afraid I cannot say. Besides, the killer must act as if he's in full possession of his faculties. Surely if he displayed signs of fae-touch or madness, he would have been caught long before now, particularly with such skilled officials on the case?"

Aunt Caris was very pale, but she refrained from interjecting. It must have cost her to let the conversation run its course. How long before she put an end to it?

"I'm afraid you're correct. He hasn't made our job easy." Mr. Burke passed the letter back to me. "Did Lady Dromley share anything else with you?"

"Nothing that would shed light on the killer." I fought to keep my voice steady. "She tried to hide it, but she was afraid."

"But she didn't fear anyone in particular?"

"Not that she told me. If I knew anything, no matter how small, you must believe I'd have shared it already." After all, I'd called upon the Magistry with the merest hint of an idea, for all the good it had done. I wasn't eager to repeat the experience.

Something flickered in his eyes—perhaps he recalled the same incident. "The day before her death, Lady Dromley painted large words on the walls of her study and bedchamber using some sort of daub-like substance. Did she confide in you her reasons?"

I rocked back slightly. What had Ibbie been about? Why would she do such a thing? I looked from one man to the other. "I'm afraid she never mentioned anything of the sort. What did it say?"

"We don't know." A slight frown appeared on Mr. Burke's face. "The words resembled the script of the alchemists, and we thought perhaps an alchemist had advised her to inscribe them as a sort of ward. You know nothing of this?"

"I wish I did. If I could examine them—"

"They exist no longer, except within our records." Mr. Ludne took over the conversation. "I had the walls scrubbed."

I blinked. "Why?"

"No sense in stirring up rumors, nor causing fear among the staff." His narrow lips tightened. "We expect you to keep this to yourself."

"Of course." But my mind whirred with theory and speculation. If I asked all the questions stirring, they'd look askance at me. No lady probed into the details of an investigation, and yet . . . "Are you certain Lady Dromley placed them on the wall? Might it have been the killer?"

"We have reason to believe Lady Dromley was responsible," Mr. Burke stated quietly.

"That would be rather out of keeping with her character," I murmured.

Mr. Burke glanced at Mr. Ludne. "Nevertheless, the facts remain."

I inclined my head and adopted a hesitant air. "Of course. I should like to help in any way I can, since Lady Dromley was so dear to me. Perhaps I could take a look at your copy and see if the runes appear to be in her writing? I'm familiar with her script."

Mr. Ludne waved a hand. "Unnecessary. They'll be examined by an expert in archaic languages."

I widened my eyes at him. "Perhaps an alchemist?"

"We'll see the inscriptions are given due attention, as we have every aspect of this case."

He'd deflected that neatly. Had they sought help from the

Avons Sect and met with resistance? Or did the Vigil shun all notion of interaction with the alchemists?

Mr. Burke remained unusually quiet, his jaw set. I sensed he was not of one accord with Mr. Ludne. Yet for some reason—perhaps orders from his superiors—he made no objection, but allowed Mr. Ludne to take charge.

All else having failed, I took a more direct approach, wondering if it would prompt Mr. Burke to speak. "But surely Alchemist Lyons would be able to answer any questions about the inscriptions or at least inform you if they were alchemical in nature. If you go to him, he—"

"That is not your concern." Something dark and unpleasant crossed Mr. Ludne's features. "In fact, you ask far too many—"

Aunt Caris stood abruptly, bringing both men to their feet. "Gentlemen, I think it's time you left. Jessa has offered you everything she knows, and I cannot think prolonging this conversation will give any fresh insight."

For a moment, I thought Mr. Ludne would lash out, but instead he gave a curt bow. "If we have further questions, we'll return. We expect your full cooperation."

With that, he departed, leaving me troubled. If the Vigil found Ibbie guilty of any *irregularities*, a polite term some used for fae-touch, would they give her death the attention it deserved?

Mr. Burke hesitated on the threshold. "I have one more matter to address—the letter you sent about Levina Tarleton. I will speak with her father, of course, but I must admonish you not to involve yourself with the families of the other victims nor seek information on the killer."

Aunt Caris clutched the arms of her chair and pressed her lips together tightly.

What reply could I possibly give? I'd not intended to unearth information on the killer then, but I certainly did now.

"Fear and grief cloud judgment and goad people to dangerous deeds," he said. "You must leave this affair for us to handle. Otherwise we cannot answer for your safety."

It seemed to me they couldn't answer for my safety regardless. I stifled the flare of anger and sought an even tone. "Of course. I understand . . . and I wish you all speed and success in finding the killer."

The faint lines around his steel-gray eyes deepened, as though he knew what I left unspoken. I'd no intention of heeding his warning. I refused to embrace an illusion of safety, when all those I cared about were exposed to a predator who could end their lives in an instant—when I'd already failed Ibbie.

Behind me, Aunt Caris simmered with emotion like a pot about to boil over. Perhaps that was his aim. Mr. Burke seemed like a man who acted with forethought and deliberation. Did he know I couldn't bear to cause Aunt Caris pain? Did he intend to provoke her by issuing this warning in her presence, thereby ensuring she kept me in check?

"If you think of anything relevant, you can contact me." He handed over his card, the black lettering and thick white paper surprisingly refined.

Though Aunt Caris gave a gracious nod, the moment the door closed behind him, she leapt up, her color heightened. "By the Crossings, Jessa! I thought you'd given up the foolish notion of interfering in this matter. What can you possibly do that they cannot?"

She was truly upset, for she'd used my given name, rather than an endearment. An ache formed beneath my breastbone. "I only wanted to keep Ibbie safe, not cause you any distress."

With effort, Aunt Caris stilled herself. "I know you loved

her, and it was natural you sought to give aid, however misguided your efforts. But you must see the folly of it now." She knelt and clasped my frigid hands in her warm ones, the letter crackling between us. "Promise me you'll forsake the matter and leave it to the Magistry to handle. Consider your family, my dear. We all worry for you."

Coils of love and propriety wrapped around me like chains. I buried my head in her shoulder and breathed in her familiar scent, a mingling of soft violet and lavender. "I am."

And because I did consider them—their lives and well-being—I could make no such promise. Her fears for me echoed mine for her, for all those I loved, in a city where anyone might become the next victim.

Would she notice my omission?

CHAPTER 7

In the three days following our conversation, Aunt Caris and my sisters hovered over me every waking hour. If I retired to work on floral arrangements, Aunt Caris appeared to offer a helping hand and a continual stream of conversation. If I went to the glasshouse to tend the plants, Ada brought her needlework or music compositions to keep me company. If I sought refuge in Father's study and attempted to distract myself with a book of conundrums, Ainslie developed a burning need to review the latest gazettes within.

More often than not, the three of them joined forces, and when they did, they filled the air with a discomfiting blend of lively chatter intended to distract and gentle reassurance meant to console, all of which provided continual pricking reminders of my loss.

Lovell added his own attempts to lift my spirits. He frequented our house even more often than usual, hovering with a purposeful air and upon every visit bringing something intended to distract me from Ibbie's fate—new books he'd fetched from the library, clippings of plants he'd found about town, or compendiums of difficult puzzles.

I couldn't speak of my desire for solitude without crushing them, but I suffocated beneath the constant outpouring of sympathy. How could I explain that their comfort brought no relief, much less confess that I would only find peace in the pursuit of answers and justice? I chafed at the delay, at the knowledge the killer could mark another at any moment. Yet to disclose the truth would only distress them further, so I remained silent.

On Sunday, I welcomed the quiet liturgies of the oratory service and the reminder that the Infinite extended mercy even in the most difficult of circumstances. That afternoon, I gently suggested Aunt Caris and my sisters might go on their usual round of calls the next day.

To my relief, they took me at my word. Their departure ushered in a blessed silence—and my first true opportunity to investigate Ibbie's death and clear up any misunderstanding about her so-called *irregularities*.

I still intended to visit Wyncourt, ostensibly to reclaim some of my sketches, but in actuality to uncover evidence within the house or in conversation with the servants. If I had time afterward, I would seek Alchemist Lyons. He might be able to answer my questions about the inscriptions Ibbie had left behind. At least, he could indicate whether she'd painted them at his bidding. And if he'd go further and divulge the devices Ibbie had requested of him, it might give some additional insight into her state of mind. Perhaps, in her final days, she'd had some inkling of what sort of attack might come and had prepared accordingly—or perhaps she'd confided something in him. Both were slim hopes, but better than none.

On my way out, Holden handed me a small pile of letters

that had arrived in the morning post. I tucked them into my portfolio and hailed a hack. The trip between the residential area that housed Wyncourt and the Alchemical Sanctum on the west side of Avons would take some time, and my correspondence would provide welcome distraction. Jade nested beside me on the leather seat, her nose twitching as she absorbed the smells left by prior occupants.

I stroked her head and then opened the first letter. The familiar looped writing of my dear friend Edith filled the pages. She offered her condolences on Ibbie's passing, and her gentle concern emanated from the page.

> *If I'd not been sent to care for Aunt Louisa, I'd attempt to persuade Mother to send me to Avons. Yet I know you have your family, and I imagine you prefer to mourn in peace. But if I'm wrong, only send word, and I shall do my best to come, despite any number of relations in need.*

Then she moved on to sharing news from Upper Northlea, a relief from my pressing sorrow. Dear Edith . . . she never failed to offer encouragement. I folded her letter and opened the next.

This envelope bore the inscription of Thornhaven, which Mother had left in trust for us after her death. Since Father forbade us to travel there after her passing, the estate manager sent comprehensive reports to us once a quarter. My sisters left them for me to review, trusting I'd inform them of any matters of import. I stared at the envelope as though it held a serpent. What would our manager have to say this time? Had the sprites kept to the bargain we'd made in Milburn, or would this missive report an onslaught of trouble?

I slit open the envelope and skimmed down the tightly scripted lines. Everything appeared in order. I let the letter drop to my lap and drew a deep breath. I'd not caused harm by relocating the sprites there, at least not yet.

If I could see for myself . . . perhaps in time we could persuade Father to allow us to visit Thornhaven once more. But even if he agreed, did I dare risk spending more time near a Crossing?

The carriage halted in front of Wyncourt, and I tucked the letter into my portfolio, a trouble for another time.

For this day held enough worries of its own, not least of which were the grim stratesmen standing guard at the door of Wyncourt. I peered through the carriage window.

Did I wish to expose my ongoing interest in the case to them? And even if I did, would they grant me entrance? I hesitated, my hand resting on the door handle.

An ornate carriage halted alongside mine and discharged a tall, unfamiliar gentleman. All confident assurance, he marched to the door. Though he spoke with an air of authority, the stratesmen appeared unmoved. After arguing with them for a few moments, the man gave up and departed.

I withdrew into the shadows of the carriage. If they'd barred the door to him, I couldn't imagine they'd give way to me simply because I'd left sketches inside, and Mr. Burke might well receive a report of all callers. If he knew I'd visited Wyncourt, would he suspect I continued to investigate and reveal my involvement to Aunt Caris?

It wasn't worth the risk, not now. Instead, I'd send Ives with a note to the housekeeper later. Mrs. Peters would inform me if they allowed anyone admittance . . . and if they intended to depart from Wyncourt.

I informed the driver I'd not be staying after all and asked him to continue on to the Alchemical Sanctum. As we drove away, I cast a glance back at Wyncourt. For a moment, it appeared shrouded by mists, its dark windows glinting like bead-black eyes in the face of a dragon. I blinked and the scene righted. Perhaps my sorrow lent strength to fancy . . . or perhaps the fae-touch exerted itself once more, distorting the ordinary and tricking my senses.

I shivered and drew Jade close. She nudged at my portfolio, and from the stack of letters, I withdrew a cream-colored missive with a small stain on one corner. The inscription was written in an unfamiliar, crabbed hand and bore the location of Milburn. The distinct aroma of pipe tobacco emanated from it—it must be from Mr. Heard, the loremaster of Milburn, whose advice had helped me confront the sprites. He'd also given me a gift before my departure, one I preferred not to contemplate, despite its generosity . . . for an unmistakable sense of Other hung about it.

Miss Jessa,

Made the acquaintance of your friends at the mill, those who were once plagued by the sprites. Thought you might want to know that they've found themselves with a number of customers in Milburn. Once that bone-headed baker relented, many followed, and right pleased they were to avoid having to travel to the next town for their needs.

As for the baker, I went to him myself and told him what's what. Couldn't see your efforts go to naught, and speaking my mind gave me a great deal of satisfaction. Of course, Mrs. Hopkins has plenty of grit and go-to, and if it weren't for her labors, no amount of my influence would bring success.

Lord Ackerley is still stubborn as a karzel, but his opinion isn't carrying the day in this matter. Rumor has it he's been in a fury over it, but what more can he do? Still, just to ensure he doesn't try anything underhand, I've paid him a visit as well. He won't want my knowledge of him to be public. Ha! It's been many a year since I've bestirred myself in such fashion. Must admit watching him puff and blow was a pleasure. Not pleasure enough to keep dealing with plaguey townsfolk, though. Don't want them banging on my door with all their needs, no indeed.

One more thing. Just because you escaped with your life once in dealing with the fae doesn't mean it'll happen again. Don't get overconfident. And never trust Otherkind.

Regards,
Leofric Heard

P.S. If you acquire any interesting lore, I'd welcome a report.

As if I would ever grow overconfident in dealing with the Otherworld. I flinched even seeing a comment on my encounter written down, though I supposed it was safe enough, given that a stratesman and an entire village family had also witnessed the final encounter with the sprites—as long as no one ever suspected what had transpired before. To outward appearances, they had been as involved, and as innocent, as I.

My sincerest wish was that I'd never encounter Otherkind again, let alone find myself forced to bargain with them, but I would welcome the chance to speak with Mr. Heard again and ask him the questions that pressed heavily on me. His zeal for Otherworldly lore matched that of Ibbie's for her antiquities. If Mr. Heard and Ibbie ever met, perhaps—

No, not Ibbie. Never again Ibbie. My eyes burned as I folded Mr. Heard's missive, and I secured it inside my portfolio as we pulled to a halt outside the Sanctum.

Jade nuzzled my hand and then clambered atop my shoulders, her presence bolstering my confidence. Welcome or not, I'd find a way within. At least here, I'd not have to fear a report returning to Mr. Burke.

We descended onto the wide walk before the Sanctum. Stark white granite walls and heavy iron gates barred it from visitors. Two guards stood watch over the gates, and when I approached, one of them motioned me forward.

His mustache bristled, unruly as gnarlroot, above a tight-lipped mouth. "What's your business here?"

I clutched my portfolio to my chest. "I'd like to see Alchemist Lyons. I'm here on behalf of Lady Dromley."

"Wait here. I'll see if he's in."

Jade and I stood in the silence that surrounded the Sanctum. Beyond the wall, it formed an enormous square around a central courtyard. The building stretched four stories high, and each side was divided into numerous sections that peaked into steep triangular rooflines, sharp angles that appeared to bristle with a warning: *keep out.*

Most streets in Avons bustled with activity, but the walk in front of the Sanctum remained quiet, almost desolate. The few passersby kept to the other side of the street, and only one carriage clattered over the cobblestones while I waited.

How had they managed to isolate themselves so completely within the city? And why would they wish it? I clutched my portfolio closer to my chest.

At last, the guard returned. "You may enter."

Once we crossed the courtyard and entered the building, he left me in a small antechamber, instructing me to wait for the footman to fetch me. The chamber wasn't designed for comfort —its narrow windows, sparse furnishings, and general lack of adornment suggested rather it was a place to fob off unwanted visitors.

Jade prowled and sniffed at the corners, her hackles rising. Perhaps she caught traces of a mouse?

An uncomfortable crawling sensation crept along my neck and down my back. To distract myself, I perched on a spindle-backed chair and turned again to my correspondence. Next in the stack lay a thick ivory envelope with precise lettering. I slipped my finger below the seal and skimmed the contents.

Oh . . . the letter fell to my lap, and I stared at it unseeing. It was a request for my presence at the reading of Ibbie's will, four days hence. Had she left me some token of personal remembrance? My chest tightened. It would be like her to consider me.

"Miss?"

With effort, I wrenched my attention from the summons to the impassive footman waiting in the doorway. Everything about him was nondescript, from his box-bark hair to his flat brown eyes.

"Alchemist Lyons has agreed to see you. If you'll come with me, I'll show you to his chambers."

Even his voice was monotone, and somehow his very blankness deepened my unease. The further we moved into the building, the more the oppressive sensations intensified. My stomach churned as though I'd eaten a full meal and then taken one too many spins on the dance floor. Had they somehow warded their buildings to repel visitors? Small wonder not many paid calls on the alchemists, if they received such an ungracious welcome.

If I'd had the social standing—and abundant funds—required to request a house call, I'd not have ventured here to begin with. I only hoped I didn't come to regret the visit.

From a nearby corridor, a high, well-modulated voice drifted out. "High fae? Nonsense."

"They're fearmongering, of course," a second man said. "The

Vigil needs to make themselves relevant to retain their power. They can't endure the notion we might one day rival them."

The footman picked up his pace, and I'd no choice but to follow, though I'd rather have listened further. Why did they discuss high fae, when none had been known in Byren in centuries? *Power enough to shake our world*—that's what Mr. Heard had said of the high fae, and all our histories and lore bore him out. Was someone spreading rumors about their presence? My encounter with low fae had been trying enough; I didn't want to consider meeting the ones even they feared.

The footman swung open a tall, heavily carved door and led me over the threshold into an opulent sitting room, where a tall, lean man stood at the window. Two tremendous ward-stones heavily scribed with runes stood on either side of the window, bristling with menace. The stomach-churning sensation intensified, and my skin stung as if I'd forged through a patch of briars. Only with effort did I keep myself from scrubbing at my arms.

Slowly, Alchemist Lyons turned toward me, his grizzled head, narrow features, and pointed nose giving him rather the appearance of a greyhound which had taken on human form. He examined the calling card I handed him. "Miss Caldwell. My footman has informed me you're calling on behalf of Lady Dromley. Most irregular, but I can only assume she wishes to commission additional work?"

His words hit like a blow, and I flinched. "You . . . you don't know? The stratesmen haven't called?"

"I'd never permit a stratesman entrance." Alchemist Lyons sniffed. "They undervalue our work and expect us to give freely on behalf of the public that which costs us a great deal in both time and resource to create—that is, when they don't seek to hinder our endeavors."

"Then they haven't called?"

He waved a hand. "Oh, I believe my assistant made mention of it . . . and he rightly informed them I was away."

Which meant if I gained anything from this visit, it could shed new light on the case—though I shuddered to think of speaking with Mr. Burke again after his warnings. Sooner or later, they'd no doubt force an audience with Alchemist Lyons, though not even the Magister himself could enter the Sanctum without an order from the king or the Assemblage of Lords.

I pressed a hand to my unsettled stomach and forced myself to voice the bitter words. "It pains me to tell you, but Lady Dromley has . . . passed on."

"My condolences." I might as well have reported the sky was blue, for all the inflection in his reply. "If that's the case, why have you troubled me? I have important matters to attend."

I swallowed against the rising tide of queasiness. "I'm here because Lady Dromley commissioned some devices from you in an attempt to protect herself from the killer. I hoped you could tell me what she purchased and anything she might have shared with you."

His whippet-sharp face narrowed further. "I never discuss client affairs with others. Discretion is everything in my work."

"But given that Lady Dromley is—"

He raised a hand, cutting me off. "You've wasted your time—and more importantly, mine—by coming here. Now run along."

The fur at Jade's neck bristled, as though she took offense on my behalf.

However improper it was to insist, I couldn't let him go, not without answers. If only I'd pressed for them sooner, perhaps Ibbie might still live.

"Wait, please." My words twisted in a discomfiting way, and relentless waves of pressure pulsed through my head. "Can you tell me nothing of what you discussed? What she asked of you?"

"I don't retain such petty details."

Petty? A wave of heat swept head to toe, and I pressed my lips together tightly. It appeared he cared for nothing except his work and his reputation. Since appealing to common decency had failed, perhaps I might press that point.

He jabbed a finger toward the door. "You may leave now."

Something wrenched deep within, as my sorrow for Ibbie wove together with my anger at his indifference, infusing my voice with something unwelcome, something that felt slightly *Other*. "Alchemist Lyons, I suggest you reconsider. Lady Dromley meant a great deal to me. Just as your business means to you. It would scarcely go well for you if word got out that she enlisted your alchemical powers to protect her from the killer—and they failed."

"I assure you my work *never* fails." But his words sounded slightly choked.

"That's not what people will think if word spreads." I choked down the bile burning the back of my throat. I couldn't worry about the fae-touch, not now. Instead, I composed my features into a pleasant smile. "All I ask is a few more moments of your time to answer my questions."

He hesitated, steepling his fingers, perhaps considering how it would reflect upon him if news of her purchase and subsequent death was spread abroad. "As I said, I recall little of our conversation, but I keep records of my devices. I'll have my assistant provide you with a list of the items Lady Dromley purchased for your reference. I trust you will maintain discretion about the matter?"

"Of course." I leaned forward, and Jade pressed herself against my legs. "But I do have one more question. Is it a common practice within alchemy to scribe words or symbols onto walls? Or floors perhaps?" I added the last as I recalled the dark lines etched into Reynold's bedchamber floor.

His wire-thin brows rose nearly to his hairline. "Inscriptions on walls or floors? Ridiculous. Such common household materials could never be a proper medium for alchemy."

"So you'd not instruct your clients to act in such a fashion?"

"Not unless I wished to be a laughingstock among my peers." A muscle in his jaw twitched. "Alchemy is a matter of precision, long hours of study, and skill—not to mention the correct use of the proper materials."

If I wanted to gain information, I must venture further. "And have those materials given the alchemists the powers of concealment they seek?"

"Who are you?" His face darkened. "Did the Wilven Sect send you?"

"No one sent me. I have my own concerns—"

"Which are no excuse to pry into the Guild's affairs." With apparent effort, he mastered himself. "If you'll excuse me, I'll send my assistant to you shortly with the information you've requested."

"But I—"

"No more questions." He stalked from the room.

Jade chuffed, apparently pleased with his departure, and I stroked her absently. He hadn't denied advancements in their ability to replicate glamour-like concealment, but it meant little. Given his pride, he'd hardly confess to failure. Still, since he suspected me of being sent to search for secrets, I found it likely that the various Sects and even individuals were competing for the breakthrough. Though I supposed one of them could have achieved it already but kept it secret—particularly if he had nefarious motives.

At least I now knew Ibbie hadn't acted at his bidding when she'd daubed the walls with mysterious runes . . . although that left me with a host of new questions. There must be a reasonable explanation, one which would not blacken Ibbie's good name.

A few moments later, a young lad entered the room with a folded, sealed paper, which he handed to me. "Alchemist Lyons says I'm to see you out, miss."

I gladly stumbled from the room and through the iron gates, with Jade trotting alongside. Beyond the Sanctum walls, the unpleasant stomach-wrenching sensation ebbed, and I rubbed my arms as the last of the unpleasant stinging departed. What a dreadful place, occupied by even more dreadful people. While I appreciated the benefits of alchemy, I no longer wondered at the king's wish to rein in the arrogance of the alchemists.

I hailed a hack, and once Jade and I were ensconced within, I unfolded the message. True to his word, Alchemist Lyons had written a list of the five devices he'd provided Ibbie. Two of the items had a more established history: the fyret sphere, which would engulf any intruder in unquenchable flame while leaving one's surroundings untouched, and a flask of haelin, a potent restorative. Fyret spheres were rare and costly—far beyond the means of most to procure—though the royal guards were supposed to possess some small supply, along with other items for protection of the king. Haelin was also expensive, but frequently used by the alchemists when they treated ailments among the nobility.

The elsinger, a protective cloak that no weapons could pierce, had recently been developed and was still rare, and the gardestones were also new. Theoretically, they offered a stronger, more advanced ward, yet no one had demonstrated the truth of these claims. How could they, when there were no fae within Avons to test them on?

The final item was a collection of ward-stones, doubtless meant to enhance the ones she already owned. My fingers tightened around the list, and the thick paper crinkled. It appeared Ibbie had acted out of caution, rather than with any specific insight. These devices indicated she'd sought the broadest protection possible, along with aids to heal in case such measures failed her.

Not that any of it had helped her, in the end. A now-familiar ache tightened my chest. I tucked the list inside my portfolio and penned a letter to Mrs. Peters. I would uncover the truth about Ibbie and about the killer, and then I would *make* the Magistry listen.

CHAPTER 8

When I received a reply from Mrs. Peters the following day, I tore open the envelope at once. Her simple, blockish scrawl filled the page.

Miss Jessa,

It's kind, you concerning yourself with us. I must say, we all wish these stratesmen gone. Without my lady to keep order, Wyncourt is at odds. She wouldn't have allowed stratesmen to tramp about the place as they pleased, much less keep us penned up here. I don't know what they expect to find, but they're determined to remain and equally determined no one else shall enter.

Mr. Broward, my lady's heir, was furious when they turned him away. He rang a peal quite soundly over their heads, but all it got him was a threat of being locked up overnight if he persisted. He's an unknown here, so it's no surprise, but Lord Blackburn himself was also sent away, and him only attempting to fetch a manuscript my lady had recovered for him. Even the simplest of household supplies must be delivered to our doorstep and brought in by the stratesmen, and I've heard more than one of them grumble about it.

Danvers asked when they'll leave us in peace, and Stratesmen Burke assured us they'll go by the end of the week. He's more a gentleman than the rest, but he doesn't stay here—more's the pity.

None of the maids appreciate our confinement, I can tell you. The footman neither. Their fears have put them on edge and given rise to all manner of rumors. It's all Danvers and I can do to keep them from quitting on the spot. My lady always allowed for a generous household budget, and we've given them extra pay if they'll remain until the matter of her will is settled, and we have word of what's to come next. I suppose we must wait and see. I do hope you'll call when the stratesmen have taken their leave.

With respect,
Mrs. Peters

How peculiar. What *was* Stratesman Burke hoping to accomplish by remaining at Wyncourt after Ibbie's death? Was he continuing to investigate Ibbie herself? Did he expect the killer to return to the scene of his crime? I refolded the letter as my bedroom door creaked open.

"Miss Jessa?" Lianne, the lady's maid my sisters and I shared, stood in the doorway.

"Yes?"

"Miss Caldwell sent me to do your hair for the luncheon."

I set the letter on my dressing table. "Thank you. I'm afraid the time rather escaped me."

I settled into the small chair before the mirrored table so she might begin the arduous process of taming my hair. Usually, I favored whatever simple styles I could manage on my own, given my thick, unruly curls, but Aunt Melisina would expect perfection—and Lianne could achieve it when I could not. She'd crafted my dark curls into a masterpiece on more than one occasion, so I didn't attempt to give instruction but allowed her creativity free rein.

As she worked, Lianne swayed gracefully. She resembled a windswept poppy, with her vivid red hair peeping from below her cap and her black-brown eyes intent on her work. She didn't so much as glance up when Ada and Ainslie swept into the room, for she was long since accustomed to our ways.

Ainslie draped herself over the bed while Ada glided to my side and rested her hand on my shoulder. "We're delighted that you intend to come today. We thought it might feel too soon, after Ibbie's passing."

It did—and yet, no one in society expected me to enter mourning, for Ibbie and I shared no blood ties. I gave her hand a gentle squeeze. "I promised Aunt Melisina, and I'll see it through."

If I could survive the afternoon without earning her displeasure, I'd count it a success.

"Perhaps you'll find it more pleasant than you expect." Ainslie crossed the room and rummaged through my small box of jewels. She selected a string of pearls—one of the few adornments I owned—and clasped it around my neck. "Since it's within Lord Cramer's gardens, perhaps you'll find new inspiration for your own, though I doubt his compares to ours, after all your labors."

I murmured my thanks, appreciative of her attempts to comfort. Aunt Melisina had described it as a small garden luncheon, yet it would surely be a lavish event. Lord Cramer was among the few with sufficient resources to have a large private garden within Avons, and despite myself, a small surge of anticipation rose at the thought of seeing his collection of plants. "I'm certain it will be lovely."

"And Lord Felix will be there." Ainslie mock-fluttered her fan. "So many ladies have swooned over him, I think it's high time I discover what the fuss is about."

I raised a brow. "So you can add him to your list of conquests?"

"And why not?" Ainslie snapped her fan shut. "Aunt Melisina would be pleased."

"If he offered marriage and you accepted, perhaps." Ada toyed with the button on her glove. "You know she grows impatient."

They exchanged a glance, and both sobered.

In the sudden silence, Lianne stepped back. "Will that be all, miss?"

"Yes, thank you."

When she left, Ada and Ainslie closed in on either side of me, their gowns rustling softly. The earnest expression on Ada's face hinted at sisterly admonishments to come.

"This won't be a terribly formal event," Ada began. "So you'll only need to concern yourself with making conversation. Keep your remarks short and unobjectionable. If you must ask questions, confine yourself to matters of wellness and weather."

Far easier in theory than in execution, when society took exception to even the most mundane of subjects. Conversing with individuals was one thing, but to enter an event with all the weight of unspoken expectation, with all the conventions that my sisters navigated with such ease—I felt as though a veritable forest of fern fronds unfurled within my belly. Yet I nodded, as if it were a simple affair.

"Above all, do not discuss the killer." A small furrow creased her brow. "If gentlemen raise the matter, don't comment. They may discuss it if they wish, but many would frown on young ladies taking an interest."

Then Ainslie broke out her sparkling smile. "And if Aunt Melisina troubles you too much, make your escape, and I'll keep you as far from her as possible."

"If I did, I doubt she'd be best pleased with either of us."

"Then I shall win her over afterward by promising to help her entertain at her next ball." Ainslie waved her hand. "And if she remains inexorable, it's no great loss. After all, sisters must come first."

With that, she helped me into my gown. Its flattering lines and pleasing color composition brought no pleasure—rather, I shrank from the touch of the cool fabric, and the reminder that the seamstress had fitted me even as the murderer claimed Ibbie. With shaking hands, I donned my gloves and fetched the beaded reticule made to match. I must force it from my mind, or I was certain to fail Aunt Melisina.

Jade pawed at my hem, her green eyes glittering with expectation.

I shook my head. "Aunt Melisina has expressly forbidden it, and I owe her this event."

She subsided, her back bristling with disapproval, and my sisters swept me out the door and into the waiting carriage.

∾

When we entered Lord Cramer's magnificent gardens, the whispers rushed round me strong as a summer gale. My cage of thorns creaked and groaned under the force, and panic stabbed through me.

Aunt Melisina spoke, but her voice faded into the background. I attended only to weaving the cage of thorns tighter and drowning out the persistent, pervasive whispers.

One moment, two, and at last the onslaught subsided to a manageable level. Aunt Melisina gripped my arm and drew me to her side, evidently unaware anything was amiss. How long could I hold the fae-touch at bay? I wanted to flee the gardens, but instead, I discreetly rubbed my throbbing temples and attempted to display an unruffled demeanor.

Aunt Melisina performed a whirlwind of introductions to ladies and gentlemen with polished smiles and sharp glances that probed for any sign of weakness or fault. I chose to say almost nothing, fearful of letting slip some unbecoming remark that Aunt Melisina would later condemn.

Meanwhile, Ada and Ainslie wove serenely through the crowd, their movements incorporating just enough liveliness to avoid appearing dull and just enough decorum to avoid drawing censure. Matrons smiled upon them—save those with marriageable daughters—and gentlemen watched them wherever they went.

From time to time, I caught snatches of conversation about the killer. After Ibbie's death, it weighed on everyone's mind, permissible topic of conversation or not. Unbearable pressure built in my chest, yet I smiled and nodded, even to the most absurd and meaningless remarks, until my face ached.

At last, Aunt Melisina released me from her grasp. Ainslie had vanished, so I slipped away into the recesses of the garden, taking refuge near a bowl-shaped fountain. The soft rush of its waters caused the voices to recede into the background, and for a moment, I could forget I needed to perform, needed to see and be seen. Just a brief respite, and then I would return and fulfill my obligations.

Before I could take my leave, a scuff of boot on the stone pavers made me jump. I turned to find an unfamiliar gentleman regarding me from deeply hooded eyes. His dark hair held a reddish sheen, like the bark of a black heselm, and though he wasn't particularly striking, some might find his air of calm confidence appealing.

I eased to the edge of the clearing, ready to make my escape, but he spoke.

"Forgive me for disturbing you."

"I have no claim on this place, so I'll surrender it to your enjoyment."

"I would by no means drive you away." He hesitated, then stepped forward. "Pray excuse my boldness, but since there is no one here to introduce us, I hope you'll allow me. I'm Mr. Upton of Bridstow."

He may have committed an impropriety by introducing himself, but I'd not commit a greater one by snubbing him. I offered a small nod. "I'm Miss Jessa Caldwell."

"Miss Caldwell." He closed the remaining distance between us. "Will you allow me to escort you back? They're preparing to serve luncheon."

I accepted his arm, and an unusual scent swirled round me —a sharp, dry fragrance, like that of a winter wind blowing down from frost-touched mountains, one that bore no resemblance to the citrus-and-spice scents favored by the gentlemen of Avons.

As we stepped onto the patterned stone path, I searched for an acceptable topic of conversation. Without Aunt Melisina to serve as a buffer, I must say *something*. "You mentioned you come from Bridstow? What brings you to Avons?"

"Business, you might say." A shadow crossed his face. For a

moment, he looked significantly older. "There was . . . a loss. A very great loss for my kin. It prompted me to come."

The pain in his voice exposed the raw places in my own heart, where the ache for Ibbie remained close to the surface. "I'm sorry for your loss, whatever the cause. And I pray you gain peace."

"I have no hope of peace nor desire for it, but perhaps I may avenge those who can no longer act for themselves." The muscles beneath my hand tightened. "I'm sure you've no desire to hear more of my difficulties."

"If it eases you to speak, I'm willing to listen."

"As it happens, there's another matter I'd like to discuss." His steps slowed. "I may as well be forthright. I intended to have a friend perform introductions, but your aunt kept you much occupied. When I noticed you leave the party, I didn't wish to lose my opportunity, so I followed you to the fountain."

What could I possibly say to that? My shoulders tightened. Did he mean some impropriety? Surely not, else why would he have offered to escort me back to the others? Besides, we were not so distant that I could not raise my voice and bring other guests to my aid. Still, I wished for Jade. She'd not hesitate to launch herself at him if he committed some solecism.

He filled the uncomfortable silence. "I beg your pardon for bringing up a matter I'm certain will cause pain, but I wish to speak of the loss you've recently suffered. I understand you were close to the killer's last victim."

I stumbled to a stop, releasing his arm. "How did you know?"

It was graceless, but surprise had loosened my tongue.

"After my arrival, it became apparent the Avons Magistry had little hope of managing the affair of the killer." The sun filtering through the branches of the trees overhead dappled his features with light and shadow. "I have considerable knowledge of matters such as these, so I've lent them what aid I can."

"I'm certain they're thankful for the assistance." What was his background, that the Magistry welcomed his involvement? Had he served them in the past elsewhere? Or was his experience more personal? Had those he'd lost been killed?

Before I could inquire, he continued. "It's further come to my attention that you're attempting to investigate the murders on your own."

Warmth crept up my neck and flooded my face. I'd attempted discretion in my activities, yet even this stranger had recognized my deeds. If he spoke to my aunts, it would be disastrous. I gripped my reticule tightly. "I've been advised to give up that pursuit. Did you seek me in order to add your own caution? I assure you it's not needed."

"I suppose I did, in a way. Burke thinks that some vague warnings will keep you from putting yourself in harm's way. I disagree." He leaned forward, and his wintry scent strengthened. "No one has the tenacity to pursue justice like those who have suffered loss. Those individuals burn with a passion impossible to quench, whatever the odds. I hardly think he's discouraged you. Am I correct?"

"Mr. Upton, I'd rather not discuss—"

"You don't have to explain. I've no authority to stop you," he said. "But I did want to speak with you myself, before your blood ends up on my hands."

"Whatever happens, no one else is responsible for my actions or their outcome. I'm not going into this blind."

"Perhaps not blind, but uninformed." He reached forth and gripped my hand so tightly that it sent pinpricks of pain along my palm. "Those with power protect themselves, even from your Magistry. They leverage their positions of authority and wealth to crush those who stand in their way. This case is no different. Do you understand?"

My mouth went dry. "I . . . I understand."

With that concession, he released me, and I stumbled back, catching my heel on an uneven stone. Did he intend to warn me that the killer was someone high in society? Someone whose attentions were doubly dangerous to draw? I steadied myself against the wicker bench alongside the path. If so, who?

I mentally reviewed the names associated with the murders. Who among the peers had taken particular interest in the case? Who showed up time and again? *Lord Blackburn.* The name sprang to mind with vivid clarity, and my breath caught.

He'd found the third victim, the solicitor. His attentions had stood out as remarkable to Lady Tarleton, given their limited acquaintance. And Lord Blackburn had attempted to call at Wyncourt after Ibbie's death, ostensibly to reclaim a manuscript she'd located for him. I knew she'd had contact with him in the past, and he could well have called on her prior to her death without raising questions. If only I could access Wyncourt and speak to the servants, perhaps I could find out how often he'd visited Ibbie . . . and when.

"Are you well, Miss Caldwell?" Concern bled into his words. "Did I alarm you? Perhaps I should—"

"No, it's not that." Did I dare ask? I looked up at him. "It's only . . . what do you know of Lord Blackburn?"

"Burke warned me you'd ask astute questions." He tapped his cane against the stone pavers. "I cannot speak of the investigation—I am bound by my word. But I suggest you stay far away from him, for your own safety."

The spring breeze worked its way through the light layers of my gown, chilling the skin beneath. Was he confirming my speculation? Yet if Lord Blackburn was the killer, why did he continue to attend the scene of his crimes? I rubbed my arms, seeking warmth. If he were depraved enough to commit these murders, then perhaps he derived pleasure from watching the families suffer.

If the killer were a lord, he'd have resources to procure alchemical devices—and it would explain the secrecy which shrouded the investigation. The Magistry would have to build a flawless case against him before they could take him into custody, given the laws that sheltered peers of the realm.

I absently plucked a dead leaf from the row of boxwood along the path. Perhaps the link between the victims was only that they'd encountered the killer at some point, that their lives had intersected his in some way, even in passing. Did any of the other victims share a connection with Lord Blackburn? It provided a starting point for further investigation.

I skimmed my fingers across the vibrant green hedge, and bitter, purgative whispers surged over me. I shuddered and withdrew. What would cause a respected lord to turn into a deranged murderer? Lady Tarleton had mentioned the loss of a child . . .

Abruptly, I came to myself, aware that we'd stood in silence for some time. Mr. Upton appeared untroubled. He stood at ease, but he watched me closely, as if absorbing my every change in expression.

I composed a pleasant smile, though it was a bit late to act as if I was unconcerned. "Thank you for your warning. I assure you I'll take all you've said to heart."

Though perhaps not in the way he'd intended.

"It was my pleasure." He offered his arm once more. "Shall we rejoin the others?"

"Of course."

As we made our way back to the party, my thoughts tumbled over one another like the waters spilling from the fountain. No stratesman would wish to pursue a peer of the realm, not if it could be avoided. Would they even be able to make a case against him? Perhaps I could find a means to speak to Lord Blackburn without arousing his suspicion, given his connection with Ibbie. There was no further time to consider, for the faint murmur of conversation strengthened, and I must rejoin the party.

Aunt Melisina looked toward me and Mr. Upton, and her lips pulled into a thin line. What had I done now? Whatever it was, she'd surely not miss the opportunity to berate me.

CHAPTER 9

Sitting by the fire on a damp spring evening and listening to the rain patter at the eaves and soak into the soil soothed my soul. Jade ensconced herself on the settee next to me, her head resting on my lap and her eyes drawn tight. A fire blazed over the coals in the hearth, driving back the chill, and Father sat in his favorite armchair nearby, muttering something about star charts as he pored over a thick tome.

The peace of my surroundings eased the residual sting from my carriage ride home. Aunt Melisina had insisted I ride back with her, rather than my sisters, so she might lecture me on my shortcomings.

Given how her gaze had burned when it fell upon me and my companion, her chastisement came as little surprise. She'd glided over to us, rigid hauteur in every line of her body, and detached me from Mr. Upton at once.

She wouldn't speak of it where she might be overheard, but once she had me alone and captive in her carriage, she'd spared nothing. "Wandering off alone and engaging with strangers?

One would think you'd been raised in a barnyard, not a perfectly respectable estate. What your mother would think, I can't say."

"I believe Mother would have enjoyed exploring the gardens with me." I struggled to maintain an even tone. "She appreciated beauty in every form."

"You well know I brought you there to engage with society, not admire the shrubbery." Aunt Melisina rapped my leg with her fan. "As for the gentleman you encountered along the way, he's not someone whose company I wish you to cultivate. He's new in town and bears no title—not at all a suitable match."

Never mind that I had no title myself, nothing less would satisfy Aunt Melisina in her matchmaking. She considered wedding a viscount her crowning achievement and wished to see us go further still.

I'd only escaped the flood of chastisement by promising to improve my performance at our next outing. Exhausted by the events of the afternoon, I forewent dinner, and afterward I crept down to the library, where I might enjoy Father's undemanding companionship and the peace found among books.

In the quiet evenings spent with Father, there was no pressure or expectation, only rare moments of camaraderie as we both immersed ourselves in written worlds. But tonight the words on the paper brought little comfort, for they held the history of the Vigil—at least if the title were to be believed.

Father remained immersed in his own book; he'd not have noticed if I'd brought in the latest scandal sheet, much less this aged copy of *Origins of the Vigil*. But if I'd attempted to read this history in the company of my aunt and sisters, one of them surely would have inquired about what so captured my interest. I paged through the volume. The ink had long since faded, making many sections near illegible.

From what I could decipher, despite the claim of its title, the book offered little on the actual origins of the Vigil. It began with records reflecting a change in power when the lines of kingship in Byren changed and the Sainsbury family claimed the throne. The new king also named a new First of Vigil, one Lord Everstone, and the book suggested that the replacement of Sir Redgrave with Lord Everstone had sowed discontent among the ranks of the Vigil.

I jotted down both names for future reference, then continued.

Nevertheless, the author recounted, the Vigil maintained a united front to the outside world, which celebrated them as the lone bastion of defense between the mortal world and the Otherworld. I tapped the page with my pencil, considering. While some parts of *Origins* read as a quasi-academic work, others held the mark of an amateur researcher, one who favored the Vigil and sprinkled opinion freely among fact.

How much could the information within be trusted? Since it was one of the few histories of the Vigil that existed, I supposed I'd have to make the best of it and cross-reference what I could.

I flipped several pages further, then bent closer to examine the script. This section referred to a Dark Era, one in which the mortal world had nearly been consumed by an Otherworldly threat, but it cited no dates, making it unclear if it had taken place before or after the formation of the Vigil. I'd never heard mention of such an era in any other history of Byren . . . how peculiar. And what was the threat? Had high fae breached our world? Their power, coupled with their cruelty toward mortals, could have caused unfathomable harm.

For all her love of conveying tales of the Otherkind, Mother had become somber when speaking of high fae, her eyes haunted on the occasions she shared a rare bit of lore about their deeds. I scribbled another note in my sketchbook.

Might it be reasonable to assume the Vigil had formed in response to that threat? It could explain why they were so celebrated, if they'd achieved a cessation of hostilities. Or perhaps the Dark Era was an exaggeration, an overstatement of an Otherworldly threat crafted by the author to paint the Vigil with more favorable strokes. But none of this provided pertinent information on the matter of fae-touch.

I forged onward, wading through a sea of theory and speculation, made choppier by the faded script, which remained undecipherable in places.

Then my heart leapt.

Despite the labors of the Vigil, some exercise the greatest of follies and continue to engage with the Otherworld. Upon them a fate most dire and deadly falls: the touch of the fae. Such unfortunates suffer most severely for their boldness.

The greatest harm appears to befall those who indulge in Otherworldly food or accept fae hospitality, if it may be called hospitality, rather than a snare laid for the unwary. Yet even the simple repetition of exposure to the environment of the Otherworld—or to Otherkind—can prove sufficient to entrap mortal minds. It is unclear what property of the Otherworld works so unpleasantly upon mortals. Some suggest that the unfortunate souls are placed under a direct glamour, but whatever the mechanism, the result is the same.

Yet I'd not engaged with the fae as a child, unless something had happened beyond my recall. Was it possible that an Otherworldly experience lay outside the bounds of my memory? That to protect me, my mind had woven a shroud around the events that had transpired?

I fidgeted with a stray strand on the embroidered pillow next to me. If only Mother were here, she would tell me. Nothing I'd said as a child ever shocked or startled her, so I'd dared inquire of her what I'd never dream of asking Father. But she was not here, and somehow I must understand what had happened . . . and when. I fumbled with the book, turning to the next page.

Over time, the very senses of the afflicted individuals alter, until they can no longer be trusted. Many crave a return to the Otherworld, though it be the cause of their doom. The signs display differently in each individual, but the Vigil reports they always end in madness.

For protection, King Ogden has acceded to the Vigil the right to maintain Institutions for the confinement of the fae-touched. They will care for the individuals so afflicted and perhaps, in time, manage to restore their sanity.

In so doing, they also hope to gain insight into the Otherworld and how they may best protect our own.

I didn't need another reminder about the inevitable outcome of fae-touch. What I required was some way to stave it off. The book suggested that had once been the aim of the Vigil, yet I'd never heard of a tainted individual restored to home and society. Had all their attempts failed? Or had they changed their aims?

Jade stirred slightly in her sleep, and I stroked her soft fur. Someone must know. But though I pored over the rest of the book, it contained nothing more about fae-touch or the involvement of the Vigil with the afflicted.

I should have known better than to hope the first obscure volume I read would contain the truth I required. The only reasonable conclusion I could draw from this information was that as a matter of self-preservation, I must shun any further interaction with the Otherworld and its denizens, lest I strengthen the fae-touch further. Both this book and all our lore suggested the more the interaction, the greater the risk.

Which explained why so few Collectors survived, despite all the protective mechanisms provided for their dangerous ventures through the Crossings. Since even the smallest scrap of leaf or mineral from the Otherworld could have powerful properties in our own when worked upon by the alchemists, Collectors took their chances, but when I'd ventured to Milburn, I'd been unaware of the truth of my condition—of all I risked.

I couldn't make such a costly mistake again.

I clutched the book to my chest and stared into the flames. Even a year ago, I'd not have imagined avoiding the Otherworld a difficult task. One must only shun Crossings and observe proper household wards. But now . . . even within the bounds of Avons, I'd sensed Other. So what was I to do?

I glanced at Father, bent over his manuscript, the flames flickering off his eyeglasses. With spectacles, one could overcome poor eyesight. Might there be a tool that could surmount the alterations in senses brought by fae-touch? Clearly, the Vigil had believed so once.

But had they ever succeeded in freeing the afflicted? And if so, why did they no longer? The flames spiraled across the surface of the coals, from orange to white to blue and back again, an endless dance that failed to warm me.

So much knowledge remained hidden, so many questions unanswered. If fae-touch afflicted those who interacted extensively with the Otherworld, was it because the time they spent there increased the risk that they'd encounter Otherkind, who in turn would deliberately ensnare them? Or was there something within the Otherworld itself, so different from our own, that simply worked an alteration? One would be an act of malice, the other a natural consequence of exposure to an unfamiliar environment, like having one's fingers frost-nipped by the cold. Certainly our tales often told of the cruelty of the fae, but if they wished to entertain themselves with our plight, why would they release victims back into the mortal world?

No one else appeared to be asking these questions. It was believed a simple fact of life: interact with Other, risk fae-touch. Receive fae-touch, descend over time into madness. Neither this book nor any other suggested a path to removing or even managing the fae-touch, once one acquired the affliction.

But there must be *someone* who knew more. I reached for my shawl and drew it close around my shoulders. Answers existed somewhere, and I would find them.

I set aside the book and found Father watching me, his auburn hair gleaming in the firelight.

"Is something wrong, Father?"

"Caris is concerned for you. She spoke with me this morning." He steepled his fingers. "She feels you haven't been the same since your return from Milburn, and she wonders if Avons doesn't suit you, if perhaps you might wish to visit your aunt Gillian for a time."

I leapt up, displacing Jade. She gave a rumbling *mrow* of displeasure.

"Please don't send me away."

When he'd banished me after Mother died, after the fae-touch first made its appearance, the grief had nearly shattered me. Aunt Melisina had offered little kindness, and no understanding. If it hadn't been for Lovell and his consideration during that time, I would have drowned in sorrow. He'd supported me as a brother would, and though it hadn't made up for the absence of my sisters, it had brought some comfort. If Aunt Melisina hadn't lost her own sister, cutting my visit short, who knows how long my banishment would have lasted?

"Surely it would do you good—time in the countryside, in the gardens you've always loved." He removed his spectacles. "Gillian enjoys your company greatly, and I thought it might offer a reprieve from your grief."

Last time, I'd been a child, bereft not only of Mother, but of the sympathetic companionship of my father, sisters, and beloved Aunt Caris. All my objections had gone unheeded. This time, I wouldn't surrender so easily.

A burning ember sparked up the chimney, and oh, I wished I might so readily escape this conversation. Instead, I drew a breath and reseated myself. "I appreciate your consideration, Father. But I have a responsibility to remain."

If there was anything Father respected, it was carrying out one's responsibilities.

"I don't deny Caris prefers to have you near, but she'll—"

"It's not to Aunt Caris. I've been summoned for the reading of Ibbie's will, which will be held in two days. I can't dishonor her wishes by refusing to attend."

"Lady Dromley's will?" His gaze drifted toward the window. "I suppose you must go if you've been summoned, but be certain to take Caris with you."

"Do you think it necessary?"

He rubbed the bridge of his nose. "Yes. It's not proper for young ladies to dash about town alone, or so Melisina says."

So she'd spoken with Father as well. No wonder he addressed me with such decision. He'd agree to nearly anything that would cause his sisters to leave him in peace, regardless of his own feelings on the matter. My weariness returned, and I leaned back into the settee. "Very well."

Jade leapt into my lap and nudged my chin. I rubbed her favorite spot between her ears, and she offered a deep, rumbling purr.

My thoughts rushed one over the other. If Father still contemplated sending me away, I must make progress on the matter of the killer. Since my conversation with Mr. Upton, I'd not been able to shake the sense Lord Blackburn was involved in some way—certainly he was the only clear suspect that presented itself.

I had an audience with Father, and he might well know something about Lord Blackburn. It would be a place to start until I could return to the library or find a way to speak to Lord Blackburn myself.

Father had walked to his desk, where he bent over a star chart, a shock of hair hanging before his eyes. I crossed the room to stand by his side, examining the riotous scribble of notes on the chart. The nearest one read: *Avaris brightness diminished 1 March and 15 March. Why?*

Why indeed . . . I shook my head. Now was not the time for distraction. "Are you acquainted with Lord Blackburn?"

"Lord Blackburn? I know him in passing. He's a bit of an odd fellow, but respected enough. Wants to better regulate the passage of Collectors into the Otherworld, thinks there are far too many losses and far too great a risk of bringing the wrath of the fae down on our heads if we continue our attempts to harvest items from the Otherworld. I daresay the fellow's right. Alchemists don't like him much for his views." He jotted another notation on the star chart before him, a sequence of letters and numbers. "Why do you ask?"

"He was acquainted with Ibbie, and—"

"I know you loved her, but it's unhealthy for you to think too much on Lady Dromley's death." He lifted his gaze but would not meet my eyes. "You may not remember, but your grief for your mother touched you in a challenging way."

May not remember? My fae-touch had shaped every day of my life since. Yet he believed it overcome, cast off as I overcame the worst of my sorrow and gained control over my emotions. I lowered my head, fearful that if he looked—truly looked, for once—he'd spy the pain I could not conceal.

"You should be thinking of marriage and family, of things that belong to the land of the living. Not the dead. You must put Lady Dromley and the killer from your mind." He turned back to his chart. "After the reading of the will, we'll revisit the matter of your travel to Gillian."

Before I could protest, he was once more immersed within his studies. For the moment, I'd secured a reprieve. But how long would it last?

∽

Before Father attempted to banish me from Avons, I must try to gather what I could on Lord Blackburn. The conviction accompanied me to bed that evening, through a restless night, and into my toilette the next morning. If I managed to find something concrete to take to the Magistry, if I could aid them in forming a case against him, then perhaps they could remove him from the streets and ensure the safety of those I loved . . . assuming he was the guilty party. Then removal from Avons would not be so dreadful a fate this time, for Father was right—the estate of my aunt was quite pleasant, despite the riot of energy brought by her five small children.

Jade and I entered the dining room to find Aunt Caris, Ada,

and Ainslie gathered to break the fast. With a swift leap, Jade positioned herself on the chair next to mine, awaiting the delicacies she knew I'd pass to her. Once Holden left, I ventured to ask Aunt Caris and my sisters if they knew anything of Lord Blackburn.

"I believe he lost his wife and son when they traveled near an edgetown." Aunt Caris reached for a jar of plum preserves. "There was no conclusive evidence of their fate, but he insisted they fell victim to fae. The Vigil could make nothing of it."

My appetite vanished. Losing Mother still brought pain all these years later. How much did Lord Blackburn still suffer from his double loss?

"How dreadful." Ada poured a cup of tea, wisps of steam curling from the surface. "Does he have any other family?"

"None, my dear. It was quite a tragedy," Aunt Caris said.

"Perhaps that's why he champions reform of fae policy." Ainslie spread jam across a scone. "Or so I've heard."

"What does he hope to accomplish?" I passed a bit of sausage to Jade, and she tugged it gently from my fingers.

"He wants the king to ban Collectors from entering the Otherworld, since so many are lost there or fall victim to fae-touch," Ainslie said.

If his deep grief had driven Lord Blackburn to advocate for reform—and his proposed changes received insufficient support—could it have driven him to more extreme action? Would he have stooped to murder just to cast blame upon alchemists or Otherkind? Could grief drive one to such depravity?

My stomach twisted. With a mind clouded by loss, he might be able to justify his actions as necessary for the greater good. After all, everything he cared about had been taken from him. What more did he have to lose? Certainly, he stood to gain support for his reforms if fear continued to spread. Many of the papers were speculating as to the involvement of the fae-touched, and some ventured to suggest the killings were the work of an alchemist gone mad. If these views gained hold, it might make his stance more popular.

I prodded at the sweet roll on my plate, and it flaked beneath the tines of my fork. "Does he have any supporters for his reforms?"

Ainslie waved her scone about. "Very few. Most members of the Assemblage claim it should be the choice of the Collectors—it's their own lives they're endangering, and many of them come from circumstances difficult enough to make the risk worthwhile."

I frowned. "The alchemists certainly see them well-rewarded. And those wise enough to limit their incursions into the Otherworld and then turn their profits to other business endeavors have improved their lot." Yet those numbers were few. It was rumored most succumbed to fae-touch or simply never managed to return to our world at all.

"I cannot fault them for wishing to better their situation. Yet I wish there were a less unchancy way." Ada sipped her tea. "After all, what use are their gains if their lives are lost?"

"And there's worse," Ainslie said. "Lord Blackburn says we're bound to incur the wrath of the fae, if we haven't already, and then where will the kingdom be? He says it will impact all of us sooner or later."

Given my recent experiences, I had to agree. I forced myself to take a bite of the sweet roll, but it held no savor. "Father said the alchemists disapprove of him, and now I see why."

"Precisely. Without the Otherworldly materials provided by the Collectors, they have no ability to create their devices," Ainslie said. "Of course they'd argue in favor of allowing passage

—and perhaps even provide financial incentives for the Assemblage to see matters their way."

Ada set down her cup with a clink. "Oh, I cannot think them so corrupt—"

"That's not for us to consider, my dears. Nor is there any need to discuss this matter further, here or most especially elsewhere." Aunt Caris spread her crisp linen napkin across her lap. "You don't wish society to think you're lacking in proper sensibility."

Ainslie dimpled. "A dread prospect indeed."

"You may laugh, my dear, but that is how unpleasant rumors spread."

None of us could argue with that, so Ainslie merrily spun the conversation in a different direction. The mood around the table lifted further when Lovell put in an appearance, imparting the latest news about town while devouring pastries.

After we rose from the table, Ainslie and Lovell collected the newly delivered papers and retired to the morning room to peruse them, Ada accompanying them to complete her needlework. I quietly announced my intent to visit the Ashton Circulating Library. While less fashionable than Spencer's, they kept an extensive collection of records on the families of Byren, which made it an ideal place to study the Blackburn family further.

Aunt Caris gave her blessing to the expedition, provided I take Lianne with me, and I did not protest. Lianne enjoyed novel reading, and I imagined she'd keep herself happily occupied perusing the newest adventure tales while I pored over the histories. Indeed, she passed the short carriage ride by telling me the details of the latest thriller she'd borrowed.

After Jade and I left Lianne among the novels, we crossed through the library toward the genealogical records. I permitted myself a small detour to examine their limited selection on

Otherworld affairs. I found only one title new to me: *The Wickford Guide to Otherkind*, which I borrowed to examine further at home.

Then, while Jade stretched herself out over the polished surface of the cherrywood table I selected—effectively barring anyone else from joining us—I examined news articles and anything else I could find on the Blackburn family history. Though a long-established family, they would die out with Lord Blackburn's passing. Despite that, he'd never remarried. Further, reports suggested that after the deaths of his wife and son, he'd isolated himself from society for nearly two years—far beyond the prescribed period of mourning.

I folded the paper, and it rustled in the stillness. I needed to delve beyond the basic facts of the Blackburn family—and their recent tragedies—and look for links to the murders. I turned my attention to searching the gazettes for reports of his views on fae policy, and I stumbled across an article in the *Observer* that included a brief statement from Lord Blackburn on the murders. No surprise, he proclaimed our meddling in the Otherworld to craft unnatural devices had resulted in a killer who could evade all of our efforts at apprehension. He didn't outright blame the alchemists, but his meaning was clear—they'd tampered with the long-standing balance between worlds, and this was the result. He insisted that only stringent reforms could offer protection.

After the murders, how many would respond favorably to any promise of safety? How much support might he gain from these deaths? Certainly, it gave him motive to act.

But if he had, there should be additional links between him and the victims. I set aside the *Observer* and sought out accounts of the victims' final days, of any coverage of their deaths or burials.

Oh . . .

My pulse quickened.

Lord Blackburn had appeared at every funeral the papers reported on. Was it an act of sympathy for the suffering? Or an assessment as to the impact of his misdeeds?

I spread the reports across the table. Had anyone else attended all the burials? I skimmed the lists of names. Mr. Burke and Mr. Ludne had attended all the funerals as well, likely in a protective capacity . . . and I couldn't rule out that some unknown individual had lurked about the burial grounds without attracting notice.

I set aside a stack of papers and rubbed my eyes. Possible motive and opportunity didn't mean Lord Blackburn was the killer, but the closer I looked, the more I found to tie him to the victims and the crimes. Had the stratesmen followed this same approach and yet failed to find any evidence to indict him?

What could I do that they could not? Could I manage to meet him socially? Even if I did, what would I say? *Lord Blackburn, have you brutally murdered citizens of Avons, preying on the city and spreading terror in order to advance your cause?*

If my earlier missteps had caused Aunt Melisina displeasure, she might enter a decline if she learned I sought such a confrontation. Jade's tail twitched in her sleep, and I began to reshelve the genealogical tomes I'd consulted. While I considered how I might approach him, I could also attempt to visit the other victims' families and perhaps uncover a clearer connection between them.

Who might I approach discreetly? I reflected once more on the list of victims and their families and landed on the most likely individual—the merchant who had lost his wife, Thomas Shipley. He sold tea and spices in the Lower Market District, an unobjectionable locale for a young lady to visit, though not as fashionable as the Uptown Market, of course.

When I collected my things, Jade roused from her slumbers and stretched, giving a tremendous yawn. Then she leapt down from the table to stand by my side.

Along with Lianne, we took a hack to *Shipley's Mercantile*, a tall, narrow building of age-darkened sovstone constructed in the old fashion, with living quarters situated above the store. I suggested Lianne remain within the carriage and enjoy her book. She accepted with gratitude that I did not deserve, since I wished her absent so I might question Mr. Shipley with greater liberty.

The bell jangled as I walked into the bustling shop. The proprietor was speaking to a small group of ladies already, so I meandered along the shelves of tea and spice. Sealed jars marked with scripted labels stood at attention on burled chestnut shelves, an impressive assortment. I needed to make a purchase to justify my presence at the shop, and why not one that Aunt Caris would appreciate? She favored soft, mellow flavors, so perhaps the rose blossom tea would appeal to her.

A prominent sign marked a display of individually packed tins: *Dunael's Finest.* Instinctively, I shrank back. Surely an ordinary merchant wouldn't attempt to source tea from near a Crossing? Yet the fine script below claimed that the herbs used in the blend had been cultivated on the outskirts of Dunhilt, the edgetown just beyond Dunael Crossing. It suggested they held special properties for energy and clarity of mind.

I gave the display a wide berth. I needed no more fae influence in my life, even were it an unfounded claim.

Jade stretched to full length and sniffed at a canister of catnip. I couldn't suppress my smile. Never mind that we had an ample supply at home, she deserved a reward for her patient companionship today.

I stepped through the throng of shoppers toward Mr. Shipley. His portly lower body slimmed as it went upward, rather like a tulip bulb, narrowing to bony shoulders and an angular face with a drooping mustache.

When he turned to me, he made a visible effort to brighten, but nothing could erase the traces of grief. "What can I do for you?"

"I'd like an ounce of catnip and a quarter pound of your rose blossom tea."

With a stoop-legged stride, he wove past the other customers to fulfill my requests.

"You seem busy this afternoon."

"Always are, miss. We import the finest of teas and spices, and there are many who appreciate our wares, particularly our new tea, Dunael's Finest."

Here was an opening, perhaps, to inquire about Lord Blackburn. Before I could formulate a question, Jade vanished amid the swirling skirts of ladies and the boot-clad legs of the few gentlemen within the shop.

Blight and rot. I whirled around to see the tip of her tail disappearing up the stairs. What was she about? I pasted on a smile. "I beg your pardon—it's most dreadful, but my cat seems to have gone up the stairs. Might I fetch her back?"

"No harm in it, miss." He scooped out the rose blossom tea. "I'd go myself, but I'm run off my feet, and I've a delivery arriving shortly. I'll have your tea waiting on the counter."

I hastened up the stairs and found the landing empty and the door to the living quarters ajar. Jade had entered his home. Should I follow?

She presented me an unobjectionable opportunity to explore, yet if I took more than a moment or two, Mr. Shipley might wonder—and possibly follow. Unless his customers kept him too busy to take note.

Whether it was utterly improper or not, I couldn't leave her in the house of a stranger. So I stepped over the threshold.

I forced myself to stop and examine my surroundings. Signs of a thoughtful mistress remained—in the perfectly crocheted doilies on the chair, in embroidered cushions arranged with care, in the collection of curios resting on the carved mantel. But her absence was equally evident, in the dust scattered over the surfaces, in the vases on the side table that no longer held flowers, in the oppressive stillness of the space.

I moved deeper into the narrow living area. A hearth with a coal grate dominated one wall, while across the room a desk of burled yew wood held a jumble of papers.

I crossed over to the desk. Though it was shockingly intrusive, I rifled through the papers, which appeared to strictly relate to matters of business. At the bottom of the stack I discovered a calling card, printed with elegant script on thick cream stock. It bore Lord Blackburn's name.

He'd called here, which suggested a much closer connection than a funeral appearance. Fingers trembling, I dropped the calling card back into the pile and returned the stack to its original disorder. Then I surveyed the room once more. A simple knotted carpet covered the floor, and Jade perched upon it, fairly radiating satisfaction. Had she acted with deliberation, coming here? All evidence supported it, despite the fact it was a great deal of credit to give to a cat.

I shook my head. "What did you wish me to see?"

Then I looked closer at the knotted carpet. It couldn't have contrasted more with the sumptuous wool rug in Reynold's bedchamber, and yet, it could as easily serve to conceal. I lifted one corner.

Nothing.

Perhaps it had been a foolish notion. I returned it to its

place, and Jade's ears pricked. She bounded onward, into the kitchen, and darted into the dim space beneath the table. In a moment, she emerged triumphant with a plump gray mouse clutched between her jaws. I wrinkled my nose, but I couldn't begrudge her the prize. Most likely, it was what she'd sought all along, rendering false my supposition she'd drawn me here for a purpose.

"Come, Jade. We shouldn't be here."

She trotted over to my side, mouse still firmly grasped in her mouth, and I hesitated in the kitchen doorway. No matter the slim odds, I couldn't leave without examining what lay beneath this rug as well. I tugged up the edge, and this time I found a dark line etched into the simple oak floor below. I pulled it back a bit further.

The line joined its fellows to form a concentric pattern . . .

A scuffle at the base of the stairs sent my heart skittering. I snatched Jade into my arms, despite her muffled *mrow* of protest, and hurried down to the shop, rounding the curve and nearly plowing into Mr. Shipley at the bottom.

"Forgive the delay, but my cat was most determined to resist departure—she was on the hunt, as you see."

"She's welcome any time, if she makes such catches."

I returned a mild pleasantry and paid for my wares, but it took a considerable time before my pulse returned to its usual rate. Everything about my excursion had felt like an unforgivable invasion of privacy. But I'd discovered matching marks on the floor in both locations—though I'd no notion what they signified—and determined that Lord Blackburn had called at the Shipley home.

Perhaps it was only coincidence, but that stretched the bounds of credulity.

And what of Mr. Shipley's recent acquisition of Dunael tea?

It was a peculiarity, like Ibbie inscribing on the walls. Could the victims share some connection lost in the obscurities of their lives, something that prompted them to act in unusual ways?

If only I'd had more time to examine the markings on the floor and the Shipley home in general. All was not lost, however, for I might be able to search Wyncourt when the stratesmen departed, depending on the generosity of Ibbie's heir. If mysterious markings were replicated there, it would offer an opportunity to study them at my leisure.

Tomorrow, her will would be read. Then perhaps I could plead with the heir for admission. I couldn't imagine the stratesmen would attempt to deny the new owner of Wyncourt his own property.

CHAPTER 10

"Do you want me to come with you to the reading of the will?" Ada lifted her head from her embroidery. "I've already begged off paying calls with Aunt Melisina, in case you wanted company."

I looked up from my correspondence, where I'd been examining the few sparse lines I'd received from P. Smith. In contrast to the rich prose and theories he'd penned in the articles I'd read, this was a bland denial of possessing any information worth sharing, written in a plain, blockish scrawl—another dead end. I sighed and tucked the letter away. "Aunt Caris plans to come, but there's something else you could do if you're willing—look after Jade while I'm gone. Aunt Caris feels her presence doesn't befit such a solemn occasion, but Holden told me she terrorized the household last time I left her behind."

Jade flattened her ears against her head and shook off my hand when I attempted to stroke her. Our partings were few these days, and she protested each one more than the last. I brushed a few strands of her black fur from my skirts, then I picked up my sketchbook. It opened to where I'd tucked my pencil, a page on which countless iterations of the crimson tattoo had blossomed as I contemplated the identity of the killer.

"I'll gladly help as I can." Ada snipped a stray thread. "She likes me no more than the rest, but I'll do my best to make sure she doesn't cause trouble."

Jade's tail twitched irritably.

"She enjoys your playing on the pianoforte."

Indeed, Ada's music appeared to mesmerize Jade—as it did many, for in addition to skill, Ada poured emotion into her music, crafting songs that entranced the hearers.

She dredged up a small smile. "Well, that will be no sacrifice. You offer me what I most love."

I studied Ada more closely. Faint shadows lurked beneath her eyes, and her shoulders bowed under weariness I'd never known her to display. I pressed my pencil into the grooves of the sketched tattoo, etching once more the ominous lines. "Are you well, Ada?"

"Of course." But she fumbled with her needle, her halting motions a far cry from her usual grace.

"I know you have Ainslie to confide in . . . but if there's something troubling you, I'm willing to listen." I moved on to sketching the bits of concentric lines I'd spied in the Shipley house. What picture would they have formed, if I'd seen the whole? I took my rubber to a stray mark. "You've listened to me often enough."

At least to the troubles of which I dared speak.

She let her embroidery fall to her lap. "Aunt Melisina wishes me to encourage the attentions of a man I find . . . deplorable."

How had I missed what was transpiring in my own household? The threat of an unwanted marriage may not match that of a killer—but it held its own pain. I brushed the bits of rubber from the paper and snapped the sketchbook shut. "Will you tell me of him?"

"He's not objectionable in appearance, though not remarkable either—but that would be nothing, if only he were kind. I fear no one ever taught him to control his appetites, much less consider the feelings of others." The words spilled from her in a rush. "He thinks me beautiful and wishes to possess my beauty as his own. Otherwise, he feels nothing for me."

"Then why does Aunt Melisina favor the match?"

"He has excellent prospects. He's the eldest son, and he'll inherit an earldom upon the death of his father, and his family is in good standing with the king." She released a pent-up breath. "I *do* want to marry and have a family, but if it's a man I can respect—and hopefully love. And I don't want to leave you and Ainslie yet."

"You know you don't have to look after us."

"Mother wished it. Perhaps you were too young to remember the sorrow that hung over her before she died, as if she knew—"

"I remember." Eight years was not so very young, certainly old enough that the weeks before and after her passing remained engraved in my memory.

"One night, when she was particularly troubled, she told me if she ever had to leave us, I must look after the two of you." Ada lowered her head, and a dark curl slipped before her eyes. "I think she knew Father would struggle."

"That was a great deal to place upon you."

"Not so very much." Ada rummaged in her sewing basket, still concealing her face. "Not when you consider her feelings as a mother. She wanted us to stay close to one another, wanted us well in every way."

I pulled my sketchbook close to my chest. If Mother had

known about my fae-touch . . . what then? "Even so, it doesn't preclude your marrying before us. Everyone will expect it, since you're the eldest."

"Yes, but I feel . . . well, I hardly know." At last, she looked at me, her rich brown eyes darker than usual. "Aunt Melisina says if I wed the right sort of man, it will allow you and Ainslie to make even better matches. But I see her unhappy situation, and I cannot resign myself to it, however selfish it might be."

"Neither of us would have you wed a man you cannot like or respect, not even if it meant we wed royalty." I tilted my head. "After all, it's not as if we desire to do so."

Ada gave a small laugh. "That's true."

"Have you told Aunt Melisina?"

"I've tried, but you know how she is—the things she says. I've discouraged suitors before, but this time . . . she's making it more difficult. And Aunt Caris agrees with her."

"She does?"

"Since your trip to Milburn, she's been more concerned with our futures, more invested in us finding partners." Ada twisted the engraved sapphire ring she wore on her right hand, a legacy from Mother. "She's not listening, not anymore."

"Our aunts can't force you to marry." Father could if he wished, but he was not a man so inclined, nor did society favor overt command in the arrangement of marriage. It was better to have the veneer of acceptance on both sides, even if more subtle arts were involved to sway the prospective partners to consent.

"No, I suppose not."

Still, familial pressure could make it difficult and painful for Ada to refuse. Those not among the gentry more often followed their own inclinations when it came to marriage, whereas those within society usually expected their daughters to heed the wishes of their elders in matters of matrimony.

We fell silent, and I rummaged among my sketching supplies, collecting my charcoals. To vent my emotions, I sketched Ada, not worn as she was at the moment, but vibrant with life, as she appeared when she unfurled melodies for her own pleasure and that of her listeners. An uncaring man would sap this life from her. Her gentle soul would be crushed by lack of love and consideration, and if it passed from indifference to cruelty—nothing could make such a match worthwhile. What blinded Aunt Melisina so?

As I put the final layers of shading upon the portrait, Aunt Caris bustled into the room to collect me for the reading of the will. While we traversed Avons, she kept up a steady patter of conversation. I forced myself to listen and to offer smiles or nods at appropriate intervals, but Ibbie filled my mind. If she were here, she'd sit in silence with me—or perhaps hand me a stack of old documents to copy so that I could lose myself in the process, instead of drowning in emotion.

But she was not.

So I fixed my gaze on the rows of honey-and-cream-colored houses outside the window, their broad white doorstones a pleasing contrast to their dark wood doors. Golden sunlight bathed the passing townhomes with a gentle glow, and Avons appeared peaceful, pleasant, the sort of place no terror could touch. Oh, I wished the illusion were truth.

As our carriage rattled down the cobbled streets of Baker's Row, the alluring scents of yeast and honey filled the air, but they failed to tempt, because it meant we drew near to the solicitor's office, to the reminder that Ibbie had left and would never return. My throat tightened.

When we descended from the carriage, Aunt Caris took the lead, her presence a greater boon than expected, since it meant I did not have to attempt to speak. She engaged with the secretary at the desk, explaining our purpose, and swept along behind him into the designated room.

Rich burgundy drapes with golden tassels warmed the oval chamber, and gilded frames containing oil portraits lined the walls. The secretary ushered us to a polished mahogany table in the center of the room and informed us the solicitor would be with us shortly.

A moment later, he entered, an older, bespectacled gentleman with brows that bushed like the culms of a bristling sedge. He offered a somber greeting, and then said, "We only await Mr. Broward, then we can begin."

While he and Aunt Caris exchanged pleasantries, the mantel clock ticked in the background. At last the door swung open to reveal a large-boned gentleman with firm lips drawn into a scowl and eyes the shade of dried hawthorn berries. Try as I might, I could spy no resemblance to Ibbie in her cousin.

"Good day, Mr. Broward." The solicitor withdrew a thick document from his leather portfolio. "Now that you're here, we shall begin."

"Very well." Mr. Broward yanked out a chair and sat, his bulky frame dwarfing the spindled seat.

The solicitor read through the formal introduction to the will. When his name was mentioned, Mr. Broward leaned forward, the movement drawing my attention to a small scar along his jaw.

To my cousin Jasper Broward, I leave Manwaring House, Hilsdale, Brownings, and all their contents.

As her sole remaining relative, Mr. Broward was the logical person to inherit the family estates. However much she'd disliked him, Ibbie's strong sense of duty had naturally shaped her views regarding the properties that had belonged to the

Manwaring family for generations. I imagined she might leave Kilmere and her research to the Antiquary Society, but . . .

To Jessa Caldwell, I leave Wyncourt, along with all my research, personal antiquities and papers, and Kilmere, as well as a trust to be used for the maintenance of these properties and the excavation of the antiquary site at Kilmere.

My pulse quickened. Oh, Ibbie . . . why? Before I could make sense of it, Mr. Broward sprang up, and his chair clattered to the floor.

"This is an outrage. That chit shares no family ties with Isabel. Why should she inherit anything?"

"Because Lady Dromley wished it." The solicitor peered through his wire-rimmed spectacles at Mr. Broward. "Wyncourt belonged to her husband, and it came to her outright after his passing. The ruins of Kilmere were given her by her father as a wedding gift. These properties were in her control to dispose of as she pleased. She expressed to me her confidence that Miss Jessa would carry on her work in the event of her death. Of course, she left the family properties to you."

"What good do they do without funds to keep them?" He laughed bitterly. "She provided better for a stranger than her own flesh and blood."

The solicitor raised his bristling brows. "She presumed you retained the ample means left to you by your own father. And the estates are well-run. Should you continue to steward them as Lady Dromley did, they'll turn a tidy yearly profit."

Mr. Broward ignored the calm explanation offered by the solicitor. He wheeled about and jabbed a finger at me. "This is your fault! You deceived her, wheedled your way into her life to gain from her death."

The accusation in his tone seared the air between us. What

could I say to that? To a man lacking both reason and composure? My hands trembled slightly, and I folded them in my lap.

Aunt Caris leapt to my defense. She might be every inch a perfect gentlewoman, but let anyone trouble one of us, and she became fierce as a wyvern defending its clutch. "Good sir, you will watch your words. I assure you Jessa had no notion of Lady Dromley's intent, much less some stratagem to wheedle her property from her. If you could have seen Jessa's grief . . ."

"Indeed." The solicitor cleared his throat. "I must insist you refrain from insulting the ladies or else depart."

A mottled red spread up Mr. Broward's neck and touched the base of his jaw, swirling round the coiled scar, but he subsided into his chair, where a glower dark as a storm cloud twisted his features.

A knot formed in my stomach, and with difficulty, I forced myself to attend to the solicitor, who picked up where he'd left off:

Though all expenses must be approved by the trustees, I have instructed them to allow Jessa Caldwell full access to Wyncourt and oversight of my antiquary affairs from this day forward. They have further received instruction to deposit a set amount in the household account each month to pay the servants and meet household needs.

After concluding the section about Wyncourt with several additional practicalities about the nature of the trust and the permission that must be obtained from the trustees before using the funds therein until I came of age, the solicitor droned on about bequests Ibbie had left to academic institutions and the Sisters of Verity, which he would execute on her behalf.

All the while, Mr. Broward simmered with rage and the knot in my stomach drew tighter.

When the reading concluded, the solicitor handed me a

thick letter. "Lady Dromley desired this delivered to you after the reading of her will."

I murmured my thanks and then tucked it into my reticule. I only hoped it offered some explanation for her decision. To receive Ibbie's personal papers meant a great deal to me, but the remainder of her bequests made me wither inside like a plant caught in a premature frost. She'd counted on me—*me*—to steward what mattered most in the world to her. Somehow, I must see it through. I couldn't let her down again.

The solicitor dismissed us, and I followed Aunt Caris from the room. But Mr. Broward caught up to me and grabbed my arm with bruising force. "You took advantage of my cousin, twisted her thoughts. Otherwise she'd never have failed her duty to her family. Relinquish what's mine—or I'll take this before the Magister."

With that, he released me and stormed out.

CHAPTER 11

On the way home, Aunt Caris watched me, the soft curves of her cheeks drawn with concern. "I cannot think your father will be pleased with this development."

Indeed not. If the unconventional nature of the bequeathments were not enough to disturb Father, Mr. Broward's intent to make trouble would certainly incur his displeasure—particularly if he must involve himself in anything that smacked of scandal. It wouldn't reflect well on him in the realm of his scholarly peers.

I picked at the fraying seam of my reticule. What happened when a will was contested? Would the trustees handle the affair on my behalf? I couldn't rely on it, not without any knowledge of them. And Mr. Broward certainly appeared to lack all scruples. If he suspected my fae-touch . . . I shuddered.

The carriage lurched over an uneven section of cobblestone, and Aunt Caris braced herself against the seat. "A home in town can be of no use whatever to you, still less ruins that must be excavated. What was Lady Dromley thinking to pass you such a burden?"

"I . . . I cannot say." But perhaps the letter held the answers I craved.

Aunt Caris patted my hand. "Well, there's no need to figure it out now. The day has been trying enough, what with this news and that dreadful man. Don't trouble yourself further—I'll sort matters with Alden."

I only hoped her view of sorting matters aligned with my own, but I murmured my thanks and we passed a quiet trip.

Once home, I slipped into the glasshouse and broke the seal of the letter.

My dearest Jessa,

If you're reading this, you have questions. And if I were a braver woman, I'd have spoken to you of what's to come, would have answered your questions in person and assuaged your concerns. Yet there are some things I find too difficult to face.

I wrote a letter explaining my will once before, when I imagined you'd receive my bequests as a woman with years to match mine now and I, old and decrepit, would depart this world for the Final Haven, the adventure that waits beyond. I pictured you well-established . . . perhaps with a family, perhaps having achieved independence through your own endeavors. Certainly, I intended to do all I could to aid your establishment in academic realms; you have the merits and need only opportunity.

But then the killer marked me.

I don't intend to surrender to him. I intend to fight, to protect myself the best I may. But sometimes, the best of efforts fail . . . and now, in the black of night, fear encroaches. I feel as though time slips through my fingers like so many grains of sand snatched by the wind.

I seize the hours that remain to order my affairs—in case.

Doubtless you wonder why I've left so much to you. If you've met Jasper, you can have little question why I chose to leave my personal estates elsewhere. Of course, I considered various institutes or even the Antiquary Society—but a group cannot care as an individual does. And though I hope otherwise, there are things you may uncover, things that I don't wish spread about by strangers, things I have confidence you'll keep hidden and safe.

But that isn't all. Sentiment plays a role, as I hope you realize. After Edward and after the passing of our child, to speak of my emotions became difficult—but now I wish I'd been more forthright with you. In case I don't have the opportunity, I'll say it here: you have become to me the child I lost, the one I've ached for these many years. So what could be more natural than to leave you an inheritance?

Beyond that, I trust you. I know antiquities are not your passion as they are mine, yet you share my thirst for knowledge and my desire for excellence. I have every confidence you'll carry out my wishes, mayhap even more effectively than I would myself.

As with Kilmere. It means a great deal to me, yet I have shunned it for the memories it holds. I should have found the courage to persevere, to press beyond my pain, for I believe what it contains will shed light on Byren's past, and possibly on our interactions with the Otherworld—though you must never hint of this to others, lest the Vigil seek to take control. You have no painful connections in relation to it, and I trust you'll do justice to the excavation.

If you'll take my recommendation, appoint Myles Tibbons

to oversee the work. He's discreet, reliable, and has proven himself worthy of greater responsibility. Further, he has no objection to working for a woman, which is a rarity.

As for all my scribblings, if you can put them in order and make something of them, you'll be a worker of wonders. I leave up to you what should be done with them.

Sometimes I fear I leave you with an undue burden, a curse, rather than a blessing. But I hope I'm wrong, hope further that I have many years left, years in which I may see you established and prepared to carry such a weight.

In case I am not, I have locked the funds in trust. Not because I think you'd mismanage them—rather, I seek to protect you. I have no intention of making you the target of every fortune hunter and bounder in Byren. My husband deceived me. He cared only for what I brought into our marriage and nothing for me. I discovered it too late, and I would not wish that fate on anyone. I pray I have sheltered you well enough from such a situation.

The trustees are sensible men, and both owe me favors. I expect they'll discharge their responsibility in this matter with diligence and respect, though who can know what lies in the heart of a man?

If the situation grows beyond what you can manage, I give you leave to pass on the inheritance as you see fit—I don't want to burden you more than you can bear, but to entrust you with that which I believe could make a difference in our world.

With all my affection,
Ibbie

I brushed the damp from my cheeks, that I might not mar

her final words. Then I lifted the pages to my face. The faintest traces of damask rose clung to them, remnants of Ibbie left behind. For all our closeness, Ibbie had held her secrets tight—and now many of them remained buried with her. Until this letter, she'd never mentioned a child, nor had she alluded to the true nature of her marriage. Small wonder she'd suffered from melancholy. If only she'd felt she could confide in me or in someone . . . but how could I cast blame for holding secrets close?

I traced the loops and swirls of her writing with a fingertip. Could I do justice to her wishes? Carry out what she had not? Certainly, I'd do everything in my power to try.

And I'd never turn over Kilmere and Wyncourt to Mr. Broward, whatever he might threaten, not when Ibbie expressly desired otherwise. Though I shrank from sharing this letter with anyone, perhaps it could shed some light on her intentions and prevent Mr. Broward from bringing the issue before the Magister. I'd have to speak with the trustees.

A gentle breeze swept through the open door of the glasshouse and stirred the branches of the sweet orange behind me. Its glossy leaves brushed my neck, and its uplifting fragrance filled the air, reminding me of one bright glimmer amid this cloud of difficulties: now that the ownership of Wyncourt had passed to me, the Magistry couldn't readily bar my access. Speaking with the servants, reviewing the condition of the house, and examining Ibbie's papers in accordance with her wishes would be viewed as good stewardship, not an impingement on their investigation—or so I hoped.

But what would I unearth?

After Aunt Caris, Ada, and Ainslie departed to attend a soiree, I left for Wyncourt in a hack, with Jade at my side. She perched on the leather seat, her back toward me and her ears pricked at a sharp angle.

"I'm sorry I couldn't bring you to the reading of the will. If it's any consolation, I wished you were there." On instinct, I did not reach for her, seeking conciliation with words instead. "There was a dreadful man—Ibbie's cousin—and I suspect you would have known how to manage him."

Jade peered over her shoulder, her green eyes glowing.

"Perhaps you could have frightened him off with one of your glares." I rubbed at the bruise he'd left on my arm. "I wish someone would, before he follows through with his threat."

Jade gave a soft trill and then marched onto my lap, where she curled up, her tail and legs spilling onto the seat beyond. Evidently, I was forgiven.

When I emerged from the carriage, Wyncourt loomed pale in the lowering sunlight, stirring in me the same out-of-kilter sensation as always, only stronger now that I knew I must enter and find Ibbie absent.

The bleeding hearts swaying in large stone planters on the doorstep murmured their sympathies, but I shoved the sensations aside the best I could, bending my attention to what I might face within. I rapped on the door, and Jade sat by my side, waiting.

In order to find any hint of what had happened to Ibbie, any connections she may have shared with the other victims, I'd not only have to search her house, but also her papers and belongings. The stratesmen must have sifted through them during their long stay here, yet she tended to tuck various notes and reflections in little squirrel holes about Wyncourt, and those they may not have uncovered.

Then there were the peculiar inscriptions. Would any trace remain, or had they done a thorough job of removal? And what possible motive could Ibbie have had for writing on walls? I pressed a hand to my aching temples. Conversely, what if she hadn't left the inscriptions at all? What if it was the murderer, as with the markings on the floor?

Danvers opened the door, jolting me from my reverie. His dour features brightened into a smile. "Miss Caldwell! I'd hoped you'd find your way here soon. Please come in."

I crossed the threshold, and a gust of chill air wafted about me. Reflexively, I clutched for the shawl I'd left at home. "Thank you, Danvers. I would have come sooner, but Mrs. Peters informed me the stratesmen were turning away all visitors."

"Ah, yes. We're quite glad they've gone." Ever the efficient butler, Danvers swept me into the sitting room. After I accepted a comfortable seat, he added, "I pray your forgiveness if I overstep . . ."

I blinked. What did he intend to say?

"Lady Dromley spoke to me the day before her death regarding the terms of her will, and Mrs. Peters and I hoped you'd be willing to discuss your plans for Wyncourt." The lines around his mouth deepened ever so slightly. "The staff are rather at odds and ends, with all that's happened, and wondering what's to become of us. I'd like to assuage their concerns, if I may."

"Of course. I'm glad Lady Dromley spoke to you." Some of the tension eased from my shoulders. "I must confess the terms of her will came as a surprise to me. I intend to honor her wishes, but I need time to make arrangements, particularly while the estate remains in trust."

"Quite right, miss."

"I'm given to understand provision has been made for staff

salaries, however." I inclined my head. "I suppose I should ask: are they willing to stay? Mrs. Peters said there's been trouble."

"After Lady Dromley received the mark, her personal maid fled in fear of the killer. Some still threaten to leave." His body drooped like the branches of a pendulous elm, attesting to the difficulties of the past few weeks. "But where else would we go, after all these years in Lady Dromley's service?"

"I imagine your skills would be welcome in any of the finest households. Still, I'm glad you wish to stay." A strange, sharpish scent mingled with the familiar aromas of Wyncourt. Beside me, Jade's nose twitched. I shook off the distraction. "Is it because of the killer or because of the restrictions placed by the statesmen that they wish to depart?"

"I cannot say for certain, Miss Caldwell." He straightened. "There have been some . . . irregularities since my lady's passing. Doubtless due to the unsettled nature of the household."

"What sort of irregularities?"

"It started off with the maids taking longer than usual on their rounds, which Mrs. Peters chalked up to distraction with all the bustle—until the upstairs maid vanished from her duties for half the day and couldn't offer any accounting for it, didn't even seem aware of the missing time." His usual assurance faltered slightly. "Then last night, after I'd done my rounds, I found the side door open. I'd secured it earlier, taken every caution. The staff all claim they didn't touch it. Perhaps they're holding their tongues for fear of trouble, but they've always been truthful in the past."

"I see. It sounds as though you and Mrs. Peters have had your hands full." In the distance, one of the servants murmured to another, a homely sound that failed to soothe. "Is that all?"

"I'm afraid not. The kitchen maid claims she's heard

someone roaming the attics night after night. I've examined them thoroughly myself—even summoned the stratesmen to do the same—but we found nothing." His gaze drifted to the polished marble mantel. "I assumed it was an overactive imagination combined with fears of the killer, but after the breach with the door . . . I'm no longer sure what to think. She's frightened, for certain. She went so far as to demand the footman accompany her into the yard when she must empty the rubbish, which displeased him mightily, I can tell you."

"I'll take a look around myself."

"Do you think it wise, Miss Caldwell? If some prowler has found his way within or if some of the servants seek to take advantage of the situation and go their own way, they might be none too happy to be discovered."

"I'll be careful. I'm certain all will be well." Despite the confidence I attempted to infuse into my words, web-wisps of unease brushed across my skin. "In the meantime, how can we calm the concerns belowstairs?"

"Perhaps if we could offer them some reassurance about your intentions . . ." He watched me expectantly.

"If you have the time now, why don't we discuss matters with Mrs. Peters? Then the two of you can inform the rest of the staff."

"Excellent." Danvers summoned Mrs. Peters.

She swooped in with a full tea tray as though she'd been waiting for his call, the usual color in her cheeks faded to a snowdrop-petal pallor. Most housekeepers might not so deeply mourn their employers, but then most housekeepers also rose to their positions after years of service, while Ibbie had taken a chance on Mrs. Peters, elevating her despite her youth. She'd brought Mrs. Peters in after she'd received mistreatment in another household, and Ibbie's compassion had been rewarded with fierce loyalty and outstanding service.

The sorrow in Mrs. Peters's features tugged at me, and I almost stepped forward to pull her into an embrace. But it would upend the proper order of things, so I restrained myself and offered a warm smile instead, one I hoped conveyed what I could not speak. "Thank you for joining us, Mrs. Peters."

Together we discussed the minutiae of household accounts, servant salaries, and so forth. The stratesmen had vacated Wyncourt yesterday, and with no one currently occupying the house, their workload would lessen. To keep the home open with no occupants save the servants seemed an extravagance, and yet, to let them go after they'd remained with Ibbie so long—I couldn't fathom she'd desire such an act.

It wasn't as if I could move in. As a widow, Ibbie remaining here on her own had raised no questions, but for a young unwed woman, it was an impossibility. Perhaps in a few years, once I came of age . . . but even then, if I left my family to set up in the same city on my own, it would create quite a scandal. So what was I to do with Wyncourt? Maybe I should consider finding a tenant once I'd consulted the trustees. But would anyone want a home where murder had struck?

I adjusted my position on the overstuffed chair and sipped at my tea. "I'll speak with you again after I consult the trustees. In the meantime, I have a few questions about what happened in the weeks before Lady Dromley received the mark. Do either of you know if she entertained Lord Blackburn in recent months?"

They were too well-trained to betray any sign of surprise at my questions. "He came on several occasions in the weeks prior to her death—once to luncheon, once again to tea, and once to call after she'd received the mark." Danvers cleared his throat.

"Then, of course, he attempted to visit after her passing, but the stratesmen denied him entrance."

"I see." Rather than attempt an explanation, I forged onward. "I also wondered if you'd ever observed Lady Dromley. . . writing on the walls."

They exchanged a look. Mrs. Peters knotted her hands in her lap, and Danvers shifted uncomfortably.

"Both of you know how much I loved Lady Dromley. I don't mean to pry without cause, but I fear what the stratesmen discovered here could give rise to false accusation against her."

"I owe Lady Dromley more than I can say." Mrs. Peters lifted her head, her russet hair peeping from below her cap. "She saw what I could be, when most would never have given me second look. So if she had her foibles, it's not for me to speak of them—to anyone."

I stroked Jade, drawing a rumble of approval from her. "Your loyalty was one of the reasons she valued your service, but the stratesmen have already begun to inquire into inscriptions they found on the wall. They spoke with me about them soon after her death."

Danvers tugged at the sleeves of his impeccable black jacket. "They asked us as well."

"And what did you tell them?"

"We told them we knew nothing."

"They believed you?"

"They had no choice but to accept it. There was nothing else for us to say."

"Perhaps there was nothing else to say to them, but can you trust me?" What mattered to Mrs. Peters, to Danvers? We shared a common goal: justice for Ibbie. I needed them to know I was fully on their side. I leaned forward. "I want to protect her reputation, not destroy it. I know better than anyone how brilliant

Lady Dromley was. If she did anything of the sort, it was with cause, and I want to know if that cause had any bearing on her death."

Again, they exchanged glances.

"Please, Mrs. Peters."

Her hazel eyes warmed to a shade like burnished copper. "You'll . . . you'll not speak of this to anyone?"

"I'll keep your confidences."

"Late one evening, not long after I first came to Wyncourt, I noticed Lady Dromley daubing the walls with a brush—or so I thought." A sigh breezed from her. "Of course, 'twas not for me to intrude upon my lady's concerns. When next morning I went into the room, all appeared in order, with no mark to mar the wall, so I thought perhaps she'd been using a brush on one of her artifacts, and I'd mistaken her actions in the dim light."

"But she wasn't mistaken," Danvers said. "Shortly after Lord Dromley passed, I'd find her working on the walls with some sort of brush and daub—only late at night, when everyone else had retired."

"So Lady Dromley periodically painted runes onto the walls?" I stopped stroking Jade, and she nudged my hand. "Then the inscriptions vanished later?"

They both nodded.

"You never asked her about it?"

"It wasn't our place, miss," Mrs. Peters said.

I stared across the room into the dim beyond the doorway. "If this had been going on for some time, it must have nothing to do with her death."

Danvers straightened. "Precisely our thoughts. If the stratesmen knew of it, they might impugn her character, with her not here to defend herself any longer."

I couldn't say they'd acted rightly—at least according to the law—but I understood their need to defend Ibbie. If she fell under accusation of madness, of fae-touch, then all her work would come into question.

"Do the other servants know?"

"Not as far as we can tell. My lady was careful, but Danvers and I often carried out our duties when the others retired. Even so, it was rare we caught her at it."

"Thank you for trusting me enough to speak." My chest ached with suppressed emotion. What did it all mean? If I'd pressed a bit more, would Ibbie have confided in me? If we'd worked together before the killer claimed her, could we have figured out his connection to her life, perhaps hidden in these peculiarities? I rubbed the place where my ward-pendant hung. "There's one more matter. I know it's difficult, but I'd like to speak to whoever put the room to rights after Lady Dromley . . . passed."

"'Twas none of our staff." Mrs. Peters blinked fiercely, as though trying to check tears. "The stratesmen insisted on an outsider. A charwoman they hired."

I set down my cup with a clink. Why had they barred the servants from the room? Why did they try so hard to conceal the method of death? It must have significance.

If I could find the charwoman, would she divulge anything? Could her knowledge provide some hint at how the killer claimed his victims? Perhaps. But if the charwoman worked for the Magistry, then speaking with her would reveal to Mr. Burke I'd not taken his counsel. Not to mention, even if I managed to locate her and risked exposing my interest to the Magistry, she'd likely have been well-compensated for her discretion.

Mrs. Peters lifted a shoulder. "I hardly liked having a stranger in my lady's bedchamber, but Stratesman Burke insisted. It would have been more proper for us to attend her, but instead they took her away without allowing so much as a goodbye."

My chest tightened further still. "Who found her?"

"One of the stratesmen," Danvers said. "They never left her alone, except to sleep, and even then they examined her room, secured it, and locked every access. Two of them always kept watch through the night outside her bedchamber. When Mary went to light the fire in the morning, Lady Dromley didn't open the door. She fetched a stratesman, who used the spare key to open it, and there he found her . . ."

Dead.

Danvers held back the word, but it resounded in the stillness. I swallowed against the tightness in my throat. "Did the stratesmen allow anyone from the household into the room?"

"Indeed not." Danvers frowned. "They kept us from that floor altogether until everything was set to rights."

"As if we'd somehow destroy a vital clue with our carelessness." Mrs. Peters brushed at her black skirt, as though ridding it of invisible dust—or the detritus left behind by the stratesmen. "We'd do anything we could to help catch her killer."

"I'm certain you would, as I'm certain they had a reason for their decision." I sipped at my cooling tea, seeking another angle. "Did they return her belongings to you?"

Mrs. Peters sniffed. "No, they claimed her signet ring was missing, and her clothing damaged. She wore none of her jewelry to bed, aside from the ring."

"I see." I'd never seen Ibbie remove the ring, so what did its absence mean? I lifted Jade from my lap. "For now, carry on as you have been. I'll be sorting through Lady Dromley's papers, so I expect to be here late."

"Very well, Miss Caldwell." Mrs. Peters stood. "Would you like more tea?"

Perhaps it would fortify me for the task ahead. "Yes, thank you. I'll take it in the study."

If I'd been stronger, perhaps I would have started in the bedchamber, but at the moment, I couldn't bear to see where her body had rested . . . and if the stratesmen had focused all their attention there, the chances of any evidence remaining were slim.

Perhaps tomorrow.

For now, I traveled down the familiar corridor toward Ibbie's sanctuary. When I opened the door, her warm, welcoming fragrance greeted me, and her presence seemed to fill the room. If only I could turn and see her cross the threshold once more . . . I choked back my grief and moved toward the one wall unlined by shelves or windows.

Though I lifted a lamp close to the surface, no remnant of the inscriptions remained. I traced the wall with my fingertips, but nothing marred the smooth surface. An unpleasant tingle worked its way across my skin, perhaps caused by whatever cleansing agent they'd used to scour away her runes.

What were you about, Ibbie?

Clearly, more had been going on with Ibbie—and Wyncourt—than I'd ever imagined. Did these irregularities connect to the case and the killer?

I spun away from the wall toward her desk. If I wanted insight into Ibbie's last weeks, the best source would be her diaries. Ibbie valued her privacy, yet she was a practical woman; if reading her personal journals spared lives, she would have permitted it.

I'd no notion where she kept her diaries, so I'd have to search for them as I worked through the mountain of papers and books within the study. Ibbie was prone to jotting notes and thoughts on any piece of paper at hand, so I'd have to pay attention to each one, particularly if I wished to locate any mention of Lord Blackburn.

Perhaps there might be a record of what he'd requested from Ibbie. A letter, by chance? Or some notation she'd made herself? If Ibbie had recorded anything that might reflect on his innocence or guilt, I'd find it.

Only . . . what else would I encounter along the way?

CHAPTER 12

I soon lost myself in sorting the wildly disarrayed papers within the study. After some time, I uncovered a parcel for Lord Blackburn wedged beneath a teetering stack of books. Quelling a momentary qualm, I undid the brown paper binding. Whatever Lord Blackburn had claimed, the parcel contained not a manuscript, but an old, crumbling collection of letters. The highly stylized script indicated the messages were hundreds of years old.

Nothing I'd read indicated Lord Blackburn had an interest in antiquities or ephemera, yet his name was clearly written on the wrapping in Ibbie's familiar hand. Was his request that Ibbie procure these merely an excuse to give him greater access to her?

I bent over the letters. They appeared to be an exchange between a military officer and his wife. Amid news of personal interest, he alluded to a violent conflict with the Otherworld. His descriptions reminded me of the references in the *Origins of the Vigil* to a Dark Era . . . interesting. I could imagine Lord Blackburn having interest in such material, given his views on fae and the Otherworld.

I turned back to the letter.

> *The courage of our men falters; I struggle to summon my own. But then I think of you, of our sons, and I know I must. Yet the defenses offered by the alchemists, so sure in times past, avail little before the threats we face. Who could have imagined such horrors? The ghouls and wights overrun our defenses, and we are undone. And there is still worse to come, if they speak true.*
>
> *The king considers an unfathomable bargain—and mayhap he chooses right. I cannot judge such weighty matters. I only pray the Infinite may take pity on us, for if He does not, how shall we thwart such monsters as they have unleashed?*

His desperation bled through the centuries, pouring into my own soul, and I shuddered. What Otherworldly monsters could have provoked such fear? The letter-writer referred to wights and ghouls—neither of which appeared in any compendium or loremaster legend I'd heard. If his account were true, why were they unknown? Why had this war he referred to passed beyond recall in Byren? We had records stretching even further into the past, and something of this magnitude should have made its way into our annals—unless someone wished us to forget.

A soft chirring sounded at the windows, and I jumped. It was only a dunnock, perhaps searching for insects in the shrubbery, and yet unease prickled down my spine. I set aside the letter I'd been reading, the last of three. It appeared the final page was missing, for there was no conclusion or signature.

Before I handed the parcel to Lord Blackburn, I'd copy the letters for my own reference. However bleak their contents, they offered a small victory—perhaps this parcel would give me an excuse to speak with him, although such a meeting would strain the bounds of propriety. I *should* send it along with a servant, but I'd dispatch a message instead. I'd request a meeting, suggesting the package was too fragile, too valuable to entrust to a servant. Perhaps it would raise questions, but it was worth the risk.

I tucked the parcel into my portfolio and then stretched and rolled the knots from my shoulders. A cold, untouched cup of tea sat on the desk before me, and outside the windows, the black of night met my gaze. The mantel clock chimed nine times, its white porcelain face gleaming in the gaslight.

Other than the letters for Lord Blackburn, my endeavors this evening had uncovered nothing of value. And I'd not located the most important item—her journals. I sighed. Perhaps I should have begun in her bedchamber, after all.

Jade had long since curled up on the chaise and drifted to sleep, her bulky form a dark pool against the cream-colored fabric. An unnatural stillness hung over the house, though surely not all the servants had retired yet. Shadows gathered deep in the corners of the study, and my mind filled them with lurking, malevolent forms.

The hairs along my arms rose. Clearly I'd spent too long contemplating the unsettling letters, yet despite the nonsensical nature of my fears, they spurred me to act. Wyncourt at night offered no welcome; it was time to leave. I shut my portfolio and knelt down to collect the stack of logbooks I intended to examine at home.

Wait.

A peculiar scent surged into the room, reminiscent of the charge in the air after a powerful thunderstorm. It mingled with the fragrances of cedar and pine, filling the chamber. The pinprick sensation of Other tingled up my spine, strengthening to a veritable flood that quickened blood and breath alike.

Flee. I should flee.

Yet something whispered: *stay*.

For every sense was awakened, quickened to life in a way I only experienced when I surrendered to the fae-touch. No, I refused to cede control. I would run, abandon Wyncourt, pretend this had all sprung from my tainted imagination. I pressed up from the floor and froze.

It was too late.

A tall, powerful figure strode toward me, his beauty unnatural. His fine features were chiseled as if from marble, and his impossibly brilliant eyes glinted with the ever-changing green of a forest pool.

A flood of Other swirled round me, waves of power emanating from *him*. I went cold to my fingertips.

High fae in Avons.

Impossible, yet he could be nothing else.

Jade bounded forward. In the flicker of gaslight and shadow, she appeared more formidable than usual. Her presence jolted me free from the unnatural stillness that had fallen upon me. His work?

Legs unsteady, I dashed toward the nearest window, fumbled with the latch. It refused to yield, the sharp metal scraping my palm. Oh, please. Open!

In a single fluid motion, the fae crossed the room. His hand closed over mine, snaring me in place. "Be still."

Command laced the words, and part of me wanted to sink into them and rest, to sleep and dream of pleasant spring days, of lush woodlands and rich flowering meadows, of ancient trees towering to the skies . . .

A deep growl snapped me to my senses. Jade bristled, her teeth bared. If she attacked him, what would he do?

"No, Jade—I forbid it."

Her tail lashed angrily, but she stilled, watching and waiting.

A flicker of curiosity sparked in the perfect features of the fae, the sort of interest with which one might examine an unexpected specimen recovered in the field.

Every muscle coiled tight. I must free myself, must protect Jade. Think, I needed to think. Why had he come to Wyncourt? The murders. It must be connected to the murders.

The cold seeped deeper, and an uncontrollable shiver racked my body. "Do you intend to kill me, as you did Ibbie?"

"Who is Ibbie?"

"If you murder someone, you ought at least know their name." Residual glamour fogged my thoughts, hindering logical speech.

"I've murdered no one." His grip loosened, ever so slightly.

It was the opening I needed. I wrenched free, grabbed the iron poker from the hearth, and clung to it, though the frigid metal burned my skin. Would iron be of any use against high fae? I'd no better weapon, so I lifted it high, my pulse thundering in my ears. "This is Ibbie's—Lady Isabel Dromley's estate. By what right do you intrude?"

A glint of amusement touched his dark green eyes. "I need no permission, not in this house."

I clenched the poker tighter, my fingers cramping. "If not to kill, then why are you here?"

"My purpose belongs to no mortal." His voice softened to the gentlest of whispers, like a breeze on a spring day. "You'll leave now and forget you ever saw me."

My mind clouded once more; a mist shrouded the room. *Let go . . . forget . . . surrender.* The words wrapped themselves around me with persuasive force, and I could no longer muster the will to resist. As my control slipped, the weave on my cage of thorns unraveled . . . and the last of my hold vanished.

A riot of color and sound flooded my soul. The joyful, lively song of the goldhearts swirled round me, and others joined in the chorus—a steady low melody from the great oak within the garden, a plucky thrum from the lawn beyond the house.

It was glorious.

The poker slipped from my grasp, clattered against the hearthstone, shattered the songs.

Stop.

I must stop.

I sought the cage within, but the strands evaded my grasp, swaying as though they responded to some other force.

Jade tensed. How much longer would she restrain herself? I couldn't let this fae hurt me—or anyone else. I must regain control. I seized the vines, and one by one, wove them back into place.

The fae watched me, his eyes narrowed. Was he considering how he might best toy with his prey? Whether he'd claim my mind with glamour or my body in death? The room wobbled at the edges.

He reached for me once more.

"Don't touch me." Despite my efforts, my voice wavered, making it more a plea than a command.

In tales of old, fae always did as they pleased—and mortals had no hope of stopping them.

Yet he halted. We stood motionless, a chair a fragile barrier between us.

Then he leaned against the mantel, casual, unconcerned, elegant. We might have been enjoying a pleasant social call, were it not for the unrestrained sense of Other permeating the air, the terror still thrumming through my veins.

"Cooperate and I'll have no need to."

"What is it you want?" I whispered.

"You'll take me to this Ibbie's bedchamber, then leave me to my work." He spoke as though my compliance were not in question. "You're not to speak of anything you've seen tonight. If you do, I'll find you, and our meeting will be less pleasant than this one."

Why didn't he try to glamour me once more? And what did he want with Wyncourt? He *might* not be the murderer—certainly he'd made no attempt on my life as yet—but for all I knew he was in league with some Otherworldly killer, conspiring to remove any trace of evidence from mortal sight. For him to appear here of all places—when no high fae had been known in Avons for centuries—it stretched the bounds of credulity that it had nothing to do with the murders. That he intended to search the scene of Ibbie's death served as further confirmation.

I should have done his bidding, then fled. After all, he could change his mind at any moment, glamour me once more or draw one of his weapons and end my life. If tales held true, he could simply end it with a word. Yet I stood motionless. "I won't help you conceal what happened."

"Why does it matter to you?"

"Because Ibbie was like a mother to me, and I intend to uncover the truth about her death, not help hide it." My pulse drummed a ragged rhythm. "What do *you* intend?"

Before he could reply, footsteps echoed in the corridor, then halted in front of the door. *Oh, please, turn back.*

Instead, the door swung open, revealing Mrs. Peters. "I've come for your tea things. Would you like anything else?"

Why didn't she scream? Flee the room? Do something besides stand there with a placid smile on her face? Realization twisted like a knot in my chest. She couldn't see him—didn't perceive the presence and power filling the room, didn't notice how the light bent and refracted around the area where he stood.

My vision blurred as I attempted to sort reality from glamour, and my temples throbbed.

Mrs. Peters remained calm and oblivious.

"I . . . well . . ."

The fae crossed his arms over his chest and raised a brow, almost as if he mocked me.

Should I try to leave with her? Best not. If I angered the fae, I'd put her and all the servants at risk. It was better to let her go about her business and hope I could emerge from this encounter unscathed. If not . . . well, I was already tainted. "No, thank you, Mrs. Peters."

With unsteady hands, I lifted the tray and crossed the room to offer it to her. All the while, his gaze burned against my back, a tangible force. I whisked the door shut and took some comfort in its solid presence behind me. I'd feel far better if it rested *between* me and the fae, yet he remained within the study, immovable as a mountain.

I braced myself against the door. "I can't leave you alone to examine the bedchamber. If I take you, I want to stay."

"You're in no position to dictate terms." He moved forward, and the lights in the study flickered, then burned brighter. "You've inconvenienced me long enough."

"Wyncourt belongs to me now. Surely that gives me some rights in this situation." Not that I'd ever heard such things mattered to fae, who viewed themselves as lords of all creation. Why should they heed such small matters as mortal ownership? Yet he grew thoughtful.

"Does it?" His fingers skimmed the dagger at his side. "I've changed my mind. You'll come with me until I'm through here."

I fumbled for the doorknob and stumbled from the room, still shaky. Had I won—or lost? At least I'd be able to watch him and perhaps learn something, gain understanding of the threat I faced . . . find out what he wanted.

Jade still glared at the fae intruder, and I snatched her up in my arms, holding her like a shield. Perhaps fear weakened my limbs, for she felt heavier than usual.

What did his presence here mean for the theories I'd conjured so far? Did it indicate Lord Blackburn was innocent? Or had the fae used him like a pawn? If he'd ventured near the Crossing where his wife and son perished, could he have fallen victim to Otherworldly influence?

I gripped Jade tighter as we ascended the stairs, and she made no protest. How was I to protect us all? I'd fallen headlong into that which I must avoid at all costs. Already his presence had confirmed my theory that interaction with the Otherworld weakened my ability to restrain the fae-touch—or perhaps it simply strengthened my affliction. Either was better than the possibility that he'd deliberately wakened the taint within, seeking to gain control. But if that were the case, why then had it cleared my mind of glamour? Or was it my struggle against it that had restored clarity of thought? I stumbled on a step.

"What's your name?"

I didn't want him knowing my name or anything about me, but there was a force behind his words that ripped a reply from me. "Jessa Caldwell."

Jade nudged my chin, and I fell silent, cutting off the urge to continue speaking, to share about my family and where I lived . . . far more than I'd ever divulge to any mortal stranger, let alone a fae. In silence, I opened the door to Ibbie's bedchamber, a room richly appointed in hues of rose and gold, with antiquities scattered throughout.

Her favorite ancient vase occupied a place of honor on the mantel, and a series of aged paintings paraded across the wall nearest her bed, adorned with rich mahogany frames. Her dusky-rose fragrance enveloped me, strong as an embrace, and I buried my face in Jade's fur.

I expected the fae to rifle through her belongings and conduct an inspection of the sort the stratesmen had—but instead he stood still, light limning his features, and surveyed the room.

He saw something I did not, I felt certain. And I doubted very much he'd tell me what he perceived. He strode across the bedchamber and cast aside the ornate rose-and-ivory rug to reveal the polished hemlock floor beneath.

A sensation like whisper-soft willow leaves brushed across my neck. The marks were here too.

The full image they formed stole my breath—a sort of fractalized web with runes woven into the upper corners. If it didn't memorialize murder, the artistry would have mesmerized me. Every line was flawless, every angle precise . . . just like the tattoos that marked the victims.

I squeezed Jade, and she gave a soft *mrow.*

Unlike the inscriptions on the wall, which appeared to be unique to Ibbie, these images had marked three of the murder scenes—and possibly all eight.

Had the murderer left them? Or did they somehow link the victims in another way? Could the victims have been chosen *because* of the marks, rather than the other way around? And how did Lord Blackburn fit into all this? It couldn't be mere coincidence that he showed himself at every turn, that he had connections to so many of the dead. Perhaps if I knew what substance formed the image, I might better determine its origin.

I lowered Jade to the floor, then knelt down and scrubbed at the markings with my handkerchief. It didn't alter in any way.

"You're wasting time—of which you mortals have precious

little. You can't remove those lines." The rich voice of the fae filled the room. "They'll remain on this wood until it rots and returns to the soil from whence it sprang."

I wanted to ask how he knew, but I'd a notion he'd shut down any attempt at questions—or require far more than I wanted to offer in return for answers. The dreadful tales of debts incurred to the fae had impressed themselves on my earliest memories. It was wiser to remain quiet until I understood his purpose than to risk entangling myself in what I failed to understand.

Then his gaze locked on something in the doorway. He left the bedchamber and stalked through the corridor. At last, he stopped before the large window that overlooked the back garden.

He examined it, then gave a brusque nod. "I intend to tenant Wyncourt. Will you bargain?"

CHAPTER 13

I wanted to shout *no*, but giving offense in such a situation might be deadly—not to mention ladies must always keep well-modulated tones, or so Aunt Melisina would remind me were she here. I rubbed my temples. Never mind that—surely I'd misheard, surely some remnant of glamour still addled my mind. I tugged the satin drapes across the window, blocking out the world beyond. "Why Wyncourt?"

"Why not?" He folded his arms, revealing a well-sculpted form beneath his silken jacket. The sprites had been unsettling, but he was something altogether different, like sunlight and storm mingled, potent in power, *more* in every way—more beautiful, more terrifying, more inhuman. "Do you intend to live here?"

Of course not. Father would never permit such an unconventional arrangement—and even were I of age and did not have to abide by his wishes, it wrenched me to think of leaving my family. "Not at this time."

"Then why not allow me?" Nothing in his face betrayed his

thoughts. "I'll offer you double the usual sum to let the house, as recompense for the inconvenience."

If a fae lord offered a glittering necklace, it was more likely to be a chain to imprison than a jewel to enrich. And yet, something tugged me to accept—some sort of compulsion, perhaps? I stepped back, putting more distance between us. "The presence of high fae within Avons will draw attention and prove more than a mere inconvenience."

"What fae?" One corner of his mouth lifted, and again light appeared to bend and flicker around him.

A wave of dizziness washed over me. Once I'd steadied myself, I beheld a transformation.

He still possessed the same presence and power, but I could only detect it if I strained, and even then, it felt like a figment of imagination. My mind struggled to reconcile his appearance and the truth beneath. In some way, he'd diminished himself, his unnatural beauty altered into the guise of a striking mortal—his features changed just enough to make them belong to our world, not his. I edged farther from him. If high fae could so easily cloak themselves as mortals, what did that mean for us? What did that mean about the claims that high fae hadn't entered our world in centuries?

"You'll introduce me as Lord Riven of Elmsford, if necessary."

"Is that your name?"

"It's what you'll call me."

"I thank you for your offer, Lord Riven, but I'm afraid I cannot accept."

"Just Riven will do." He appeared entirely untroubled by my denial. "Consider my offer. You have something to gain, if you accept—and a great deal to lose otherwise."

I kept quiet, though everything inside longed to agree,

simply so I might flee his presence and the alluring call of Other. But though I'd been fortunate in my dealings with the water sprites, I was unlikely to emerge unscathed from another bargain with Otherkind, particularly high fae. All the tales agreed: fae only bargained for their own gain, and no mortal escaped entirely unharmed.

Further, if he was willing to bargain, Wyncourt must hold something he desired, something he couldn't just seize by force. Some motive must govern his actions, and I dared not consent without understanding it, not when I risked so much.

"I'll grant you two days." From his tone, it would seem he thought this generous. "Then I'll call upon you, and I expect a favorable response."

"There's no need for you to call—we could meet here."

"Your home would be better, I believe."

He didn't await my reply, but strode around the corner. When I ventured to look after him, he was gone.

Blight and rot. He intended to call on our townhome—how did he know where I lived? Perhaps he didn't, at least not yet, but he appeared confident he could find me. I sank to the floor and leaned against the wall. I'd intended to protect my family by declining his bargain and keeping the Otherworld as far from them as possible, but I'd already failed.

Why had he granted me time to consider? Fae exercised no compassion, no generosity, which meant there was a great deal more to this situation than I understood.

Jade crept into my lap, sniffing at my face as if she conducted an examination for any hidden harm. At last satisfied, she curled up against my chest.

I held her close. At least she'd listened and restrained herself in our interactions with Riven. If this night had stolen her from me . . . no, I refused to consider it.

Cradling her bulky frame, I struggled to my feet. I shouldn't linger, no matter how leaden my limbs. I'd two days to determine a course of action, two days to figure out a way to keep the Otherworld far from my family without entangling myself further with fae or endangering the inheritance Ibbie had left me. But how?

I forced myself to descend the stairs, Jade wrapped like a stole over my shoulders.

As I reached the first landing, the entryway clock chimed eleven times—I'd lost hours. I rushed into the study and snatched up my belongings. If I wished to return home before Aunt Caris and my sisters, I'd have to hurry. If Aunt Caris discovered my absence at this hour, she'd sound the alarm—and she and Father might consider all their concerns justified.

Though I urged the driver to as fast a clip as was safe, I arrived home as Aunt Caris, Ada, and Ainslie ascended the steps to the townhouse door, Lovell serving as escort.

They turned to watch my approach, and my chest tightened. Would the trials of this day never end? I pasted on a smile as I descended from the hack. "Did you have a pleasant evening?"

Aunt Caris ignored my question and bustled toward me, her silk skirts rustling, her lips pinched in a fine line. "Where in the Crossings have you been?"

"I only went to Wyncourt to tend to Ibbie's affairs." The gaslight spilled out onto the streets, shimmering in puddles left by an earlier shower. "I'm afraid I lost track of the time."

"Lost track of—what were you thinking, roaming the city unescorted at this hour? And with the killer still at large?" She examined me as though the mark might already have bloomed across my neck. "He could have ensnared you with none the wiser."

Lovell stepped toward us. "Now, aunt—"

"Killer aside, you exposed yourself to all the ordinary dangers of Avons at night." Ada clutched the iron railing tightly. It wasn't like her to interrupt, so she must share Aunt Caris's concerns. "You didn't even have a footman to look after your safety. It's not like home, not here."

"And it's not proper. If anyone saw you, it could lead to all sorts of rumors." Aunt Caris lifted her hands. "What am I to do with you?"

I dropped my gaze to the cobbled stones beneath my feet. Stars danced in the pools of water below, and I longed for the freedom they enjoyed. Yet I didn't belong in the heavens, so somehow, I must find a way to fit into the world I inhabited. Recalling extensive plant catalogs and libraries of lore required little effort, but attending all the intricate proprieties society required . . . I tightened my lips to still a tremble.

Once again, I'd disappointed those I loved. And I couldn't even excuse my behavior with the truth—that I'd been detained by a fae lord, that I'd nearly allowed my fae-touch to overtake me. So I said nothing at all.

Ainslie tilted her head. "Discussing our affairs on the doorstep could give rise to unwelcome remarks as well."

"Quite so." Lovell extended an arm to me. "Won't you come, Jess? It appears Holden has anticipated our arrival."

I accepted his arm, and we turned to find Holden standing behind us with the door held open, his face impassive.

Aunt Caris swept ahead and shepherded us into the drawing room. Ada and Ainslie settled on the chaise, and Lovell stood behind me.

And then Aunt Caris collapsed into her favorite chair. For a long moment, she remained silent, as though collecting her thoughts. "I know this matter with Lady Dromley has caused you great upset, my dear. It's only natural. Regardless, you cannot allow your grief to cloud your judgment. I'd be failing you if I did not speak of the dangers of your behavior."

Jade glared at Aunt Caris, the slightest twitch to her tail. I stroked her to calm us both. I couldn't protest there'd been no danger, not with the fae I'd encountered—though Aunt Caris and I had altogether different threats in mind.

"Your father and I are concerned that Lady Dromley's death has brought up painful memories of your mother's passing."

"It has been painful, but—"

"You must exercise greater care to avoid any . . . troubles."

A veiled reference to the affliction they believed vanquished? "Yes, Aunt Caris."

"Given the current circumstances, you're not to go out without first obtaining permission for your errand." I'd never heard her use so firm a tone. "Your father says you don't wish to leave Avons, but you must show better judgment if you're to stay."

A frown tugged at Ainslie's lips. "Aunt Caris, I don't think—"

"No, my dear, you must not interfere." She straightened and clasped her hands in her lap. "I'm quite right in this. You'll see in time."

The restraints closing around me stung like bonds woven of thorn and nettle. I wanted to protest, but what would it accomplish, except confirm to Father he was right to banish me to Aunt Gillian's? Small wonder so many women welcomed the chance to wed—at least then they had greater liberty, provided their husbands were not tyrannical. I fought to maintain an even tone. "I'm sorry for causing you worry, Aunt Caris. That was never my intent."

"I know, dear," she said. "Now get some rest. You look entirely done in."

She was right. The reading of the will and its attendant threats, the Otherworldly encounter, and now the family scuffle, all in the course of one unending day—it was sufficient to weary the hardiest of souls. Fatigue settled across my shoulders like a yoke, and I struggled to move from my chair.

After Aunt Caris's chastisement, no one wanted to venture further speech. We all made our escape, Lovell departing for home, and Ada and Ainslie ascending the stairs arm in arm, while I trailed behind with Jade.

Once secure in my bedchamber, I collapsed into bed fully clothed. Jade nestled herself alongside me.

Never mind the trouble I'd caused already, what greater difficulties might befall us when Riven came to call? Would he seek to glamour my family? Would he wake my fae-touch once more, by intent or by virtue of his presence? What if it strengthened beyond my control? I shut my eyes, welcoming the dark and the silence.

Whatever it required, I must keep him from harming my family, from afflicting them as I was afflicted—or worse.

～

AUNT CARIS HAD ALWAYS REMINDED me of a sunbloom, her coppery hair sharing the sheen of its petals, her full figure its graceful curves, her face its radiance. But this morning, the bloom absented itself from her cheeks, and she drooped like a blossom in drought.

Whatever troubled us, troubled her. I wanted nothing more than to restore peace and alleviate her worries, so I choked back the request that she permit me to return to Wyncourt and attended instead to the simple homely tasks in which she delighted.

In time, her color returned—at least, until Aunt Melisina sent a carriage to fetch her. Reluctantly, she departed, after securing a promise that I'd remain sequestered with my sisters for the afternoon.

We retired to the morning room, Ada to practice the pianoforte and Ainslie to re-trim one of her hats. While I might not be able to examine Wyncourt further, I could still attempt to work out the case—and the additional difficulties of Riven and my fae-touch.

I fetched my writing supplies and sat down to pen a letter to Lord Blackburn. One way or another, he was involved, and if I met him, I might be able to determine how.

I penned a brief note explaining my connection to Lady Dromley and her estate, adding that I desired him to call at his convenience so I might deliver directly into his care a parcel from Lady Dromley. I folded it at precise angles, then hesitated. Could I remove him from suspicion now that an Otherworldly connection had emerged?

I tapped the end of the pen against my lips. There were oddities about Wyncourt that appeared to stretch far beyond this case, but it was far too soon to rule anything out.

If I could persuade Aunt Caris to let me return, I might find some of the answers I required within Wyncourt—and Ibbie's diaries, if I located them. But if I tenanted Wyncourt to Riven, would I be able to conduct a further search? Surely I needed to stay as far from him as possible.

In Milburn, sensation had overtaken me like a flood when I'd chosen to open a chink in my cage of thorns. Yet when I'd encountered Riven in Wyncourt, it had started to unravel without my consent. Had Riven forced open the cage, or had the fae-touch itself continued to strengthen despite my efforts to constrain it?

I studied the red splotch of wax that sealed my letter. I took for granted my ability to correspond, to communicate, to think rationally . . . but what if my control failed? What if the burgeoning fae-touch snatched my reason?

Suddenly, I ached for Mother, for the cool, soothing touch of her fingers, for her melodious voice offering reassurance. Somehow, even when I resolved to remain silent, she'd always drawn my feelings from me—and she'd never condemned them.

But she wasn't here, would never be here, and I required more than reassurance; I required information.

Who could I ask? When I'd composed a plan to find information on my fae-touch, I'd considered inquiring of loremasters, though it was a riskier endeavor than burying myself in the library stacks.

If they perceived my fae-touch, surely the loremasters would have no compunction about summoning the Vigil. Mr. Heard had certainly seemed to suspect *something* in our interactions, though he'd not pressed for answers nor suggested the authorities examine my life. But I couldn't count on others expressing such tolerance.

If Mr. Heard were in Avons, I'd inquire of him, no matter my fears of betraying myself further. Perhaps I should write. Even apart from my pressing questions, I owed Mr. Heard a reply. I reached for the small ink pot, uncorking it once more and releasing its faint mineral scent.

Mr. Heard,

> I trust this letter finds you well. I was delighted to receive your report on the mill and the recent successes of the Hopkins family, yet I write on another matter.
>
> Doubtless you've heard of the difficulties we face in Avons,

and I thought perhaps you could shed some light on our present situation. There's a great deal of speculation about the nature of the Crimson Tattoo Killer, but since the Vigil has involved themselves, I cannot help but wonder if there's some Otherworldly connection. I'd hoped you'd share your opinion on the matter.

Is it possible the killer might be fae-touched? Could you suggest resources about fae-touch and its influence on the mortal mind? Do you agree with the conclusion that it always leads to madness? Could it have led the killer astray or made him vulnerable to some manipulation of the fae? Do you know of accounts of Otherkind preying so directly on mortals in this way in our world? Forgive the bounty of questions and the trespass on your goodwill, but any knowledge you may have, I'd appreciate.

If I can do anything for you in return, you have only to tell me. Since you requested I share any lore I uncovered, I will say I've stumbled across references to a Dark Era and an open conflict with the Otherworld in some old documents. I wish I had more to share with you, but beyond such rumor—and a reference to Otherkind dubbed ghouls and wights—I know little else. I thought it might interest you, yet perhaps you're already familiar with such tales?

Finally, I assure you I'm taking your warnings to heart. I desire nothing more than to avoid Otherkind, forever if possible.

With respect,
Jessa Caldwell

If only avoidance of Otherkind *were* possible; if only the sincerity with which I embraced his warning could extend to action. I folded and sealed the letter and stacked it with the missive for Lord Blackburn. I hoped Mr. Heard's unusual perceptiveness didn't extend to the written word—that he would not read between the lines and see reflected my fears for myself and my sanity. Regardless, by framing the letter as I had, at least I'd not expose myself to accusation, if another should read it.

A moment later, Danvers announced dinner, and we all followed him to the dining room. Aunt Caris swept in unusually late, her full green skirt sweeping around her.

After joining us in prayers, she turned to Ada. "Melisina and I have been speaking of your many suitors. She tells me you won't encourage Lord Bradford, even though he's an excellent prospect."

Ada unfolded her linen napkin and placed it neatly on her lap. Only a faint stain of color on her cheeks hinted at her discomfort. "I haven't rejected his attentions as yet."

"But do you have some objection to him?" Aunt Caris asked gently.

Ainslie leapt to Ada's defense. "Indeed, she does! As do I, on her behalf."

"I would never wish you to wed a man you find distasteful, but surely there's someone among your suitors who has caught your interest, someone whom you could respect enough to wed." Aunt Caris gripped her glass tightly. "Don't you wish to establish yourself?"

"Of course I want a family, but not enough to marry a man who leaves my heart untouched, nor whose character leaves a great deal to be desired. If he were a man I could respect, I'd agree to a match, but otherwise—"

"For my part," Ainslie announced, "I'll not marry for anything aside from love. Why should I bestow myself on someone who cares for nothing more than a glittering trophy, one that he'll likely placed on the shelf when the thrill of acquisition fades and a more attractive prize crosses his path?"

"By the Crossings! Between the three of you, it's a wonder I'm not already wrinkled and gray. I only hope you come to your senses before it's too late. I know better than to hope your father will put his foot down, as he ought." Aunt Caris ran her fingers across the simple gold locket about her neck. "I'd by no means see you wed to a man of ill character, but love can deceive. Find a good-natured gentleman, one well-established, and you won't come to regret it—but if you trust your feelings, you may be led astray."

Did she hint at the secret that had led her to Milburn, the one which she'd gone to such lengths to keep concealed? I leaned forward. "Did you ever fall in love, Aunt Caris?"

"That's neither here nor there, my dear. I'm far too old to consider such things." Yet her coppery-gold curls, gleaming in the gaslight, and her smooth creamy skin belied her claim of advanced years. "I suppose for all my rearing, you're still your mother's daughters. She always was headstrong."

Ainslie swirled the minty spring soup with her spoon. "If she were here, I'd imagine she'd do her share of scaring away suitors on our behalf."

A familiar ache squeezed my chest. What would Mother have advised us? We'd never know, not for sure.

"You may well be right," Aunt Caris said. "But she wanted the best for you, and I'm certain she would have exerted herself to find a pleasing match."

"There will be time enough for me to find a man I respect, if only you'll be patient . . . and perhaps put in a good word for me with Aunt Melisina?" Ada asked.

"Melisina is set on Lord Bradford, but perhaps if I suggested a more promising suitor . . ." Aunt Caris brightened. "Lord Riven would be an excellent choice."

I choked on my soup. "Whom did you say?"

"Lord Riven—a charming gentleman I met today. He's new in town, but wealthy and titled." She turned to Ada. "He'd make any woman a fine husband."

Only if she wished to find herself bound to a fae who would use her for his own ends and discard her, for fae could do nothing else. They'd certainly not stoop to wed a mortal. I fumbled with my spoon. If Riven wished to make his point, he'd done it. Not only could he determine where I lived, he could also reach any member of my family at any time—and they might not be able to resist his glamour. If there was one favor the fae-touch granted, it appeared to be my ability to peer through glamour to some degree. They didn't have even that limited protection.

When he called tomorrow, I'd have to bargain with him, and later persuade the trustees I'd acted rightly in letting Wyncourt. But I wasn't going to take his first offer, not if I could help it.

CHAPTER 14

When the last hint of pearl-gray vanished from the horizon and lampposts scattered about the garden cast great pools of shadow, Riven appeared. Though I'd spent endless hours rehearsing the ways our conversation might unfold, I still didn't feel prepared. I gripped my trowel like a weapon, though I knew it would accomplish little against an Otherworldly foe.

As he stalked down the garden path, the flickering gaslight drew out the reddish glints in his warm brown hair, a rich hue better suited to oils than watercolors. He'd assumed his veiled form, power hidden but pulsing beneath the surface. I hoped he concealed not only his power but his presence from possible onlookers—or that no one happened take note of a gentleman with me. The walls and shrubbery provided a great deal of concealment, but still . . .

Jade rushed forward and placed herself between us, motionless except for the tip of her tail, which twitched uneasily.

He halted a half fathom away. "I trust you've reconsidered, mortal."

No pleasantries, then. Did fae ever observe them, or were mortals simply too far beneath their notice to deserve simple courtesies? I set the trowel on a nearby bench and brushed the dirt from my hands. "Will you remind me of your terms?"

The question was mere form, and perhaps he knew it, for the slightest hint of amusement flickered in his eyes. Was this a game to him?

"It's quite simple. You give me the tenancy of Wyncourt through midsummer's eve. I'll give you double the usual sum to let it. There are no other requirements." His scent, like that of a sun-warmed forest after a storm, filled the air between us.

The sense of Other strengthened, a compelling draw to . . . what? Allow the fae-touch to consume me? Doubtless that would suit his purposes, for if it did, if I were stripped of reason, I might consent to anything.

He stepped closer. "Perhaps you fear that I've woven some snare within the bargain, but I don't require a mortal plaything. I have only one purpose in your world, and I'll leave once it's fulfilled."

Did that mean if he hadn't come for a purpose, he would have sought a plaything? Never mind, it made no difference to our bargain—but his intent did. "Last night, you never answered me. Are you in league with the killer?"

The green of his eyes darkened till it resembled shadowed pines. "No."

Yet it couldn't be coincidence that had brought him to Wyncourt. "But you do know something about him?"

He appeared to weigh his words, then said, "Yes."

My pulse leapt. This was what I must bargain for.

"My patience is dwindling, mortal." His voice deepened, and the gas lamps flickered. "Do we have a bargain?"

I breathed in the soft fragrances of lavender and budding

rose and struggled to maintain calm. "Not yet. I'd like to propose an alternative. I'll allow you tenancy of Wyncourt in exchange for information about the true nature of the killer, but I have two conditions: if we enter into this agreement, you'll not remove or conceal any of Lady Dromley's papers from me, and you'll not harm my family or any of the servants at Wyncourt."

"You concern yourself a great deal with the affairs of others."

"Because they matter to me. I have a responsibility to those I love." Surely even fae could understand such things—there must be those they cared for.

Yet he remained inscrutable, the flicker of the gaslight across his chiseled features reminding me of his Other nature. At last, he gave a curt nod. "If you want information, I require more than Wyncourt. In return, you'll answer any questions I have regarding Lady Dromley or any of the other mortals in Avons. I'll not withhold her papers from you, but I require access to them as well."

A rising tide of sensations battered at my cage of thorns. Soon now, and our dealings would be over. "Very well."

"As for your other concerns . . ." He shrugged, as though my requests were trivial. Perhaps all mortal concerns were, to fae. "They are of no consequence. I will add them to the bargain. Now, do you consent?"

"Yes."

"Then it is done."

A strand of light as brilliant as liquid gold passed between us. It twined about my upper arm in a pattern of swirls, and I fought the urge to claw at it, struggling to still my thrumming pulse. "What have you done?"

"It's merely the outward sign of our binding."

My skin tingled, and I rubbed the slender lines of gold that shimmered along the edge of my sleeve. After a moment, they dimmed, but when I moved my arm, they gleamed in the gaslight.

Like the scar on Ainslie's arm—only hers was tinted silver, rather than gold.

I staggered back and braced myself on the wrought-iron bench. The cool metal sent a chill down my arm. "Is this sort of marking customary among your people?"

His eyes narrowed. "All bargains among high fae have a visible binding, if that's what you're asking. Though glamour may conceal it."

"Then will you do so? Otherwise it will give rise to questions, and I cannot think you wish to draw attention to your presence."

"As you wish."

Even as he spoke, it faded. Only when I strained could I perceive the faintest traces of glamour weaving round my arm and hiding the sign of our bargain.

I'd bound myself to Riven, and Ainslie . . . what had befallen her? When had she encountered fae? Unless I was much mistaken, her scar was no scar, but a binding mark. Jade offered a soft *mrow*, but it failed to comfort.

Whatever my fears for Ainslie, I couldn't let this opportunity for gathering information slip from me. I'd learned from the sprites to assume an air of confidence, so there was no need to veil my questions, nor conceal them beneath the careful delicacy of a lady. For once, I could take a direct approach. I straightened. "Tell me of the killer."

"I'll tell you, but I'll also caution you. You care about the death of your friend, but any attempt by a mortal to apprehend the killer will only result in more death. He comes from my world, and he claimed his first prey there."

I drew a shuddering breath. Ever since Riven had appeared,

I'd wondered if the killer was an Otherworldly predator. Now I had confirmation, but could it be trusted?

Never trust a fae. The warnings were clear. Yet Riven hadn't tried to craft an exacting bargain, and he *appeared* to offer information in a forthright fashion. Perhaps that in itself should worry me. I clasped my hands to still them, ignoring the smudge they left on my gown. "Is the killer high fae?"

"He's of our world."

Fae doublespeak. He'd said the killer came from his world, but what did that truly mean? After all, a mortal could have entered the Otherworld, then returned here and continued a murderous spree . . . and still conceivably be said to have come from the Otherworld. And yet, I couldn't imagine a mortal successfully killing fae, not even when equipped with the most advanced weapons of the alchemists. Perhaps one might succeed once, if particularly fortunate, but beyond that? Unless Riven meant he'd killed low fae . . .

I rubbed my temples. "Do you know what sort of creature he is?"

"His identity is unknown at this time."

Fae couldn't lie, but Riven continued to select his words with care. What did he hide? "Does he conceal himself with glamour when he moves among us?"

"There's no indication he uses glamour."

"Yet he must conceal himself or the Magistry would have uncovered him by now."

"Otherkind, as you call us, possess many methods of concealment. Not all rely on glamour."

I blinked. What else didn't I know about Otherkind? I suspected the knowledge I did *not* possess could fill vast libraries. "How would he—"

"That's all I can offer you about his nature. Anything else would be speculation."

"Then what of the marks on the floor?"

Riven lifted his broad shoulders. "He leaves them at the site of every murder."

So much I'd already surmised. "But why?"

"Surely you don't believe I can read the mind of a murderer?" The faintest trace of mockery laced his tone.

"As you've pointed out, mortal knowledge about fae is limited. *Can* you read minds?"

"No." But there was a flicker in his eyes, like the glint of sunlight on a forest pool. He might not read minds, but he could perceive something beyond mortal ken, I was almost certain. I didn't wish to press my good fortune by inquiring beyond the bounds of our agreement. What else might I reasonably ask?

The soft chirping of a cricket issued from the bushes behind us, and Jade pricked her ears but kept her glowing gaze focused on Riven.

He might not be willing to divulge anything else about the nature of the killer, but what about the nature of the murders? "Do you know how he's killing them?"

"He's draining their bodies. He takes their vitality and leaves a husk behind." The slightest shadow touched his face. "It's not a pleasant sight."

Blight and rot. A vivid image of a mummy I'd once seen on display at the Royal Museum flashed through my mind, its features gaunt and desiccated. If the victims bore a similarly distorted appearance, it would explain why the statesmen refused to let anyone in the chambers until the bodies were removed. If so, then the Magistry *must* know the killer wasn't mortal, despite the denial of the Vigilist. Or perhaps not—for alchemy gone wrong could provide an alternate explanation for the disfigurement of the bodies.

And Ibbie . . . oh, Ibbie. I looked away from Riven, toward the pale arch of the birch branches against the dark sky. How much had she suffered, when the creature drained her life? Icy fingers clawed at my heart.

Jade pawed my hem, and I lifted her, her warmth driving away the biting cold. "Why . . ." My voice faltered. I collected myself and tried again. "Why would he kill in such fashion? Does it fill some sort of need?"

"I can't say, not for certain." His voice carried an edge, a warning. "I believe he takes pleasure in pain—and he could as easily take pleasure in yours as that of others, if you interfere with his aims."

"But if no one interferes, he'll kill again and again." And so many I loved were within Avons and vulnerable. I inhaled the grass-sweet scent of Jade's fur. "Do you intend to stop him?"

He might as well have been carved of oak for all the reaction he offered. "I've told you of the nature of the killer. That was our agreement. I'll collect my information on Lady Dromley later."

Although he clearly held much back, Riven had offered this information with surprising readiness. Why? Fae had no interest in helping mortals. Perhaps he knew I'd no hope of convincing the authorities of the truth. After all, I could hardly confess to having bargained with high fae without drawing down the wrath of the Vigil. Perhaps it was why Riven felt it safe to share what little he had.

Certainly, no one would expect a lady with little power or influence to attempt to stop an Otherworldly killer. But if Riven would not act, then where did that leave me?

The garden rustled to life, the whispers becoming melodies, strong and sure.

No, no, no.

I sank onto the bench. I'd made it so far in our interactions without succumbing; I only needed to last a few moments more. Yet the melody of the roses strengthened—a prickling sweetness in their song—and I struggled to tighten the weave of the thorned vines within. I couldn't afford another slip like the one I'd experienced at Wyncourt, not absent a clear path to safety. I clutched Jade closer and rehearsed my favorite passages from the Script forward and backward.

Riven broke into my thoughts. "At noon tomorrow, you'll meet me at Wyncourt to inform the staff of my tenancy."

Then he strode from the garden before I could protest. In his absence, the pressing, pricking sensation of Other eased, and the melodies subsided back to whispers.

My thoughts spun and swirled like leaves caught in a river eddy. Somehow I must determine what sort of Otherworldly predator preyed upon us—and how it could be stopped, a seemingly impossible task. I brushed at the dirt on the front of my gown. And what of Lord Blackburn? Did he play a role in this still? Had the killer found a way to use a mortal in his schemes?

A nightjar rasped in the tree above, and I startled. Something brushed my shoulder. I gasped and whirled toward the threat, nearly dropping Jade. But it was only a low-hanging limb, swaying in the breeze.

The fur on Jade's neck lifted, and she nudged me, as if to propel me back withindoors.

"I quite agree. Neither of us should be out here any longer."

Not when the killer could be lurking in the shadows, concealing himself from mortal eyes. Cat senses were far superior to those of humans, so if something discomfited her . . . I hurried down the dimly lit garden path and into the house.

Somehow I needed to persuade Aunt Caris that an errand to

Wyncourt the next morning would be harmless—and prevent her from trying to accompany me. I wanted to keep Riven away from my family, if at all possible. I already bore the taint of fae-touch, but they didn't need to join me, or worse, find themselves enslaved to the bidding of the fae . . . as Ainslie may well be already.

The thought stopped me in my tracks. I wanted to flee to the safety of my bedchamber, to shut the door and bolt out the world, but I couldn't retire without speaking to her, without confirming my theory.

Though what could I do to extricate her if I was correct and she had made such a bargain?

∾

I forced myself onward, hastening up the stairs to the bedchamber Ada and Ainslie shared. If what I suspected about her mark was true, then it upended everything the authorities of Avons had asserted about our relations with fae. Riven's appearance alone could have been excused as an aberration, but if Otherkind had intruded more than once, it not only indicated fae were far more involved in our world than the Vigil claimed, it also lent credence to Riven's claim about the nature of the killer.

Before I jumped to conclusions, I needed confirmation about Ainslie's mark. I halted on the woven carpet in front of her door. How could I broach such a sensitive matter? I knew all too well what it was to fear the Vigil; I didn't want Ainslie to suffer as I had. Would she want the truth? It didn't matter—I must know, if she was to be kept safe.

I clasped the ornate brass knob and eased open the door. I'd hoped to find Ainslie alone but wasn't so fortunate. She and

Ada, already wearing nightclothes, perched in the enormous four-poster bed that dominated the room, its crisp white linens contrasting with the dark, intricately carved posts.

Knees bent to her chest, Ainslie concentrated on a sheaf of paper, scribbling notes furiously across the pages, while Ada studied a new piece of sheet music, making occasional notations.

Ada glanced up and bestowed her gentle smile upon me. "Have you just come in from the gardens?"

"Yes—there was much to be accomplished." I crept into the room, reluctant to disturb their peace.

Ainslie put the final flourish on the page before her. "Come join us for a lovely gossip before bed. I've had interesting news from Aunt Gillian—"

"I can't, not yet."

Ada set aside her music, a slight frown crossing her perfect features. "Is something troubling you?"

More than I could ever confess. I climbed onto the end of the bed, careful not to muss the linens. "It's about your scar, Ainslie."

She waved her hand. "Oh, Jessa. You've already poured more time into it than I ever expected—and if your concoctions can't fade it, then nothing will. I've made my peace with it."

I smoothed the wrinkles that fanned onto the linens around me. "I've learned something that makes me think it's not a scar."

"Nonsense." She pulled her knees closer to her chest, and the papers rustled. "What else could it be?"

"A scar requires an injury, and you cannot recall one." Unable to still myself, I continued smoothing the linens. "Unless you simply don't wish to recount what happened."

"I don't remember everything that ever happened to me."

"Of course, certain things are inconsequential—but an

injury of that sort, you would recall under ordinary circumstances."

"What do you think it is, Jessa?" A note of unease threaded Ada's voice, and she edged closer to Ainslie.

"I think it signifies a bargain with fae."

Ada gasped. "Surely not! She's never ventured anywhere near the Otherworld, not even to an edgetown."

But Ainslie's vivid coloring washed to a pale ivory, and she drew her hand across her eyes.

"Could it be?" I asked.

"I . . . I don't know," Ainslie said. "But the scar frightens me. It always has."

Thus she'd made light of it in our previous conversations, pretending it was of no consequence, asking me if I might rid her of it—but only if it were no trouble. It was her way.

"Please try to remember." I leaned forward and gripped her hand. "You didn't have it when you and Ada came to spend the season with Aunt Melisina."

"I . . . I can't remember anything. That's the trouble."

I looked past her to Ada. "When did you notice it?"

"Perhaps a fortnight before your arrival in Avons. I don't recall exactly."

"Think, Ainslie." That unfamiliar, discomfiting note crept into my voice, carried against my will on a tide of fears for my sister. "Remember."

"We were walking in Calcot Park." She spoke slowly, like one in a dream. "Ada went ahead with Aunt Melisina to meet Miss Hastings, and I was about to follow when I saw . . . something by a stand of elms. It didn't seem to belong, so I felt I must investigate."

I held my breath, willing her to continue.

"An old woman stood beneath them. She wasn't like the

others in Calcot. Something about her didn't belong. She was unnaturally still and watched the crowd like she was searching for something or someone. I felt I should speak to her, see if she needed assistance." Ainslie leaned back against the headboard. "But then everything becomes unclear."

"Did you agree to do anything for her?"

"I can't remember. I might have done, but attempting to capture the memory is like trying to catch a butterfly. Every time I approach, it flutters away."

The mingled frustration and fear convinced me of the veracity of her words, and the haze that hung over her memory hinted at fae glamour. But what had she unknowingly consented to? Just how great was the danger?

This wasn't a puzzle I could solve with logic and research; it was a threat lying in the shadows, obscured by whatever blocked Ainslie's memories.

Ada nestled closer to Ainslie. "Are you sure this has to do with fae, Jessa?"

"Quite." But if I confided the evidence in full, the truth that I'd consorted with fae, they might tell Father and Aunt Caris—and my banishment would no longer be a question, but a fact. I brushed at a smudge I'd left on the pale linens. For once, my interest in uncovering obscure information could act in my favor. "I've only just learned from . . . an expert on the subject that high fae seal their bargains with marks like your scar. The fact that it refused to alter in any way, no matter how we treated it, always struck me as peculiar—but if it's not a scar, then it's perfectly reasonable. May I touch it?"

Ainslie gave a small nod, far more subdued than her wont. She'd never allowed me near the scar, always applying the salves and unguents herself. I ran my fingers across the marking, and it shimmered at my touch. My stomach twisted. How heavy a glamour had the fae laid upon her, that she'd failed to realize it didn't even *feel* like a scar? There were no hardened areas beneath the skin, no sensation of puckering or tightened tissues. Only a smooth expanse threaded with lines of silver, binding her to . . . what?

Ada looked at me over Ainslie's shoulder. "We can speak of this to no one."

CHAPTER 15

Ada and Ainslie wished to keep our knowledge of the binding a secret, and in this, we were of one accord. Ainslie displayed no other signs of fae-touch, but the Vigil would find the mark of a bargain highly suspect.

After our conversation, my mind had conjured all sorts of dire possibilities the bargain might represent, and my worries roused me early. It would be another hour before the servants set out breakfast, and I'd no desire to remain abed that long. I required some sort of activity to distract myself, so I dressed and went down to my tiny compounding room. It was belowstairs, near the kitchen, so I need not worry about disturbing my family. I rummaged through the drawers, seeking the ingredients to make a simple salve for the chafed hands of our lady's maid. I might as well accomplish something useful.

Jade leapt upon the table, nosing a jar of mugwort, then sneezed at the pungent aroma.

"I have something far more pleasant for you." I offered her a stalk of dried catnip, and she rubbed her face against it with a purr.

I crossed to the small table set below the single window. Beyond the pane, a scarlet dawn burned away the dark with a furious flare that matched the one kindling within me. How dared the fae force a bargain on Ainslie without her awareness, ensnaring her with glamour? Granted, the old tales told of such, but they always spoke of the victims committing acts of folly—venturing near Crossings or even into the Otherworld itself. Certainly, they never told of fae invading fortified bastions like Avons or lurking among ordinary park-goers and waiting to ensnare innocent mortals.

Though why not? If the fae were everything rumor held, wasn't that precisely what they *would* do? It was only the protection of the Vigil and the military that kept us safe—or at least they claimed to do so.

I could speculate endlessly about the changing interaction between our worlds, but if I was to find the killer, I required more information. Assuming the Otherkind hadn't made Lord Blackburn complicit in these crimes, would he possess answers about the presence of high fae within Avons? Certainly his request to Ibbie to procure the old letters for him indicated he conducted research of his own—unless the killer had swayed him to collect evidence to destroy so mortals would remain ignorant of fae interactions with our world. Nothing seemed too far-fetched at this juncture.

I plucked the calendula from the shelf.

If Lord Blackburn didn't call upon me soon in response to my message, could I find some way to inveigle an audience with him? It would be the height of impropriety for a lady to call upon a gentleman, but if I could unearth some sort of mutual connection . . .

I shook some of the dried calendula into a jar, along with lavender, then poured oil overtop, the familiar motions soothing.

What did I know for certain? Ainslie had been marked by fae. Riven had appeared, and I'd bargained with him. As for the Otherworldly nature of the killer, I had only the word of a fae.

Could it be trusted?

Fae were experts in twisting the truth to suit their circumstances, so I couldn't fully embrace what Riven had said without some sort of verification. Yet his explanation fit the facts, and it opened a path of investigation. I must seek information on Otherkind that drained the bodies of its victims and disguised itself without glamour—and further, I must determine if Lord Blackburn investigated the case himself or had fallen under the influence of the killer.

At least I had a path forward. Perhaps I could consult with a loremaster for information on more obscure Otherkind, if I could find some way to conceal the reason for my interest. And then there were Ibbie's diaries. If she'd known or suspected something of the Otherworld within our own—a thin thread of speculation at best—perhaps I'd find additional information contained within.

I closed the jar and carefully placed it where the sun would illumine it, drawing forth the healing properties of the herbs. If only I could so readily concoct something to heal my fae-touch.

Yet for all the dangers it posed, it also appeared to offer some protection. Certainly it had permitted me to perceive and bargain with the sprites in Milburn, and it seemed to assist in repelling glamour—though I didn't know how far such protection extended. If Riven had continued to press, would I have been able to resist?

It was impossible to predict, which brought me back to my original conclusion: I must avoid *everything* related to the Otherworld, a challenge if I intended to investigate a killer allegedly Other in nature.

I sealed the canister of calendula and returned it to the shelf. It would be all the more difficult if I intended to help Ainslie. In some fashion, she was also entangled with fae, and I'd yet to land on a notion of how I might identify the Otherkind who held her binding.

As though the thought conjured her, Ainslie appeared in the doorway. "Holden said you hadn't gone out to the gardens, and you weren't in your bedchamber, so I imagined I'd find you here."

She flitted into the compounding room as if she hadn't a care in the world, her wild-rose fragrance swirling between us. Yet . . . she'd fashioned her hair into the simplest of twists, rather than the elaborate styles she usually favored, and her gown lacked adornment, as though she'd dressed in haste. Perhaps she was more concerned than she let on.

She sank into the single chair I kept in the room and glanced over her shoulder, as if to ensure we were alone. "I've been considering all you said last night, and I wondered if perhaps I've already done whatever I bargained to do, and that's why I can't recall anything. If so, the scar cannot signify any cause for concern."

Jade perched on the narrow table, and one of her ears twitched. If only she could share her opinion. I felt sure she had one. Yet perhaps I gave her too much credit, as doting pet owners were wont to do.

It was possible Ainslie was right. I hadn't asked Riven if the mark would vanish once our bargain was fulfilled. "But what if you're wrong?"

She lifted a slim shoulder. "What can we do, short of invading the Otherworld and shouting an inquiry to the winds? It would be utter madness."

"I wasn't considering such an approach, but—"

"What then?" She caught her lower lip between her teeth. "I know you, Jessa. You don't like unanswered questions. But I don't want to cause trouble. If we start prying into this, word could get out and . . . that would bring its own dangers."

She didn't need to remind me of the risks, for I shared her fears. To wait for the fae to return and require the fulfillment of the bargain went against every instinct, yet she was also right: our inquiry could give rise to unwanted attention—or bring down more Otherworldly wrath. Perhaps I could find another way to keep her safe? Perhaps we could acquire stronger wardstones? Or . . .

"Promise me you'll let it rest?"

"It doesn't trouble you?"

"I refuse to worry any longer. What will it gain me?" A sparkling smile lit her face. "The Mansforth Ball is tomorrow night, and I mean to enjoy it to the full."

I *almost* believed her determined good cheer—but for all her enjoyment of society, she had a quick mind. She wouldn't so readily brush this aside, not unless glamour influenced her to do so—or she was more frightened than she let on.

I brushed a few scraps of lavender into my hand, then poured them into the small wooden rubbish bin. "I won't take any action that could expose you to danger."

"Very well." Ever persistent in her efforts to win Jade over, she stretched a hand toward her. Jade only glared at it. Ainslie shook her head and laughed. "If it weren't for the affection she shows you, I'd be convinced she held the world in scorn."

With that, she retreated from the compounding room. Absently, I began plucking dried mint leaves from their stems. I'd do my best to find a path forward that didn't expose her to further risk. Yet however frightening the notion of her bargain with an unknown fae, the presence of the killer within Avons threatened not only Ainslie, but my entire family, and I required understanding of his identity above all else. To that end, I must return to Wyncourt and seek Ibbie's diaries before Riven laid claim to them.

As I'd recounted our bargain in my mind time and again, I'd had a sinking feeling that Riven could choose to interpret my specification of papers as those loose, not bound into books like her journals, which meant if he found them first, that loophole could allow him to withhold them from me.

Perhaps they'd contain nothing pertaining to the case, but with such scant evidence at hand, I couldn't afford to pass by anything that might offer insight on the killer or evidence to support or invalidate Riven's claims. Not to mention, any account of Ibbie's interactions with Lord Blackburn could direct my inquiries further.

No, I wouldn't leave claiming her diaries to chance, nor the goodwill of the fae. Somehow, I must locate them before Riven did—which meant persuading Aunt Caris to allow a visit.

Jade gave a plaintive *mrow*.

"Yes, I know you're ready for breakfast. Let's go."

∽

After breakfast, I paced the morning room, Jade twining between my ankles, at times nearly tripping me. She seemed to take my restlessness as a personal affront and nudged me toward a chair, but I couldn't bring myself to sit while I awaited Aunt Caris.

At last, she put in an appearance, a basket of plain sewing tucked under her arm. She'd broken the fast in her bedchamber, as she did on occasion when she was more worn than usual, but she seemed in good spirits.

I fetched the basket from her and presented my request, settling in with some stitchery to show my goodwill.

Aunt Caris frowned. "My dear, I cannot think it wise for you to visit Wyncourt alone, not after you were so overcome last time that you lost all sense of the hour and your own safety."

I jabbed my finger with a needle and winced, tucking it in the fold of my skirt before the bead of blood could stain my work. "I understand you don't want me to linger there, but I thought perhaps I could fetch some of Ibbie's belongings and bring them home."

"Wait until calling hours this afternoon, and we can all visit Wyncourt together after we're through," Aunt Caris said. "Melisina and I think it's time you join us to go calling, at least on occasion."

She was right, of course. I should have made a formal entrance into society some time ago, but having two older unwed sisters had offered me some protection from that expectation. On the face of it, her request was reasonable enough—paying calls was the least I could do.

Yet Riven expected me at noon, and if I didn't arrive at Wyncourt to hand over tenancy when he'd demanded, he might well view it as a violation of our agreement. He might come here to fetch me, or he might disturb the staff at Wyncourt—both disastrous. But what excuse for urgency could I offer? I fumbled with the needlework. "Aunt Caris—"

The door swung open, and Lovell breezed in, his juniper scent a bold counterpoint to the soft violet and lavender fragrances Aunt Caris favored. He brushed her cheek with a kiss and then dropped into the seat next to mine.

"What brings you here so early?" I asked.

"Mother sent me to fetch the invitations Ada addressed for her. In truth, I was glad to escape before she changed her mind and enlisted me to play escort to her friend's daughter, who has an unfortunate tendency to cling. Her stay has already felt an eternity." He winked. "But don't tell Mother I said that."

Aunt Caris shook her head, but the corners of her mouth twitched.

Lovell's gaze swept between us, as though seeking any sign of residual strain. "While I'm here, I thought I might take Jess out for a bit."

Jade chuffed her approval.

And I offered a genuine smile. "That would be lovely. I was hoping to call on Wyncourt this morning."

"Excellent. We can drop the invitations at home, then make straight for Wyncourt," he said.

Aunt Caris visibly relaxed. "Well, I suppose if Lovell is with you, you can't come to any harm."

"There you have it." Lovell pushed to his feet. "Shall we go, Jess?"

"Yes, please."

In short order, he'd settled me within his curricle. An empty satchel sat at my feet, one I hoped to fill with Ibbie's journals, and Jade perched on my lap, gazing beneficently upon Lovell. Evidently, she approved of his support.

He kept the horses to a brisk pace, and it wasn't long before he'd deposited the invitations into the hands of a footman, and we were on our way to Wyncourt.

The morning already proved a warm one, and sun bathed my face as I considered my options. I couldn't risk Lovell encountering Riven without explanation—nor did I want my family exposed to him at all. I'd have to find some way to keep the two apart without betraying my purpose. I unfolded a careful explanation about introducing a new tenant to Wyncourt, and he accepted it readily.

"I'm impressed. Mere days after receiving an unexpected inheritance, you've located and installed a suitable tenant." He flicked the reins. "Perhaps Father should enlist *you* to put his northern estate in order."

"I've no desire for estate management."

"Nor do I." A languid grin tilted his mouth at the corners. "But Father refuses to believe me."

"Perhaps if you proposed some other course of action? Some other skill you'd rather attain?"

"Brilliant." His lips quirked further. "I know . . . I'll announce I intend to become a Collector and join the team venturing into the Fens Crossing."

I raised a brow. "They'd never take a gentleman—and even if you managed to conceal your identity to join them and then somehow survived your venture into the Otherworld, your mother would kill you afterward for taking such a risk."

He laughed. "Only if she had an alchemist on hand to revivify me."

"Only in rumor can alchemy accomplish such feats."

"True. Perhaps she'd settle for taking me to death's doorstep." He tightened his grip on the reins. "But anything I proposed after that would surely be seen as more reasonable. They might even consent."

A hint of something more sober in his tone suggested he had some purpose in mind. "Consent to what?"

Any trace of seriousness vanished, and he flashed a grin. "Why, to me remaining permanently a gentleman of leisure, of course."

Lovell might act the part, but I couldn't believe he'd be satisfied with such a life. Since joining my family in Avons, I'd noted hints of restiveness in him that I did not recall seeing before. Yet if he wished for something more, he didn't want to divulge it—and I couldn't blame him.

In short order, we halted in front of Wyncourt, and Jade draped herself over my shoulders. Lovell extended a hand to help me disembark, and I accepted, since Jade's position and the satchel draped over my arm made my balance more precarious.

"This won't be entertaining for you, I'm afraid. Do you want to take a turn about Avons until I'm through?"

"Not a chance." He passed off the horses to a waiting footman. "Aunt Caris would have my head. Where you go, I go."

I couldn't protest without raising suspicion, so I simply nodded. How was I going to escape Lovell before Riven arrived? And what if I lost control of my fae-touch in front of him?

Never mind that now—I'd best address the servants and move through business as swiftly as possible, if I wished to find the diaries before Riven did. I informed Mrs. Peters and Danvers that I'd let Wyncourt through midsummer's eve, and the tenant, Lord Riven, would be arriving this morning.

"I apologize for the short notice, but he wished to let the place at once. I truly hope you'll continue to serve here." If they refused, I'd have difficulty replacing them—finding trustworthy servants was the complaint of every lady in Avons.

Danvers gave a stilted nod, appearing less than enthused about a new master. "Certainly we will, as long as he proves reasonable. Lady Dromley would have wished it of us."

"Thank you. I'll perform introductions when he arrives, but in the meantime, I intend to examine Lady Dromley's bedchamber."

"Quite right." Mrs. Peters inclined her head. "I had a time putting it to rights after the stratesmen left. If you're displeased with its condition, you've only to let me know."

"I'm certain all will be well." I stopped at the base of the stairs. "One more thing—please prepare tea for my cousin and have it served in the drawing room."

Danvers and Mrs. Peters departed, but Lovell examined me closely. "Don't think you can shake me off so easily, Jess. Do you think it a good idea to go to her bedchamber? I know that's where she was found."

"It's something I must do, but I'd welcome your company. I'm seeking Ibbie's journals. If you're willing, I could use assistance with the search."

"It would be a welcome diversion."

He claimed the satchel, and side by side, we ascended the wide marble staircase. When we entered the bedchamber, my gaze drifted to the rug that concealed the fractalized mark below. Dreadful images filled my mind—Ibbie, alone and vulnerable, drained of life by a monster, lying on the floor, her features distorted . . .

My throat tightened.

If only I could have one more moment with her . . . if only I could have found the killer, before he found her.

But longing would not bring her back, so I forced myself farther into her bedchamber, seeking her diaries in all the likely places: within the drawers of her secretary, on her bedside table, and in the shelves filled with books. Then I moved to the less likely, inspecting beneath the mattress, within her wardrobe, and inside the chest of blankets at the foot of the bed.

Lovell searched alongside me, and even Jade joined in, nosing about the room—likely in search of mice, not that Ibbie would ever permit such creatures in her house.

After a few moments, Jade leapt upon the gilded mahogany secretary situated near the fireplace. She sat upon the top, twitching her tail so it beat upon the surface with a dull, repetitive thud. Then she gazed upon me and offered a soft *mrow*.

We'd already examined the secretary, but . . .

Oh.

Ibbie had appreciated the solving of secrets, the arts of concealment and discovery. The secretary could well contain hidden chambers. Mother had possessed a similar one and made a game of hiding us little notes in its secret compartment, often scribed in various codes or ciphers. When we uncovered and solved them, she would exclaim her pride and delight.

I ran my fingers across the ornate carved buttons and gilded woodwork, seeking an element that would depress. In time, I found three. I tried first one sequence, then another. On the fourth attempt, a strongbox sprang forth from the surface of the desk, one large enough to contain a stack of fifteen leather-bound books.

A quick peek inside one of the volumes confirmed it: I'd found her diaries. Or more truthfully, Jade had.

Lovell gave a low whistle. "Nicely done."

"You should credit Jade, not me." I stroked the soft fur between her ears, and her purr rumbled against my fingers. It was an impressive feat. How had she done it? Had she scented Ibbie on the diaries, perhaps?

Swiftly, I collected the journals and deposited them into my satchel, tightening the straps to conceal the contents. Then I restored the secretary to its original state. Once I'd had a chance to read them, I'd share them with Riven, so I might not come under accusation of breaking our bargain.

"It appears your tenant has yet to arrive. Let's take tea while we wait." Lovell lifted the satchel. "Best not linger here, now that you've found the diaries."

"Why don't you go to the drawing room? Mrs. Peters will have set tea. I need to collect a few items from the study. I'll join you shortly." And with good fortune, I'd spy Riven before Lovell did and avoid the two of them meeting.

A shadow of concern crossed his face. "Jess, I'm not sure—"

"I promise you I won't be overcome by grief while rummaging among the stacks. And I've never known you to turn down a good tea. Ibbie's cook is a fine one."

"We can take it together once you're through."

"Lovell, please. I need a moment alone."

He gave a slow nod. "Very well."

Before he could think better of it, I swept him down the stairs and left him in the drawing room to enjoy the lavish tea spread by Mrs. Peters. As I approached the study, a firm rap echoed through the corridor and a now-familiar prickle crept up my spine.

Riven had arrived.

Danvers marched past me with the air of a man resigned to his fate.

"If that's Lord Riven, please bring him directly to the study." I hurried down the corridor so I might wait there to greet him— well out of sight of Lovell.

A moment later, Danvers ushered Riven into the study, while on their heels Mrs. Peters bustled in with another tea tray.

The aroma of cinnamon drifted from the pastries, and a little curl of steam rose from the teapot, all perfectly ordinary, even homish—unlike Riven.

In his presence, the pinprick sensation of Other strengthened. On instinct, I tightened the weave on my cage of thorns as I performed the introductions.

With a few well-timed words, gracious gestures, and perhaps a measure of glamour, Riven charmed the servants. Danvers unbent so far as to bestow a smile upon him, and Mrs. Peters practically glowed.

I straightened one of the stacks of paper on the desk. If I'd not recognized he was fae, would he have glamoured me into cooperation so easily? I wrenched my attention from Riven and the servants and looked out the tall sash windows.

Though there was no breeze, though nothing beyond them stirred, the bushes outside the glass lifted curved boughs and waved at the windows, beckoning, reassuring, alluring.

The room dimmed at the edges.

No, no, no.

As I'd feared, Riven's presence roused the fae-touch, provoking it to press against the bounds of its cage.

I clenched my hands tightly and drew one deep breath after another. The songs from the garden wended through the window glass and swirled round me, drowning out the conversation within the room.

Riven shot me a gleaming glance. What did he perceive? No matter, after I settled him into Wyncourt, I'd have no need for further communication with him—no need to allow the Other to impinge further upon my senses. Or so I hoped.

Jade pawed at my legs, and I snatched her up, holding her like a shield against the encroaching Other. I would not listen to the enchanting melodies; I would attend to the servants. Someone needed to make sure Riven didn't mistreat them.

Slowly the fog lifted; slowly the voices became clear.

Mrs. Peters was promising to have rooms prepared for Riven right away, and then Danvers offered to take Riven about the place.

"No need. I've a few matters to attend to this morning." Riven drawled the words as any gentleman might, his assumed air of languor well-suited to the title he claimed—and a sharp contrast to the power and purpose below the surface. "My belongings will arrive this evening. I'll view the house then."

"As it pleases you, my lord." Danvers bowed slightly. "May I summon a carriage for you?"

"Not today, I'll take my own transportation." Riven slid to his feet with easy grace. "And I'll see myself out."

When he left, the pinprick sensation vanished and the tension in my middle eased. Apart from his assumed mortal guise, he'd not attempted to manipulate the servants, and were it not for the surging fae-touch, I would have viewed the encounter as unremarkable—shocking when one considered high fae involvement.

Mrs. Peters gave a soft breath of relief. "He seems as though he'll be easy enough to please."

If only she knew. She and Danvers went about their duties, and I poured myself a cup of tea, adding a generous measure of sugar. The warmth and sweetness brought a measure of calm—until a vigorous pounding at the front door nearly caused me to upend the cup on my lap.

Danvers entered a moment later. "Miss Caldwell, I beg your pardon, but there's someone here requesting an audience with you."

I set down the cup. "Someone here?"

Who would seek me at Wyncourt, rather than my own home?

"I've put him in the sitting room." He hesitated. "I didn't know if you'd wish to see him with your cousin or without."

"Very well, Danvers. I'll see him alone." I didn't want to drag Lovell deeper into my affairs, not when there was the slightest chance they could be of an Otherworldly nature.

Jade gave an inquisitive *mrow*, and I stroked her head. "Let's go see this mysterious visitor."

When we crossed the threshold, I found not a stranger, but

Mr. Broward. I stopped short. His hulking form dominated the delicate furnishings and pale colors of the room.

He wheeled to face me, his black brows lowering. "I see you've hoodwinked the servants as well as you did my aunt. Her butler won't even turn over my belongings without your permission."

"What is it you need, Mr. Broward?"

"I've only come for what's mine."

Did he refer to Wyncourt and his belief Ibbie owed it to him? I wasn't sure how to respond.

Jade glared at him, becoming weightier in my arms.

His hawthorn eyes bored into me. "I'd left several things in keeping of my aunt. I'll take them and be on my way—for now. But we have a reckoning coming, girl."

I pasted on a pleasant smile. "What is it you left with Ibbie?"

His gaze shifted to the side, then returned to glower at me. "A few antiquities, that's all."

He expected me to believe that? He'd not visited Ibbie even once since I'd known her, nor did he seem the sort to share her interests.

I hesitated in the doorway, unwilling to draw any closer to him. "I'm confident Ibbie would have referenced your belongings in her will, if she'd kept them in trust. After all, she mentioned the items on loan from Lord Haversham."

His features crimsoned with rage. "Are you calling me a liar?"

Yes. Unequivocally. But ladies did not express themselves so bluntly, and to state it outright would only fuel his fury. Still, I owed it to Ibbie to keep him from stealing items from her collection for his own gain. They should be displayed for research, as she'd wished. I drew myself up to my full height, wishing it were more impressive. "Can you describe these antiquities to me?

When and where did you find them? And do you have articles of provenance?"

"Articles of—" The flush deepened. "Ibbie was *my* family. *Mine.* You think families quibble with such matters between them?"

Jade dug her legs into my middle and sprang down to place herself between us.

"Perhaps not most families. But Ibbie did, always. She was meticulous in cataloguing her antiquities."

He stomped across the oak floorboards, rattling the glass figurines on the mantel with his steps. "You have one more chance to give me what's mine."

"Mr. Broward . . ."

He grabbed my arm much as he had before, with bruising force, and something snapped within. How dare he? My fingers wrapped around one of Ibbie's metal-ferruled parasols, neatly positioned in the door rack. I lifted it and slammed it against the side of his head just as Jade sank her teeth into his ankle.

The howl he released rang in my ears. He staggered back, blistering the air with curses.

Before he could close the distance between us once more, Lovell charged into the room. "What in the Crossings is happening here?"

"This chit assaulted me."

"This *lady* is my cousin, and you trespass in her home." I'd never seen Lovell riled before, never seen his casual demeanor give way to more intense emotion. But now he practically bristled, his hands fisting. "Leave now, unless you want me to cast you out by force."

For a moment I believed Mr. Broward would challenge him then and there, that there would be blood drawn between them. I clutched the parasol tighter.

But Mr. Broward appeared to think better of it. He crammed his hat down on his head. "There will come a day when you'll wish you'd cooperated with me. I'll see you before the Magister."

Then he stormed from the room.

"I thought you said you'd come to no grief rummaging the stacks?" Lovell shook his head. "Catch me being lured away by promises of tea again. Aunt Caris would have me hung if she knew I'd allowed you to fall into an altercation with a brute like that."

Jade stood in the doorway, licking her lips, looking for all the world like she yearned to sink her teeth into Mr. Broward once more—and I'd certainly not bestir myself to stop her.

I returned the parasol to its stand. "I don't think he'll show his face here again, but I'll speak to Danvers about denying him entrance."

"Even so, he seems quite serious about dragging you before the Magister." Lovell's lips drew into a stern line, an unfamiliar expression for him. "I don't like it, Jess. And Mother and Aunt Caris will like it even less."

I lowered my head, rubbing the aching spot on my arm. "What choice do I have but to defend that which has been left in my care?"

I should have already spoken to the trustees about mounting a defense, but the threat of action in court had paled before the incursion of fae and Otherworldly dangers. I'd neglect it no longer. Perhaps speaking with my trustees could serve more than one purpose—they might also be able to help me gain an audience with Lord Blackburn, if I told them he'd a connection with Ibbie's estate. "Please, don't tell Aunt Caris about this yet. If he's as serious as he seems, she'll find out soon enough."

Lovell folded his arms. "Only if you swear to come to me if he troubles you again."

"I promise." I would consult him, and gladly, for this was an ordinary sort of trouble, one with which he might assist, unlike the matters of the killer and the fae binding. "Perhaps . . . perhaps we'd best go home. I've done what I intended here."

And if the Infinite were gracious, I'd never see Mr. Broward —or Riven—again.

CHAPTER 16

After my unsettling encounter with Mr. Broward, I wanted nothing more than to examine the diaries in some quiet, solitary location to see if I could find a clear path forward before another disaster struck. Instead, I owed an afternoon of calls. On a scale of things to dread, paying calls ranked rather higher than rooting out a field of plith saplings by hand, even on the best of days, which this was not.

Yet my promise bound me. Even if Aunt Caris had taken pity on me and released me, Aunt Melisina certainly would not.

With crisp precision, she marched into the sitting room and announced that she intended us to call on Lady Bradford first. "She tells me she wishes to make greater acquaintance with the young lady who has caught her son's eye."

Ada immediately looked stricken. "Aunt, I don't think—"

"Pish, child." Aunt Melisina rapped her fan against her leg. "Playing hard to get may work for a time, but he'll need encouragement if he's to come up to scratch."

Ada and Ainslie exchanged one of their knowing looks.

"But that's the trouble, Aunt Melisina," Ainslie said. "Ada doesn't *want* him to come up to scratch."

"Don't be ridiculous, Ainslie." She motioned to the door. "Come along, time's wasting."

Why did it matter so much to Aunt Melisina to see us wed above our standing in society? As Ada had stated before, nothing indicated her own marriage was a happy one, for all that she'd successfully raised her station by it.

Ada pulled on her gloves. "Aunt, please let it rest. I don't wish to call on Lady Bradford today nor give her any false impressions about my interest in her son."

"Foolish girl." Aunt Melisina wheeled on her sister. "What did I say about poor influences, Caris? Alden should have left them in my charge."

"It's not so bad as all that." Aunt Caris plucked at the lace near her throat. "If Ada doesn't believe Lord Bradford would suit, then perhaps—"

"Perhaps she's a great deal too choosy for a girl with only a modest dowry."

A tide of heat swept up my chest, but to release the swell of anger would only reflect poorly on Aunt Caris. How might I sway her? I stepped between them. "Aunt Melisina, if we call upon Lady Bradford while Ada is . . . undecided, she won't make the best of impressions. Perhaps we'd better postpone the visit to another day?"

Aunt Melisina opened her mouth, then shut it tightly. Doubtless she wished to argue all the more since the suggestion came from me, but one look at the pinched pallor of Ada's features confirmed she was in no state to meet a prospective mother-in-law.

"Very well—but this conversation is not at an end." With that, she stalked from the room.

We followed in her wake to the waiting carriage, where her footman ceremoniously assisted us up the steps and then closed the door behind us.

As we traveled down Camden Row, Aunt Melisina fixed her attention on Aunt Caris. "I inquired about Lord Riven at your suggestion, and I discovered that of all things he's taken tenancy of Wyncourt. Were you aware of this?"

"Indeed not." Aunt Caris brightened. "But surely this is good news."

"Good news? I hardly think so. Will he wish to further the acquaintance of a family who allows their youngest daughter to conduct matters of business?"

Did they truly consider Riven as a possible suitor for one of us? For once, I didn't feel grateful that my aunts considered it important to marry off Ada or Ainslie first, not when they lacked any means of defense against fae artifice. My fingers curled within my gloves. "You're quite right, Aunt Melisina. Undoubtedly he won't wish to further the acquaintance."

Better to have her angered by my behavior than inviting fae into our home.

Aunt Melisina's lips pinched. "It's as I've told you, Caris. This is what comes of holding the reins with too loose a hand."

"You cannot blame Aunt Caris—"

"Cease interrupting, Jessa."

Aunt Caris made conciliatory murmurs, and we subsided into fraught silence. After one or two attempts, even Ainslie gave up on trying to make conversation. When we entered the first house, everyone donned an air of determined good cheer. Ada was more subdued than usual, but Ainslie charmed all those we met. I offered polite smiles and the occasional remark on the weather, all the while contemplating what sort of Otherkind could skulk about concealed without using glamour.

Perhaps I could turn this outing to my advantage by persuading my aunts a trip to the library was in order after our calls. I could seek tales that matched the sort of killer Riven had described—though if records existed, they must be obscure. Certainly, I'd never encountered them before, nor had Mother shared of any such fae.

Three houses and a blur of new faces later, we entered the home of one Mrs. Winters. A gentleman sat in her drawing room already, engaged in easy conversation. When he rose to greet us, I found he was none other than Mr. Upton, whom she introduced to us all.

He bowed. "I've had the pleasure of meeting Miss Jessa before, and I'm delighted to make the acquaintance of her family."

Aunt Melisina looked displeased to find him there, but she could scarcely cut him in the home of a friend, so she perched on a stiff-backed chair, her body rigid.

"Do you still keep abreast of the news, Miss Jessa?" While a seemingly innocuous remark, the glint in his eyes suggested that he spoke of certain news in particular.

"I always attempt to keep well-informed, but I've no doubt there's a great deal I don't know."

"One with your . . . determination will always find the knowledge sought." His deeply hooded eyes remained as unreadable as ever.

I shifted uncomfortably in my seat. Did he mean to betray me to my aunts? But no, for in the next instant, he turned to address Ainslie, and she beamed upon him with the generous goodwill she bestowed upon ladies and gentlemen alike.

I studied him.

Mr. Upton had spoken to me of the case before, more

openly than Mr. Burke. Might he again, if I asked the right questions?

When Mrs. Winters crossed the room to display her new pianoforte, my aunts and sisters followed, but Mr. Upton made no move to rise, and I seized the opportunity.

"You mentioned the news, which brought to mind an oddity that's troubled me—the degree of interest the Vigil has taken in this case." I tilted my head. "Given your work with the Magistry, you must know—do they suspect Otherkind?"

"Otherkind." He spoke slowly, as though the word held an unpleasant taste. "No one has confided such in me. They say they cannot manage without additional men, which the Vigil provides. Though between us, I believe they'd get on better without them."

"You find them incompetent?"

"I didn't say that."

But he didn't deny it either. Nor had he strictly denied the involvement of Otherkind. Could he share my suspicions?

Before I could form another question, Aunt Melisina bustled past. "Jessa! Come along."

Since she and the rest of my family moved toward the door, I'd no choice but to join them. I cast one glance over my shoulder to find Mr. Upton watching our departure. Would he have spoken more, if we'd had the time?

∼

OUR CALLS COMPLETE, I made my request to visit the library. Ada and Ainslie added their pleas to mine, Ada because she wished for the latest Penworth novel and Ainslie because she desired to browse the stacks. Despite Aunt Melisina's displeasure, Aunt Caris gave her consent.

I did *not* confess that I wanted to research the sort of Otherkind that might drain its victims dry—and how one might defend against such a foe. No sense in stirring trouble.

Once within the library, I strolled toward the history and lore sections. I bypassed all the familiar books on Otherkind; any mention of a creature as ghastly as the killer would have stuck in my memory. I'd have to find something I hadn't read before.

Finally, I located a slim volume entitled *Observations on the Otherworld and Its Inhabitants*, its thick layer of dust suggesting it had remained wedged behind larger books for some time.

On a whim, I also selected a history of the lakes region, where Bridstow was located, and paged through until I located a brief report on the Upton family. By all accounts, they were unexceptionable. On the face of it, Mr. Upton was as he represented himself: a gentleman of middling prospects, worthy of a minor mention in the annals of Bridstow, but no more. Yet some tragedy had befallen him, motivating him to involve himself in this case. What lay hidden in his past? What knowledge did he possess of value to the Magistry?

I tucked both books under my arm. Ada and Ainslie had already checked out their materials at the circulating desk, so I hurried to do the same, only to be halted by a voice speaking about fae.

In one of the side rooms reserved for lectures, a prominent loremaster addressed a small group. I took a half step in his direction. Would my family have patience for yet another detour? I glanced over to find them immersed in conversation with an acquaintance and decided to take my chances.

In such a setting, my interest in Otherworldly matters would be less likely to draw notice. After all, a whole throng was gathered round to listen to his tales. I slipped into the room in time to hear the end of the story of Matilda of Hemsworth and the bargain with faefolk that left her mute and enslaved to their whims till she died. Despite the disturbing subject matter, appreciative applause met his tale. He then launched into a lecture about how one must travel in groups when venturing near edgetowns, claiming there was safety in numbers. He even crafted a yarn about a large company of individuals who had intimidated a passing low fae and escaped unscathed.

I frowned. By all accounts I'd ever heard, a larger group would only offer more entertainment for any sort of fae, high or low.

A stout, matronly lady fluttered her fan vigorously. "I'm delighted to hear it. My son must travel near the Morven Crossing next month, and I'll be sure to tell him never to wander alone."

I willed the loremaster to confess it was only a tale, yet he flashed a smile at her. "He's fortunate to have such a concerned mother."

I clutched the book closer to my chest and stepped forward. I wouldn't contradict him outright, but if I could plant a few seeds of doubt . . . "You say groups might deter a single low fae, but don't low fae favor moving about with companions of their own?"

He spread his hands. "Who can say what a fae will take in mind?"

I inclined my head and lowered my voice, as though I repeated some fearful rumor. "Well, I've heard that some Otherkind can pull the very life from their victims, leaving only a husk behind. Is it true?"

"As I said, anything is possible when it comes to the Otherworld." He stroked his smooth chin with tapered fingers. "Though that does put me in mind of the breath-stealers."

He spun a vivid account of how these creatures whisked the breath from their victims as a form of play, but he said nothing about leaving desiccated corpses in their wake, and that seemed a bit too specific a detail to ask. His polished words dripped honey, yet held little substance. I craved the sound information Mr. Heard had offered, however brusque its delivery.

I tapped my fingers against the etched binding of the books I held. *Pemberton's Encyclopedia* and several others discussed breath-stealers in passing, but they relegated them to the realms of unproven Otherkind. Besides, according to lore, they were more animalistic in nature, certainly without the cunning to pull off a series of murders. It wasn't impossible, but quite unlikely that the killer was among their number.

Ainslie gesticulated to me from the doorway, and I allowed myself to be drawn away. It didn't appear this loremaster knew anything helpful, and any further questions risked drawing more attention than I desired.

On our ride home, I paged through the book on the Otherworld. Toward the end, I located a brief account of Otherkind the author dubbed *deerings*, due to their deerlike hooves, the only oddity on their otherwise maidenly forms. They were said to drink the blood of their chosen victims, but not to the point of death. Nor were they described as having glamour. Though Riven had said the killer used a different form of concealment, I couldn't imagine a mortal distinguishing between the two.

I shut the book with a snap. Nothing quite fit. I knew all sorts of accounts of predatory fae, but none that matched Riven's description. Given the limitations of our knowledge regarding the Otherworld—and the increasing evidence there was confusion of fact and fiction among it—how could I determine what sort of Otherkind preyed upon us, much less how to stop it?

I mulled over the problem throughout dinner, then trudged

up the stairs to my bedchamber, seeking solace in solitude. Despite my exhaustion, I forced myself to lay out Ibbie's journals in order by date . . .

Wait.

The last journal entry was dated six months before the murder. But Ibbie wrote in her diaries nearly every day, which meant the most recent—and most important—one was missing.

Why wasn't it kept with the others? And where might Ibbie have stashed it? I stacked the diaries I did possess in order.

All the things I didn't know, many of which may not have the least importance in finding the killer, settled on my shoulders, and I bent under the weight.

While the nature of the killer—and how to stop him—weighed foremost in my mind, I couldn't help wondering how many of the peculiarities that had cropped up since he'd appeared in Avons intersected with the case.

Perhaps my mind sought to make connections where none existed, but it all appeared to tie into some larger encroachment of the Otherworld into our own as evidenced by Riven's appearance within Avons, Ainslie's binding mark and bargain, and my own fae-touch. Even the involvement of the Vigil suggested perhaps the authorities feared more than they spoke.

Did that mean the oddities in Ibbie's behavior and the inheritance she'd left me also held some Otherworldly tie? She'd suggested something within Kilmere might shed light on our interactions with the Otherworld. Then there was the mention of the Dark Era in the history of the Vigil she'd procured for me. Could I assume it held truth about our past? If so, might another such perilous time fall upon us in the future?

Or did my grief over Ibbie and my fears of the killer have me conjuring dire possibilities with no just cause? I rubbed my throbbing temples.

Mother used to ask *how does one eat a dragon?* And then she'd answer her own question: *one bite at a time.* Though of course if one did manage to conquer a dragon and then bring oneself to eat the flesh of a sentient creature, the most likely consequence would be some sort of dreadful transformation.

But I didn't seek dragons—at least not to my knowledge—and I would do my best to work through each unanswered question one at a time, until some order and logic emerged from the chaos of possibility.

~

THE MOMENT I descended the stairs the next morning, I was waylaid from my quest for answers.

"Oh, Jessa, there you are." Ainslie flitted to my side, her ivory gown swirling about her ankles. "It's not like you to miss breaking the fast, but I'm glad you're here now."

I'd read Ibbie's journals into the small hours of the night, but given her dense script and my desire to attend to every detail, I only made it through two of them before I drifted off sitting upright. Subsequently, I'd slept past breakfast, which had prompted worry from Aunt Caris. Only a promise I'd join my sisters shortly reassured her enough that she went belowstairs to speak with Estine about the menu for the week.

I'd stacked up the diaries and gone in search of my sisters as promised, but it didn't appear Ainslie intended to let me read. She hurried me into the morning room.

"I want to practice the Ansforth Reel—it's the newest dance. Before long, all the fashionable hostesses will include it, and I simply *must* master it!" Ainslie extended her hand. "Will you partner with me while Ada plays?"

I set the stack of diaries on the nearest table and accepted her proffered hand. She began instructing me on the intricate movements, and after several false starts, we fell into step with one another.

While Ada played the lively melody and Ainslie spun me about the room, I could forget my worries. The rhythm of the music drummed from me all my speculation about the killer and Ibbie and fae. After countless iterations of the dance, we were both breathless.

Ainslie whirled me into a chair. "There now, that should be sufficient."

"Indeed." After a moment's rest, I pressed to my feet. "I need to catch up on my correspondence."

"I'll join you." Ada closed the top of the pianoforte.

While Ada wrote to her friends, I jotted short missives to the two trustees of Ibbie's estate, requesting a meeting at their earliest convenience.

With that accomplished, I immersed myself in Ibbie's journals once more, while Ainslie browsed the society paper, adding her commentary to the articles she perused.

My late-night reading on Ibbie's early days had revealed nothing out of the ordinary about her, aside from her burning passion for antiquities. Certainly, nothing of the Otherworld appeared to have influenced her life as a young debutante.

This morning, I chose another approach. Rather than studying each line of the oldest diaries in depth, I instead skimmed one of the more recent volumes. When my own name caught my eye, I halted.

I met a young woman today. Jessa Caldwell. In some ways, she reminds me of myself as a girl. When she speaks of what she loves, of her plants and drawings, her eyes kindle with beautiful fire. And I ache, remembering the warmth of the similar flame that once burned within me. I've been cold for so long, cold and dark inside—but Jessa, she is light and beauty and warmth. So was I, once.

Gentlemen will see her loveliness and be drawn to it, but unless she conceals her bright, inquisitive nature, they'll as swiftly fall away. Her intellect will bring condemnation from those who believe a woman should only speak of the most mundane trivialities. I know, for I endured their scorn. Yet my position sheltered me in ways hers will not. A pity.

I intend to call upon her aunt again and forge an acquaintance while we are both in the country. Perhaps I can ease the way for her, make her path a bit smoother.

My eyes burned, and the letters blurred beneath my gaze. Even at our first meeting, Ibbie had understood more than I ever dreamed. She'd so rarely spoken of her emotions or of her past. If only we'd had more time together.

"I'm certain I don't know." Ada sealed a letter. "What do you think, Jessa?"

I blinked away the damp gathered along my lashes. "I'm not certain . . . what did you ask?"

Ainslie waved the paper. "There's a story about karzels appearing near the Fens Crossing. I asked why you thought rumors were spreading about all manner of Otherworldly monsters."

"Perhaps such tales have simply become the mode." I let the diary fall to my lap. "The gentlemen of Byren have always sought to one-up each other—in racing, marksmanship, sword-play, and the like. With the restoration of alchemy driving Collectors into the Otherworld and leading them to boast of their prowess, perhaps these tales only reflect a desire to display superior knowledge and courage without taking any true risks."

Ada lifted a brow. "I'll grant that the young blades of the kingdom have more means than sense and would do anything to best one another, but these tales haven't just spread among the nobility. And then there's Ainslie's mark . . . it happened right here in Avons."

Her skepticism was justified, but I needed to discourage her interest, lest her questions draw her down a treacherous path. "Are you worried that we may be in danger?"

"Of course we're not in danger." Ainslie spoke a bit too briskly, and the pages of the gazette crackled as she turned them. "It's only that I've noticed the voices advising caution about the Otherworld are drowned out in favor of those suggesting we now have the knowledge and experience to confront Otherkind and come off victorious."

She paused, then turned another page. "It strikes me as rather odd. What can we claim to know about the Otherworld that generations before us did not? Even alchemy is nothing but a revival of lost knowledge, and one only restored to us twenty years ago, yet the alchemists claim their advances are such that they can send increasing numbers of Collectors through the Crossings with no consequence."

"I knew the alchemists wanted more resources, but I hadn't realized the views in society shifted so strongly in their favor." Nor had I realized Ainslie reflected so much on these matters. I studied her as she bent once more over the gazette.

Her easy mannerisms could engage others in speaking far more than they intended—I'd observed it time and again. Perhaps she wielded her engaging nature to accomplish more than social success. I traced the seam of the journal in my lap. We'd forgotten the art of alchemy, beyond a few token skills, just as we'd forgotten the Dark Era referred to in the history of the Vigil. Could the revival of alchemy lead to another such tumultuous time in the future? Did the two relate? Or was I seeking connections where none existed?

Perhaps Ainslie had considered the same. "Ainslie, do you think—"

"Oh, look." She'd returned to the society paper. "It appears netted hats have made a comeback. How interesting."

She rattled on about the styles of hats most suited to each face and how netted hats increased the allure of a select few, but on many they merely looked ridiculous, leaving me to wonder if her more serious remarks had been a mere figment of my imagination.

Then Holden strode into the morning room. In Aunt Caris's absence, he addressed Ada with a small bow. "Miss Adamina, a Mr. Ludne has come to call on Miss Jessa. Shall I show him in?"

I jumped as though he'd thrust a thorn into my side.

Jade roused herself and blinked at Holden.

"Mr. Ludne?" Ada piled her letters into a tidy stack. "I don't believe we're acquainted with a Mr. Ludne."

"He's a Vigilist." I forced the words from a suddenly dry throat. "He came once before, with Mr. Burke from the Magistry."

"A Vigilist? I cannot think Aunt Caris would approve." Ada turned back to Holden. "Tell Mr. Ludne we're not at home."

As much as I'd rather avoid him, turning him away would only postpone the inevitable. I couldn't imagine he'd give up so readily.

Nor did he.

Moments later, Holden returned, a slight stiffness in his voice hinting at his displeasure. "He says it's a matter of some urgency. He intends to wait until you return."

I closed the diary. "Ada, perhaps I should see him?"

"He can wait until Aunt Caris comes home," she said firmly.

"If he's so inclined. Holden, you may show him to the drawing room."

"Very good, Miss Adamina."

What could he want? Had he discovered that I'd continued to investigate matters—or worse, did he suspect my fae-touch? Surely if it were the latter, he'd not have agreed to wait but would have seized me at once. I roamed the room, conjuring all sorts of dreadful notions about his intent.

Ada shook her head. "Wearing a hole in the carpet won't bring her back faster."

Yet I couldn't settle, not with the endless conjecture my mind spun.

Just when I prepared to plead my case with Ada, Aunt Caris hurried in, her rose-tinted cheeks flushed a more vivid hue than usual. "Holden informs me we now have a Vigilist paying calls. Whatever will people say?"

"Perhaps no one will notice," Ada said. "He doesn't wear a uniform or any sort of insignia that reveals his identity."

"We must hope you're right." Aunt Caris removed her hat and set it on the table. "However little I like it, I suppose you must see him, my dear. But I intend to accompany you."

Given her ease in maneuvering social situations, perhaps I would come off unscathed after all. She summoned our housekeeper and sent a tray ahead of us.

"Men don't like to be kept waiting, and I imagine Vigilists like it even less." She brushed a strand of Jade's fur from my skirts and smoothed one of my unruly curls away from my face. "Perhaps some refreshments will put him in a better frame of mind."

She waited a few moments more, then bustled down the corridor. I followed in her wake, content for once to let her smooth the way. After all, if she failed to charm him, I'd no hope of it.

"How dreadful that we've kept you waiting." Aunt Caris glided into the drawing room. "I only hope you're not too fatigued."

He refused to acknowledge her pleasantries, and he hadn't touched the tea—so much for improving his frame of mind. "Pressing matters await my attention, and I'll thank you not to waste my time further."

"Of course." Aunt Caris offered a gracious smile. "If only you'd come during calling hours—or perhaps sent a message announcing your intent—you would have found us at home."

He ignored the slight barb and tented his fingers. "Miss Jessa, we require all of Lady Dromley's papers at once. Her solicitor informed us that she bequeathed them to you."

My breath hitched. I poured a cup of tea, taking refuge in the familiar action while I sought an acceptable protest. Jade settled on my lap. Could I even grant him permission when I'd already bargained their access to Riven? Would Riven hold me to our bargain if circumstances unfolded outside my control?

Regardless, I could scarcely confess to a Vigilist that I'd bargained with high fae. I took a sip of the tea, hot and bracing. "I must confess, I'm surprised. I didn't realize the Vigil took interest in antiquities."

"This isn't about antiquities. It regards the murder investigation." His fingers clenched around his iron-headed cane. "That's all you need to know to do your duty."

I carefully returned the teacup to the saucer, assessing him. If I resisted directly, he'd only attempt to bring his authority to bear—yet I couldn't let him take the papers. His very interest betrayed their importance. Perhaps if I dissembled slightly? I blinked my eyes, as though staving off tears. "Oh, must I truly part with them? They mean so very much to me, for Lady Dromley was an exceedingly dear friend."

"Duty to one's kingdom supersedes sentiment. Your cooperation is required." His narrow lips thinned further. "The only possible reason for withholding evidence would be a desire to conceal some truth about the killer—or Lady Dromley."

Jade growled softly, and Aunt Caris drew a swift breath. "That's absurd, and I will not permit you to insult my niece in her own home."

As much as I appreciated Aunt Caris's defense, facts were not required to damage a reputation, especially when one possessed the authority of a Vigilist. If he chose to accuse me of wrongdoing, then the Vigil could claim it necessary to seize everything—Wyncourt, Kilmere, the whole lot—and I'd never be able to honor Ibbie's requests. I folded my hands in my lap. "Of course, I want to do my part in helping find the killer—"

"That's fortunate, because as it stands, you have no choice in the matter. Should you choose to be difficult, we have the authority to requisition whatever we require." The jet-black eyes set in the raven's head on his cane glared at me. "I've informed you as a courtesy."

And perhaps as a test. Had he wished to assess my response? Clearly I needed a new approach, since my earlier attempt to dissuade him had failed. What did I know of him? He relished his authority, that much was clear. He'd not relinquish control easily, but perhaps if he saw me as a vulnerable and senseless young lady, he might be swayed to some sort of concession. I chose my words with care. "Of course, you've done me a great courtesy, but you must understand my attachment—"

"We will return the papers to you once we're through. That should be sufficient."

"I appreciate your consideration." I forced a smile, determined to allay any suspicions he might hold. If he thought poorly of Ibbie, he might view me as tainted by association. "Only, I thought the stratesmen had already examined everything within the house after Lady Dromley died."

"I wasn't present then—and they would not have known what to seek." He spoke with brusque precision. "I'll send some men to collect the papers this afternoon."

My shoulders tensed. Would his men recognize the presence of fae in the house? Could the Vigil peer through the glamour Riven donned? I couldn't take the risk.

"Oh dear." I pressed the tips of my fingers to my lips. "I've only just recalled . . . I did not think before . . ."

Aunt Caris looked at me, bemusement evident in her face, and I willed her to keep quiet.

"Did not think what?" he asked.

"A tenant already occupies Wyncourt, and I do not wish to earn his displeasure. If he must entertain visitors he neither expects nor desires . . . I don't want any trouble to arise." Had I babbled on enough to engage his sympathy? Did he have any to give? I leaned forward, widening my eyes. "You don't think he'd break his lease over the matter? Then I suppose my trustees would be greatly displeased, and they might even blame me for the whole affair."

Jade's ears twitched slightly, and she tilted her head at me as though amused.

He waved a hand. "It's of no consequence. We're accustomed to managing reluctant individuals."

"Of course," I murmured. "But perhaps . . . if there was a more convenient way . . . might you consider it?"

"Go on." He rubbed his pointed chin.

"I only thought I might remedy the situation if I asked the housekeeper to pack all of Lady Dromley's notes and papers for you to collect." All the emotions swirling within, those I worked so hard to constrain, surged through my body, and my voice altered, shaded with the discomfiting tone that didn't belong. I clenched my hands, digging my nails into my skin. Not now. If this unwilling change signaled some new manifestation of the fae-touch, then to expose it before a Vigilist could undo us all. With effort, I kept my words light. "It would spare your men the inconvenience of an inconsequential task, and the tenant wouldn't be troubled, nor my trustees. If you approve?"

"A kind offer." A thin smile sliced across his face. "Yet I trust only my men to handle this matter."

"I see." I lowered my gaze to conceal the rising fear within. "I . . . I hope you'll tell my tenant that I attempted to leave him undisturbed, if he issues a complaint."

"Of course." He surveyed me with those winterberry eyes. "We appreciate your cooperation."

Blight and rot. Coercion and cooperation were not the same thing. I checked the stinging words rising to my tongue, the desire to tell him what I thought of him and his methods alike. Instead, I murmured a polite farewell.

When Mr. Ludne left, Aunt Caris let out a huff. "What a detestable man. I'm sorry, my dear. I know Lady Dromley's research meant a great deal to you, and I regret he's forced it from you."

"As do I." A familiar ache formed beneath my breastbone. "I can only hope he means to keep his word and restore them to me once they're through."

"I'm certain he will." She stood, frowning at the doorway. "After all, the Vigil must maintain a high standard."

But who held them to that standard? Who checked their power? And why did they want Ibbie's papers? Did they seek to prove a case of fae-touch? I couldn't fathom what that would gain the Vigil after her death . . . unless it were to permit them to seize her assets. Or was I correct in my suspicion that something in Ibbie's life had drawn the killer to her? I lifted my now-tepid tea and took a mechanical sip.

It was a mercy I'd already fetched Ibbie's journals. I'd no intention of surrendering those. But what of Riven? He wanted her papers also, and I couldn't imagine he'd simply give them over because the Vigil demanded it. What trouble might he unleash?

CHAPTER 17

After concocting and discarding various madcap schemes to interpose myself into the situation at Wyncourt—which would only confirm Mr. Ludne's suspicions—I steeled myself to wait until the following morning, when I was certain the Vigil would have departed.

I only hoped Mr. Ludne didn't return, breathing rage and ready to condemn me for letting Wyncourt to a fae lord. Over breakfast, I ventured to propose a call upon Wyncourt, omitting my desire to ensure no all-out war between fae and Vigil had taken place overnight.

Yet Aunt Caris firmly vetoed the suggestion.

"If your tenant was discomposed by the visit from the Vigil, then you'd best give time for his irritation to fade." She nibbled at a sweet roll. "Better yet, allow your trustees to manage the gentleman. Doubtless he'd receive an explanation far better from them anyway."

If he were an ordinary gentleman, she would be right, but since he was not . . . I stirred a swirl of milk into my tea. "But Aunt Caris, I feel that I—"

"Besides which, what if that dreadful Mr. Ludne hasn't finished his business? I don't wish you caught in any altercations."

"I'm certain he's through by now."

"My dear, it simply won't do. We're at home to callers this afternoon, and you're needed," Aunt Caris said. "If you feel you must go, we can call together another day."

Yet another day or two might be too late, for I not only needed to assess the state of affairs at Wyncourt, I required Ibbie's missing diary before Mr. Ludne or Riven seized it—assuming it was concealed somewhere within Wyncourt and not already claimed by another.

I passed a bit of egg to Jade and considered a new approach. Aunt Caris and my sisters had a dinner party to attend this evening, and if Father remained in his usual abstracted state, he'd grant his permission readily. I'd wait until then, for I'd no other choice.

Jade and I slipped from the table and made our way to the morning room. I yearned to throw convention to the wind and not only descend upon Wyncourt at once, but also call directly upon Lord Blackburn following. I settled for penning him another missive, a gentle reminder that I held his letters in trust . . . and did he still wish to receive them? If he continued to ignore my messages, then perhaps I could prevail upon Uncle Milton to perform an introduction, though that would raise questions I wasn't prepared to answer.

After depositing the sealed letter with the footman, Jade and I walked down to the compounding room, where I removed some dried herbs from the hanging rack and prepared them for storage. I soon lost myself in the pungent fragrances and familiar motions.

And then Holden wandered in to join us. How odd. Holden

never wandered; rather, he marched from place to place with efficiency and precision. He stumbled to a stop before me. "You're needed in the gardens, Miss Jessa."

I affixed a label to the nearest jar. "By whom?"

But he only repeated, "You're needed in the gardens."

What had brought on this bemused state—oh. Could Riven have come? I could think of little else that would account for Holden's condition. I snatched up my hat and hurried up the stairs. Jade bounded before me, the fur on her neck already raised.

I halted abruptly, and she turned to face me. "Jade, if you come, you must *behave*. There'll be no attacking Riven—no matter how provoking he is."

She yowled a protest.

Could she understand, or did I give her too much credit? "Please, Jade. Just do as I ask?"

She inclined her head and ceased bristling. I let out a breath. What a mercy—this interview was likely to be tense enough without her returning his offenses.

It took a moment for me to find Riven, but the peculiar refracted light within the glasshouse drew my eye. I dashed through the door and shut it promptly behind me.

The familiar fragrances of orange and lavender were drowned out by the sun-and-storm scents Riven brought. He lounged on a bench across from the door, utterly at ease. "Care to tell me why you sent your Vigil to Wyncourt?"

"I didn't . . . That is, I did my best to dissuade Mr. Ludne, but he refused to listen to reason." All the dreadful scenarios I'd dreamt about through the night roiled through my mind, clouding clear thought. "Did he—did you—"

"He left unscathed, if that's what you're concerned about—though in my view, his sort are a blight on all worlds." The green of Riven's eyes lightened with a faint hint of amusement. "He and his men found they had an urgent need to take tea before collecting your Ibbie's belongings."

He'd glamoured them.

And they *hadn't* known. Our stalwart Vigil, meant to guard against every wile of the fae, hadn't recognized Riven or his glamour.

But I had.

I locked that disconcerting thought deep inside. "I'm sorry I couldn't stop him."

"Why?"

"Because I don't want trouble, nor do I want attention drawn to Wyncourt." I stroked a sprig of jasmine, and it curled round my finger. I wrenched free. Was this Riven's doing? I buried my hands in the folds of my skirt. "I suppose now they have Ibbie's papers. He's promised to bring them back once they're through, but I have my doubts."

"Did you imagine I'd turn them over?"

"Then you kept them? But how?"

"I summoned assistance." His lips quirked slightly. "He has copies of the most boring, tedious documents in her collection and a few others besides—all in her writing, of course. It should keep him busy with trivialities for some time to come."

I sank onto one of the crates that held my gardening supplies. It seemed having a fae tenant held some reward to go along with the risk. "I am . . . relieved to hear it."

And even more relieved that he'd glamoured them to take tea, not dance over hot coals till they were consumed, like the legend of Gentleman Tom, nor hurl themselves in the nearest river and swim shore to shore till their strength failed and they drowned, as said the tale of the Lowery Brothers. Perhaps he'd truly meant it when he said he didn't seek mortal playthings—or perhaps the tales overstated the deliberate cruelty of the fae.

Suddenly, he leaned forward, lessening the distance between us. The air crackled with the charged-storm energy familiar now as his . . . and all sense of relief vanished.

"I didn't come here merely to discuss your Vigil." He braced his hands on his knees. "What did you remove from Wyncourt?"

How did he know about the journals? Never mind, something in his stance warned me it would be unwise to dissemble. Yet it wouldn't do to show fear, so I straightened and regarded him evenly. "I brought Ibbie's diaries home to examine."

"You didn't think I'd take interest in them?" he asked.

My arm throbbed beneath the bands of gold, a painful reminder of the binding between us. I'd best tread with care. "Rather, I was concerned you might not consider our bargain to include her diaries, and I couldn't afford their loss. I merely intended to examine and then return them, not withhold them altogether."

"I thought you wanted to avoid trouble—not provoke it." All trace of emotion disappeared from his face, leaving it a disconcerting blank.

An ivy-tendril of unease sprouted inside. How greatly had I provoked offense?

I inhaled, drinking deeply of the mingled sweet orange blossoms and rich, intoxicating jasmine. If I allowed myself to reach out and touch them, to lose myself in their scents and songs and escape . . .

Jade nudged me, her nose warm and slightly rough against my cheek.

I cradled her close and willed the allure of the blossoms to lessen. "I spoke the truth. Although I needed to read her diaries,

I don't wish to have trouble with you or anyone else, and I didn't break our bargain."

Though I might have bent it slightly, depending on how one interpreted such things.

"I know." He surveyed me, almost as if he were reading the air as it shifted between us. "It would be impossible for you to do so."

The ivy-tendril of unease grew, snaking its coils through my stomach. What dread fate awaited if I made a misstep in our dealings?

As though it were of no consequence, he continued, "What have these diaries revealed?"

"Very little so far." Should I confess the rest? He'd not yet acted in the malicious manner recounted in our tales of the fae, but I did not wish to test his patience, and it appeared I'd never succeed in searching Wyncourt without his knowledge. "However, her most recent one is missing. I'd hoped to examine Wyncourt for it. Unless . . . have you already found it?"

"No." Silence stretched between us for a moment. Then he said, "Come, we shall seek it together."

I rocked back, and the crate creaked beneath me. Fae never acted out of kindness, so did he intend to claim something unknown in return? Or did he perceive the weakening of my control and intend to erode it further?

More than anything, I needed to avoid him, to avoid the Otherworld altogether. And yet, what choice did I have? Clearly, he didn't mean to let me search without his involvement, and I couldn't abandon Wyncourt and the diary to him. I'd simply have to remain alert and do everything in my power to ward off the fae-touch.

I pressed to my feet. "I have family obligations, and it will be evening before I can come."

"Very well. I'll expect you before the moon rises."

∼

When I returned withindoors, lively banter between Ada, Ainslie, and Lovell echoed through the corridor, broken at intervals when Aunt Caris slipped in a well-modulated remark. I brushed the lingering cobwebs from the crate off my skirt and joined them in the morning room.

Aunt Caris welcomed me with a smile. "A footman has just come from Wyncourt, with a message from the butler there. He says these letters arrived for Lady Dromley, and he thought they should go to you."

She handed me two small letters, seals intact. I imagined it must have cost her to remain ignorant of their contents, and I gave her hand a squeeze of appreciation. Then I sank into the chaise, and Jade nested beside me, kneading my leg with her paws as I opened the first missive.

It was short and businesslike, penned with a crisp, precise hand. The writer informed Ibbie that his company wouldn't be able to fulfill her request for a press until late summer or perhaps early autumn. Did she still wish to place an order?

An ache settled in my chest. The letter dropped into my lap, and Jade nudged it with her nose.

"No bad news, I trust?" Aunt Caris brushed a coppery curl from her face.

"Not bad news, simply unfinished business." I folded the letter. "She'd intended to place an order she'll no longer need."

Ibbie had used her last days attempting to support my goals and desires. Now I couldn't bear the thought of pursuing them —not with the killer still free to cause further harm. Perhaps later, I could consider the herbalism manuscript again . . . but there would be no funds to purchase a press and all the necessary materials for a print run, not anymore. She'd left a generous sum in trust for the restoration of Kilmere and maintenance of Wyncourt. Even if the trustees would agree to such a plan, I'd not seek to use those funds for my own endeavors.

No, my work must stand on its own merits—or not at all. Perhaps that's how it should have been all along.

I unfolded the second missive, this one on coarser paper, its letters looser and less refined.

Lady Dromley,

 I regret to inform you my time in Carlsdale has proved fruitless. In the end, Sir Alfred refused to hand over the documents for any sum. In truth, I'm not convinced he possesses them. He seemed willing enough to talk about the curse on Kilmere, but when it came time to provide evidence, he became evasive. I'll continue on to the Fens and see what I can unearth there while I await your instruction. You can send word to me at the Rose and Crown.

With respect,
Mr. Myles Tibbons

Myles Tibbons. He was the man Ibbie had recommended to oversee the work at Kilmere. But a curse? Why hadn't Ibbie seen fit to mention that in her letter to me? I clasped one of the chaise pillows to my chest. What sort of inheritance had I been given? Perhaps it was only rumor . . . but rumors often carried a seed of truth.

Regardless, I owed them both the courtesy of a reply, though I'd no notion of how to instruct Mr. Tibbons. Perhaps I should request he return to Avons to discuss the whole affair. Ibbie must have covered the cost of his travels, though, and I'd have to request the necessary funds from the trustees when we spoke. Would they approve such an expense, when I didn't yet understand what Ibbie had employed him to do?

Before I could order my thoughts sufficiently, Holden ushered in the first caller. I took refuge in the convention that permitted one to take up needlework or other simple tasks during calls, and I reached for my sketchbook, tucking the letters inside.

I attended to the conversation, attempting to interject banal remarks at appropriate intervals and allowing my pencil to roam the page freely. This time, I found myself sketching Wyncourt—yet somehow, I failed to capture its essence.

I abandoned the attempt and had turned to a blank leaf when Holden opened the door and announced Mr. Upton.

Jade pricked up her ears and surveyed him as he walked into the room, eyeing him with the wariness she did most strangers. I patted her head to reassure her, then snapped my sketchbook shut.

He took the chair nearest to me, while Aunt Caris poured him a fragrant cup of tea.

He accepted with thanks. "I hope I find you well this afternoon?"

"Indeed, though I might wish for more pleasant weather." Aunt Caris sipped at her own tea.

"I find the chill invigorating." His long fingers curled about the cup. "Indeed, I've found my time in Avons quite restorative."

She beamed upon him with her usual good cheer. "I'm delighted to hear your spirits remain strong."

"Ah, yes. It does seem that a pall has fallen over many, and it's not surprising." He gave a nod toward the gazette Ainslie held. "Have you read the latest theory?"

Aunt Caris clucked softly, but she was too polite to directly correct a visitor, however improper his choice of conversation.

"About a mad alchemist committing the murders?" Ada frowned. "It seems incredible that an alchemist could succumb to lunacy without his compatriots taking note, but perhaps no less incredible than this whole affair. Whoever did it simply *must* be mad."

"Of course the Alchemist's Guild vehemently denies it." Ainslie looked as if she wanted to say more, but instead she folded the gazette and placed it on a side table.

"Naturally they'd issue a denial. Any implication of guilt allows the king to interfere more in their affairs," Mr. Upton said.

"Precisely." Lovell leaned forward, displaying more interest than he had toward any of the earlier conversation. "And it may well sway the opinions of the Assemblage of Lords to be less lenient in their policies toward the Guild."

"A difficulty indeed. Such is the nature of politics—easily swayed by public opinion." Mr. Upton examined me, his hooded eyes intent. "What is your opinion, Miss Jessa? Do you believe the killer is an alchemist?"

Jade's eyes narrowed, and her tail twitched.

Heat prickled up my chest. Did he mean to reveal my interest to my aunt? I clutched my sketchbook, and the letters within crackled. "I believe there's a great deal of contradictory evidence, and it's no wonder the Magistry struggles to find the killer."

"A very . . . carefully stated view." A small smile tugged at his lips.

He was needling me. But why? "I believe we should exercise restraint in speaking about those things we fail to fully understand."

"An admirable trait."

"Indeed." Aunt Caris evidently felt she'd permitted this conversation sufficient leeway. She extended a plate of pastries toward Mr. Upton. "Won't you have a tart, Mr. Upton? Our cook has a light touch, and I think you'll find them to your liking."

"My thanks." He accepted with a nod.

And I ventured a question of my own. "How goes your work in Avons? I trust it progresses?"

"Certain aspects of it proceed marvelously well. Others have been more difficult." He shrugged. "But that is only to be expected."

Then he turned his attention to the room at large, recounting an entertaining tale of his travels. A few moments later, when Holden returned to announce new visitors, he took his leave.

When the last of the callers blessedly departed, Aunt Caris and my sisters retired to prepare for their dinner party, as did Lovell, after claiming a few of the more obscure gazettes Father subscribed to. Once I'd seen them off, I joined Father in the dining room.

He watched me as I settled into my seat, for once appearing to truly *see* me. "Sometimes you remind me so much of Kensa."

I nearly dropped my spoon. Mother had passed down to me her deep blue eyes and dark curly hair, though mine was more unruly, but Father had never acknowledged the resemblance before. "I wish I could have known her longer. I forget, sometimes, what she was truly like."

"You share so much of her determination and brilliance. If she were here, she would know what to do for you." The gaslight drew out the red-gold sheen of his hair and concealed the fine lines in his face, making him appear younger. I could almost imagine him as the dashing young gentleman he'd been when he and Mother courted. Then he shook his head, and the illusion faded. "Now it's left to me to do the best I can for each of you."

I swirled my spoon through the bowl of white soup before me. Though the fragrances of thyme and bay rose from the surface, my appetite diminished. Why did he bestir himself now, after all these years of distraction?

"Caris is worried. She says a man from the Vigil called to make demands upon you." The furrows around his eyes deepened. "I've written to Gillian to see if they intend to remain in their country home for a time. If so—"

"I can't go, Father. Don't you see?" My control over my emotions frayed, and all my longing and fear poured into my voice, infusing it with a discomfiting, increasingly familiar tone. "You don't to need to worry about me. The Vigilist has no interest in further conversation, he only wanted some items belonging to Ibbie. And I can't imagine leaving all of you in Avons—please don't make me go."

His expression softened. "Well, perhaps . . ."

"I've promised to go calling again with Aunt Caris next week, and I'm endeavoring to do all my aunts wish. I'm beginning to grow accustomed to Avons, and besides, my home is where you and Ada and Ainslie are." The discomfiting note in my voice strengthened, and I struggled to rein in my emotions. "Surely it's better for us to remain together."

Father nodded slowly. "I suppose you're right. Avons is the place to settle your future, or so your aunts say. But if he keeps troubling you or other issues arise over Lady Dromley's estate, you're to come to me, and I'll address the matter. Caris reminds me a young lady should not be burdened by business affairs, and she's quite right."

"I can manage, Father." The band around my chest loosened,

and I breathed a bit easier—despite the reminder that my aunts wished me wed to someone they deemed suitable. I couldn't bring myself to consider that obstacle now. I gripped my goblet. "To that end, I'd like to make sure all is well at Wyncourt. There's a new tenant, and I want to see that he's settled in, among other things. I intend to visit tonight, if you'll grant permission."

He rested his spoon in his empty bowl. "I won't have you going to Wyncourt alone, not when the Vigil might still be there."

As if an afterthought, he muttered, "They should have come to me to begin with."

A little pang of disquiet struck at the degree of his concern. Could he know the truth about me, about the fae-touch? Had his insistence that my grief over the loss of Mother triggered the peculiarities I experienced been a deceit for my benefit? Or did he fully believe his premise that they were aberrations brought on by emotional distress, then and now?

Either way, he had cause for concern about the Vigil, who did not approve of any deviation from the standard. "I cannot imagine they'll still be there, but if you feel a chaperone is needed, I could take Lianne."

He'd never cared about such proprieties before, but Lianne was a safe choice, as I could sequester her in the servants' quarters, far from Riven.

"No, the Vigil isn't to be trusted." Father rarely roused himself from the world in his mind, but now his eyes lost their dreamy, half-focused look and snapped to full alertness. "They may protect us from the Otherworld. But who protects us from them?"

"I'm certain it will be fine—"

"I'm taking no more chances. I've told Caris to send for me

at once if they come again. And I certainly won't permit you to venture to Wyncourt alone at this hour, when they might lie in wait. I'll go with you myself."

I stared into my mostly full bowl. Many times as a girl I'd longed for Father to offer his companionship—to show interest in my occupations, as I attempted to do with his—but now, it could only cause trouble.

Holden brought in the fish course, and I dragged the tines of my fork across the pale flesh, flaking off small fragments. The fervor that had crept into my words earlier subsided utterly, leaving me cold and empty. "Of course, Father. I . . . I appreciate your consideration."

CHAPTER 18

When we arrived at Wyncourt, Riven opened the door. An electrical charge seemed to crackle in the air, as though a tempestuous summer storm had blown through, and the pinprick sensation of Other intensified to a gale-like force.

I drew upright, bracing against the intangible assault. What had happened here? Never mind—it was one evening. I could manage.

I must.

As I murmured a greeting to Riven, I wove the vines within tighter to bolster my cage of thorns. The sooner I found the diary, the sooner I could cut ties with Riven—the sooner I could protect myself from this onslaught.

A low rumble rose from Jade. She scrambled from my arms into her favorite position, draped over my shoulders like a stole. From her perch, she glared at Riven.

His glamour thinned until it was the merest veil over the power beneath, and the tight lines of his body indicated disapproval. I should have found a way to come alone.

Before I could attempt to smooth over the situation, Father stepped forward, scowling. "Who are you? Don't try to tell me you're the butler."

"I'm the new tenant of Wyncourt. I would bid you welcome, but you are not." The green in his eyes brightened until they resembled the new leaves of spring. "You'll forget we've spoken. All is well with your daughter; all is well with Wyncourt. Remember only that."

A sigh gusted from Father like a breeze across autumn boughs. "All is well."

"You should rest in the sitting room. Perhaps take a nap until Jessa returns to you."

A surge of power laced his words, and Father yawned and wobbled toward the sitting room, his boots shuffling across the polished floor.

"Why did you glamour him?" The words ripped from me, unbecomingly sharp. A lady never accused another, never censured a gentleman. But Riven was no gentleman, so perhaps I might be excused. I fought the urge to clutch my ward-pendant. "He's done nothing wrong."

"You don't approve? It will do him no harm and will keep him from interfering." He lifted one shoulder, a smooth, elegant motion. "Or did you intend to explain to him why you're housing fae and hunting for evidence of a killer?"

I'd spent the entire trip here attempting to figure out how to avoid just that . . . to no avail. But I could scarcely confess that to Riven and justify his deeds. I stepped back, putting another pace between us. "You concealed your true nature with the servants and the Vigil—I'd hoped you'd manage it with my father as well."

The faintest gold light shimmered about him. "I've no intention of constraining myself to mortal form or power this evening. All the staff are likewise indisposed. They'll be content in their slumbers till I waken them."

"But you will waken them?"

"Of course," he said. "I require their services."

"Then perhaps we should be about our business, so they need not be held in thrall longer than necessary." Would being subjected to glamour trigger fae-touch in the servants? I'd bargained for their well-being, but perhaps he did not consider that harm. I moved away from the door, deeper into the great echoing entry. "I searched the study and came up with nothing. The diaries I did find were hidden in the secretary in her bedchamber."

"If the others were in the bedchamber, mayhap the missing one will be also."

"I examined it thoroughly."

"So you say."

I pressed my lips together. Were all fae this infuriating?

"Tell me. How many rooms does Wyncourt possess?" He gave a casual motion of his hand that encompassed the elegant marble staircase and the corridors that branched from the entry.

"I . . ."

Jade's tail twitched, tickling my cheek, and I clutched at it to still her while I attempted to calculate the number. Ibbie had taken me through Wyncourt on multiple occasions, so this should be a simple matter. Yet each time I counted, I came up with a different number. At the last, I subsided with a nagging pain at my temples. "There's something . . . wrong with Wyncourt."

"Very good."

The gaslight flickered, and in the dance of its flame, the statues placed at intervals around the entry appeared to shift within their dim nooks. I shuddered and looked away.

Why had Riven prompted me to this conclusion? What did *he* plan for this evening? Whatever his scheme, it likely boded ill for me. My stomach sank as though I'd stepped off the edge of a cliff. "Is that why you said you'd no intention of limiting yourself to mortal ability?"

"Precisely."

I mistrusted the glint in his eyes, but I couldn't shrink back now. Ibbie had left Wyncourt to me, which meant I was responsible for whatever it contained, for good or ill. If I wanted answers, I couldn't cower for fear of what I might discover. And if something with Wyncourt—and by extension Ibbie—was amiss, perhaps it had some connection with the killer.

I pressed my hand flat against my stomach, as though I could settle it by force. "Then I suppose we must examine her bedchamber once more."

I straightened to my full, unimpressive height and marched up the stairs. Although I'd previously searched the room, I examined every crack and crevice once more, even scouring the rest of the furniture for signs of hidden compartments.

When I bent to look beneath the bed, my ward-pendant slipped from the bodice of my dress. It hung stark black against the pale muslin of my gown—a clear affront, should Riven choose to take offense.

Before I could tuck it away, Riven closed the distance between us, his speed disquieting. He lifted it, and it dangled in midair between us.

I should have pulled back from such disconcerting proximity, yet I froze. Riven was striking, even more so up close. But what did it matter? A fine physical form did not signify character; indeed, the legendary beauty of the fae, along with their glamour, lured many a mortal into their coils. And more dangerous by far, Other emanated from him, alluring, beckoning, reminding me of the vibrant sensations I experienced when I allowed the fae-touch great liberty. For a moment, I could not catch my breath, could only struggle to maintain my unraveling defenses.

Then he let the pendant drop. "Don't rely on this. It will do you no good."

Quickly, I tucked it away and rounded the bed to put distance between us. I'd always wondered about the efficacy of ward-pendants, given their affordability and wide usage, when most alchemical devices required a substantial sum. Were they entirely inert, a placebo to placate the masses? I smoothed the bedquilt, which I'd rumpled in my search. "And you've warned me out of . . . kindness?"

"I've warned you because I've no mind to have another dead mortal on my hands. It's too great an inconvenience, and I've been delayed enough already."

Death was an inconvenience? I plumped a pillow rather more vigorously than necessary before tucking it back in its proper spot.

Unruffled, he continued, "Do you mean to conduct your search just as you did before?"

"What do you suggest?"

He leaned against the substantial pillar of the bed. "Among the fae, we have a saying: great reward comes only with great risk."

"And what does that mean?"

"You tell me."

"Do all fae take lessons in obscure speech?"

"No lessons are required." The slightest uptilt of his lips hinted at amusement.

For one who did not want a mortal plaything, he appeared to enjoy stringing me along. Why couldn't he simply be forthright? Clearly, the old tales hadn't been mistaken in their suggestions that fae delighted in trickery and concealment. I paced the bedchamber.

What had I missed? What required risk?

Oh . . .

The back of my neck prickled. If I was dealing with an Otherworldly element within Wyncourt, I had to consider the uncomfortable possibility my fae-touch might be required. With the sprites, it had allowed me to perceive what I could not with mortal senses and thereby survive the encounter—albeit at a cost.

Was that what Riven meant when he spoke of risks and rewards? I must risk the madness of fae-touch to gain the reward of answers? That would indicate he could perceive the taint within me . . .

Again, I pressed the palm of my hand to my stomach, a vain attempt to calm its churning. I didn't have to lower my guard completely, but perhaps if I relaxed my hold on the cage of thorns the slightest bit . . .

The room appeared to warm, the gaslight taking on a more golden hue, and little shimmering lines gleamed along the wall surrounding a . . . door?

A little shiver worked its way down my spine.

I closed my eyes against the deluge that sought to flood my senses, reweaving the loose vines back into the cage one by one. The effort left me slightly sick, and I swallowed hard. Just a little longer, and then I could go home.

I crossed over to the door, now visible even to my mortal senses. How could I have overlooked it before? I should have considered seeking a connecting door, should have remembered Ibbie's husband and the convention of adjoining rooms. Yet somehow, it had never occurred to me.

"Good choice," Riven murmured silkily.

I swung back toward him. What did he know? What was he waiting for me to find?

Jade leapt down and sniffed beneath the door. Her pupils dilated, and she chuffed softly.

I twisted the ornate brass knob, but it refused to give. "Perhaps if you woke Mrs. Peters, she could give us the key."

"The servants have no recall of these chambers, much less a key."

My attention snapped back to him. "Did you glamour them into forgetting?"

"No." His eyes gleamed in the gaslight. "That's what's intriguing."

Intriguing? I could think of other words to describe it. I turned to survey the door once more. "Have you been inside?"

"No," he said. "I believe it's a task best suited for the owner of Wyncourt."

I tilted my head. What difference did it make who opened the door? I'd let Wyncourt to him, and by law, he had access to the entire house. Unless some Other law governed his actions. I traced the cool metal of the knob with one finger.

Although Riven directed me for his own ends—which he refused to be forthright about—he'd given me the opportunity to gain information I might use to protect Wyncourt and its inhabitants when he departed. I couldn't turn back now. So I walked back to the secretary, where I'd seen a small brass ring of keys earlier.

I tried each one in sequence, but not a single key fit. Not once did Riven bestir himself to offer aid. He only watched and waited in silence. I returned the keys to the secretary, where they clinked as I set them in the drawer.

Then I moved back toward the door, frowning at its impenetrable surface.

Jade stretched up on her hind legs and batted at the lock above the knob. I bent to study it more closely, and the fae-touch encroached on my senses against my will. Perspiration slicked my palms as I struggled to rein it in.

Intangible gossamer-like threads wove around and about the lock. They drifted above a pattern etched around the keyhole. I reached out to trace the etchings, and like the quick stab of a needle, pain spiked through my finger, over and gone in an instant, leaving a drop of blood in its wake.

The tumblers inside the lock clicked and released.

Riven swiftly stepped past me and shoved open the door. Had he known all along what was required?

Of course he had. Why else allow me to come on this expedition? I scrubbed my hands against my skirt.

The fusty smell of a long-enclosed space wafted through the doorway, unwelcoming. Yet I followed Riven into the room. Once inside, the smell strengthened to a repellent, desiccated odor. My stomach turned, and I instinctively clutched at the ward-pendant, despite Riven's warning that it was inert.

No lamps remained to light the chamber, even if the gas had been turned on. Our only illumination was the light pouring from the open door behind us, and it scarcely pierced the shadows of the room.

All the furniture within bore shrouds, not the customary white linens draped over the furnishings of unused rooms, but thick black material that gave the whole room a funereal appearance. Even the enormous four-pillared bed was heavily draped in dark curtains.

I edged closer to Riven. He might be fae, but I'd proven

useful to him, so I hoped that meant he'd see to my safety—at least as long as I served a purpose.

In the gloom, the large-bodied furniture appeared like slumbering beasts in the night, ready to rouse when called upon and devour unwary intruders. Riven muttered something and a fae-light appeared at his shoulder, a gleaming orb that contained swirls of whites and golds, like someone had captured living sunbeams within a glass.

I forgot everything else. I gazed upon it, its shifting hues and tones, the vibrancy of the colors within. Unbidden, the vines on my cage began to unfurl. With great effort, I wrenched my gaze away.

Not now. I couldn't afford a misstep. If I lost myself, I'd be utterly at his mercy.

Jade stalked in front of me, and I followed in her wake. The luminous glow from the fae-light revealed cobwebs draping the corners of the bedchamber and dangling down along the walls. As we moved deeper into the chamber, we stirred up layers of dust, and the silvery motes drifted thick through the air, clouding my vision.

I blinked several times in a vain attempt to clear it, and the dull heaviness that overcomes one just before sleep turned my limbs leaden. If I could only rest . . .

"None of that." Riven spoke sharply. Then he cupped my elbow, and a pulse of energy surged through my veins, a shock sharper than static in winter. It was as though the charged-air sensation around him transferred into me. At once the chamber seemed gloriously alive, awake, and vibrant, though its colors had not changed.

I shivered and pulled away. If he could so alter my perception in a moment of contact between us, what would happen if I spent more time in his presence, more time close to Otherkind?

Despite my fears, I forced myself to take one step forward, then another.

Whatever he had done cleared the dust from the air, and this time, when I surveyed the room, the trailing strands of long-dormant cobwebs bobbed and swayed as though some invisible breeze stirred them. The threads all moved in unison, drifting toward the farthest corner of the enormous chamber. Though the windows were sealed tight and heavily draped, a draft must be coming in from somewhere.

Riven forged a path through the room, his stride purposeful. He halted before the tall bookcases that bracketed the farthest corner and studied them a moment. Then with an abrupt motion, he tugged at two scripted volumes, and the right-hand bookcase swung back.

Despite all sense and reason suggesting danger lurked ahead, I couldn't restrain a small smile. I'd always wanted to step through a secret door hidden in a bookcase, never mind the woes that befell heroes of literary lore on similar ventures. Sometimes, surely, they must conceal wonders.

But when I stepped closer, all consideration of wonders fled. The scent of dust and decay deepened, and my throat tightened, rebelling against the stench. Narrow stone stairs ascended to a sharp turn, which concealed their final destination.

Jade wove between my ankles, growling low, and I had no reassurance to offer. Whatever was hidden here would not be pleasant. I faltered out the first remark that came to mind. "I . . . I can't fathom Ibbie concealed her diary here."

"No, she would not have been able to enter."

"Then that was never your aim."

"For the moment, my aim is the truth about Wyncourt." Riven paused on the first step and angled toward me. "Will you turn back?"

If I turned back, if I allowed him to uncover the secrets of Wyncourt alone, I'd never know the truth about Ibbie's life . . . or her death. How much had she known about what went on here? How much had it changed her?

Despite Jade twining beneath my ankles and doing her best to block my way, I shook my head. "Wyncourt is my responsibility. Ibbie left it in trust to me. And how can I let the servants stay when who knows what is lurking within the walls?"

A muscle shifted in his jaw. "Fine. Stay behind me."

My fingers brushed the stone, and it was smooth and bitterly cold, a stark contrast to the pleasant warmth we'd left behind. Halfway to the landing, I stumbled to a stop.

Why was I here? I should have fled while I still had the chance . . . and now, what horrors awaited? Perhaps it wasn't too late. I could still flee—but no, I didn't want to run. Why was I even considering it? Despite my reasoning against it, the urge strengthened, fear prickling up my back and into my neck.

Blight and rot, what was this? Jade pawed at my hem, and I lifted her. She scrambled to my shoulders.

Riven turned toward me once more. "Will you surrender to the compulsion?"

"I . . ." Again, an ache nagged at my temples.

He shrugged. "No surprise. You're only mortal, subject to the weakness of your kind."

"We are *not* weak, simply because we lack Otherworldly powers. It takes far greater courage to face danger without the tremendous arsenal of weapons you fae are privileged to possess." The thorned vines unraveled slightly before the tide of emotion, and the light from the orb took on a more golden cast. I drew in a deep, even breath. Why had I allowed him to discompose me?

Regardless, the pressing urge to turn back subsided. Riven

gave a satisfied nod and continued the ascent. Just before he reached the landing, he paused as though examining something.

What did he see—oh. Some sort of shadow swirled at the far end. I stepped onto the landing, to take a closer look.

The dark fog surged forth to surround us. I gasped, but nothing filled my lungs. The cloud settled over me, and a burning sensation started deep within my chest, then surged up into my throat. The thick mist scalded me from within, stealing my very breath.

Air, I needed air. But however deeply I inhaled, nothing filled my lungs except that dreadful fog, biting, choking, mocking my futile efforts.

Light limned Riven's features and coiled round his fingertips, vibrant and gold. He sent it hurtling into the mist.

From somewhere behind, a quiet moan sounded, then a soft creak. What now? Was there a creature concealed in the dark fog?

I struggled to turn toward the sound, every muscle straining for a single clear breath. Dark blotches filled my vision, blotting out sight.

Then the mist receded, driven back by the light pouring from Riven. He spoke something, but my pulse pounded in my ears, drowning out his words.

I heaved a great breath. Sweet air flooded my lungs, as cool and refreshing as a glass of water on a summer day. I gulped in, my vision clearing.

And then I saw it.

A form flickered where the miasma lingered in the corner of the landing. Something *was* in the gloom. Riven stepped in front of me.

I wasn't equipped for this fight—what had I been thinking

to come? I edged back toward the stairs, toward safety. My arm caught on a protrusion in the wall.

A stab of pain pierced tender flesh. Then a door of stone caved open behind me. Off-balance, I fell through the newly formed opening—and the door slid shut, locking me in.

Rot-scented air surged about me. I fumbled along the edge of the door, seeking the knob. My fingers closed around etched metal, but it would not yield, nor did any locking mechanism reveal itself. I was cut off from Riven and all possible aid.

Jade gave a low, rumbling growl and sprang from my shoulders.

The skin at my neck crawled. I should have examined the room, should have considered what dangers might lurk.

Thud-thunk.

Thud-thunk.

I half-spun, too late.

Clawed fingers, cold as ice, gripped my arms. The scent of decay intensified, twisting my stomach, pulling bile into my throat. Thick, corded arms closed about me.

I was trapped.

CHAPTER 19

Thick burlap wound about my face, chafing my skin, cutting off light and air. The hands of my captor drew the fabric tight, then clenched about my throat.

I scrabbled at the relentless grip. With a grunt, my assailant hurled me to the floor, and the cold stones drove any remaining breath from my lungs. Before I could scramble away or withdraw the binding from my face, he was upon me once more, his hands seeking my throat.

From somewhere over my shoulder, Jade—could it be Jade?—snarled, a deep, resonant growl of rage. Then a thud resounded behind me, and a bitter, earthy scent flooded the chamber.

Where was she? Was she hurt? Oh, please, no . . .

Unseeing, I fumbled in my reticule for my penknife.

My assailant pressed his advantage, his grip around my throat biting deep.

My fingers closed about the penknife, and I lashed toward the hands pinning me in place. Over and over, I jabbed my penknife into solid flesh.

He didn't flinch, not once.

This was no natural foe. And if it didn't respond to pain, if its strength far exceeded my own, how could I ever escape? The drumbeat of my heart in my ears drowned out the sounds of a scuffle behind me. My throat burned beneath the grasp of my assailant; my body went cold.

And the vines in my cage wavered.

Faint and far in the distance, songs whispered, a reminder of a world of living color beyond this chamber. If only I could reach out and touch it, could draw from that strength . . . but I was encased in a fortress of stone, fighting blind, trapped far from any living thing.

Another snarl rumbled through the air. Glass shattered. Something hit the floor with a tremendous thud.

From my left, a sharp blade pierced my side. Like a flame, the heat of pain licked up my body, and the penknife dropped from my grasp.

Who . . . how? Was there more than one of these *things*?

Damp spread outward from the wound—blood. I thrashed against the inexorable being holding me captive. If I could not free myself soon . . .

A sound like thunder cracked the air, and the whole room shook.

Riven.

His voice resonated above the chaos as he spoke a command in the fae tongue. The world stilled.

My pulse thrummed, my throat burned . . . but the iron grip released at last. I was free.

I ripped the burlap from my face and hauled in a deep breath. A bolt of pain shot from the gash in my side. Where was Riven?

I pressed upright. He stood over a shattered door of solid stone, strands of gleaming light unspooling from his hands.

The threads of light wove themselves into a tremendous snare around four appalling apparitions.

I froze in place. What were they? The shape of their frames vaguely recalled that of mortals, but there the resemblance ended. Murky greenish skin stretched over cords of muscle and protrusive ribs and traveled down disproportionately long limbs, the flesh darkening as it edged away from the torso. Black veins stood stark in arms and faces, and thick shocks of wiry hair bristled above white-and-gray marbled eyes, which lacked both lashes and lids.

Like beasts, the creatures snarled and clawed at the bonds of light, which seared them each time they hurled themselves against the restraints. Soon the stench of burned flesh filled the air, mingling with the odor of rot.

My stomach lurched, and I pressed my hands to my mouth. We'd found something, but not the killer—unless he used these monsters for his own ends.

Three of the four creatures bore tremendous gashes along their heads and sides from which brown-black ichor oozed. But they paid no heed to their injuries, only hurled themselves relentlessly against their bonds, their hands bent into clawed hooks, the nails thick and black.

Perhaps they didn't need to pay heed, for the injuries began to seal themselves, and the flow of ichor ceased. I wrapped my arms around my legs and rocked in place. What in the Crossings were these creatures? And how . . . how were they here, in Wyncourt?

Riven crossed the room in a few strides and pulled me to my feet. "Are you injured?"

"A bit bruised." The words rasped their way out of my chafed throat. In truth, my body throbbed all over—where the creature had restrained me, where it had hurled me to the floor, where its hands and those biting nails had dug into my neck. But nothing hurt as much as the wound in my side.

His gaze flicked to the darkening patch on my gown. "Looks like more than a bruise."

Without awaiting a reply, he ran his finger over the gash and then began to unbutton my damaged spencer.

"Don't . . . please." I stepped back. "I assure you, I'm well enough."

"It cut you." His voice dropped low. "And your kind are dangerously fragile. Let me look."

I limped farther away. "I'll tend it myself, when I return home."

I'd no intention of making myself more vulnerable to him, but my plans were undermined when my legs wobbled, refusing to hold my weight.

He reached out to steady me, his features shadowed. And at his touch, the pain ebbed slightly.

"Jade! Is she here? Did they harm her?"

"Not even close."

I peered around Riven. Jade perched in the center of the room, her starflower patch gleaming white in the inky blackness of her fur, her green eyes aglow. Thank the Infinite she remained unharmed. Dark blood stained her paws, doubtless from where she'd walked through the patches on the floor. She daintily lifted a forepaw and started to lick it clean.

I shuddered and looked away.

The horrors attempted to hurl themselves against their restraints once more, and Jade paused her endeavors long enough to glare at them.

"You were fortunate your *kit-isne* distracted the other three, else you wouldn't have lasted until I could breach the door."

Distracted them? What did he mean? And . . . he'd had to break down the door? Why, when I'd stumbled through, without purpose or intent? "Was this room sealed, like the bedchamber?"

A curt nod.

"Then you could have forced the bedchamber door also."

"Yes, but I would have risked bringing Wyncourt down about us, depending on the strength of the working that bound it shut." Riven looked at the creatures, his mouth tightening to a grim line. "Fae workings within mortal structures are . . . risky at best. Which is why most won't attempt them. Too many unforeseen consequences."

"Yet you breached this door?"

"Risks and rewards, Jessa."

I swallowed hard. The risk was clear, the reward from his vantage less so. Yet given the outcome, I'd not protest. If he hadn't risked bringing Wyncourt down around our ears, I'd be dead. Yet to think of Father, of the servants, crushed by the weight of the collapsing house . . .

A chill crept deep into my bones. Better not to think of it, not now.

I turned once more to the slavering creatures. Guttural sounds escaped their sharp-toothed maws. I averted my eyes. "What are you going to do with them?"

"I'll bring them to my world, where they can be dealt with in a way befitting their sort."

"Their sort? What are they?"

"Ghouls."

Ghouls. The writer whose letters Lord Blackburn sought to procure had mentioned ghouls and wights. These were certainly abominations, as he'd suggested, but were they as deadly as he claimed? I took a shallow breath, trying not to smell the singed flesh. "Can they be stopped, aside from confinement?"

"They're among the undead. They cannot be killed by any conventional means."

The undead—the stuff of the most bone-chilling legends bandied about at inns and taverns. The Vigil, and subsequently society, claimed such creatures were a fiction, but these were terrifyingly real. I pressed my hand to the splotch of blood on my bodice, and its warmth seeped over my fingers. "What makes them impossible to kill?"

For a heartbeat, I thought he'd refuse to answer. But perhaps he felt he owed me something for using me as a human key, or perhaps near death granted one the privilege of knowledge, or perhaps he intended to purge all this from my memory later. Whatever the cause, he spoke.

"Their own word binds them, animates them." His jaw tightened. "In exchange for a promise of immortality, they surrendered their hearts. But they made a corrupt bargain, for they became neither living nor dead, doomed to exist forever enslaved."

"By whom?"

"By the fae who created them."

Fae did this? Deliberately fashioned these monsters? Against my will, my gaze traveled back to their marred visages. Something uncomfortable nagged at the edges of my awareness. "What were they before they became this?"

"What do you think?" Weariness crept into his voice. "What sort of being craves immortality?"

My pulse surged. It was impossible, surely, and yet . . . "Were . . . were they once human?"

"Yes."

I stood motionless in the middle of that dreadful chamber,

my hands pressed to the wound in my side. The snarls of the creatures echoed in the emptiness and resounded in my soul. For so long, we'd thought we understood the threat represented by the Otherworld—and yet this was a fate worse than any our lore had ever conjured. "Is there any possibility of their restoration?"

"If their hearts were found and returned to them by a practitioner of sufficient skill, they would become mortal once more. Most would die in the process, however, as the weight of their years descended upon them at once."

But death with one's mind and soul restored, with the assurance of rest in the Final Haven, would be preferable to *this*. Tears stung my eyes. Since Riven had struck a reasonable bargain, part of me had begun to imagine that the cruelty of the fae in our tales had been heightened for impact, to create enough fear to prompt mortals to stay well within proper bounds. But this . . .

It was unspeakably vile.

And yet, if Riven was to be believed, the mortals in question had entered the bargain of their own free will.

Jade sauntered to my side and curled up on my feet to finish cleaning herself. Her solid form anchored me, and yet I couldn't stop shivering. "They covered my face, like they didn't want me to see them while they . . ."

While they tried to kill me.

"Their master may have commanded them to in order to keep their nature concealed." Riven brushed his fingers across a low stone shelf, then shook his head. "It's time we left."

What did he perceive? Apart from entrapped ghouls, the chamber appeared barren. On one side, a long, low table stretched out, on the other rested some shelves, empty except for a few glass jars. But what else lay hidden within this space—or beyond? If I left now, I might never know.

Certainly I doubted the wisdom of returning without Riven.

If he'd not been present to dismantle the trap on the landing, it would have finished me before I'd even reached the ghouls. Which meant although I wanted to collapse into bed, this was my best chance at uncovering the truth.

"We've come so far, and there must be more to find. Surely all those wards were not merely to prevent us from discovering the ghouls?" I straightened, wincing as the movement pulled the wound in my side. "Could this chamber have been crafted by the killer?"

"These workings bear the mark of high fae, not the killer. Nor would he have been able to access this space, not without causing clear destruction." His gaze flicked to an empty expanse of stone wall. "Nothing else remains within. It was a work chamber, but whatever else the fae created here is long since gone."

"Then why leave the ghouls?"

"Convenient storage, mayhap, till they were needed for some other purpose."

Storage? Once, these had been living beings—now they were weapons to be tucked away, mindless in their malice. "Still, there could be something else, hidden nearby."

"It's likely." He spoke calmly, as though the notion of hidden horrors in one's house was no more troubling than a leak in the roof. "But we're through for tonight."

I would have asked why he bothered to bring me at all if he intended to shut me out at the crucial moment, but I already knew the answer: I was a tool to be used, like all mortals. Now he had no more purpose for me. I pressed my hands to my hips, ignoring the stab of pain. "You expect me to leave simply because you say so? Since Wyncourt belongs to me, surely I have some right to—"

"Not until midsummer. You've given away your rights."

"That's not how it works."

"Perhaps not with mortals, but our bargain binds you. If I bid you leave, you must." His voice became stern, unyielding. "Do not test me."

The gold binding along my arm tingled. I drew a deep breath, which proved a mistake, since it pulled at my injuries and caused the room to wobble around me. "And when you leave? Then Wyncourt will be my responsibility once more, along with whatever dangers it contains. Will you tell me then what might threaten us?"

"We'll discuss later what bargain might be made." He strode toward the door. "It's time to go."

Time to go, now that I'd allowed him access to what he desired. I wanted to stay, yet I'd no more strength to object. Body aching, I limped over the shattered remnants of stone, all that remained of the barrier that once sealed this chamber from the world. I trailed him back down the stairs, now devoid of the cloud of darkness and the lurking form, whatever it had been. How had Ibbie lived alongside all this? How much had she perceived? She must have known something, else why had she scripted runes on the wall?

It took all my effort to keep one foot moving before the other, to concentrate on the smooth seams between steps so I did not stumble. My eyes burned with tears I refused to shed. I'd tried so hard to avoid the Otherworld, only to meet it at every turn. If I were out-of-doors, every plant I met would doubtless batter down the feeble defenses I still possessed . . . and perhaps I would welcome them, for the comfort they brought. As we descended into Wyncourt proper, their whispers teased my senses through walls and windows, and I could not drive them back.

Jade gave a quiet *mrow*, and I lifted her, stifling a gasp at the hot pain that seared my side. Yet her closeness, the very ordinariness of her bulk and the sweet-grass scent of her fur, steadied me, and the whispered songs stilled.

We trailed Riven into the study. Embers burned dull red in the hearth, and the gas lamps cast a familiar, welcoming glow through the room—dull in comparison to the brilliant orb Riven had conjured, yet comforting in their homeliness. The scents of leather, ink, and parchment permeated the chamber, chasing away the remembered stench of rot and scorched flesh.

Utterly spent, I eased into a chair. And yet, I couldn't lower my guard, not while I remained in the presence of fae. I removed my bloodstained gloves and stared senselessly at them while Riven crossed to the decanter on the side table and poured two small glasses of brandy.

It wasn't customary for ladies to indulge in this sort of drink, but I accepted his offering. Its slightly sweet taste warmed me, and at last, I stopped shivering.

Riven added coal to the fire, coaxing it to a comfortable blaze, and then took the chair across from me. "The fae who imprisoned the ghouls had a great deal of power. I think it's time for you to answer some questions about your Ibbie. Was she Other?"

I clenched my fingers around the glass, and its ridges dug into my skin. "She wasn't fae."

"How do you know?"

"Because she cared for others—she cared for me."

"And fae are incapable of feeling." He'd gone cold and expressionless once again.

Had I caused offense? I ventured forward slowly. "I didn't say that. Only, I had the impression that mortals mattered nothing to fae."

And worse yet, they did active injury to mortals, used them as playthings, took advantage of them—made them monsters, as

I'd learned tonight. Nothing could contrast more sharply with the kindness Ibbie had displayed.

"As you say." He shrugged. "Do you have further evidence?"

"Unless she constructed her diaries as a complete fiction, they record the life of an ordinary woman, apart from her interest in antiquities. And if she used any glamour, I . . . I could not see through it." I lowered my gaze to the familiar medallion pattern of the carpet below, one I'd trodden over countless times while assisting Ibbie. "In every regard, she behaved as a mortal. I never caught the slightest hint of power that didn't belong."

"Mortals shouldn't perceive such things." He inclined his head. "Did you expect to?"

Already, I'd misstepped. I carefully set my glass on the side table. "It . . . it just seemed like I would have noticed a difference in her. We spent a great deal of time together."

"That signifies nothing." He sipped at his own brandy. "Tell me of her husband."

"She didn't like to speak of him. I had the impression their marriage wasn't a happy one," I said slowly. "In a letter, she spoke to me of her husband deceiving her, caring only for what she brought into the marriage. I thought she spoke of her fortune and position, but perhaps not."

If I'd been mistaken, did that mean . . . was it possible for a fae to enter so deeply into our world as to wed a mortal? Nothing in our lore suggested fae would willingly share any intimacy with humans, nor be drawn to mortal beauty, which paled in comparison to their own. Yet after tonight, nothing would shock me.

Riven nodded, as though this came as no surprise. "Did he construct Wyncourt?"

"I'm not certain." I reflected back. "It's possible. Her solicitor said Wyncourt had belonged to him."

"Does she mention her husband in her diaries?"

"I would assume so, but I haven't read of their meeting yet."

"I'll need to see them myself."

"Why?" Exhaustion tugged down my defenses, frayed the edges of my words. "It appears the peculiarities of Wyncourt have nothing to do with the killer, so why are you so interested in Wyncourt and Ibbie? Even if they had ties to your world, what can it matter to you? Unless . . . you're not here because of the murders."

"The presence of the killer brought me to Avons." Unlike me, Riven chose his words with care, as unruffled by the events of the evening as if we'd taken a moonlit stroll through the gardens. "It's possible the killer chooses victims with Otherworldly connections. Therefore, it's worth understanding any aberrations in their lives. Your world offers far more limited means of gathering information—I'll take what I can to complete the picture."

I rocked back. Could Otherworldly ties be the missing link between victims the Magistry had sought? Ibbie had strong connections to the Otherworld, and the Shipleys had engaged in Crossings-trade. What of the other victims? Weeks ago, I'd not have considered it possible that so many within Avons held links to the Otherworld, but now . . . nothing would surprise me.

But how would I ever prove such to Mr. Burke, without betraying a dangerous degree of knowledge? I'd once intended to find evidence to support the case the Magistry built, then turn it over to them so they could take the killer off the streets, but that was fast becoming an impossibility.

Unable to remain seated, I crossed to the low table beneath the windows where the pot of goldhearts rested. They'd flourished here, and their blossoms gleamed vibrant in the silvery light shining through the windows. I caressed their petals, too weary to battle the allure. Their song crept into my heart—a triumphant, joyful melody.

It chased away the cold horror of the ghouls and the terror of near death. Even the pain in my side vanished, and though the muslin of my gown remained stiff with drying blood, nothing new seeped through its layers—one more peculiarity to add to the others of the evening, though at least this one worked in my favor. The flowers' spiced scent filled my lungs, and my mind cleared.

In the sanctuary of the study, surrounded by everything familiar, I could imagine the Otherworld distant, separated from our own by the boundaries of Crossings and the protections of the Vigil—but in truth, Otherkind lurked just beyond the confines of this chamber, and within it.

Either by willful deceit or lack of knowledge, the Vigil misled the folk of Byren with their assurances that they held the Otherworld at bay. It appeared true, given that the invasions commonplace in earlier eras—dragon incursions, karzel attacks, elemental sprite raids, and the like—had all but vanished for centuries, aside from occasional intrusions near the Crossings.

And yet, the Otherworld was *here*.

Perhaps not as in years of old; perhaps some of the safeguards still stood. But something had eroded our protections and allowed this incursion of Other. Jade bumped my skirts with her nose, a reassuring nudge. I stroked her absently.

If I didn't attempt to find answers, who would? The Vigil, who'd not detected the presence of a single high fae in their midst? The Magistry, who'd never even made a pretense of handling Otherworldly affairs? Or the alchemists, who'd perhaps driven us to this end with their hunger for Otherworldly power?

I ran my fingers over the stained muslin of my gown. If I wanted answers, I could no longer flee from any hint of the

Otherworld—I'd have to work with Riven and embrace my proximity to Other. And if I did, I risked strengthening the fae-touch beyond control. I risked setting it free before I'd gained any knowledge of how to protect myself. I risked madness, I risked shaming my family, I risked the Institutions.

Yet what was the alternative?

If I walked away from Wyncourt and Riven, from investigating the killer, from the growing realization that Other had already invaded our world, then I risked far more. I risked the lives of those I loved and the lives of those who depended on me—not only my family, but the servants who continued to work here at my request and the many other lives that intersected with my own. Further, I'd let down Ibbie and the trust she'd placed in me. Astute as she was, she must have known at some point I'd perceive the peculiarities within Wyncourt. Had she counted on it?

I plucked a dying leaf from the goldhearts, and they surged stronger into my awareness. I could attempt to flee the truth. Pretend I'd not seen or heard any of this. Do as my aunts wished and immerse myself in society. Forget everything I'd learned.

If I truly embraced an ordinary life, were such a thing possible, the fae-touch *might* remain manageable—or it might strengthen on its own with time and overcome me anyway. If I chose the path of apparent safety, who knew how long that safety would last?

I couldn't shrink back, couldn't retreat to the illusion of shelter from the encroaching Other. Not after what I'd seen. Not when failing to act meant endangering all I loved, when the very fact that I was fae-touched might draw the killer to them . . . or to me.

Before, the danger to my family had been theoretical—a blind, unreasoning terror that the killer would somehow find and choose another victim I loved. Now it seemed altogether too grounded in reason. My fingers skimmed the rent in my spencer as each beloved face flashed through my mind—oh.

Ainslie.

Not only did she have a fae-touched sister, but she bore her own binding mark. If Otherworldly ties drew the killer to his victims, she was doubly in danger. My pulse beat ragged at the base of my neck.

I had to stop speculating.

Seeking comfort, I stroked the goldhearts once more, and their sheen became more brilliant, little threads of gold shining amid the creamy expanse of their petals. But perhaps that was just an illusion, the taint of the fae-touch altering my perceptions at a subtle yet steady pace.

My eyes slid shut.

Perhaps an alliance with Other would result in my fae-touch consuming body and soul; perhaps it would not. But regardless, it was a chance I must take. I gently tugged one of the blossoms free and cradled it in my hand.

Then I turned to face Riven, who appeared untroubled by my long silence. He'd refilled his glass and was sipping it slowly. That was one benefit of interacting with fae—they did not expect or require adherence to our social conventions. Riven wasn't surprised by my interest in the killer, nor my forthright speech. I didn't need to pretend to be a senseless young lady, which was fortunate, since at the moment, I lacked the capacity for pretense.

"If this killer is from the Otherworld, what I've seen tonight has convinced me that it will be difficult, if not impossible, for the Magistry and the Vigil to stop him. You said as much before, and I'm starting to understand why."

"Their endeavors don't concern you."

"Perhaps not, but their success or failure impacts all of Avons, myself and my family included." The spice-sweet fragrance of the goldheart swirled around me, strengthening me. "I intend to help."

A shadow crossed his features. "You shouldn't interfere."

"You can't force me out of this, not unless you claim my will and mind alike. I won't risk losing someone else I love to this killer." Nor to the encroachment of fae into our world, but I'd leave that part out, along with the fact that interaction with him might give insight into just how deeply the Otherworld invaded our own.

"I've no intention of claiming your will or your mind—if you recall, your bargain protects you." The firelight played across his features, and in the flicker of light and shadow, his features seemed to sharpen, becoming wholly Other.

"Very well, but you represent fae interests—and you won't even tell me what that means. Who represents mortals? Who looks out for our well-being?" I lifted my shoulders, despite the protest from my scored side. "I can seek information on this killer alone, but since this concerns both our worlds, I'd rather work with you."

Work with was perhaps a stretch, but however fae might downplay the usefulness of mortals, two minds were better than one. In the Otherworld, I couldn't imagine being of use, but in my own, surely there was some advantage I could lend. And Riven was the best chance of seeing this killer defeated, assuming that was his intent.

He became perfectly still. When he spoke at last, his tone was even, betraying no emotion. "I don't require mortal aid."

"You've made that clear." This was the sticking point: what did I have left to offer? I didn't want another bargain, didn't want to bind myself further to him. I struggled to order my thoughts, to present a reason that would sway his views. "But what if you require more access to Wyncourt?"

"Then you will give it."

"I'm not bound to do so, but I'll cooperate—and that's my point." I cradled the blossom in my palm and found strength to continue. "Surely having a mortal whom you don't have to glamour or coerce into assisting you would be helpful upon occasion. And the killer may come from your world, but he's entered mine. However vast the knowledge of fae, there's much about the mortal realm I don't think you understand. If you want insight on victims, on mortal families, I can help."

It was a weak argument, but in my weariness I could come up with nothing stronger.

And yet Riven leaned toward me, his sudden focus disconcerting. "Then tell me about your family."

"My family?"

"If you want me to consider your proposal, tell me of your family."

I returned to my chair and sank into the welcome support offered by the cushions. "There's nothing particularly noteworthy about us. My father has no title, but a respectable estate. Two of his four living siblings are wed. His youngest brother has no family and spends his time at sea, and his youngest sister, my Aunt Caris, keeps house for us."

"And your mother?"

"She passed away when I was a child, and we have no kin on her side."

"None of them spent time in the Otherworld?"

"Of course not." My pulse drummed at the base of my throat. "Why would you suggest such a thing?"

"I find your response to all of this . . . interesting."

I felt certain that he guessed at my fae-touch—but I refused to confess. To speak of my shame would make it real and give him further leverage to use against me. I lifted my chin. "How would you have me respond? Even if I closed my eyes to the danger, it would still remain."

"I'll grant that much." Riven tented his fingers, and his twisted-gold-and-emerald ring glinted in the firelight. "I'll enter no bargain on this, nor bind myself to a partnership. But I concede your mortal connections and information could have a use—for a time."

Perhaps I would have felt relief, were it not for my certainty that nothing in my limited argument had persuaded him, but rather something about *me*. He perceived the peculiarities about my person, and in some way, that prompted him to agree to my proposal.

Jade drew herself into a tight circle on my lap, and I stifled a yawn, weariness clouding my thoughts. I glanced at the mantel clock—it was half past ten. "I must go."

"You still owe me answers about Lady Dromley—and her diaries," he said. "If you intend a cooperative effort, we shall explore them together. You'll answer any relevant questions about her life in context."

"Tomorrow?" I gently stroked the furrow between Jade's ears. "It will draw far less notice than at this late hour."

He gave a clipped nod. "I suggest you amend your appearance before you go. Though my glamour may sway your father to overlook it, the greater the distance between reality and glamour, the more strain it puts on the mortal mind."

Oh.

I struggled up from the chair and stumbled into the drawing room, where a large looking glass hung upon the wall. Though the polished surface didn't provide a perfect reflection, it was sufficient to confirm that my appearance desperately needed more than simple amendment.

My hair had tumbled free and curled riotously around my face, which bore a streak of dirt along one side. My spencer was ripped and bloodstained, my skirt was rent at the hem, and my gloves were beyond repair—not to mention the rather large patch of blood marring the side of my gown.

Even if residual glamour prevented Father from taking note, no amount of explanation would reassure my sisters as to my safety, to say nothing of Aunt Caris.

To make a proper job of repairs, I'd require a washbasin and a new wardrobe. I could have borrowed some of Ibbie's garments, but given her stately, imposing figure, I'd appear like a child playing dress-me-up—which would raise even more questions. What could I do with what I possessed?

I withdrew a handkerchief from my lined reticule and scrubbed the dirt from my face, then stuffed it and my gloves deep into the bag.

Then I pulled the remaining pins free from my hair and let it tumble down my back. My eyes stung as the movements tugged at the gash—though the pain was far less than before—but I did my best to remove the bits of dust and detritus from my curls. Then I wove it into a braid, which I coiled up and secured precariously with the few pins I still possessed. And as I did, I rewove my cage of thorns and the tattered edges of my emotions. When they were under as careful check as my appearance, I moved away from the looking glass.

Riven watched me as though he calculated an impossible sum . . . and something in his expression unsettled me more than the discoveries I'd made tonight.

He offered me one of Ibbie's voluminous silk shawls, which

he must have fetched from the bedchamber while I'd made my repairs. "You might want this."

"Thank you." I removed my spencer and tucked the disreputable bundle under one arm, after which I swathed myself in the shawl to conceal the worst of the damage.

Then I fled the room as though the hounds of the hunt snapped at my heels.

CHAPTER 20

The rim of the sky had only just tinted pink, and already I buried myself in the gardens, weeding, trimming, and deadheading flowers. The dewdrops shimmered like jewels, drawing forth the vibrancy of the varied shades of green. Not a single voice nor clatter of carriage over stone broke the silence. And on so quiet a morning, I might *almost* believe the events of the night before a troubled dream, were it not for the lingering tug of the gash in my side.

A night of deep sleep had worked wonders, and much of the pain of my encounter with the ghouls had faded. When I'd examined the injury to my side this morning, I'd found it nearly healed. What precisely had Riven done when he'd touched me? The legends of fae held they could heal swiftly . . . however, it seemed more prudent not to inquire, but to simply accept the small victory.

As I took relief in the fact that Father appeared to emerge from the glamour unscathed. At a word from Riven, he'd roused, though a fog had hung over his thoughts through the carriage ride home. He'd appeared under the impression that he'd toured the house with me and found everything in perfect order. Time and again, he'd repeated a few simple phrases about how all was well at Wyncourt, as though the words had taken on a life of their own within his mind.

By the time we'd arrived home and I'd served him a strong cup of black tea, he'd seemed back to his ordinary self, speaking of complex star theory with ease. The only lingering effect appeared to be some sort of veil hanging over his recall of the evening.

However distressing, the events of the night before had borne fruit. I no longer held any doubt Riven spoke the truth about the nature of the killer, not given the mounting evidence in support of his claims, but that meant I couldn't seek this killer in the way most comfortable—by research and analysis alone. I required connections to the Otherworld, which meant a return to Riven and Wyncourt as swiftly as possible.

I skimmed my fingers across sprightly stalks of chamomile, and their soft fragrance swirled through the air around me, an invitation to peace my soul refused to embrace. For my fae-touch ran up against the edges of its bounds time and again. With each touch of leaf or blossom, a snatch of song wove its way through my defenses.

If I had any sense, I'd flee the gardens, yet I found I could not. The melodies drew me irresistibly, and only out-of-doors did the restless ache inside still.

I couldn't help but recall a snippet from the history of the Vigil: *Many crave a return to the Otherworld, though it be the cause of their doom.*

I could only hope I'd not share the end of the others so afflicted. A tiny weed poked its head among the chamomile, and I uprooted it. If only I could find some confirmation that I didn't embrace false hope . . . that some fae-touched lived with their affliction and still retained their reason.

The sky brightened to red-streaked gold, and I brushed the dirt from my gown and hastened upstairs to change before seeking Father's permission to return to Wyncourt. As I drew the laces on my sturdiest pair of walking boots, one snapped. I sighed and unwove it from my boot.

Perhaps Ada or Ainslie would have another. I walked down a flight of stairs to their shared bedchamber. A thin seam of light beneath the door suggested they were awake, despite the early hour. I rapped softly.

"Come in," Ainslie called.

I found her alone, only half-dressed, her dark curls in disarray, and several political papers spread over the bedcovers. She hurriedly swept them up. "Oh, good, you're here. Ada has already gone down to help Aunt Caris prepare for the picnic she's planned for this afternoon, and I simply can't decide whether to wear the sprig muslin or the white."

"Definitely the white. It's more striking with your hair and eyes."

"I knew you'd have the answer for me." She smiled, but it lacked its usual luster.

"Ainslie, is something wrong?"

She pulled in a quick breath. "No, indeed. Only that I've dawdled abed long enough, given all I must accomplish today. When you go, will you send in Lianne?"

"Of course." Yet I'd fobbed off questions in such a fashion too often to believe her. My gaze drifted to her binding mark. Would it draw the killer to her? Could she possibly suspect? Or did something else altogether trouble her? "But first, do you have a lace I could borrow for my boot?"

"I believe I have an extra pair somewhere." She spun about

to rifle through the clothes press. "Perhaps here or in the bedside table . . ."

While she rummaged deeper, I moved to the bedside table, sifting through the drawer. I lifted a pencil case and found a note resting beneath.

Angular crimson letters sliced down a cream-colored page.

Have a care—or you'll be next.

My fingers went slack, and the pencil case crashed into the drawer. I snatched up the letter and whirled around. "Ainslie . . . where did this come from?"

Some of the color left her face, but she shrugged. "Oh, that. It's some sort of prank, I suppose."

"Who would be so cruel as to send a threat of this sort when the whole city is on edge over the killer?" It crinkled in my grasp. "Did the message come addressed to you? Or to Ada?"

"It was sent to me."

"From whom?"

"Someone anonymous, which is why I imagine it must be a jest in ill taste."

She was far too intelligent to consider any such thing. Who would think it a jest to threaten a lady? She knew more than she was saying, that much was clear. I decided to be blunt. "Ainslie, this could mean the killer has fixed his attention on you."

"Oh, Jessa, you worry too much. We've no reason to think he's ever done something so mundane as send notes to his intended victims—he appears to favor the dramatic, given the tattoos." She folded the shawl she held, creasing the lines with unnecessary vigor. "I'm not concerned about it."

"Well, you should be." Was her dismissal of this threat, vague though it may be, evidence that the killer toyed with her mind? Or did she know the identity of the writer? Did she have reason to suspect she'd made an enemy in another way?

Someone aside from the killer who would want to antagonize her or make her suffer? A jilted suitor with a vengeful streak, perhaps? It was far out of the ordinary way, but anything was possible. "At least consider the danger—after the binding, and now this letter. You cannot continue as if nothing has happened. Perhaps if we—"

"I can and will do as I please." Her dark eyes flashed. "You certainly do."

I dropped my gaze to the letter, and its harsh lines glared back. She was right, of course.

"Forgive me." A hint of regret crept into her features. "I don't mean to be unkind—but please, let it go."

I'd make no such promise, but nor would I press her when she'd only refuse to answer—and perhaps make a point of pressing me in return.

She turned back to the clothes press and sorted through the jumble at the bottom with even greater determination, while I examined the ominous message. Had any of the other victims received written threats? Surely Mr. Burke would know, given that the Magistry had examined the scenes of every death. Yet I could not think of a way to disguise such a direct inquiry. Perhaps Riven might have a notion.

I returned the letter to its place and pressed a hand to my stomach to still the churning within. If Ainslie would take no precautions, I'd even more reason for haste.

"Here you are." Ainslie popped up from the clothes press and waved the laces with a flourish. "Now I must dress if I'm to help Aunt Caris."

Despite her light tone, the tight grip she had on the laces betrayed her tension. It cost her to speak so carelessly, I was certain. So why did she choose to deny any threat?

With my boot repaired, I made my way to Father's study, where I found him buried among his papers as I'd expected. He didn't lift his head when I slipped into the room, far too preoccupied with whatever the tome before him contained.

Jade hopped onto Father's desk and batted at a pen, but he still took no notice.

"Father?"

"Ah, Jessa." With visible effort, he wrenched his gaze toward me. "Has it gotten so late already?"

"Not so very late, but I'd hoped to tend to a few matters of business for Ibbie. May I return to Wyncourt this morning?"

"Of course." He flipped a page. "Things are remarkably well there."

He echoed Riven's words without awareness they'd been imprinted on his mind. I instinctively touched the healing wound at my side. Things were far from well, but I couldn't confide in him, no matter how I longed to spill my soul. If he knew the truth about me, he'd surely banish me—if he did not feel himself duty bound to call in the Vigil. He may be swift to condemn their power, yet he'd also summoned them for Mrs. Murton when she succumbed to fae-touch. I might be his daughter, but he had a whole family to consider and protect. I wove my arms around my chest. "Thank you."

"One moment, Jessa." Father blinked as though clearing a fog—residual glamour?—from his mind.

Jade knocked the pen from the desk, and when it cracked against the wood floor, I jumped. Then she moved toward the inkwell. I grabbed her up before she could create a disaster, and she gave a slight *mrow* of protest. "Yes, Father?"

"If you have time this evening, will you transcribe a fresh

copy of my notes?" He handed me a stack of folded sheets, all over scribbles and ink blots. "I've promised Wiltshire the latest version."

"Of course." I stuffed the papers into my reticule, welcoming the idea of the simple, soothing ritual of copy work. For time out of mind, I'd transcribed Father's notes for him, my writing being far more legible than his own.

Jade wriggled free from my arms and sought a sun patch on the rug.

"Will you tell Aunt Caris I've gone to Wyncourt with your permission?"

"Of course, of course." He bent over his book once more. "Why would the pattern shift?"

Perhaps I'd best ask Holden to inform Aunt Caris when she emerged from her bedchamber—he'd be more reliable. I snatched up the pen Jade had knocked onto the floor and placed it back upon a stack of letters.

In ordinary circumstances, I might have spent the afternoon sorting Father's correspondence for him, but now . . . it was impossible. I couldn't afford a delay, when the killer could strike again at any time. So I wrapped up all the errant strands of emotion, all my desires for normalcy, all that I longed to pour out to my family, all that they would never understand, and stuffed them deep inside my chest, where they throbbed and ached against my breastbone.

Then I lifted Jade and held her close. She nuzzled my chin. Somehow, I would investigate these murders and my fae-touch —and avoid giving him cause to send me away.

∼

To my relief, when Danvers opened the door at Wyncourt, he appeared no worse for his experience with glamour. Nor did he display any sign of surprise at my uncommonly early arrival. "Good morning, Miss Caldwell. I trust you're well."

"Indeed." I offered him a bright smile. "I'm here to speak with Lord Riven on a matter of business."

Danvers gave a slight bow. "I'm afraid he's out."

"So early?" I shifted the heavy satchel of journals from one arm to the other. "No matter, I'll wait for him in the study. Please inform him I'm here when he returns."

"Shall I send tea?"

"That would be lovely." I hesitated in the entry. "Danvers, how have you fared with Lord Riven?"

"He's clear in his expectations, and otherwise an undemanding master. The staff is well-satisfied to work for him until his lease concludes." Danvers folded his hands. "Even better, his presence seems to have steadied the household. We've had nary a report of peculiarities since his arrival."

So Riven had taken it upon himself to keep the Otherworldly incursions at bay, a small mercy. Lighter of spirits, I ventured into the study, where Mrs. Peters delivered a tray laden not only with tea but a rich assortment of pastries.

I repeated the question to her.

"When I first clapped eyes on him, I won't deny I had some concerns." She set the tea tray on the polished scallop table. "Attractive men are wont to view serving girls as playthings for their pleasure—if you'll pardon my speaking so plain, miss. But he's left them alone and lets us go about our business undisturbed. I can't ask for more than that."

Aside from glamouring the servants, it appeared he'd kept his word and done no harm—and I couldn't rightly say the glamour had harmed them. At least, they showed no signs of it.

When Mrs. Peters left, I lifted the blue-and-white scrolled pot and poured a cup of tea, the fragrances of cinnamon and sweet plum drifting about me. I considered again the wall which Ibbie had scripted runes on. Had she somehow sought to stave off the encroaching Otherworld? How much had she known of Wyncourt's strange nature?

The rich flavor of the tea bolstered me, and after a moment, I crossed to the blank expanse where Ibbie had painted runes. I removed a glove and traced the wall with my fingers.

Faint and far off came the sound of murmured voices, as though they whispered through the wall and poured themselves into me. I snatched back my hand as though I'd been scalded. Was this another manifestation of fae-touch, another way it warped one's senses, or a peculiarity of Wyncourt itself?

I allowed my fingers to trail the wall once more. It shivered under my touch and became transparent, fading away to reveal another set of stairs. I wavered. Did I have the fortitude for another encounter such as I experienced last night?

At my feet, Jade sniffed the air, and I followed her example. No scent of rot or must emanated from beyond the wall; rather, a clean, springlike fragrance beckoned us onward. Perhaps it was a trap, but I required more information, and I didn't have confidence Riven would be forthcoming.

Before I climbed the stairs, I armed myself with the iron poker from the hearth, its cold metal sending an ache up my arm. Even this small means of defense boosted my confidence. Once at the top, I found myself in a narrow hall of sorts, with small peepholes alongside. I looked through the first set, and it revealed one of the guest bedchambers. Each series of peepholes appeared to overlook a set of rooms, which meant not a single visitor to Wyncourt could be assured of privacy.

I tightened my grip on the poker. If one wished to gain

knowledge to wield as a weapon, this would be an excellent way . . . but what sort of disturbed individual would find it necessary?

As I moved down the corridor, I caught the occasional snatch of voices. Then I peered through the final peephole and found Riven and another figure standing in the suite of rooms he'd chosen, surrounded by a sort of luminous haze. Clearly, he hadn't gone out, whatever Danvers believed.

Though they stood only a few ells away, their voices were too muffled and indistinct to distinguish words, as though they issued from underwater. Some sort of protection to prevent eavesdropping, perhaps?

In which case, whatever they discussed must be important. I pressed my hands against the walls of Wyncourt and strained to *listen*. The walls beneath my touch quivered, quickening with a sort of eagerness . . . as though Wyncourt itself wished to help.

I pulled back, then chided myself. I had decided last night: I wasn't going to flee from the enrichment of Other into my life, no matter the risks. I removed my other glove, tucked it into my reticule, and pressed my palms to the walls once more.

It felt as though Wyncourt itself surged up to meet me, the sounds throughout the dwelling taking on sharp clarity as though I leapt into each room at once—Mrs. Peters consulting with the cook, Danvers instructing the footman, the scullery maid flirting . . .

No, it was too much.

A wave of dizziness assailed me. I needed one thing only—Riven and the mystery figure with whom he conversed. I attended to them only and closed my ears to all else. I'd a great deal of practice blocking that which I did not wish to perceive, and it stood me in good stead now.

"Your king has proclaimed the death of this killer will be

long and painful, and so he placates your court." The other figure turned, and his face came into view—his inky-black hair and silver-gray eyes a striking combination. Like Riven, he was unmistakably fae.

All my qualms against listening in faded. Fae did not abide by our rules, and if I was to keep my family safe, I needed whatever advantage I might gain. This might be my best chance at finding out if Riven acted with honesty in our dealings or if he sought the trickery for which the fae were renowned.

The other fae—Silver-eyes, I dubbed him—continued. "That's not your usual approach. Yet here you are."

Riven toyed with an orb of light, and it flicked in and out between his fingers. "I've come as my king bids. Yet I'll dispense justice, not vengeance."

"He'll be angry." A swift smile flashed across the face of the fae. "Which will please my queen."

"Mayhap, but he has no other arbiter. He'll accept it in the end."

"You tread a sword's edge." Silver-eyes shook his head. "One might almost imagine you intend to provoke him into removing you."

"Imagine what you please." Riven lifted a shoulder. "My desires are immaterial. As are his, in this. No others possess the affinities for the role. He won't chance bringing greater turmoil to our court, nor risk giving your queen an opportunity to seize greater power."

What *was* Riven? Was arbiter a role? A title? Clearly he held greater influence in his realm—court?—than I'd ever dreamed. Yet this other fae appeared to belong to a rival court, so why did they talk so freely, as if no enmity existed between them?

"He might not be able to replace you," Silver-eyes said. "But he'll have no compunction against inflicting whatever suffering he can, if you choose your own course."

Riven turned a cold, expressionless face toward Silver-eyes. Evidently, he didn't reserve that remote detachment for mortals, but used it as he pleased to cut off undesirable lines of conversation. "Don't tell me your concern for my fate brought you here."

"No concerns here—just a body. Came across it on the queen's hunt, and it looks like the work of your killer."

"Recent?"

"Not very. From before the killer crossed into the mortal world, best as I can tell." With a twist of his wrist, Silver-eyes released lines of deepest shadow and drew them into an animated scene, like a charcoal sketch brought to life.

My breath caught.

Riven paced the recreated scene. "The killer left his mark."

"And that was about it." With a flick of his fingers, Silver-eyes made the image vanish. "Any other traces in the essence had faded before I came on the scene."

"I'd guess this was his final victim before he crossed between worlds."

"Did he steal a passing prism? We had watch on our Crossings, and I'm certain you did yours."

Riven nodded. "He killed its owner, then claimed it for himself, near the border between our courts. Perhaps your dead fae was someone who stumbled upon him in the process. Does your queen consider the death in her court cause for involvement?"

"Not at this juncture, as I understand it. The dead fae was inconsequential. Should we find evidence he preyed on others, she may change her mind. Still, I've been instructed to keep a watch for signs he's crossed back."

"You'll inform me?"

Silver-eyes nodded. "Have you identified his kind?"

"He's some sort of shape-shifter. Were it not for the binding of the Netherworld, I'd almost consider . . ." Riven drummed his fingers against his leg. "His true nature remains unclear. But since coming here, he's shifted to mortal form. He's also taken full advantage of the fact this world cannot retain traces of his passing."

Shifted to mortal form? I froze in place, the smooth surface of the wall pulsing beneath my fingers. I'd assumed when Riven spoke of Otherkind, he'd meant some sort of monster with powers of concealment. But if there were Otherworldly beings who could take on human form at will, what did that mean?

Lord Blackburn.

It brought him squarely back into the suspect category. I'd thought the evidence that the killer was Otherkind had cleared him of anything but possible fae influence swaying him to act on the murderer's behalf, but if the killer could become mortal, then he could be Lord Blackburn.

He could be anyone.

My breath came rapid and uneven. I struggled to steady it, to stay still and quiet. I couldn't afford to betray myself, not now.

"You've always enjoyed pitting yourself against crafty foes." A half-smile crossed Silver-eyes' face, enhancing the perfection of his features, were such a thing possible. "Seems you got your wish."

"Not this. It's too messy with mortals involved. They're fragile at best, fools likely to dig their own graves deeper at worst."

"Better you than me dealing with this accursed world." Silver-eyes buffed his fingers against his black coat. "But why dwell in a mortal home? Seems like an unnecessary complication."

"Reach out," Riven said. "Does it feel like a mortal home?"

Shadows deepened around Silver-eyes. "Kel's teeth! Who did this?"

"A fae arrogant enough to take extraordinary risks. One arrogant enough to think a mortal structure could be interwoven with fae workings, even expanded by them, without fracturing under the strain."

"Someone tried to construct a demesne in the mortal world?"

"Precisely."

Silver-eyes let out a soft whistle. "And the impact on the Accord?"

"Unknown. Likely the fae in question was canny enough to circumvent it. But it's my business to be sure. I won't leave it to chance."

What in the Crossings? The Accord? Demesnes? I didn't think they referred to the mortal sort of demesne, not with fae involvement, and not with Wyncourt surging about me, as if something living had been woven amid the stone and wood that made up the house.

"What are the odds the killer happened to claim the occupant of a half-mortal, half-demesne estate?"

"Small," Riven said. "Either way, it bears investigating."

"Thought you knew better than to get entangled with mortals." Silver-eyes lifted a brow. "Unless the rumors are true."

A muscle leapt in Riven's jaw. "I've no intention of entanglement, only of preventing future complications."

"One of the many reasons the king tolerates your generous interpretations of his commands." Silver-eyes smirked. "You've saved him from trouble enough times."

I staggered back from the wall. It sounded as though their conversation was winding down, and I didn't want to be found here when they finished. I dared not test Riven's tolerance of mortals to that degree.

With Jade at my side, I stumbled down the stairs, passing through the open wall and into the study. *Oh.*

What now?

If Riven returned and found a gaping hole in the wall, he'd surely have questions, ones I did not wish to answer. He'd spoken of Wyncourt almost as a being with some degree of sentience—so perhaps it could help? "Can you . . . would you close the wall?"

Nothing happened.

Jade chuffed, and I frowned at her. "You don't have to look so amused. It's not as though I have experience with fae houses."

Touch had appeared to waken Wyncourt upstairs, so it was worth a try now. I brushed my fingers over the borders of the opening, attempting to coax the surface back into place. Slowly, the edges rejoined, and the wall lost its translucence, becoming solid once more. After a moment, any signs of the staircase had vanished.

On shaking limbs, I returned to my now-tepid tea, which I sipped without thought or taste.

What would Riven do if he suspected I'd overheard him speaking so freely? Would such a notion occur to him, given the protections set in place? Perhaps it was better to leave and return. But if I did, the servants might wonder about my peculiar behavior and might even mention it to Riven, since I'd stated I was here to see him.

Then again, Riven might be the least of my concerns. There was another fae in Wyncourt, one with whom I had no bargain and no means of protection against. What was to stop a horde of them from descending upon the place?

Blight and rot.

How could I possibly watch over Wyncourt and the servants without raising alarms with my own family? I was ill-equipped in any case. I wanted to shout my frustration, but instead I forced myself to draw in a long, even breath. Could I pull off a calm facade?

I must try.

But shape-shifting? If we faced a monster who transformed into a mortal and mingled with us to make his kills, I couldn't imagine the Magistry had the tools to uncover him, much less apprehend him. His choice to come to our world appeared to shelter him in some way from Riven also, since Riven had alluded to the limitations of our world when it came to tracking such creatures. Did that mean even Riven wouldn't be able to distinguish the killer from an ordinary mortal? After all, if the Otherkind truly changed his form, there would be no residual glamour to detect. Assuming that was how shape-shifting worked . . . perhaps I could find a way to inquire of Riven.

And what of Lord Blackburn? Could he truly be a monster in mortal guise? Why then would he champion reform of fae policy and reportedly care deeply for his wife and child? Unless the Lord Blackburn who had come to the murder scenes *wasn't* Lord Blackburn, but Otherkind bearing his form. I set down my teacup with haste, and it rattled against the saucer.

Just because Lord Blackburn had a connection with the case didn't mean he was the killer. A shape-shifter might have instead taken the guise of someone else who could more easily access the crime scenes. Perhaps a member of the Magistry? Or the Vigil? How would we ever know?

A bitter taste filled my mouth, and the last remnants of

chilled tea couldn't chase it away. I shifted and my foot bumped the satchel of journals.

Since I was bound to Wyncourt until I could speak with Riven, perhaps I'd best turn my thoughts to something more useful than this endless speculation. I settled back in my seat and selected the third journal in chronological order. Soon, Ibbie's straightforward descriptions pulled me into her world—and into the mind of a younger, more naive version of the woman I'd known. She'd kept her head about her as she began to move in society, until she met a dashing gentleman, Edward Dromley. Whatever became of their marriage in the end, she fell for him heart and soul soon after their meeting, dedicating pages to his virtues. The very cadence of her words changed when she spoke of him, of his dedicated attention, and of his interest and support of her works, a rarity among gentlemen.

When I'm with Edward, time seems to lose meaning. Hours become as minutes in his presence. I ache for him in his absence, and my heart thrills whenever he appears, at the sound of his voice calling me "my dove." I think he will ask for my hand soon, and I long to hasten the day. To have both the joys of marriage and motherhood and the liberty to pursue my passions . . . it's beyond anything I dared dream. And Edward has granted it to me.

I returned to the first two sentences. If Riven hadn't planted in my mind the notion of fae influence, I wouldn't have considered them noteworthy. Perhaps they were only figurative. And yet, they troubled me. What if Edward *had* been fae? What if he'd glamoured her, clouding both her thoughts and perception of time? Could I uncover the truth, these many years later? Was it at all relevant to the case?

In one particularly poignant entry, Ibbie described her dreams of excavating Kilmere, of the significance she believed it held. Yet she'd never carried out her plans. Why? In her letter to me, she'd spoken of painful memories. Was it an association with her husband and the unpleasant turn their marriage had taken?

Oh, if only I could see her once more and hear the truth from her lips . . . if I could only ask her what she would have me do.

Vision blurring, I looked up from the pages, and the shadows at the edge of the study shifted, their movement unnatural. I blinked, and the fae I'd witnessed in Riven's chambers took shape among them.

How had he entered? And when? I was certain no one had opened a door or window—I'd not been so lost to the world that I wouldn't have observed it. How long had he observed me, reading who-knows-what emotions on my face?

"So you're the mortal who owns this place." Without awaiting an invitation, he crossed the room in a few long strides and took the chair across from mine. The air stirred between us, seemingly at his bidding.

Jade stalked to the space on the floor between us and sat, immovable as if she were sculpted from stone. Then she narrowed her green eyes at him.

"Your *kit-isne* doesn't appear to appreciate the company."

Riven had used that term for Jade as well. *Kit-isne*—was it the fae word for cat? While loremasters believed that fae had their own tongue, mortals didn't know even the smallest scrap of it. However curious I might be, I wasn't about to ask this strange fae for linguistics instruction, not when he might take that as an opening to bargain—and not when I shared Jade's sentiments. I snapped the journal shut. "Who are you?"

His teeth flashed white in a brash, almost feral grin. "You can call me Nikol."

"I expected Riven."

"Oh, Riven's gone." His voice lowered. "He had an errand."

Unease rippled down my spine, and I wished I'd kept the iron poker at hand. "So Danvers told me. I intended to wait for him, but I didn't realize he'd taken a houseguest."

"I won't be staying long. Just long enough to enjoy making your acquaintance."

A shadow curled out from him and crept along the floor like a vine, reaching toward me. All the while he watched me, waiting . . . for what?

Jade rumbled low in her chest, and I pulled in a quick breath. I'd better act before the situation spiraled out of control. What would Aunt Melisina do? She was an expert at putting unwelcome callers in their place. She'd draw herself up and adopt a chilling tone—so I'd do my best to emulate her example in this one instance. "Perhaps you're not familiar with the conventions of the mortal world, but it's impolite to touch others without their permission. I suggest you keep your shadows to yourself."

Whatever I'd expected, it wasn't the lightning crack of laughter that followed. "Do you indeed?"

How was I supposed to respond to that? I curled my fingers around the smooth leather of the journal and chose to ignore it. "Would you care for a cup of tea?"

"The only beverage this world has worth imbibing is frostwine."

"I don't believe Lady Dromley kept frostwine." Indeed, I'd only ever encountered it in Milburn. "But I could ask Danvers, if you wish."

"No need." He leaned back in his chair, the shadows still stirring unnaturally around him. "Unless you're so inclined."

I tilted my head, changing tactics. "If I did, would you use those shadows to snare my servants? Do they allow you to glamour mortals more easily?"

"Riven may choose to give you bits of information as it suits his purpose, requiring nothing in return, but I offer nothing for free. If you wish to know, there's a price." Though his tone remained light, my skin chilled.

Legends spoke of courts with greater and lesser enmity toward mortals. If Riven belonged to a more cordial court and Nikol to one more hostile . . . it was better to avoid striking any sort of bargain with him. In fact, it would be far better to avoid conversation altogether, avoid provoking him while Riven was absent.

But if I left, he might well roam the house and harass the servants. I forced a smile. "If you're not interested in tea, perhaps you'd prefer a book while you await Riven's return? Ibbie has an extensive collection."

"I favor action." He picked up a centuries-old statuette worth a considerable sum and tossed it from one hand to the other. "You're not like most mortals I've encountered. Shall we find out how deep the differences run? It might prove . . . entertaining."

Jade paced between us, the fur on her neck raised as the air around us grew heavy, even oppressive.

A knot formed in my chest, oppressively tight. If he truly sought the source of the differences he sensed, he could upend my control over the fae-touch in a moment. Would it amuse him to watch me descend into madness? My temples throbbed. "You're a guest here, and I don't think—"

"If it's location you protest, I'd be happy to take you home. Only say the word." The shadows deepened, spiraling toward me.

Jade rumbled low and bared her teeth. I fumbled for her, not daring to take my eyes off Nikol for a moment.

"It seems the *kit-isne* doesn't approve."

A pulse of energy fairly crackled in the air, and Riven strode through the door. "Nor do I."

The knot in my chest loosened, and Jade ceased growling.

"You're no fun." Nikol tossed the statuette to Riven.

He caught it effortlessly. "And you're interfering where you have no business."

"One would think you tire of my company."

"One would be correct."

"Very well. I'll take my leave." Nikol sprang to his feet in a single lithe motion. "But now that I know how you've been entertaining yourself, expect another visit soon."

With a swirl of dark shadow like the gathering of a tumultuous storm, Nikol vanished.

I breathed more easily . . . until Riven turned toward me with a frown.

"What are you doing here?"

CHAPTER 21

Every rational thought fled before a compelling need to pour forth thoughts and feelings irrelevant to the matter at hand—and dangerous to reveal. I was here to offer the diaries to Riven, before he could attempt to fetch them from my home. That was all. I kept my thoughts confined to that path before opening my mouth. "Last night you said you wished to look through the diaries. So I brought them."

"I didn't expect you so eager to return."

"I'm eager for answers." And to keep him as far from my family as possible. I drew the book to my chest. "Is Nikol a friend?"

"An associate." His tone made it clear Nikol wasn't a matter for discussion. "Have you unearthed anything in her diaries so far?"

"Nothing of note." I motioned to the satchel. "But if you want to examine them yourself, I brought them all."

One by one, he lifted the books from my satchel and turned them over in his hands. Light spilled from his fingers across the pages.

"Is anything amiss?"

"The books themselves are perfectly ordinary." He kept the first volume. "As for what's recorded—we'll see."

While he was distracted by his reading, perhaps I could venture a question. It was risky, but then, so was this whole endeavor—and I couldn't expect our mortal libraries to have information on the nuances of fae abilities. If I wanted information, I'd have to get it from the source. I let the diary fall open on my lap. "What's the difference between glamour and shape-shifting?"

Riven looked sharply at me, and I did my best to maintain a mildly curious facade.

"Why do you ask?"

"Something Nikol said," I murmured, leaving out *when* he'd said it.

"He needs lessons in discretion," Riven muttered. Then he flipped a page. "Glamour alters perception. Shape-shifting alters true form."

So it functioned as I'd feared. I stared at the page, the words becoming indistinct. Whatever limited ability to see through glamour I possessed by virtue of the fae-touch would not serve in the case of a shape-shifter—for there was nothing to see through. The Otherkind would in fact become human, for a time. Could fae perceive them in their altered state, or did no discernible trace of the changes remain?

Riven pointedly lifted the book to conceal his face, effectively cutting off further conversation. While he paged through the diary, intent on its contents, I returned to my own. In silence, we read through our respective volumes, and despite the irregularity of the situation, despite my pressing questions, my tension eased. In some small way, it felt like all the other times I'd studied in this room, Ibbie and I each absorbed in our own work and sharing noteworthy findings at intervals.

Only I must remember—this time, I did not work with a friend, but a fae. His conversation with Nikol might have confirmed that he shared my goal of apprehending the killer, but beyond that, I could trust nothing.

With a rustle, I turned to the next page. Ibbie had recorded Edward's proposal and her wedding, her words incandescent with joy. And why not? She had found someone who understood her, who accepted her eccentricities, and even loved her for them—a remarkable feat.

Then, for three months, she wrote nothing at all. When she picked up again, the entire tenor had changed.

> *My husband. How long I dreamt of saying those words about someone I loved more than life itself, someone who loved me in the same way. When Edward came into my life, he embodied the fulfillment of my dreams—or so I thought. But now those dreams have turned to ash, and I cannot speak of the cause, cannot even write it. Some days I feel as though the weight in my chest is unbearable, that I must speak, lest the burden suffocate me.*
>
> *And I tried, once.*
>
> *So foolish. My tongue cleaved to the roof of my mouth and all breath left my lungs. He warned me I was constrained, and he spoke truth. I will not risk it again.*
>
> *Now I must simply endure. And pray for an end.*

My throat constricted. How long had Ibbie suffered in silence? Had this constraint bound her from speaking the truth, even after her husband's death? It sounded like some sort of compulsion, so did that mean . . .

When I looked up, Riven watched me, again with that unnatural perceptiveness. "What did you find?"

I didn't trust my voice, so I offered the book to him, tapping the appropriate section.

A slight frown creased his brow. "This Edward, does she speak of his family? His history?"

I shook my head. "It's as if he appeared from nowhere. She describes him bursting onto the scene of society and capturing the attention of countless ladies. She speaks of losing her sense of time and self when with him, and of her confidence he loved her as deeply as she did him. He supported her works as well, which meant a great deal to her."

"What sort of work did she undertake?"

"She was interested in antiquities and wanted to continue her studies, as well as carry out excavations. She was particularly interested in the ruins of Kilmere, which her father purchased for her as a wedding gift."

A flare of interest kindled in his green eyes, but he said only, "I see."

"Do you know something about Kilmere or about Edward?"

"I have no interest in mortal excavations." He returned the diary to me. "However, it's likely this Edward was fae. This morning I visited your archive and confirmed he designed and oversaw the building of Wyncourt."

I caught my lip between my teeth. Riven confirmed my suspicions, but why would any fae want to snare a mortal in marriage, when they viewed humans with scorn? I couldn't fathom fae ever forming any sort of attachment to a mortal, and certainly Edward's mistreatment of Ibbie confirmed that. It was not marriage, not in any true sense, but a most dreadful form of bargain. He must have chosen her to further some sort of unpleasant scheme, and once he'd snared her, she could not escape. Had she tried?

Wait, the inscriptions on the walls . . . Had Ibbie sought to protect the inhabitants of Wyncourt in some form? What might have caused her to think the runes would offer protection? Was it something in her interactions with Edward?

I clasped my hands in my lap to still their shaking. "Then it wasn't only Wyncourt that tied Ibbie to the Otherworld, it was also her husband. Do you believe the killer chose her due to the strength of those connections?"

"I find it likely."

My gaze drifted back to the wall that concealed the staircase. What other workings had Edward woven into Wyncourt? And how much bearing did all this have on the murders? "Did you confirm that the other victims share her connections with the Otherworld? I know the merchant did, since his shop contained tea sourced from the Dunael Crossing."

"The sailor and solicitor also appear to have ties. As for the others, it remains to be seen," he said. "Your—what do you call it? Your newsboy? He had no remaining family, no one who knew him outside his place of employment. He slept on the streets. It will be difficult to ascertain if one such as him had ties to my world, when so little evidence remains."

"But if we can connect the other victims to the Otherworld . . ."

"It would be confirmation of a pattern." Riven reached for another diary. "The killer seeks his prey for a reason. If we can unlock it, we'll be one step closer to finding him."

Should I ask him about Lord Blackburn? Perhaps he would know something about him, or perhaps it was a matter we could tackle together. I leaned forward. "There is a gentleman connected with the case—"

Abruptly, the door swung open, and Mrs. Peters entered, bearing a luncheon tray.

"I thought you and Lord Riven might be wanting a meal, Miss Caldwell." Her hands trembled as she lowered the tray to the table, and the china clinked slightly.

"Thank you, Mrs. Peters. Has there been any more trouble in Wyncourt?"

"It's nothing, Miss Caldwell."

Mrs. Peters never displayed signs of agitation—something must be unsettling her. "I'm certain Lord Riven would wish to hear if something has gone amiss."

"It's not about Wyncourt," Mrs. Peters said. "It's only that there's been another murder, and this time the body was left in front of the Magistry—not even an hour ago, so the delivery lad told us. And I cannot help but remember my lady . . ."

Another victim, another murder. What family had suffered loss this time? How many loved ones grieved? Assuming our Otherworldly connection theory held true, some other poor soul had possessed ties as strong or stronger than those within my own family. How long would that be the case? I swallowed hard against the bitter taste filling my mouth. "How dreadful."

Riven turned his gaze upon Mrs. Peters, with all its gleaming intensity. "What else do you know?"

"Nothing, my lord. The lad was fair shook up, said his mum talks of leaving Avons altogether to go to her brother in the country. But he'd heard nothing else."

"Very well. That will be all, Mrs. Peters." Every line of Riven's body had coiled tight, poised for action. "We won't need anything else today, you understand?"

"Of course, my lord." She gave a small curtsy and left the room.

When Mrs. Peters left, Riven sprang to his feet. "Are you coming?"

I wavered a moment, caught off guard. I'd expected to have to justify my interest, to convince Riven of the acceptability of a lady viewing such a scene. Instead he took it for granted that I'd want to be there, and it inclined me in his favor.

Before I could think better of risking exposure to the Magistry again, I nodded. I couldn't pass up this chance. It hadn't been long—perhaps the killer had left some trace. Perhaps he'd even lingered at the scene of his crime.

∽

Outside the Magistry, a restless throng milled, fear and agitation emanating from the individuals clustered within. Doubtless, the word of the new victim had spread like knotweed through the troubled city.

Riven and I halted at the edge of the crowd. From her perch on my shoulders, Jade surveyed the gathering and gave a soft hiss, as though the restive energy of the assembly unsettled her.

Stratesmen had blocked the street immediately surrounding the Magistry from public access, and they'd assembled in greater number than I'd ever witnessed, pressing back the crowd.

"You'll have to wait here."

I didn't argue, because it was plain that no one without glamour could get close enough to examine the area before the Magistry. But I still might gain something from my vantage nearby.

While Riven bent light around him in the peculiar way that allowed him to vanish from mortal sight, I turned to survey the crowd. Instead, two stately elms in the courtyard nearby caught my eye.

In Milburn I'd once perceived a scene that had happened before my arrival by connecting with the witness—a stately linden. It had almost overset me, most likely would have, if it hadn't been for my companion. I wavered.

I'd already chosen to expose myself to Other; I didn't need to deliberately free the fae-touch, didn't need to risk further damage. And yet, if I could catch a glimpse of what had happened here . . .

Before I could dissuade myself, I crossed to the courtyard and reached for the nearest elm. Just as my fingers brushed the low-hanging limbs, a nearby voice spoke my name. My heart leapt into my throat, and I pulled free, nearly stumbling onto the street.

"Easy, Miss Caldwell."

It was Mr. Burke. He grasped my elbow to steady me. "Why am I not surprised to find you here—and unescorted at that?"

"Mr. Burke." I stepped back, more gracefully this time. "I was at Wyncourt, and the housekeeper spoke to me of another victim. I suppose it's true?"

"There has been another victim, yes." His kestrel-sharp gaze pierced me. "You came all this way to determine the veracity of her tale?"

I shifted uncomfortably. "I came to ease her mind and my own."

For nothing brought the same comfort as information and understanding, the possession of facts and the comprehension of them—but I could scarcely explain that to Mr. Burke.

What did I know of him? He appeared to care deeply for justice and for the protection of Avons. The anger of the populace—the accusations of incompetence, given the murders were ongoing—must be troubling. If I pressed upon that point, would it move him to speak to defend the Magistry? I brushed a bit of bark from my gloves. "Has the Magistry come any closer to apprehending the killer? With such a bold step, surely he's unmasked himself."

"We're doing all we can." His words took on a slight edge. Evidently, I'd found a tender spot. "The Magistry has pulled in outside assistance, and the Assemblage of Lords has pledged its resources."

"I believe you've employed a Mr. Upton? I've made his acquaintance, and he says he's familiar with the case."

"Mr. Upton is one such, yes. But you need not concern yourself with the particulars. We will find the killer, rest assured."

But I had no such assurance, not when I knew the killer was Otherkind. And if Lord Blackburn was in fact the shape-shifter in disguise, how better to cover his tracks than by involving his peers more deeply in the whole affair? "Did Lord Blackburn propose the assistance of the Assemblage of Lords?"

Mr. Burke became very still. "Why do you ask?"

"I've only noted he seems to have an . . . avid interest in this case."

"As do you. How is it you still give so much attention to this investigation?"

The sun beat hot upon us, and I removed my fan from my reticule and waved it, a lacy shield for my face. "All of Avons speculates in some fashion, Mr. Burke. Don't we all have ideas and theories and fears?"

"I'll grant that much. But not all of Avons takes it upon themselves to pry into the affair with such determination."

I unfurled the fan more widely. "Then you haven't noticed Lord Blackburn show any particular interest in the case?"

He huffed out a breath.

Jade's sides quivered, as if she were amused. At least someone was entertained.

"I've noted that Lord Blackburn has many friends in high places," he said in a clipped tone. "He's made himself indispensable in certain quarters. It's better you stay away from him."

Friends in high places meant that the dictates of position and power limited any queries the Magistry might make into Lord Blackburn—even in a circumstance as dire as this. To charge a member of the peerage would require unassailable proof, and if he was Otherkind, that proof might be impossible to come by.

I needed to speak with Riven about him. Out of guilt or preoccupation or simply lack of concern, Lord Blackburn hadn't deigned to reply to my missive about his parcel. If he were innocent, then we needed to remove him from the list of suspects. But if he were guilty . . .

Mr. Burke sighed. "Since you've listened to no other cautions of mine, please tell me you'll come to me directly with any concerns or questions. Don't do anything rash."

"I never act rashly." I folded my fan. I might take risks, but I considered them beforehand, so they could not be deemed impulsive.

"Doubtless you think me interfering, but I act only out of concern for your well-being and the rest of this city." Mr. Burke examined the throng before us, and the slight furrow between his eyes deepened. "I mistrust the look of this crowd. As you've aptly pointed out, all of Avons concerns itself with this case—and fear can easily spark anger. Allow me to hire a hack to see you home."

Where had Riven gone? I couldn't spy him anywhere, nor the telltale shimmer of light that might conceal him. If I protested Mr. Burke's kindness, I'd draw unwanted attention.

For all the inconvenience of his presence, I believed his concern sincere.

Perhaps he'd even saved me from making a dangerous error in attempting to connect with the elms. I could have exposed myself before a crowd, and worse still, I might have risked so much and yet found nothing. To think that I could so easily exercise control over the fae-touch—and use it to my advantage without paying the price—defied reason.

In any case, I didn't want to stir further suspicion in Mr. Burke, so I accepted his proffered arm. "Thank you, Mr. Burke. You're most kind."

As we wove through the crowd, I ventured one more question, too concerned for Ainslie to conceal my purpose. "Aside from the tattoo, have any of the victims received any other sort of warning from the killer?"

His gaze sharpened. "Why do you ask?"

"I only wondered." If I spoke of the letter, Ainslie would be furious—as would my aunts, when they found out I still engaged with the case.

"You . . . wondered." He raised a brow. "Have you received any threats?"

"No."

He sighed. "You should know by now I can't discuss the case with the public. Only be assured we've overlooked no possibilities."

Which gave me no reassurance whatsoever about Ainslie. Mr. Burke handed me into the hack, and on the trip home, my mind spun with a multitude of questions that had no answers. As we halted in front of the house, I glanced up to see the profile of Lord Blackburn as he descended the polished stone stairs.

Everything froze.

What was he doing here? Had he come to fetch the parcel of

letters after all, with no response or forewarning? Or was his intent far worse?

Forgetting the propriety of waiting for the driver to open the door, I fumbled with the latch. It stuck, refusing to give way.

"Sorry, miss." The driver appeared outside the door. "If you'll allow me."

The door shuddered as he forced it open. It was too slow; I was too late.

By the time I emerged, Lord Blackburn had disappeared into the bowels of his own carriage. If I wished to run down the street shouting like a town crier, perhaps I might gain his attention—and scandalize all of Camden Row in the process. Instead, I hurried up the stairs, nearly tripping at the top.

Holden opened the door to me. "Good afternoon, Miss Jessa."

"Was that Lord Blackburn?"

"It was. He called upon Mr. Caldwell."

With a murmured thanks, I rushed toward the study, Jade keeping pace. If anything had happened to Father, how could I forgive myself? I should have gone to see Lord Blackburn sooner, should have confided in Riven about him earlier . . .

Oh, what had I done?

But when I charged into the room, Father sat hale and whole, bent over a star chart and sticking it in places with map pins, muttering about how the constellations should not alter.

"Father, was that Lord Blackburn?"

"Mm, yes."

"What did he want?"

"Only to speak of some concerning trends he's observed and inquire about my star findings." Father jabbed another pin into the map. "He's quite right to be concerned about these incursions into the Otherworld. The Collectors are fools, as are the alchemists for urging them onward. One would think the lives lost sufficient deterrent, but I suppose the lure of riches is irresistible."

"I suppose so." But this time I cared nothing for theories about the Otherworld. I inspected Father for any sign of a tattoo, any sign of Other attaching itself to him, and found nothing. Still, I found it difficult to catch my breath. "He mentioned nothing about a parcel from Lady Dromley? Nor wanting to see me?"

"No, nothing of the sort." He leaned closer to the chart, inking a mark onto the paper. "I must go out."

"But you'll return in time for dinner?" In such an abstracted state, I didn't trust him not to climb into the carriage of the killer rather than his own—assuming the killer even used one.

"Of course. I only have to fetch a reference book from the library."

Which meant we'd be fortunate indeed if he rejoined us before full night. I wanted to plead with him to stay home, but I had no just cause. Nothing appeared amiss. Yet Lord Blackburn's presence here—with no true acquaintance between him and Father and no mention of my missive—it couldn't be coincidence.

CHAPTER 22

When we gathered for dinner that evening, Aunt Caris ordered the curtains drawn, as though by avoiding the eye of the killer we could keep from receiving his mark. Once she'd heard of the newest victim, she'd begun to talk of the failures of the Magistry to keep the townsfolk safe, and worse still, of the necessity of leaving Avons.

I kept looking to the door, hoping I would find Father, wanting to examine him again for any sign of peculiarities. At last, after Holden had drawn the curtains and laid the first course before us, he entered the dining room.

The moment Holden withdrew, Aunt Caris launched her attack. "Alden, thank the Infinite you're well. Jessa told me you went out, and I cannot think it wise. You've heard about what happened?"

"You mean about the appearance of the Haydon Comet? Why yes, though I'm rather surprised you have."

She sighed. "No, not that. The killer has claimed another victim—and he had the audacity to leave the body in front of the Magistry."

Father paused with his fork halfway to his mouth. "That's unfortunate indeed."

"More than unfortunate." Aunt Caris snapped open her napkin. "Given the situation, I cannot think it safe to remain in Avons. Perhaps we should all withdraw, either to Caldwell House or to visit Gillian together. Once the Magistry has apprehended this madman, we can return to Avons."

I should have known Aunt Caris wouldn't let this go, but I hadn't expected her to approach Father so swiftly and in front of us all. I stirred the rich chestnut soup, my spoon making ripples across the surface. Given his recent admittance to the Royal Society of Astronomers, I couldn't imagine Father would leave—nor would Lovell and Aunt Melisina or many of the others I cared about. To leave Avons, with Wyncourt in disarray, with the killer free to strike those I loved, with the Otherworld encroaching on our city unbeknownst to those charged with its safety . . . it would be disastrous.

Given her delight in Avons, I expected Ainslie to protest, but she remained quiet, watching Father from the corner of her eye. Perhaps it was better she refrained from speech, since she and Father were rarely in accord.

"Nonsense. It was one thing to consider Jessa paying a visit to Gillian to ease her past the worst of her grief. But I refuse to have my family flee in direct opposition to the stated wishes of the king. If he keeps his own family in Avons, surely we have no need for flight." Father took a bite of soup. "Of course, if you wish to go, Caris, I'll make arrangements on your behalf. You must make your own choice. My daughters will stay, but we will manage if you feel you must leave."

To avoid inciting panic, King Everill and the Magistry had assured people it was safe to stay and issued demands that the Assemblage of Lords and other governmental activities continue as usual. A mass exodus of the wealthy would lead to social unrest, with possible rioting among those who couldn't afford to leave or had nowhere to go. Some men had quietly sent their families away and some few had departed altogether, but for the most part, the actions of the crown had been effective. No one with the means to relocate wanted to earn the disfavor of the king or lose face in society by appearing overly fearful. If Father departed, he would risk losing standing within the Royal Society of Astronomers, whose members were appointed by the king, and also with the rest of his academic peers, whose opinions he valued above all others.

Aunt Caris's lips trembled slightly. "Of course, you must do what you think best for your children, Alden. I know I have no authority to decide for them—I only thought to keep them safe."

"There are greater odds of them meeting their death in a carriage accident than being selected by the killer in a city the size of Avons. Simple mathematics, Caris." He thumped his glass down. "It's folly to run."

What made Father so adamant? This seemed to be more than concern about what his peers might think. I wasn't surprised that he wanted to stay, but it was odd that he was so determined we remain. Something didn't add up. Did Lord Blackburn's presence earlier today have any bearing on the matter? Could he have planted some notion in Father's mind?

Aunt Caris had lowered her gaze, peering into her bowl as if it contained the answer to the mysteries of the universe. Father's lack of care must sting, after all she'd done to tend us.

I offered her a smile and reached over to place my hand atop her own. "Of course, we know you only thought of what would be best for us. You always do, and we appreciate you for it."

Never mind that her notion of my best and my own didn't always align; her love remained steadfast.

Ada and Ainslie chimed in their agreement, and Aunt Caris toyed with her napkin. "Thank you, my dears."

As it happened, I preferred that Ada, Ainslie, and Aunt Caris remove from Avons, regardless of the equation Father might have used to assess the risks. I sipped my own soup, the fennel and chestnut flavors soothing. "Perhaps Ada and Ainslie might accompany Aunt Caris on some pretext of assisting Aunt Gillian. It needn't look like a rejection of the king's edict. I could remain to lend face and assist you with—"

Ainslie set down her glass with a clink. "I can't leave Avons now, with the . . . social season in full swing. Father's right, it wouldn't do."

"And I certainly won't go without my sisters," Ada announced.

"Then the matter is settled," Father said. "Unless you wish to depart, Caris?"

"I'd never know a moment's peace, leaving all of you here with that vile predator roaming the city. Someone needs to see to the girls. I'm staying." Nevertheless, she cast an uneasy glance at the shrouded windows.

When Holden brought the second course, Aunt Caris made an attempt at conversation. "How was your dress fitting, Ainslie? Melisina told me she was most pleased by the unique pattern the seamstress achieved."

"The dress fitting?" Ainslie looked at her blankly.

"You went this afternoon? To your fitting?"

"My fitting. Oh, yes." She blinked, as if trying to clear a haze from her eyes. "It was . . . ah . . ."

Ada frowned at Ainslie but swiftly filled the silence. "For my part, I cannot think how the seamstress does such intricate lacework. When I consider the hours she must spend on each piece, I'm quite astonished."

"As am I, my dear. Of course, Melisina would accept nothing less," Aunt Caris said.

She chattered on about lace while I prodded the roast on my plate with the tines of my fork, my appetite vanished. Something was amiss with Ainslie. Even if she'd had a change in plans she'd rather Aunt Caris not know about, she would have come up with some adroit misdirection to distract from further inquiry. Her confusion reminded me all too much of fae meddling. Could it relate to her binding mark? Or the killer?

If he found Ainslie before I found him . . .

We all subsided into silence, each one apparently as troubled by their thoughts as I. Although Father expressed a logical view about the odds of being selected by the killer, he didn't know that the victims weren't chosen at random, but by their connection to the Otherworld—nor did he know of all the ties within his own household. And if Lord Blackburn were somehow involved, his appearance here could only bode ill.

∽

When everyone retired for the evening, I found myself restless. The moon rose large and low on the horizon, a pale golden disk as remote as the Otherworld. After a long, exhausting day, I should have collapsed into bed, yet I perched at the window in my bedchamber, staring out at the gardens.

Had Lord Blackburn unduly influenced Father? If so, why? If not, what had brought him here? I couldn't speak with Riven about the matter until morning, which felt unbearably far away.

Jade sprang onto my lap and kneaded my legs with her paws.

"What do you think, Jade?"

I stroked her head, and she purred. As we sat together, an urge crept over me to visit the glasshouse. Images of moonbeams on blossoms filled my mind; the impression of their soft fragrances whispered on the wind. The room became as stifling as a prison, and the glasshouse an invitation for release.

"Do you want to go outside?"

She leapt up with a *mrow* and batted at the door. Remaining inside might give the illusion of safety, but the murders had all occurred within the confines of familiar spaces, with the victims surrounded by people who should have heard or seen the killer, but had not. I'd be as safe inside the walls of our garden as within the walls of my bedchamber.

Jade appeared to agree, for she bounded eagerly through the corridor and down the steps, leading the way toward the glasshouse.

Silvery moonlight bathed blossom and bough, and the scene was every bit as magical as I expected. The fragrance of the princess-of-the-night blooms whispered a greeting, their song a promise to ease breathing and relieve discomfort. As I passed through the doorway, I caressed their petals, and they swayed toward me.

But something intangible marred the perfection of the moment, an uneasy sort of murmur sweeping from the potted plants on the center table. What trickery did my fae-touch conjure now? I pressed my fingers to my temples.

A low rumble resounded in Jade's chest, and she rushed ahead. She leapt upon the table and looked back at me, her eyes aglow. Once again, she'd scented something amiss.

A leather-bound book nested among the plants, a crisp white sheet of paper bound to its cover with a crimson ribbon. Every muscle in my body tensed, and I whirled around, seeking an intruder.

But I could find no one.

I inched closer to the book and plucked it from its nest. It was all too familiar, a perfect match to Ibbie's diaries. Spidery lettering scrawled across the paper bound to its surface, an inscription bearing my name: *Miss Jessa*.

And I knew.

It was the killer. He'd left this to taunt me. Who else could it be? An uneven breath shuddered my chest. The moonlight took on a harsh, ominous tint, and the shadows it cast became dangerous patches of concealment in which the killer might shelter.

With trembling fingers, I unraveled the ribbon, unfolded the note. The spidery writing continued inside:

Oh, Jessa. You enchant. Your fear is delicious, your sorrow delightful, your cause hopeless. You should surrender now, but I hope you do not—for you give the game such savor. Indeed, it is lifeblood to me.

Beneath the writing was a sketch of a small crimson tattoo, utter perfection in every stark line.

The glasshouse walls closed in on me, shimmering in a dance of light and shadow. I gripped the table edge hard, fighting to remain upright.

Jade nuzzled my hand, her pupils wide in the dim light, but I could not find my voice to reassure her.

No question remained—it was no longer surmise, but fact. The killer had been here. *Here.* Was he lingering, even now? Did he lurk beyond sight or perception, waiting to make his mark? If so, what hope did I have of escape?

The slightest of sounds sighed behind me.

My stomach gave a sickening lurch, and I spun toward a

figure in the shadows. A militant murmur swirled from the plants about me as I snatched up a shovel.

Then he stepped into the light.

Riven.

It was only Riven.

I sagged back against the table, releasing my hold on the shovel.

"What's wrong?" His voice rumbled, low and soothing.

I thrust the note at him.

He skimmed it, and his grip on the page tightened. The charged-air sensation increased. "Did you see anyone in the glasshouse?"

"No . . ." But perhaps Lord Blackburn had left this earlier, when he'd paid his call on Father? No servant would have questioned him, not after he'd been admitted by Holden and welcomed by Father. Before I could bring up his visit and my suspicions, Riven began to prowl the glasshouse. Brilliant faelights sprang up around him, bathing our surroundings in a rich golden glow.

"Did he leave some sign, something that might signal his identity?"

"There's little left to reveal his passing." Riven snapped his fingers, and the lights vanished. "In your barren world, few currents of power remain to direct the course of the investigation or to trace the paths of those who cross them."

He halted before me. "That's the missing journal, I assume."

"I believe so." I flipped it open to find Ibbie's familiar writing, and then turned to the final entry, dated the day before her death. Riven crossed the space between us and stood close, reading over my shoulder.

I'm not myself. The tattoo seems to burn my skin, throb-

bing and aching more with each passing day. And I wonder. When the pain reaches its zenith, is that when the killer will appear? It's a fancy, I know. But unnerving. I can't shake it.

    Lord Blackburn called this afternoon. The Magistry suggested I deny all visitors, but he pushed his way in. Robart and two other stratesmen supervised his visit the entire time, a reminder of the danger that stalks me. I couldn't conceal my feelings, not in full. He insisted this whole affair was the natural outcome of our unnatural meddling in the Otherworld. He seemed almost pleased to have evidence of it. On and on, he ranted.

    His visit harrowed me still more, and I almost summoned the stratesmen to have him evicted, when he abruptly took his leave, forgetting the parcel for which he came. Such was my state of mind that I only remembered it an hour after he departed. I shudder at the thought of another call from him once he recalls his errand.

    I've prided myself on my strength for so long, but now I find myself weak of will. I long for Jessa, for her steady, calming presence. Twice, I've almost sent for her, only to check myself. I refuse to endanger her, however much I desire her company. I know it's best to keep her away until this is over—one way or another. If she were harmed . . . I would rather go to my grave than live with more deaths on my conscience.

Ibbie left a gap, as though some hours had elapsed. When she resumed writing, her hand was unsteady, the letters wobbling across the page.

    Oh, it burns.
    I see its pattern etched against my eyes when I close them. There is no rest. No sleep. No peace.

Only pain.
And waiting.
Sometimes I hear phantom footfalls, intruders not present. Folly and nonsense, yet my mind will play tricks.
I've always relied on it, on sound intellect and quickness of thought, but now at the end, it betrays me—if this is the end.
Only one thing remains: the mercy of the Infinite.
I shall cast myself upon it.
For only there can I find rest.

Tears burned my eyes, and one escaped against my will, searing a path down my face, betraying weakness to Riven. But the ache burrowed so deep, I could no longer care.

I should never have stayed away, should never have left Ibbie to suffer alone. *I'm sorry, Ibbie.*

"You couldn't have stopped him, even if you'd gone to her."

"But I could have made her last night more peaceful. Instead, I left her alone and tormented by her fears." I dashed away the tears before more could fall. "I left her to die without the comfort of a friend."

"She sent you away." Riven plucked the journal from me. "She was right to do so—and you were right to respect her wishes. The choice was hers, and she chose to die with the knowledge that she'd protected those she loved."

Logic supported his claim; emotion did not. "What if she regretted it, in the end?"

"Then console yourself with the knowledge her killer will pay for his crimes." Riven snapped the book shut. "He's observed you and your efforts, now he taunts you."

"That's no comfort."

"His interest in you makes him vulnerable. Gives us a greater chance to uncover his identity."

I wasn't sure I liked the notion of drawing the killer out, but if it ended everything, then perhaps it was worth it. I inhaled the perfumed air. "If he's interested in me, then my family might be at risk. Aunt Caris thinks we should flee Avons. Do you agree?"

"He could find you as easily in the country as the city. If he intends to mark you or your family, your departure will not preserve you."

I almost wished he were a gentleman inclined to give false comfort to a lady in distress—but better by far to have the truth, no matter how it stung. I sank onto the bench. "But he's confined himself to Avons so far."

"So your Magistry says." Riven's words took on an edge. "But your Magistry wouldn't hesitate to lie, if it suited them. They already have. It's why the killer left the body in front of the Magistry this time."

"What . . . what do you mean?"

"There was another victim between this one and Lady Dromley, one whom your Magistry concealed. Evidently, the killer doesn't want his work to remain unnoticed."

They'd lied to everyone. I gripped the bench, a splinter from the wooden slats stinging my skin. "Who was the other victim?"

"A young woman, a charitable case taken in by your Sisters of Verity. Once I found the information within the Magistry and spoke to the Sisters, they were inclined to talk. They bear a grudge against your Magistry for concealing her death, for the constraint of silence."

"Why would they lie?"

"There are many possible reasons, not least of which is an attempt to avoid a citywide panic," he said. "There may be other, less commendable causes. Those with power always have motivation to keep it."

I sprang up and paced in the confined space between bench

and table. The note caught my eye. It had already begun to crumble at the edges, as though it were centuries old, rather than hours. "What's happening to the message?"

"It will be gone by morning."

"Gone?"

"There's an aging compulsion upon it, meant to prevent any trace of lingering evidence. It may not even last that long."

How . . . unsettling. I turned my back on the aging note. "There's something else, something I wanted to tell you this afternoon before Mrs. Peters came. Someone mentioned Lord Blackburn to me in connection with the killer, even going so far as to warn me away from him. And he called upon my father today, although he shares no great acquaintance with him."

All his attention locked on me. "Who else had connections to him, aside from your Ibbie?"

"He attended all the burials, at least those of which there are record. And he called upon both the merchant and the Tarleton family. There may be more ties that I have yet to uncover."

"Why didn't you tell me sooner?" There was no mistaking the glint in his eyes—I'd stirred anger.

I rushed on. "Because I have no evidence to support his guilt, nothing except his connections to the victims and my own theories. When you told me the killer was Otherkind, I thought at first it ruled him out . . . but when I considered shape-shifting, I realized the killer could have taken Lord Blackburn's form. Yet his connections to the victims, his lack of care about being seen in connection with them—it appeared almost too obvious."

"The killer enjoys the reactions of his victims and their families. Perhaps he even gains strength from it." Riven gestured toward the missive. "The note he left you confirms it. He'd want to be as closely involved as possible. Even if your people discovered he was the killer, it would matter little to him. They can't stop him."

"Will you know if he's the killer? Can you identify a shapeshifter, if you see one?"

"No." Light kindled in his eyes, like flickers of green fire. "But I can press him to defend himself—and that will reveal the truth."

He spun to depart, and I caught his arm. "Wait."

He stared as though I'd slapped him. I released him and stepped back, alarmed by my own forwardness. I folded my hands together. "If he's not the killer, then you'll have to glamour all recall of your interactions. And what harm might that do?"

"Don't worry, I won't leave a mess behind."

"I'm not worried about that." I was concerned for the fate of Lord Blackburn if he was innocent. Riven answered to his king —would he care about hurting mortals in the process of finding justice? "If he's truly Lord Blackburn and not Otherkind wearing the lord's form, then he's suffered enough at the hands of Otherkind."

"That's for me to determine."

"Please, if you'll just wait until morning, I have the perfect excuse to call on him—some letters Ibbie procured on his behalf."

"There's no need for your involvement."

"But I'm already involved. If it's Lord Blackburn, he knows where I live, and he has full access to my home and my family." And if I was wrong about Lord Blackburn, I couldn't endure the thought that I'd set him up to face an angry fae. I needed to know that if he were innocent, he'd remain unharmed. "Wouldn't it be simpler not to force your way in? Would it hurt anything to try a gentler approach first?"

The set lines of his face suggested he'd issue a flat denial, but then he abruptly said, "We'll try your way first. I'll call for you tomorrow. Be ready."

Light coiled from him, and I closed my eyes against its burning brilliance. When I opened them, he was gone. I collapsed onto the bench, and only then did it occur to me . . . why had Riven come to the glasshouse in the first place? What had he sought?

CHAPTER 23

By dint of keeping vigil at the front window, I managed to slip from the house when Riven approached in a curricle. He'd chosen a mortal means of conveyance, rather than the Other means I suspected that he adopted when on his own, yet I could never mistake him for a mortal, not even with the veil of glamour altering his appearance.

I'd approached Father rather than Aunt Caris this morning, securing his permission to go about on some errands, and he'd readily agreed, though I wasn't certain how much he heard of my explanation.

I climbed into the open curricle, and Jade readily leapt up beside me. She positioned herself between Riven and me on the seat and surveyed the scenery.

The air around us flickered in a peculiar manner, like the shimmer of heat above cobblestones on a scorching summer day. Riven must have used some sort of glamour to disguise our passing, and for once, I welcomed it. But the concealment did nothing to soothe the agitation within.

Riven had consented to use my letters to gain admittance to

the house, which protected the servants from glamour and its possible repercussions . . . but how would he deal with Lord Blackburn, once we'd gained access?

One look at his set jaw, and I dared not ask. I'd pressed my way this far into the matter, now I'd wait and observe.

At the door, an elderly butler with skin as seamed as a walnut hull greeted us. He took our names without blinking an eye. From his impassive demeanor, I couldn't imagine much *would* make him blink an eye—perhaps not even the discovery that his employer had carried out a series of brutal murders.

Riven handed over calling cards and presented a request for an audience with Lord Blackburn, along with the tidings that we brought him an item of value at his request. To hear Riven avail himself of mortal pleasantries, when the power he held could destroy the entire house . . .

A sudden absurd urge to laugh seized me. I choked it down.

"One moment, if you please." The butler vanished into the depths of the house, leaving us to wait in the grand entrance.

The glittering chandelier overhead, the carved vines and flowers in the arch of the ceiling, and the cream-and-gold color scheme combined into a bright sort of beauty that should have cheered me. But my dread of what might lie ahead cast a pall even over this lovely space.

Riven surveyed the entry, and his eyes narrowed. As best as I could guess, he sought signs beyond mortal ken. What did he perceive? I could scarcely ask with so many possible listening ears about. A house of this size would have servants everywhere.

At last, the butler reappeared and beckoned us onward. "His lordship will see you now."

Riven stalked after the butler, and I forced myself to follow. My heart thrummed hard against my ribs. Were we about to confront a murderous Otherworldly monster or an innocent, much-bereaved gentleman?

"Miss Jessa Caldwell and Lord Riven of Elmsford," the butler intoned as we entered a large study, appointed with richly hued oil portraits and heavily carved furniture in dark tones.

Up close and with the afternoon sun slanting across his features, Lord Blackburn appeared older than I'd expected. Like a tree weathered by age but still rooted deep, he held himself erect despite the storms he had seen. A strong, craggy nose perched above a determined mouth and chin. Nothing about him indicated he was Other, but since we dealt with a shapeshifter, that told us nothing.

He looked from one of us to the other. "I don't know you, and I cannot fathom how you have something that belongs to me. I should warn you I have little tolerance for those who waste my time."

My mouth went dry, and I struggled to form words. Why wouldn't Riven speak? He just watched and waited, the air fairly crackling around him with currents of energy.

Jade sat at my feet, quiet also, assessing Lord Blackburn.

"Forgive the intrusion, my lord." I withdrew the parcel of letters from my portfolio. "I recently inherited Wyncourt from Lady Dromley, along with her papers and journals. She had among them a parcel of letters she'd procured for you, and I wished to deliver them into your keeping."

"Ah, yes. Indeed." He accepted the proffered package. "My thanks. I attempted to call to fetch them after she passed, but the dashed stratesmen wouldn't allow anyone entrance."

"I sent a letter to inquire about a meeting to return them to you." I eyed the teetering piles of paper scattered across his desk. "But perhaps it was misplaced."

"It never reached me. You could have sent a footman, no need to come yourself."

"Given the items within have a great deal of value, I wanted to see the matter properly handled."

"I appreciate your diligent efforts."

The dismissal was clear, but neither Riven nor I moved to leave. Why did Riven wait? Lord Blackburn appeared nothing out of the ordinary, but he could easily be toying with us . . .

"That concludes our business, unless I'm mistaken." His pale brown eyes locked on mine and then flicked away. "There's something else. What?"

Riven stepped forward, and the pressure in the chamber increased, like the air before a storm. "Are you aware that some believe you are the Crimson Tattoo Killer?"

I expected fury, outrage, a summons to have us removed . . . not the seams of exhaustion and pain that made Lord Blackburn's face fold in upon itself.

Jade chuffed softly, and my chest tightened.

"So that's it." He gave a humorless laugh. "How could I not know? I'm no fool, despite what my detractors say. I don't know where the rumors started, but those of my peers who wish to discredit my reform work have seized upon them. The Magistry hasn't dared question me yet, but it's only a matter of time."

"Do you want to find the truth about these murders? No matter the means required?"

"Yes, of course," he said. "I'm loyal to the people of Byren in every way—and I weary of this cloud of suspicion."

"Excellent." Riven leaned forward, and it seemed as though the air between them glistened slightly, as though some shift transpired beyond the edge of perception. "Did you carry out these murders?"

Lord Blackburn sputtered. "Of course not!"

"Then why are you under suspicion?"

"I told you, there are those who wish to discredit my name to advance their own agendas."

I rocked back. He appeared earnest, but how could we know if he spoke truth or wove a web of lies? I interjected a question of my own. "Why did you visit my father—Alden Caldwell—yesterday?"

"Alden Caldwell?" He peered at me. "Young lady, I don't even know your father, and I certainly didn't call on him yesterday."

"Forgive me, I must have been mistaken." But I knew I was not—I'd seen him, exact in every detail. What did it mean? That the killer had come to our home, in the guise of Lord Blackburn, while the true Lord Blackburn had remained elsewhere? My heart leapt painfully.

If so, how could I discern the true individual from the imposter, should we meet in the future? How would I know when to engage and when to flee? I locked my arms in front of my chest.

Lord Blackburn sagged in his chair. "You and many others."

"Tell me about the others." Unmistakable command laced Riven's words.

"A friend of mine—he's held off the Magistry—but he's told me they're building a case against me. He says they believe that I've shown up at many of the murder locations in the days leading up to and following the deaths. But that's impossible."

"What about Lady Dromley?"

"I considered her a friend, certainly a woman of sense beyond most of the lords with seats in the Assembly. She shared some of my concerns about the Otherworld. So yes, I visited her." His mouth firmed. "But the other individuals in question—no."

"Is it possible you've forgotten?" The words came silky-smooth from Riven.

"I may be getting older, but my mind's as sound as ever."

Yet I could hear uncertainty in the quaver of his voice, a hint that fears preyed upon him in wake of these accusations.

"Is it? Tell me there are no gaps in your memory. No lost periods of time." His voice was like steel now, sharp and unyielding. "Well?"

Lord Blackburn rubbed his temples. "I . . . I cannot. There are intervals I cannot recall. Times that hours have passed in a moment, and I don't know what has transpired in these . . . blanks."

"So you could be the killer."

His face became pale as parchment, and I feared he would topple from his chair. "I would never, could never."

I believed him. Unless . . . was it possible that some creature had seized control of body and mind and forced him to act, like a weapon in the hand of a warrior? Riven had mentioned a shape-shifting fae creature to Nikol, but what if he was wrong? What if it was something more sinister? What if it stalked Ainslie? My hands clenched as her confusion of the day before returned in vivid color—a lapse that had occurred right after "Lord Blackburn" visited our house. With effort, I dragged my attention back to the conversation.

"Never? You could never have blood on your hands, no matter the circumstance?" Riven watched Lord Blackburn as though he could peer through skin and bone to see the soul beneath. I'd assumed Riven meant to physically press Lord Blackburn to defend himself, but perhaps he meant merely interrogation and verbal defense.

"Anyone could, I suppose, in the right circumstances . . . but

I didn't . . . I know—that is, I believe . . ." Lord Blackburn subsided, uncertain and tormented.

The silence stretched unbearably. Even Jade sat motionless.

Lord Blackburn now lacked color even in his lips, a grayish pallor creeping over his features. Something in his face reminded me of Father after Mother's death. He suffered, and I could not bear it. However much I wanted the killer brought to justice, I no longer believed Lord Blackburn was the murderer—at least not *this* Lord Blackburn. "Could he have done it, Riven?"

I willed Riven to be forthright, to put to rest the dreadful possibility that clearly haunted the man.

"He's not the killer. You are absolved, Lord Blackburn."

The utter confidence in Riven's voice brought a tangible shift in our host. He exhaled and passed a hand over his face.

Riven continued. "Lord Blackburn, someone is framing you—and taking care to plant doubt in your mind as well. I suggest you remove from Avons for a time and make your departure public. Say you're withdrawing from the Assembly for your health, or whatever is required until the killer has been found. Make sure you have companions to vouch for you wherever you go."

"Yes, yes. I'll do as you say." He still looked haggard, as though a score of years had been added to his account.

"Good." Riven pivoted, as if he intended to leave.

But I couldn't go yet, couldn't leave Lord Blackburn in such distress. "Lord Blackburn, it doesn't matter what the Magistry or the public believes—truth will win out in the end."

"That's kind of you, but that's not the way it works. Not always."

And I remembered his wife and son, lost without answers, the truth hidden before an onslaught of assumptions. How much had that increased the pain of his loss? "Perhaps not always, but I won't rest till I find this killer."

The words slipped from me unbidden, exposing far more than I'd intended. Fortunately, he was too troubled to issue more than a token protest.

"Why should you concern yourself? It is not . . . usual for a young lady. Certainly not safe."

"Perhaps not, but this is personal to me." More than I'd ever confess to a stranger. Oh, how I hoped I was wrong about Ainslie. Yet she had one too many ties to the Otherworld to ever judge her safe, even if I discounted the letter and her recent lapse in memory. I tucked my fears deep inside and attempted to speak in a composed tone. "If you should need a place away from gossip and speculation, our home is always open, though I should warn you that my father believes you've already come."

Riven glanced between us, the faintest tightening of his lips suggesting he disapproved of the direction of the conversation.

"So someone truly is imitating me?" Lord Blackburn clutched at the edge of his desk. "On what pretext was I supposed to have called?"

"To inquire about my father's star findings and discuss concerns about the Otherworld."

"Hmm . . . my views are public and easy enough to imitate. Perhaps I have some look-alike out there, some by-blow from elsewhere in the family tree whose features are close enough to mine to be convincing." He warmed to this theme, to the possibility he might take some tangible action. "I'll set an investigator on the matter at once."

I opened my mouth to reply, but Riven cut me off. "Jessa. It's time we go."

"Wait." Lord Blackburn stood. "I don't know why the two of

you have chosen to involve yourself in this matter, but I owe you thanks—and I never forget my debts."

Riven gave Lord Blackburn an appraising look, and my stomach sank. He'd admitted he owed a debt of gratitude to a fae—what would come of it?

Riven inclined his head. "I accept."

And then he swept from the room. I hastened after him, Jade at my heels like a rear guard.

When we were seated in the curricle, once more concealed beneath the veil of glamour, I turned to Riven. "You forced him to speak with such forthrightness, somehow."

"Yes."

"Can you do that to anyone?" Had he done it to me? I recalled the times I felt a compulsion to speak, to share far more than I'd intended to divulge.

"That has no bearing on this case." Riven flicked the reins. "Besides, if you're concerned for him, he gave his permission. He clearly stated he wanted the truth revealed by any means necessary."

"I doubt he meant by having his mind laid bare!" How would he feel when he realized he'd poured forth his thoughts and speculations so freely to two strangers? I shuddered at the notion of such forced vulnerability.

"I permitted you to come." His voice was a low rumble. "I'll not permit you to question my methods."

There would be no gain in attempting to force a fae to acknowledge the error of his ways. Instead, I clutched Jade close and attended to my other questions. "Could . . . could you perceive if he spoke truth or not?"

"Yes. There's no question. I've no doubt the killer has taken his form before—and ensured the true Lord Blackburn would not show up elsewhere for the duration, thus the gaps in memory. But the man we spoke to is innocent."

"Are you quite certain the killer has taken only his form? Not taken control of his body and mind and compelled him to act?"

Either option was dreadful, but at least with the former, Lord Blackburn could take comfort that he'd had no part in the murders, even under coercion.

"All evidence points to a shape-shifter, rather than one who seeks to control the mind. Some remnants of *ilusne* remained in his house. Only the most powerful sorts of shifters use *ilusne*, those who have the ability to alter more than just their own appearance."

"Then you know the creature we seek?"

He shook his head. "Many Otherkind—as you call them—can take on a variety of forms. Some few can adopt any form they please with perfect likeness. Even fewer can wield *ilusne*. It narrows the field, but doesn't yet provide the answer. There are elements that don't fit."

If he didn't know the answer—or wouldn't share it with me—what hope did I have of uncovering the truth? I'd assured Lord Blackburn I would, but he had been our best lead. "Would it be possible to set a watch over Lord Blackburn till he leaves Avons? Do you think the killer will return to his house?"

"Perhaps. A watch will be set." Riven turned to survey me. "But I believe he's more interested in you at the moment."

The words hit like a blow, nearly unseating me. Jade gave a soft *mrow* and nudged my chin. I collected myself. "In that case, might I be of use in catching him?"

"Yes—with care."

He rumbled some low words in the fae tongue and with a snapping, sparking sort of light, a small figure emerged from the ether to perch on Riven's shoulder.

Jade's ears went flat against her head; my breath caught in my throat.

The fae was translucent gold and feminine in form, as brilliant as a sunbeam on a summer day. Her golden hair flowed freely around her as she swirled on the breeze, her long wings fluttering like miniature flames behind her.

"She's magnificent."

The little fae glowed even brighter.

A half-smile tilted his lips. "Her kind are vain enough already. They require no encouragement, however much they crave it."

A tiny spark drifted from her fingers toward Riven, a clear act of protest.

Despite the circumstances, I couldn't restrain a soft laugh. "What is she?"

"A sun sylph. They're allies of my court. She'll remain with you," Riven said. "Should the killer act, she'll alert me."

Jade glowered at the sylph.

"With your permission, *kit-isne*." Riven extended a hand toward her. "It's for the safety of your mistress."

Jade's pupils narrowed, then she condescended to give a slight bob of her head.

I studied Jade. All doting owners of pets considered their beloved beasts smarter and more personable than average, but Jade appeared to understand every word we spoke. Not for the first time, I wondered from whence she'd come, and not for the first time, I refused to consider.

Then the sylph darted to hover a hand's breadth away from my face, inspecting me as I inspected her. Despite the serious situation, despite our lack of leads, despite the fact that our best hope was that I use myself as bait for a monstrous murderer, I was enchanted by my new companion—and I should not be.

Any lady of sense might accept the necessity of protection, but what reasonable individual would find a glimmer of delight in a fae companion? Was it another sign the fae-touch altered my desires? I lowered my gaze to my lap. "Will she be able to perceive the killer, if he's in mortal guise?"

"Not as such, not unless he makes a move to threaten you. Then she'll fetch me."

So no one would intervene on my behalf, unless the danger were dire. Yet having a means of contacting Riven brought some comfort. I stroked the starflower patch on Jade's chest, and she rumbled a purr.

"Won't the presence of a sylph draw attention?"

"She can conceal herself. No one else will be able to perceive her," he said. "She won't be able to offer any direct protection though, so don't grow too bold. Our killer is powerful."

I didn't need the reminder, not after all I'd witnessed. Could I find myself branded like Ibbie? Alone as the killer approached . . . no. I refused to allow my imagination to conjure dire fates.

"You're quiet. Do you object to the plan?"

"What use would my objection be? If the killer has taken an interest in me, you cannot deter him."

"But?"

"I'm afraid." The whisper escaped without my permission. I should have restrained it, should have refrained from showing such weakness to an uncertain ally—but I could not, not when my mind filled with visions of the killer closing in, seeking my family, seeking any signs of weakness, savoring my suffering.

"Mortals should fear fae. It makes them wiser, more wary. Less likely to become prey."

"And yet he takes pleasure in my fear. He said as much."

"Yes." Riven stared into the distance, faint lines forming

about his eyes. "Not all fae are so entertained, but many are—which is why you should remain wary."

How I wanted to believe Riven was among the fae that didn't entertain themselves with mortal suffering. But did those truly exist? Could I take the word of a fae on the matter?

Either way, better to keep my emotions buried deep. I lifted my chin. "I've no intention of becoming prey to this monster. I will see him stopped."

"Good. You'll need all your resolve." He flicked a glance at me. "But you shouldn't have wasted time offering assurances to Lord Blackburn. When the killer is found, he'll face fae justice. I doubt your Magistry will arrest Blackburn, particularly if the deaths stop. But some cloud of suspicion may always remain."

"Not if I can find a way to clear his name."

"Why do you care?"

"The innocent shouldn't suffer for the guilty. If I were under suspicion and someone had knowledge of the truth, I'd want them to make it known."

"It's a wonder any of you mortals survive, blundering about driven by emotion, heedless of the dangers you heap upon your heads." Riven shook his head. "Attachments are dangerous, yet you form them with a stranger, on a whim."

"Why do you say attachments are dangerous? Aren't our connections what give meaning to life?"

"Can you say your love for your family doesn't make you vulnerable? Even now, if I were to threaten them, you'd make any bargain I required for their safekeeping. Can you deny it?"

I bit my lip. I could not, yet took some comfort in the knowledge I'd already bargained for their safety. "In one sense, perhaps, they make me vulnerable. But in another, they give me strength."

"So you say, as you hide your actions from them."

The barb sank deep. "Any concealment I undertake is for them, for their safety. And it cannot be any concern of yours."

Yet even as I spoke, I knew it wasn't the full truth. I kept my investigation and my fae-touch hidden, not only for their sakes, but also to protect myself from the sting of rejection and banishment, from the shame of having my taint exposed before those I loved.

Riven's green eyes glinted, but he only lifted a shoulder. "As you say."

I fumbled to recover. "Surely there must be something we can do to find the killer, aside from waiting for him to act."

"You may do as you please, which is what I intend." His tone forbade further questions, yet I'd no doubt he'd some plan of how to proceed.

As before, he'd been remarkably forthright up to some predetermined limit. And since much depended on his continued goodwill, I'd not press further. "And if I discover something?"

"You know where to find me."

I subsided into silence. True to Riven's word, the sylph faded as we drove, but the pulse of her presence created a faint pricking disturbance in the air around me, a sense of Other that never fully subsided, even after Riven deposited me on the front steps of my townhome and drove away.

I watched him depart. What did he mean to do next? No matter, I must act in any way I could. And I *would* find a path forward. I refused to sit around simultaneously hoping and dreading that the killer would come to me. Though that would be far better than if he targeted Ainslie first. If there was a way to uncover him before he could act, I'd find it.

CHAPTER 24

Inside, I found my sisters and aunts assembled in the drawing room, all frowning at a poor soul who appeared as though he might be a young clerk or office assistant. A sheen of sweat had broken out on his pale forehead, and he kept shoving his spectacles farther up his beaked nose.

What now?

Aunt Melisina turned her frown of disapproval from him to me. "At last you've returned. This *individual* will not depart without speaking to you directly."

"I have my orders from the Magister, my lady, begging your pardon."

A shaft of ice struck my heart. "The Magister?"

Had they deemed my interference with the case too great? Or did they suspect my fae-touch? I rubbed my temples, which suddenly throbbed unbearably.

"Aye." Another shove jammed his spectacles higher on his face. "You must verify—are you Miss Jessa Caldwell?"

"I am." Somewhere in the corner of my vision, the air shimmered, the little sylph bobbing near my shoulder. Oh, I hoped

Riven was right that no one else would perceive her. If I wasn't in trouble now, any sign of her presence would surely land me there. "What did you need to discuss?"

"No discussion, miss, only a summons to appear in court on the matter of your inheritance from Lady Dromley." He handed me a thick cream paper. "The Magister will hear all arguments and make his judgment, which shall be deemed final."

So Mr. Broward had followed through on his threat and sought to undo the will Ibbie had left. With what evidence? Of what did he mean to accuse me, in order to carry out his aims?

Jade rumbled low, glowering at the messenger as if *he* were responsible for contesting the will. He looked as if he'd like to leap from the chair and flee the room, but to his credit, he remained seated until I accepted the summons.

"What utter nonsense." Aunt Melisina arched a brow. "You've said your piece, now you may go."

"Aye, my lady." The clerk scurried from the room like a beetle from beneath an overturned stone.

But no, that was uncharitable—he only carried out his duty. I sank onto the chaise beside Aunt Caris.

"There was no need to be so cross with him, sister," Aunt Caris said. "He was obliged to deliver the message."

"He was impertinent—and he seeks to compel my niece's involvement in an altogether improper affair." Aunt Melisina's mouth twisted. "As for this Mr. Broward, I cannot fathom what he thinks he'll accomplish with these shenanigans. Most unbecoming."

"I'll need to find a barrister."

Aunt Caris pressed her hand to her chest at my words. "A barrister?"

"Young ladies do *not* engage barristers," Aunt Melisina announced.

"But if I'm required to appear in court, I must be prepared to make a defense."

"Perhaps so." Aunt Caris patted my hand. "But it would be much better to allow the trustees to make any necessary arrangements, my dear. They can sort out any defense needed."

As it happened, I did require their involvement—at least for permission to use the necessary funds, which I did not possess on my own. But would it matter to the trustees if Mr. Broward claimed Wyncourt? It would make their lives easier if they didn't have to oversee my inheritance. And whatever Ibbie had thought of them, they might well share the common view that it was improper for a young lady to involve herself in such affairs. Certainly, they'd not exerted themselves to respond to my earlier messages with any haste. Though to be fair, it had only been a few days.

I shrugged off Aunt Caris's gentle touch. "Ibbie left her work to me because she trusted me. She wanted me to steward her legacy, so I must find a way to carry out her wishes."

"I cannot fathom what she was thinking." Aunt Melisina stiffened, her back straight as a drake stem. "With one careless act, she's set you down a path toward ruin. If some taint of scandal attaches to you through this case—or if you allow yourself to be drawn into her academic concerns and become branded an intellectual—your hope of a suitable match diminishes considerably. It's not as if you have a fortune to offset such flaws. She could have done you that favor, yet she chose instead to hang a millstone about your neck."

"She didn't see it as such, nor do I. She knew I'd want to carry out her work and honor her good name."

"I'm sure Lady Dromley meant well, and I know her kindness to you." Ada looked up from her embroidery. "But her position in society and her widowhood sheltered her from society's censure. She may not have considered what her bequeathment would mean for you."

"Or for your family." Aunt Melisina lost no time in pressing upon my weak point. "Do you want to be their ruin? Do you want to see the Caldwell name blackened by your unbecoming deeds?"

Of which appearing in court would be the least. What if my choices harmed the chances of my sisters making choices for their futures? For such was the nature of scandal in society.

Aunt Melisina rapped her fan against the arm of her chair. "If you persist in making a public spectacle of yourself by engaging barristers and appearing in court, then you drag not only your own name through the mud but also those closest to you. I'd not believed you entirely devoid of feeling."

In my lap, Jade tensed, her muscles coiled as though she prepared to spring on her prey. I clutched at her and shrank deeper into the curve of the chaise. I knew well enough that I didn't conform to the expectations of my family without having Aunt Melisina constantly cast it in my face. But how could I disregard the trust Ibbie had placed in me?

"Now, aunt." Ainslie's eyes sparked. "Jessa isn't making a spectacle of herself—it's this Mr. Broward causing all the trouble. If you wish to see matters settled, perhaps you could ask Uncle Milton to speak with him and see this resolved out of court."

"You expect me to drag my husband into this unseemly affair?" She shook her head. "It's absurd. A young lady without a husband shouldn't be managing an extravagant townhome, much less overseeing excavations and sorting academic affairs. Only fortune hunters will be drawn to such a spectacle, and when they discover there's no fortune to go alongside, matters will go from bad to worse. The inheritance should be surrendered. The sooner, the better."

"Would you desire to see your wishes disregarded after your death?" Ada spoke gently, but the question appeared to nettle Aunt Melisina.

"I'd never act in such a senseless fashion."

Senseless? Ibbie had never lacked sense in her life. The throbbing spread from my temples down my neck.

Jade sprang from my lap and perched on the edge of the chaise, her gaze locked on Aunt Melisina.

"Jessa has every right to decline a bequeathment that can only blight her future. And she should have done so from the beginning," Aunt Melisina said.

"I won't dishonor Ibbie so."

"You'd rather disgrace us all?" Her voice lashed unmercifully. "Bring shame upon the memory of your mother? Were she here—"

Jade's claws flicked out and caught the lace at Aunt Melisina's wrist. She avoided sinking her claws into flesh—a small mercy—but with one tug of her paw, she unraveled the costly imported lace of the sleeve.

Aunt Melisina sprang up with a gasp. "This—this is what comes of keeping untamed beasts in one's household!"

Jade lifted her tail at a lofty angle, the jaunty curve at the end signaling her satisfaction.

I could not bring myself to chastise her. Instead, I tugged her onto my lap. "I'm dreadfully sorry, Aunt Melisina. It won't happen again."

Or at least, I hoped not.

Whatever Jade's intent, she'd effectively distracted Aunt Melisina from the matter of the court case.

Her lips pinched tight, Aunt Melisina clutched at her

damaged sleeve. "I shall return tomorrow. I expect to find more sense displayed—and that creature absent."

She swept from the room, her head held high, nearly bowling over Holden as she departed.

A storm churned within, only this was no time or place for release. Was I bringing shame upon the family? If Mother were here, what would she say?

Ainslie muttered something that sounded suspiciously like an improper word, and Ada jabbed her side. Aunt Caris shot them both a warning glance, and poor Holden acted as though he saw nothing amiss. Finally, he cleared his throat.

Aunt Caris looked wearily at him. "What is it, Holden?"

"Mr. Upton has come to call. Shall I show him in?"

Of course, a visitor *would* choose this moment to call.

Aunt Caris brushed her hand over her hair to smooth it, as if her clearly ruffled spirits might have manifested in her coiffure. "He must know we're at home . . . yes, show him in."

However undesirable the timing, Aunt Caris was far too kind to give a direct snub to a caller. I stroked Jade, doing my best to even my breathing. It would never do to display signs that an altercation had taken place.

A moment later, Mr. Upton strolled in, giving no indication he'd overheard snatches of our heated conversation—even though he must have done so.

He offered a bow to us all, but his gaze lingered on me. "I hope I've not come at an inconvenient time."

"We're always most pleased to receive you," Aunt Caris said. "Do be seated."

"Thank you, Miss Caldwell." He settled into a tufted chair of white and gold, resting his cane on the floor beside him. "I shan't detain you long—I came only to extend an invitation."

Did his gaze cant toward my shoulder? I kept my own

straight ahead, forcing myself to ignore the pinprick sensation of the sylph hovering there. If I imagined every errant glance a sign someone espied my new companion, I'd never have a moment's rest.

Ada offered him a gracious smile. "How very kind of you."

"I intend to hold a small dinner party in my home Saturday evening, and I'd count it an honor if all of you would attend."

Aunt Caris handed him a cup of tea. "We'd be most pleased to accept."

For once, I did feel pleasure at the prospect—for perhaps I could gain an audience with Mr. Upton and learn more about how the investigation was progressing with the Magistry, perhaps even find a way to broach the subject of the Otherworld.

"Excellent. My home will be honored by the presence of four such lovely ladies."

"You intend to remain in Avons, I take it?" Ainslie asked.

"I cannot leave until my business is concluded." He sipped his tea, then rested the cup and saucer on the table beside him. "And I must confess, I find Avons to my liking, despite the difficult circumstances."

Ainslie beamed. "As do I."

Then my sisters engaged him in lively conversation, and my thoughts drifted back to the killer. I needed to find another angle of approach, another way we might locate him, despite his ability to shift forms.

Would a visit to a loremaster provide any insight on the sort of shape-shifters that inhabited the Otherworld? It was dubious. Not once had I come across hints of such creatures in our libraries, nor even in the tales Mother delighted to tell of the Otherkind. While loremasters held a vast store of knowledge, if they were to impart such a tantalizing fact, the stories would have spread.

What of the Sisters of Verity? If I called, might I be able to ask them about the hidden victim? Riven said they'd been displeased with the way the Magistry had handled the situation.

Perhaps something in the life of the victim would give fresh insight . . . or perhaps the Sisters had witnessed something of note. I might not gain much insight, but it would be preferable to waiting for the killer to strike—or to call again on our home. Had he taken on the forms of others as well as Lord Blackburn? Could he? If that were the case, who could ever be trusted? I shivered.

"Have you taken a chill, Miss Jessa?"

I looked up to find Mr. Upton's dark eyes riveted upon me. To hide my face, I crossed the room to fetch a shawl. "It's a bit drafty, that's all."

"Of course." But he watched me from beneath those hooded eyes, considering. What did he know?

∽

ONCE MR. UPTON DEPARTED, I penned another missive to each of my trustees and sent them with our footman, requesting in rather stronger words that they call this afternoon. Aunt Caris had no intention of releasing me from our day at home to callers, so instead of seeking them, I must rely upon their goodwill instead. They might still choose to avoid me, but at least I'd tried.

While Aunt Caris and Ada bent over an embroidery project on the far side of the fountain, I discreetly eyed Ainslie for any signs of change within her binding mark or any hint of a tattoo. The creamy skin of her neck remained unmarred and the scar unaltered. Could her lapse in memory be related to her binding or to the killer? Either way, it boded ill—but one danger was far more pressing than the other.

Perhaps I should confide some part of my fears to Lovell. He and Ainslie planned to attend the symposium together this afternoon, and if I told him my concerns, he'd keep a close watch over her rather than let her flit about, as was her wont. Yet it would betray her confidence, not to mention raise questions about how I'd come by my knowledge.

"Why are you looking at me like that, Jessa?" Ainslie asked.

"Just woolgathering." I dredged up a small smile, then forced my attention back to my correspondence. A small spot of comfort awaited there in the form of a letter from Levina. She shared that her family had removed to their country home. Although grief still bled through her words, it sounded as though their departure from the city had brought her a measure of peace. I tucked away the missive to reply to later.

While a steady stream of callers passed through our doors, theories and fears about the killer wove through my mind like wintercreeper roots. Only with effort did I remain at my station, smiling and nodding at all and sundry.

Shortly past four, Holden fetched me, saying two gentlemen had arrived to see me about Lady Dromley's estate. Aunt Caris was occupied with her guests and couldn't protest my departure —not without drawing unwanted attention to my undesirable dilemma.

I slipped into the corridor, leaving the hum of conversation in the drawing room behind.

"I've put them in the morning room, Miss Jessa. Shall I bring refreshments?"

"I don't expect they'll stay long. If they do, you may send in a tray."

I entered the morning room to find two older men, one rather rotund, with a shape resembling the gourds that flourished in the gardens of Caldwell House, and one a lean man with hair whitening at the temples and the extravagant attire of a dandy.

The second wore an ornate quizzing glass on a gold chain, through which he examined me. "Miss Jessa, it's a pleasure to meet you. I am Sir Reginald, and my fellow trustee is Mr. Penwick."

Mr. Penwick gave a ponderous nod. "We received your message and thought it best to come without further delay. You'll forgive our lack of response to your first message; we wished to speak with Mr. Broward to better understand his claims and the facts of the situation before we called—but it was never our intent to cause you distress."

"Of course," I murmured. "I'm certain your affairs keep you quite busy. Now that you have spoken to him, what do you intend?"

Sir Reginald lowered his quizzing glass. "We found him a most unpleasant man."

"Quite," Mr. Penwick said. "But he's all bluster and bombast—he has no case at all. There's no need to worry."

"Yet I've received a court summons just this morning, which is why I wished to consult with you and receive guidance." I folded my hands in my lap. "I'm certain you'll know the best way to go about hiring a barrister to defend the will."

"My dear girl, we don't need to go that far." Mr. Penwick smiled beneficently. "Any man of sense would dismiss the matter outright, so you've no cause for concern."

"But the Magister hasn't dismissed his claims, else I wouldn't have received a summons."

Sir Reginald waved a hand. "The Magister may need to go

through the motions of the case, but any man of reason would grant that Lady Dromley possessed full control of her faculties and the right to leave her property as she wished. Penwick is right—there's no need to worry, none at all."

Perhaps the repeated incursions of the Otherworld into my life had conditioned me to find even the most mundane matters suspect, but the way they kept repeating *no need to worry* unnerved me—it reminded me of how Father had spoken after Riven glamoured him. I was certain Ibbie wouldn't have appointed men lacking sense as trustees. So why were they steadfastly refusing to take the logical step of hiring a barrister—unless more was at work than met the eye?

"Of course, we will attend court on your behalf, so you'll have no need to expose yourself to the unpleasantries there. We'll call afterward to inform you of the proceedings," Mr. Penwick said. "It's the least we can do."

"It will be a simple matter, you'll see." Sir Reginald twirled his quizzing glass. "No need to worry."

If they said that one more time . . . I pressed my lips tightly together. Perhaps it was no Otherworldly device; perhaps they only imagined that I required the simplest of reassurances repeated endlessly, as if it were a panacea to soothe overwrought nerves. My jaw tightened further still as I choked back my frustration. "I am . . . appreciative of your offer. But this is my responsibility, and I have no intention of shirking it. If you'll not engage a barrister, I'll argue on my own behalf. Lady Dromley left me a letter expounding upon her wishes—perhaps that will help."

"No one would think you shirked your duty, indeed, it's not the thing for young ladies to appear in court—much less speak before the Magister. You shouldn't even consider it."

"Then I am requesting that you hire a barrister to protect my interests in this matter."

"You simply don't understand the way these things work—not that we'd expect you to." Sir Reginald leaned forward, an earnest expression on his face. "There's no barrister needed, none at all. It's merely the petty act of a vindictive man, soon settled."

"And we'd be doing you no good turn to allow you to squander the finances Lady Dromley left for Wyncourt and Kilmere on a bit of nonsense," Mr. Penwick added.

Scathing words rose, and the effort of checking them sent the throbbing ache of earlier pulsing into my shoulders. If they did not act to protect Wyncourt and Kilmere, there would be no need for finances to steward them.

Yet what more could I do? If they refused to act, I'd have to find another way. I stood, and they both rose in accord.

"Thank you for calling. What's the best way to reach you if I have future concerns?" Not that I'd any assurance they'd take a request seriously, after their handling of this matter.

"You may send for us anytime." Sir Reginald straightened his jacket. "You may be assured we will make ourselves available."

"Am I to understand the servants' salaries and upkeep of Wyncourt will continue to come from the estate?"

"Yes, of course," he said.

"And Mr. Myles Tibbons was also employed by Ibbie." I might as well attempt to handle the other matters of business, since I'd received no satisfaction in the situation with Mr. Broward. "He requires traveling funds."

"Have him submit his expenses to us, and we will see them paid."

"And you'll find we're right in the matter of the will," Mr. Penwick added. "We'll report in full after the judgment of the Magister."

I'd not argue with them, but no report would be needed—I fully intended to appear in court myself, proprieties notwithstanding. After a small exchange of pleasantries, I summoned Holden to escort them out.

Something was amiss with the trustees, but what . . . and why? I collapsed into the nearest chair and closed my eyes, seeking to ease the ache in my head. Why couldn't anything be simple?

CHAPTER 25

In the morning, I asked Father if I might visit the Sisters of Verity. "And perhaps I'll spend some time in the library afterward. I may well be gone for the day, if you'll grant permission."

He set down his pen. "Caris believes your time better spent at home."

I could advance a number of arguments, but I settled on the one he was most likely to sympathize with. "Aunt Melisina is . . . not best pleased with me, and she intends to call again this afternoon."

"Ah, I see."

He'd received Aunt Melisina's blasts of displeasure on occasion himself, for a variety of reasons—and he always endeavored to escape her ill moods.

"In that case, I suppose there's no harm in going out. But don't take a hack—Caris says the young ladies of Avons don't often go out on their own. She rang a peal over my head the other day after I consented to you going about your errands without escort. Have Simms drive you in the carriage, and take the groom for further protection."

"Certainly, Father." I kissed his cheek and hurried from the room before he changed his mind about the possible dangers.

For myself, with Jade at my side and the sun sylph hovering at my shoulder, I felt as safe as I could under the circumstances—though were Riven here, I'd feel safer still. However formidable the Otherworldly predator, I imagined Riven could stand against him.

Simms navigated us through the crowded streets of Avons with ease, finally halting before the Kelforth Cloister, home of the Avons Sisters of Verity. It bore the gentle curves and arched domes of early Avons architecture. Many-paneled windows swept up in arches to match the tower, creating a pleasing aspect. Its gracious courtyard invited visitors—the iron gates were open wide to welcome all comers, and the lavish gardens within beckoned.

I descended, venturing into the Cloister courtyard with the groom at my heels. The fragrance of lemon balm hung heavy in the air, drifting from the extensive gardens the Sisters cultivated. It sang a somnolent song, and I blinked back sudden drowsiness as I ascended the sovstone steps.

At the top, a central door of dark wood mounted in white stone was flanked by two smaller ones, and when I approached the largest, a doorman bade me enter.

The groom took up station alongside him, evidently considering the Cloister a safe enough locale that he need not hover at my side.

As I moved deeper into the enormous pillared-and-arched entry, Jade keeping pace, a Sister with a gentle smile and a slanted half-moon scar near her right eye approached.

"How can I help you, my child?"

"I wished to speak to you about a delicate matter."

"Of course." The half-moon tightened. "Won't you come with me?"

The Sisters heard all sorts of personal and private affairs, bound to discretion by the regulations of their Order and their firmly held beliefs. She ushered me into a small antechamber, where two small chairs huddled around a table carved with a rose-vine pattern.

She took one and gestured toward the second. "Please, unburden yourself."

I sat and Jade hopped onto my lap. There was no discreet way to broach the subject, so I might as well plunge in. "I have some questions about the Crimson Tattoo Killer and his next-to-last victim, the one who sheltered with you before her death."

Her gentle smile faded. "How do you know of her? The Magistry has sought to keep knowledge of her fate hidden."

"Does not the Script say hidden things will come to light?"

"Indeed." She inclined her head. "But I possess few facts, and speculation should not be shared."

"The Magistry forbids you to speak?"

A spark formed deep in her honey-gold eyes, burning contrary to the serene exterior she otherwise presented. "The Magistry may desire that we forget Marian, but their choice to engage in wide-scale deception and so dishonor the dead means we refuse to bind ourselves by their strictures."

The Sisters were a force unto themselves, revered in society for their good deeds—and I doubted the Magistry could give a binding order for their silence, since speech was not a crime. I nodded. "I understand that you would never engage in gossip or idle speculation, nor break any confidence, but I don't ask for your opinion out of idle curiosity—it's a matter of great importance."

"Indeed." She traced the pleat of her gown with one hand. "I see this truly troubles you. We will speak further, but not here. Please, come with me."

"Thank you, Sister—"

"Margery."

"Sister Margery." I dredged up a smile.

We moved past the common areas and deep into the heart of the building. Given that I'd asked her to disregard the instructions of the Magistry, her desire for greater privacy than the small antechamber offered was logical.

We entered a small, lovely room, one wall lined with books, the other with a series of arched windows overlooking the back garden. Perhaps this was her personal space, for she moved with grace and confidence in it, and its serenity suited her own.

"While we may not bind ourselves by the whims of the Magistry, I've no wish to stir trouble with them—or with others in my Order who take a different view. Here we may speak freely." She motioned toward a chair. "Won't you sit?"

Jade and I settled ourselves once more, this time into an armchair with delicately spindled legs.

"Why does this gruesome affair concern you, child?"

"I lost someone I loved to the killer, and I've been . . . thinking about the case a great deal. When I learned one of the victims had sheltered with the Sisters of Verity before her death, I thought perhaps you might be able to shed light on what happened."

"Her identity isn't public knowledge, so I'll ask again: who told you?"

"I'm bound to keep my source confidential."

"I see." Again she regarded me with her honey-gold eyes, as though she sought some truth hidden within. "What do you wish to know?"

"Did the woman who was killed have any sort of connection to the Otherworld?"

Jade pricked one ear toward Sister Margery, as though she shared my curiosity.

"A peculiar question." She favored me with a piercing look, the half-moon tightening once more. "I'll grant that she was a bit . . . disturbed."

"Some would say disturbed individuals belong in the care of the Vigil."

What did Sister Margery believe? What she said next would guide how much I dared ask her.

"The Vigil has no place in caring for afflicted souls." Sister Margery rested her hands in her lap, calm and unruffled—at least, on the surface. "They have no compassion in them, no desire to heal or restore."

So she didn't favor the Vigil, did not venerate them as some did. "You don't believe they should confine the fae-touched?"

"We don't ascribe to such labels here. Each individual is made in the image of the Infinite. If the image becomes marred or broken—whatever the cause—we will offer whatever aid we can. Perhaps we can even be a means of restoration for some."

I inclined my head, considering her words. Perhaps I should become a Sister. At least then Aunt Melisina wouldn't hound me about becoming a proper lady and securing a husband—and the Sisters would care for me without judgment should my quest to manage the fae-touch fail. An ache formed at my temples once more.

Jade rumbled softly.

Sister Margery's face softened. "What a remarkable cat."

"She's been a more faithful companion than I could have dreamed."

The Sister reached for her, and Jade growled.

"But faithful to one mistress, I see." She laughed, then turned somber again. "Just as you must hold some things in confidence, so must I. Those souls who choose to disclose personal matters to me do so with certainty of my discretion. I'm afraid I can discuss the victim no more. Indeed, I know little else of consequence."

She'd given me nearly nothing, except the conviction that the individual in question *had* been fae-touched. Had Riven ascertained as much? Almost certainly, which meant my visit had accomplished little. If only Sister Margery would reconsider her decision to keep hidden the details . . .

A loud clatter resounded in the corridor behind us, and then the door wrenched on its hinges, slamming against the stone wall.

A woman staggered into the room and tumbled down at the feet of Sister Margery. "Please! Please! Get it off me."

Sister Margery's hand went to the emblem of her order emblazoned on the front of her gown, and her features tightened. "Miss Caldwell, please take yourself to the corridor and wait for a moment. I must assist Dreda, and I'm afraid she cannot wait."

But I could not wrench myself away, however reasonable the request, for the woman—Dreda—was fae-touched. I was sure of it. Her frantic motions mirrored the erratic, irrational movements of Mrs. Murton all those years ago, right before the Vigil took her away. A quivering sensation started in my belly and worked its way upward.

Jade *mrowed* low in my ear, nudging my chin, and I drew in a shuddering breath.

Dreda moaned. Her disheveled hair bristled from her head like corkscrew rushes; her clawlike hands clasped at Sister Margery's skirts in supplication. "You must make it stop."

"My child, I will do what I can." Sister Margery rummaged in what appeared to be a chest of simples. "Only rest."

But Dreda remained on the floor, wringing her hands and muttering inarticulate sounds.

If I could not govern the fae-touch, would my condition come to mirror hers? A bitter taste flooded my mouth, and I thought I might cast up my accounts.

"Please, please, please. Make it go."

Her distress pierced my heart, tugged me from my own troubles to hers. How could I help? I shoved aside my fear and knelt beside her. "You said you want it to get off. What do you wish to remove?"

She clutched at me, tears filling her eyes. "The creature, the Otherkind! It won't let me sleep nor rest, but always conjures the most dreadful images, day and night. Please, please get it off!"

My own eyes stung, and my chest burned. I took her clawed, grasping hands in mine and bent my head close to hers.

And then I perceived it—a glamour.

It wove its way through her corkscrew curls, concealing a diminutive Otherkind, which had attached itself to Dreda. Its translucent wings were divided into panels with dark brown strips between, like lines of lead came on a stained-glass window.

Was this what tormented her? My surroundings faded, and all that remained was Dreda, worn ragged by her suffering. Heat swept my body, and the glamour took on more detail before my eyes. Small lines and filaments wrapped around the Otherkind, binding it to Dreda.

Jade churred low.

"Don't worry, Dreda. I'll remove it."

A tear trailed shimmering down her cheek. "You will?"

"Whatever it takes." How dare this Otherkind afflict an innocent woman so? I reached forth and touched the filaments of glamour. They sparked against my hand. Had others felt the same? Surely not, else they'd not have left Dreda to suffer.

The creature lifted its head, revealing disturbingly humanoid features. From its mouth, long incisors protruded, and its enormous sunken eyes were pools of dark amber.

It drew back its lips into a snarl.

I rocked back on my heels and studied the Otherkind. Its hind limbs sank into her scalp with sharp claws. Surely it would be unwise to rip the creature out. How much pain would such an act trigger? Could it cause other damage? But if I left it alone, it would only continue to torment her—an unacceptable option.

I pressed through the strands of glamour and wrapped my fingers around the repulsive creature. My throat tightened.

It shrieked and then snapped its teeth at me.

From somewhere behind, Jade growled.

Sister Margery spoke, but her words didn't pierce the haze around me.

"You will release her," I said.

It snapped again, but unclenched its grip. It flailed its barbed legs at me, scrabbling against my gloves for some hold on the flesh underneath.

What could I do with the wretched thing?

I must confine it somehow, must keep it from harming others till I discovered what in the Crossings it was. My reticule—I wrenched it open and stuffed the creature inside. Then I drew the strings tight and did my best to ignore the unseemly bulge that wriggled about within.

Dreda collapsed against me. "You saw it. You did."

"Yes." I stroked her hair. "And it's gone—you'll be well now."

Sister Margery stared, her lips slightly parted. "How did . . . something did afflict her. I thought the fae-touch had addled her wits and conjured torments. But that . . ."

"What did you see?" I asked.

"I'm not certain—nothing distinct. After you touched Dreda, it was as if a shadow had fallen over your hand." Sister Margery clutched at the small vial she'd withdrawn from the chest, then looked at Dreda. Already the furrows in her face had relaxed and the tightly clawed hands unfolded. "I suppose this will no longer be necessary."

"What is it?"

"Just a simple tincture of valerian and hawkbit. It soothes the agitation to a degree. As I said, we do what we can, little though it may be. But you—" She broke off abruptly.

What would Sister Margery do now? The creature's glamour had kept it partially concealed, even after I'd pulled it free from its workings. Yet she'd perceived enough to turn me over to the Vigil. I'd made myself dangerously vulnerable—but Sister Margery had said she was no friend of the Vigil, and she cared deeply for those suffering. Surely she'd not spread a report of what she'd seen.

Dreda still rested her head against my shoulder, her ragged breathing becoming steadier.

The Vigil would have labeled her fae-touched, and in the strictest sense, she was not only fae-touched but also fae-tormented, unable to free herself from the parasitic Otherkind which had fed from her. But surely not all fae-touched were so afflicted? Nothing I'd ever read or encountered suggested the presence of actual fae causing the affliction.

Before I could begin to sort my thoughts, a much younger Sister hastened into the room. "Sister Margery, I cannot find—oh, I see she has come to you."

She glanced at us, in our huddle on the floor, and took a half step forward. "Do you want me to return her to her quarters?"

Sister Margery joined us on the floor and gently touched the woman's shoulder. "Are you willing, Dreda?"

Dreda drew back from me and peered up at Sister Margery, her eyes unclouded. "Yes. I should like to sleep."

"Very well, my child." She turned to the Sister. "You may take her, Sister Elaine. The Infinite has shown mercy through one of His own. I believe she'll be able to truly rest now."

When they left the two of us alone, I pushed myself up from the stone floor. "Do you have others here who share her condition?"

"I should tell you no. Everyone knows the care of the fae-touched belongs to the Vigil, no matter how much we dislike it." Sister Margery spoke slowly. "But you have given her a great deal of comfort. If you wish to see the others we tend, I will not deny you—and if you're able to help, I'd more than welcome it."

If I wished to see them? I wanted nothing more than to flee and immure myself in the glasshouse or the library, away from people, away from Otherkind, away from the roiling fears within. "If there's anything I can do, I will. Only—was Marian among their number?"

Sister Margery opened the door. "She was, and more troubled than most, poor soul. I trust you will keep that to yourself."

I nodded and joined her in the corridor. "I have only one more question—did you know Marian had been marked?"

"I wish we had, but she refused to let anyone near her. We did not wish to disturb her further, so we gave her distance, leaving food and drink and allowing her to roam the tower as long as she didn't bother the others. If we'd known, perhaps—but it's no use thinking of what might have been."

"Even if you'd known, I don't think you could have protected her."

"But we might have tried."

I couldn't argue with the sentiment, not when I felt it so strongly myself.

"You may know that we keep a constant watch over the tower. I cannot think how anyone gained access without our knowledge, let alone the killer. It has troubled me many a night. As it was, he left no trace except his mark on the stones beneath her—and her disfiguration." Sister Margery drew a hand in front of her eyes. "But now, we should cease such talk. The ladies we seek to help need no more cause for disquiet."

Together, we ascended a tall central tower, the winding stairs leading to a circular open space broken at intervals by doors. Two Sisters sat at a small table, mending clothing and keeping watch.

They rose to greet Sister Margery.

"All is well, Sister," said the taller of the two. "You've brought a visitor? Is she a relation to those within?"

Sister Margery shook her head. "No, but she may be able to render them aid. We shall see."

The doors led into small wedge-shaped rooms, comfortable and quiet. The first we entered held a woman in a state of despondency. She refused to glance at us when we entered or respond to Sister Margery. Her gaze was locked on the far corner.

Try as I may, I could perceive no glamour over her, no evident affliction. Nor by following her gaze could I detect any trace of fae-presence.

Sister Margery looked at me hopefully, and I murmured, "I'm sorry."

In the other room, a Sister did her best to calm a sobbing woman of advanced years who kept saying, "They're coming, I know they are. Why won't you listen, why, why, why . . ."

Again, no visible signs of Otherworldly affliction rested on her, no tangible glamour, certainly no Otherkind like the one who had entwined itself with Dreda. Which suggested most fae-touch came about as our lore held—by exposure to the Otherworld and its kind, to its food and drink, to its very essence—rather than some overt affliction.

If so, what might be done to help?

My heart twisted as I shuffled after Sister Margery. Her shoulders slumped, hinting she shared my sorrow. I ached to bring them relief, but I had no answers—not yet.

And if I couldn't check my own strengthening fae-touch, couldn't find a way to exist alongside it, I would join their ranks. I tripped over the threshold and faltered to a stop in the circular corridor.

Jade stood on her hind legs and nudged my fingers, which had gone icy within my gloves. I stroked her head, and they slowly warmed.

"You could see no sign of their affliction?" Sister Margery asked.

"I'm dreadfully sorry, but I couldn't. I couldn't perceive any means of relief for them, not as I did with Dreda. As much as I wish otherwise, I have no answers. But their suffering grieves me."

"I believe it does, and I'm grateful you tried."

"I . . . I wish there was more I could do."

"Your compassion alone means a great deal. Not many share it. Most believe the fae-touched chose their fate, by willfully disregarding the instruction concerning our interactions with the Otherworld. And perhaps some did."

"But you don't think that's always the case?"

"I believe there's much we don't understand—including the increase of the fae-touched in a time the Vigil claims we are safer than ever."

An increase of fae-touch? Certainly, I'd heard it much discussed, but I'd not known it had increased to a measurable degree, except among Collectors. "Have you always sheltered the afflicted here?"

"Not always, though perhaps we should have done. Sometime we may talk of how it came to pass." She hesitated, then continued. "In the end, we Sisters agreed that to follow the ways of the Infinite means we cannot abandon those in distress."

I'd never heard the Sisters speak to any sort of current event, never hint that they were dissatisfied with the rule of the Vigil, and I never would have dreamed that the Sisters acted against them, even in the smallest of ways. But her sentiments gave me hope she'd keep hidden my intervention in Dreda's case and made me feel as though I'd gained an ally, however unexpected. "I am grateful you hold that view. There's much I don't understand, but I intend to find answers."

"If you should come across anything that might aid in the future, will you return?"

"Of course."

She pressed my hand. "Surely the Infinite has smiled upon our meeting today. If Dreda continues to fare well, it's my desire to see her restored to her family—with none the wiser as to her former affliction."

"I hope it may come to pass." Together, we began to descend the stairs. "If she is well enough, please tell her she's always welcome to call on me at 68 Camden Row."

"It would be my pleasure." Then Sister Margery gently touched my forehead and spoke a familiar blessing from the Script.

A curious warmth spread through my chest, driving back the lingering tendrils of fear.

Jade purred softly, her satisfaction evident. She unbent so far as to incline her head toward the Sister.

Sister Margery withdrew. "I pray you find the truth you seek, my child. There is one thing more. I cannot promise it will hold answers, but we maintain an extensive library, along with our Brothers. Would you like access?"

The Cloister libraries were legendary, as were the restrictions on their use by those outside their Orders. If the Sisters attempted to treat fae-touch, perhaps they kept records of their endeavors. Might they also have knowledge about the origin of the Vigil and our interactions with Otherkind?

"It could help a great deal."

"Very good. Our Brothers house the library. Call upon them and tell Brother Lyndon I sent you, and I have given consent to your access."

"Thank you, Sister Margery."

Hope quickened my steps as I departed. Could the library provide insight on my affliction and the threats Avons faced?

CHAPTER 26

Within the blessed solitude of the carriage, my eyes slid shut, but I couldn't block out the forms of the distressed women. Their pain was my own, and I could not purge it.

So instead I forced myself to consider the situation rationally. Why were there more fae-touched now than before? Once it had been a rarity, but now there were three afflicted women sheltered in the Avons Cloister alone, and those were only the rare few not taken by the Vigil. How many more had been Institutionalized across Byren?

I rested my head atop Jade, her fur a soft caress against my cheek. Was this a sign that our incursions into the Otherworld were causing far-reaching damage, even to those who kept their distance?

All evidence appeared to confirm that the victims held a connection to the Otherworld. But aside from Marian, who had been marked by fae-touch, the other connections were buried deep.

Yet the killer appeared to have some way of uncovering

them. Was there any way we could use this link to predict his next victims and protect them from harm? Would Riven be able to perceive others who bore ties to the Otherworld? Even if he *could* find them, how could one fae keep watch over all who might hold such connections in a city the size of Avons?

The creature jabbed me through the fabric of my reticule, but the thick waxed canvas reinforcing it from the inside held strong. I only hoped it would keep the creature contained until I could find Riven and figure out what to do with it. I couldn't set it free to afflict someone else, but nor could I bring myself to kill it outright, since it appeared to have some degree of sentience.

"What shall I do, Jade?"

She fixed me with her steady green gaze, and I couldn't push back the thought that she, like me, had some undue influence of the Otherworld tainting her, altering her cat senses as it had done my mortal ones. What if she'd received her injury near a Crossing—or what if some fae creature had hurt her? Even were it true, how would I ever know? It wasn't as if she could confide in me.

A moment later, Simms halted in front of Belsay Cloister, which housed the Brothers of Fidelity. Once admitted, I asked if I might speak with Brother Lyndon.

In short order, a small, wizened man bounded over with unusual energy, given his age. His balding pate was surrounded by white tufts of hair like the down from a thistle, and his nut-brown eyes were set among deep furrows. He beamed when he greeted me. "Good afternoon to you, my child. How may I offer aid?"

"Sister Margery told me to seek you, and she bade me inform you that she grants me permission to use your library."

One wispy brow rose. "Did she, indeed? You must have risen

high in her esteem. We don't often welcome those outside our Orders into our library."

My reticule squirmed, and I clutched it close, willing the creature to remain hidden. I'd little time to take my usual cautions. Sister Margery had chosen not to take exception to my interest in the Vigil, and I'd have to trust Brother Lyndon shared her views on them, as she'd indicated. "I'd love to see any books you possess on Otherkind—or the Vigil."

"Would you, indeed?" A gleam of curiosity sparked in his eyes. "In my day, young ladies didn't often take such interests."

"Nor do they now." I forced an expression of calm I did not feel, given what I risked. Sister Margery cared for the fae-touched, and she indicated Brother Lyndon also carried this burden. If he knew I shared their concerns, perhaps it would allay any suspicions. "I'm concerned for the afflicted, and I felt . . . if I gained knowledge, perhaps I could help."

I did not mention I was among their number, but his gaze bored into me nevertheless. "Such compassion does you credit. Follow me."

When we entered the library, I stopped short, mesmerized by its beauty. Some skilled artist had painted the arched ceiling to resemble a brilliant sky, with a radiant sun stretching its beams across the expanse. It extended down to meet shelves of white stone, filled with books of dark leather. Polished marble set with intricate medallions that wove together the emblems of the two Orders formed the floor, and all joined together to form a harmonious whole.

Jade's ears flicked forward as she surveyed the space. The sylph maintained her position at my right shoulder, but she fluttered her wings with evident pleasure as multihued light from the stained-glass windows spilled over her. Her glow brightened, and I tensed.

But Brother Lyndon appeared to take no note, just as Riven had promised. He led me up to the third level and into a sheltered nook, which held a small table for study, tucked amid the shelves. "You will find this area contains some of the older histories."

Then he gestured to a trunk that stood at the base of the nearest window. "And this is my personal collection. You might find something of interest within."

"Thank you, that's very generous."

"It's nothing. Sister Margery and I share certain interests, and if she sent you, who am I to turn you away?" His nut-brown eyes brightened. "I must attend to my duties, but you are welcome to stay as long as you like."

When he descended the stairs, I turned to the trunk. How did the personal collection of a Brother have bearing on the Otherworld? I lifted the lid, and a cloud of dust swirled in the air.

Jade sneezed and my own nose tingled, but I didn't dare open my reticule to withdraw a handkerchief. I didn't want those sharp teeth to latch themselves onto my hand—or worse still, the creature to escape and ravage the library. So with a slight sniff, I knelt down to examine the documents contained within.

A small leather-bound diary caught my eye. I opened it to find the records of a young Brother of Fidelity. I flipped through the pages until the words *fae-touch* leapt out at me. He chronicled the fate of one Mr. Moore, afflicted by fae-touch and kept within the Cloister. Being a personal record, his account was frustratingly scant on details and presupposed a great deal of knowledge, but after several months, a favorable report caught my interest.

Mr. Moore keeps his regimen with all diligence, though

sometimes it seems to me the remedy is as dangerous as the ailment. He progresses well, though still subject to occasional attacks. They seem to occur at even the mention of the Otherworld, and we keep him sheltered from such, at his own request.

It heartens me to see him return to himself, after so many have been lost forever. His family looks with anticipation to his return home, and I have every expectation of his success.

Then the Brother proceeded to detail some of the more mundane events of life within the Cloister. No more mention of Mr. Moore occurred, except for a brief notation:

Mr. Moore has returned home, all are filled with joy.

The dates confirmed that everyone involved with his case would be long since dead and gone, but this record indicated that at least one who bore fae-touch had been restored. It was the hope I'd dreamed of finding, yet it did not relieve me as I had expected. Far too many questions remained.

What dangerous remedy had they used? What regimen held the fae-touch at bay? The Brothers had helped him, yet the Sisters seemed to have little knowledge of how to aid the afflicted. Did that mean the techniques had been forgotten?

Clearly, the Brothers had kept him far from any interaction with the Otherworld, a necessity supported by my earlier readings. Did that mean I'd disqualified myself by my continued exposure to the Otherworld?

No matter—it was a choice I'd make again. I'd simply have to find the killer, and then I could put Riven and all Otherworldly influences aside and attempt to address the fae-touch.

I placed the diary on the floor and lifted out the book that had been below it. It appeared to be a logbook, its binding decrepit and spotted with age.

With a gentle touch, I opened it to the first page. Scripted runes met my gaze, similar to those I'd seen Ibbie reference in her antiquary studies. Though she'd shown me a few of the basic components, I'd never be able to translate this dense writing.

If Ibbie were here . . .

I shut out the thought, before the tightness in my chest could give way to tears. She wasn't here, so how might I decipher the pages before me?

Jade pawed at the page with the pad of her foot and then stared pointedly at the sylph. Again, a nagging sense of unease crept over me. If something Other influenced Jade, causing her to sense things and behave in ways a cat should not . . . No, this wasn't the time for speculation about what might shape her behavior. I didn't have long to examine the contents of the library, and I must make the most of it.

What of the sylph? Was it possible she could help in this matter? How would fae know about ancient mortal languages? And if she was able to understand, would she respond to a mortal's request? I'd little to lose in the attempt.

"Sylph . . . I'm not sure of your name or proper address, but might you aid in translation of this manuscript?" I kept my voice to the lowest of murmurs, so I should appear only to be talking to myself, if someone passed by and took note—eccentric perhaps, but not fae-touched.

She brightened slightly, but didn't descend from my shoulder. Jade chuffed at the sylph, and she fluttered her wings.

What did I know of fae? They required bargains in exchange for aid—but how could I bargain when she couldn't speak? Even when interacting with Riven, she'd listened but made no audible response, only flicked her light at him. I rocked back on my heels.

The last thing I wanted was another fae bargain, but perhaps a simple exchange of favors would do the trick without the need for a bargain. She had appeared to appreciate my compliments when we met, and Riven had suggested sylphs had more than their share of vanity. Perhaps I could repay her in that form? I'd read my share of overblown poetry and dramatic narrative, so why not attempt a few flowery compliments, inspired by those sources? "Oh lovely and most luminous of sylphs, one with your great charm and exceeding beauty must surely possess great knowledge to match—would you render your aid in the translation of this manuscript?"

Her light became brilliant, and she fluttered toward the logbook. Somehow, her light—or her glamour?—shifted the appearance of the words on the page, and I could discern their meaning. "Thank you, most magnificent sylph."

She preened, clearly pleased.

And I immersed myself in what proved to be a logbook kept during a war with the Otherworld. Was it the same as the conflict the letter-writer had described? I could hardly fathom one open conflict with the Otherworld, let alone two. If they spoke to the same situation, perhaps an alchemist had kept these logs, for they used runes even in that era.

The columns were tedious, covering conditions of weather, gains and losses, terrain traversed, and the like. The simple notations gave little insight, except that the battles were extensive. Of more interest, the writer included a column regarding the Otherkind present in each conflict—he not only mentioned the ghouls and wights, but also creatures of destruction, ones who shifted form to carry out their dark works. He called them auvok.

At the very end, he'd noted: *They propose Binding. I hold the cost too great.*

After that, the log ceased.

I stared at the words. What had transpired so long ago? Could this auvok, whatever it was, be the same sort of predator that stalked Avons now?

And how had we lost so much knowledge of the Otherkind? Was it because the Vigil hid information? Or the king? Or had they also lost sight of the truth?

I gripped the edges of the logbook as though I might force the answers from it, and then a voice broke the stillness of the library.

"Step aside."

It was disturbingly familiar—Mr. Ludne was here. My mouth went dry. Why had he come? I peered over the railing.

"I must request you depart." A young Brother hurried after him. "You disrupt the sanctity of Belsay."

"I come with the authority of the Vigil. Keep out of my way." Mr. Ludne pressed forward, his heavy tread disrupting the peaceful hush that hung over the chamber.

I shrank back. I had a sylph at my shoulder and some mysterious Otherkind in my reticule, and I was poring over ancient scripts that pertained to the Otherworld. Even lacking evidence of fae-touch, he'd have enough to confine me, if he observed the signs. Quickly, I bundled the papers back together and into the trunk.

"Hide yourself," I whispered to the sylph, and she dimmed to the smallest of flickers.

I latched the lid and scurried to the nearest shelf, withdrawing the first book my fingers touched and popping it open just as Mr. Ludne rounded the corner.

"Miss Caldwell." Mr. Ludne gave the slightest of bows. "At last."

Fear prickled up my spine, jabbing as sharp as thorn-weed spines. He'd come here, seeking me? Riven had said Mr. Ludne was low in the order of the Vigil, and yet he'd not hesitated to breach the Cloister just to find me. Did that mean I'd given him cause for great suspicion? Or was it simply a declaration of power, something he did because he *could*, without a care for whom it might impact?

"You're an unusually active woman."

"I have many interests." I offered a gentle smile. "What of you? Do you often frequent the Belsay library?"

I spoke as if I'd no notion of the offended Brother, who hung back and glowered at Mr. Ludne.

"Never." His eyes hardened. "And I'm surprised to find you do."

"Oh, this is my first visit. I make it a point to call upon every library I can—each holds such a vast array of interesting materials."

His gaze dropped to the book in my hands. "You're interested in the economics of trade in old-era Byren?"

"You must admit such books are not readily found elsewhere."

"For good reason."

Again, I offered a demure smile. "However did you find me here?"

"Investigation is a necessary part of our role of protection." He clasped the raven-head cane, its heavy iron clanking against the marble floor.

Disquiet stirred. Did he mean to emphasize that they could find me and apprehend me any time they wished? "Of course,

I'm certain you're most diligent in your endeavors. But I must confess I'm puzzled. Why have you sought me?"

"I have some questions about Lord Riven."

"And they were so urgent you must track me down across Avons?"

"One never knows when it comes to the Otherworld."

At once, the room stifled me, and the sun filtering through the stained-glass windows became overbright. "What does my tenant have to do with the Otherworld?"

"That's what we would like to ascertain." The lines about his mouth tightened. "Have you observed anything unnatural about Lord Riven?"

"On the contrary, nothing could be more natural than his words or deeds." For high fae, that is. "I believe his manners are generally agreed to be pleasant and engaging."

"So you've noticed nothing peculiar at Wyncourt?"

"Mr. Ludne, if you observed nothing when you and your men gave it the most minute inspection, I don't know how you imagine I would." I forced myself to shrug. "Wyncourt is as it ever was."

"We have to investigate every suspicion in times like these—you understand."

"Of course. But where is all this coming from?"

"We received an anonymous letter detailing concerns about Lord Riven."

"What sort of concerns?"

"Those that belong to the Vigil, Miss Caldwell."

"Who made this . . . suggestion?"

"We do not divulge accusations to the public."

And therein rested the problem. Anyone might accuse and remain hidden from sight, destroying others by slander in secret.

Only in this case, the accusation was true. Who could have guessed it? Perhaps the killer? Did he seek to remove Riven from the equation? If Riven must withdraw, he could continue to kill unchecked.

I hugged the book to my chest. "Might it not be someone who simply wished to cause trouble for Lord Riven and took advantage of these tumultuous times to level an accusation?"

"It might."

Just then, the creature within my reticule gave a dreadful thump against my side and commenced thrashing about. If Mr. Ludne noticed, if he sought to examine my reticule, how could I deny him?

Jade leapt upon the nearest table and pressed hard against a stack of books, toppling them to the floor.

Distracted, Mr. Ludne looked toward her.

I tucked the reticule firmly under one arm, while the Brother gave a groan and hurried forward to collect them. "Perhaps you should take your cat outside?"

And the Vigilist too, his tone suggested.

"When we're through." Mr. Ludne turned back to me. "It's my experience that when there's smoke, there's fire. Have a care. If you should notice any signs of Otherworldly incursion, you're required to report it at once."

"I assure you, I understand my duty, Mr. Ludne." However, his views of duty and mine did not align. I returned the economic treatise to the shelf.

"I trust that you not only understand it, but also the consequences of shirking it." He studied the shelves once more, showing no sign that he was inclined to depart. "What did you hope to find here?"

"I merely wished to browse the stacks—this isn't a circulating library, so one must peruse within its walls." I beckoned

Jade, and she bounded to my side. "But it grows late, and my family expects me at home."

If he wouldn't leave without me, then it was no use remaining.

"Excellent. Allow me to escort you back to your carriage." His pale winterberry eyes glinted like frost at sunrise. "One can't be too careful in times like these."

"Thank you," I murmured. Though I'd rather have wrestled an angry karzel, I accepted his arm. I dared not turn my head to check on the sylph, nor release any of the pressure I kept on my reticule. A few moments longer, and we would be well away.

As we strolled out of the library, I considered the matter of the accusation against Riven. He possessed the ability to conceal his nature from mortals, and further, to glamour them into a sense of peace and security with his charm, so I couldn't imagine a mortal sending an accusatory note to the Vigil. Who did that leave?

Someone who was themselves Otherworldly, which made the killer the most likely culprit. Did that mean Riven had made a discovery that threatened him?

Then another chilling possibility occurred. What if there had been no accusation against Riven? What if Mr. Ludne had noted something peculiar at Wyncourt and suspected *me* of being the source? I stumbled over the last step.

"Careful." His eyes narrowed. "Is something troubling you?" There was no care or compassion in his words, only sharp suspicion.

"Nothing more than that which concerns the rest of Avons—when might this killer be caught?" I clutched his arm tighter, as any simpering miss might. "Do tell me you've found something that will lead you to him?"

"I have nothing to say about the investigation. When the killer has been caught, all Avons will know."

Mr. Ludne handed me into the depths of the carriage, which was dark as a tomb with the curtains drawn. He spoke with confidence, but what if the killer wasn't caught until it was too late? What if the killer—or the Vigil—ensnared me first?

∼

Since I was desperate to remove the Otherkind from my possession, I requested that Simms stop at Wyncourt. But Riven was out, and I dared not linger, not when Aunt Caris expected me for dinner. If I failed to appear, she might well summon the Magistry herself, in belief that I had succumbed to the attentions of the killer.

"Shall I tell him you called?" Danvers asked.

"Yes, inform him I have a matter of business to discuss at his convenience." While I wanted him kept away from my family, I also didn't want to hold a captive Otherkind within our home overnight, so I hoped he'd visit discreetly.

To that end, I escaped to the gardens right after we finished our meal. And when the shadows lengthened, I sensed him. The prickling presence of Other impinged on my awareness, followed by the distinct sun-and-storm scent that always accompanied Riven, one which I welcomed this evening.

A moment later, he strolled around the elm, light bent about him to conceal him from mortal view. My eyes strained to adjust, then he made some alteration in his working to engulf both of us within it, and I no longer struggled to perceive him.

How did he . . . Never mind, it wasn't relevant. I resisted the desire to trail my fingers across the gleaming strands of glamour and instead tucked my hands into the folds of my gown. "Thank you for coming."

"Do you have information?"

"Not exactly, but I encountered an Otherkind this afternoon."

While his relaxed demeanor didn't alter, the charged-air sensation around him intensified, as though he gathered his power to strike. "What sort?"

"I was hoping you could tell me." I described the creature to him, and the pent-up tension surrounding us released.

"It sounds like a dread-aught, a pestilent sort of creature that must feed on the blood of a host to live. Unpleasant, but no great threat to fae."

"Do they afflict Otherkind?"

"When they can. Think of them like your biting flies. They may nip and harass, and leave a stinging welt. Yet we can easily swat them away."

"And what of their interactions with mortals?"

"Mortals have no ability to repel them, and something in their saliva triggers hallucinations in your kind—visions and dreams of terror. If a dread-aught is fortunate enough to find a mortal host, they remain and feed until they drive the mortal to its death."

I drew back to the edge of the glamour that enclosed us. How much longer would Dreda have survived, if I'd not removed the dread-aught? Small wonder mortals fared so poorly in the Otherworld, if one of their minor pests could torment a mortal unto death.

"When did you encounter one?"

"This morning, attached to a woman in Avons."

He closed the gap between us. "What did you do when you perceived it?"

"I removed it." I lifted my reticule from the sealed basket I'd placed it in for extra security. "And put it in here."

He surveyed the wriggling material, and a slow smile spread across his face. It lightened his eyes to the enchanting green of spring. "You put a dread-aught in your reticule?"

"Well, what else was I to do with it? I couldn't have carried it through Avons."

His eyes gleamed. "Why not? Most mortals are blind enough to miss the whole spectacle."

Yet I was not, and the reminder of the influence of the fae-touch stung—even though in this instance I'd turned it to good purpose.

"Were you able to inquire if the woman had ventured into the Otherworld?" he asked.

"Does it matter?"

"Dread-aughts shouldn't be able to enter your world on their own, but they might attach themselves to the unfortunate individuals who choose to enter mine." He shrugged, a careless motion that contrasted with his words. "So yes, it matters."

"I may be able to ask Dreda later—I extended an invitation for her to call. But I'm not certain she'd confess if she had visited the Otherworld, regardless of the truth."

"Ah yes, you mortals and the stigma you attach to association with the Otherworld. And all the while you crave its power."

The glamour woven about us intensified, and the world beyond faded, as though I peered at it through a dark glass. I wrapped my arms around myself.

"Tell me how you removed the dread-aught." It was a command, not a suggestion.

"I just . . . pulled it off."

"I see." The speculative look on his face sent a shiver down my spine. "Did you perceive its glamour?"

"I suppose I must have done, for I found it readily enough." I didn't want him to press me about how I'd managed such a thing, so I hurried on. "What should I do with it now?"

"I'll dispose of it, unless you'd rather."

"Indeed not." With a shudder, I handed over the reticule. "While you're here, I did have one other question. Could our killer be an auvok?"

He raised a brow. "You have been busy. But auvok no longer exist, not in my world nor in yours. They were imprisoned many years ago, far from the both of them."

Was this then the creature he'd described as bound in the Netherworld? I dared not betray any knowledge of his conversation with Nikol, nor ask the questions it stirred within me. "Could it have escaped?"

"There's no escaping this prison."

But could any prison bind so effectively? I supposed if it *were* another world, with no means of passage between, it might be possible. As soon as I could, I'd return to the Cloister library and dig deeper in hopes of finding additional references to these—or other—shifters. "There's one thing more. I encountered Mr. Ludne again today."

"The Vigilist?"

"Yes. He said someone raised concerns about you, but he refused to divulge his source."

"Is that so?" His gaze sharpened.

"After I spoke with Mr. Ludne, I wondered if he truly has a source or if he acts only on his own suspicions." I omitted the part about my own fae-touch being what might have triggered these concerns. "And if he does have a source . . . could it be the killer? Who else would know you're fae?"

"Good questions. Ludne seeks to hide a great many things. His lies color the air around him." A little spark formed between Riven's fingers and danced across the back of his hand. "I'll pay him a visit."

"But he already suspects you. If you go to him, it will only make matters worse."

"How so?" He gave me a searching glance, as though he read something in the very air around me.

I wanted to step behind the elm and hide, but I stood firm. "As you said earlier, association with the Otherworld brings condemnation. If it escaped that I let Wyncourt to a fae, it would draw unwanted attention to me and my family—and that attention could land us in a great deal of trouble."

He lifted his shoulder. "You've no cause for concern. I'll go in a form he won't recognize."

"But—"

"Do you want the truth?"

If the killer had pointed Mr. Ludne in our direction, perhaps Riven would find some trace of him there. I couldn't reasonably continue to protest, nor did I believe Riven would listen if I did. So I inclined my head. "Of course. Will . . . will you tell me what you find?"

"You gave me this lead, I owe you what I uncover."

With that, he stepped from the glasshouse and vanished. I stared after him, wrestling with the knowledge that my future hinged on a fae lord behaving with circumspection in his dealings with mortals.

If only I'd more confidence he'd exercise care.

CHAPTER 27

When I finally retired that night, I struggled to force away images of catastrophe—of Riven and the Vigil locked in open conflict, of the killer creeping into our home and savoring my fear as he left his mark on me, or worse, on Ainslie, leaving me to bear the weight of another failure. I propped myself up in bed with my sketchpad in my lap and Jade at my side, drawing at a furious rate. I poured forth images of the dreadful creatures I'd encountered since Ibbie died: the ghouls, the dread-aught, and last, an amorphous shadowy being.

The shape-shifter.

I'd no knowledge of his true form, but the act of transferring his imagined image to the page unburdened my mind. Slowly, I crossed from waking to sleep.

I dreamt of a gentleman, polished and smiling. He approached me for a dance, but as he held me close, his features melted away. His form became dark and shadowed, and his clawed limbs scrabbled at my neck. Alongside my feet scarlet flowers bloomed, resembling little droplets of blood scattered in a field of green.

With a gasp, I woke.

Something rasped at the window, and I clutched the quilt to my chest. Wait, it was only the limbs of the oak brushing against the pane, as though it sought to gain entrance. For some time, I listened to the sweep of its boughs, its gentle song. I couldn't bring myself to strengthen the cage of thorns, not when the oak sang of earth and water and sunlight and growth, all the things belonging to the realm of life.

With the moonlight bathing my face and the song of the oak in my ears, I drifted back to sleep. When I woke again, the sun poured into my face—the hour had grown late.

I completed my ablutions in record time and hurried down the stairs, reaching the breakfast table just before the servants cleared away the dishes.

But any hope of returning to the library today—or of calling on some of the other victims' families—soon evaporated. Father was out and Aunt Caris promptly wrung from me a promise I'd stay home until we attended dinner with Mr. Upton this evening.

I occupied myself the best I could, but as the day unfolded, it became apparent none of us were at our best. Evidently, the tension sweeping Avons had affected us all. Ainslie ruined her best hat attempting to remake it, Ada thumped tumultuous tunes on the pianoforte, and gentle Aunt Caris snapped at her lady's maid when the unfortunate soul scorched the gown she'd intended to wear to the dinner party.

After I'd shattered one of my favorite vases while attempting to assemble a bouquet for belowstairs, I escaped to the gardens. I sat on the bench and let the soft breeze caress my face. The welter of emotions refused to subside, but at least I wasn't subjected to the turmoil of my sisters and aunt as well as my own.

Part of me hoped Riven would appear. He'd said he'd return to inform me about his conversation with Mr. Ludne, yet most of the day had passed, and he'd made no appearance. Had something gone dreadfully wrong?

I couldn't just sit and worry, so I fetched my writing supplies and penned a brief missive to Mr. Tibbons, instructing him to apply to my trustees for his expenses. I added that he was to continue investigating whatever Ibbie had wished him to and report to Avons if he uncovered anything of note.

When the sun concealed itself behind a bank of charcoal-colored clouds that roiled on the horizon, I returned to the house to prepare for dinner, consoling myself with the knowledge that I'd have an audience with Mr. Upton tonight. One way or another, I'd find an opportunity to speak with him and gain answers. And if he refused to be forthright, I'd explore what I could of his house.

If the killer had impersonated others involved in the investigation like he had Lord Blackburn, then he may well have visited Mr. Upton's home. Perhaps I could find some scrap of evidence that Riven might examine more closely. I could also ask Mr. Upton directly if he'd ever experienced gaps in memory.

After Lianne styled my hair, I dressed in an ivory gown while Jade watched, contemplative. When I crossed to the door, Jade bounded ahead of me and planted herself firmly in front of it. She refused to budge until I consented to bring her along.

Perhaps it wasn't quite the thing, but I didn't think Mr. Upton would object. I collected my wrap and gloves, and together we descended the stairs to where my sisters and Aunt Caris awaited.

We passed the short drive in relative silence, and when

Simms halted before Mr. Upton's townhome, we found it as well-ordered as his person. The dark red door contrasted with the pale sovstone and modern white trim, and symmetrical columns of windows marched up the front of the house in glittering array.

The butler ushered us into a sumptuously appointed drawing room. Avons favored deep, rich colors for decor, and someone had designed this room in perfect keeping with the current style. Furnishings, rugs, and even curtains were all in hues of burnished gold and crimson, kept from overpowering the room by cream wallpaper lightly patterned with medallions of palest gold.

Mr. Upton stepped forward and greeted us with warmth. As promised, it was a small gathering—our family made up the majority of the women present. Mr. Upton had included a few familiar faces, Mrs. Winters, an acquaintance of my aunts, and Mr. Burke among them. Evidently, his work with the Magistry had given him some closer tie to Mr. Burke, if they also mingled socially.

I didn't have to inveigle an opportunity to speak with Mr. Upton. When I stepped across the room to examine a landscape hanging on the far wall, he approached. "How do you find my home?"

"It's lovely." Though the color scheme didn't match my own preferences, an artistic eye had pulled it into a pleasing whole. "Who designed it?"

"I oversaw it myself. I've long since learned not to trust important tasks to others."

"Mr. Upton." I lowered my voice. "I know you warned me to exercise care when it comes to the killer, and I respect your view. But I have come across some disturbing information, and I must ask—have you experienced any lapses in time? Any moments that have slipped outside your recall?"

The lines around his hooded eyes etched themselves more deeply. "Why do you ask?"

"Because . . . it's happened to others who have concerned themselves with the case."

He scrubbed the back of his neck with one hand. "You're certain it's the act of the killer?"

"Quite certain."

"Blast."

I kept my gaze on the landscape so that we might not draw undue attention. "It's happened to you?"

He gave a clipped nod. "I'd chalked the oddities up to the strain of my endeavors or the rare overindulgence. But this—"

Before I could inquire further, Aunt Caris linked her arm through mine. "What a lovely painting."

"My thanks." Mr. Upton gave her a slight bow. "I procured it from someone who no longer required it and count it an excellent find."

With that, Mr. Upton excused himself to speak with his other guests. He'd not even begun to answer the questions that crowded my mind. Somehow, I must find another moment alone with him—but it proved difficult. We were soon summoned to the dining room, where the table was elaborately set. A cobweb lace covering rested atop a creamy linen underspread, and an enormous centerpiece of deep red roses in an epergne of silver sprawled across the table.

Like the decor, the meal was well planned. We received delicately seasoned soup, herbed fish, perfectly roasted joints of meat —an endless succession of pleasing dishes accompanied by meandering conversation.

Toward the end of the meal, two young gentlemen led the

conversation to the matter of the killer. "Quite a shock to find a body before the Magistry. What do you say about it, Burke?"

"I say it's not fitting dinner conversation." His kestrel-sharp eyes bored into the man, and he wisely subsided.

But his companion, more than a little in his cups, jabbed his fork in the general direction of Mr. Burke. "I say the citizens should take the lead. You at the Magistry have had your chance. If we all rise up together, surely this monster doesn't stand a chance."

"I can think of no course of action more reckless," Mr. Burke said. "Nor more guaranteed to cause trouble."

"I've heard rumor the Vigil has gotten involved," the first gentleman added.

"About time someone did something," the second muttered.

It was scarcely a fair remark, given the labors of the Magistry—and the opponent they faced.

Mr. Burke sipped his wine, his hand clenching tightly about the cup. To his credit, he refrained from comment.

Meanwhile, Aunt Caris fidgeted with the linen napkin in her lap, her strain evident. This careless conversation stirred her fears afresh.

We received a momentary reprieve when the butler brought in the final course of fruits and sweetmeats. Before the gentleman could press further on the subject of the killer, I interjected. "Mr. Upton, I couldn't help but notice you have a lovely pianoforte in the drawing room. Might we have some music after dinner?"

"I'd like nothing better—if one of you ladies could be persuaded to play."

"Ada has quite a gift with music." I looked at her pleadingly.

And as always, she rose to the occasion. "I would be delighted."

"Excellent."

As though they perceived my line of thought, Ada and Ainslie took the lead on further conversation, discussing various schools of music and instrument preferences until the meal concluded.

Then Mr. Upton stood. "Let us retire to the drawing room."

While the other guests appeared enthralled by Ada's music, Mr. Upton looked distracted. Halfway through the second song, he slipped from the room. Without a moment's consideration for the proprieties, I followed, Jade trotting alongside. If I didn't seize this opportunity, I might never find a chance to speak with him alone.

A faint scuffle sounded down the hall—Mr. Upton? At the end of the corridor, a door stood ajar, leading to a well-lit study. In one corner, a rosewood desk stood, its expansive surface devoid of the usual papers and writing implements. The only item on its surface was a translucent vase that appeared spun from strands of glass. Inside, a collection of small items glittered in the gaslight.

Mr. Upton wasn't here—perhaps I should go. The room felt . . . wrong in some way, as though it were an imitation of a study, rather than the actual thing.

But as I turned to leave, a flicker of red within the vase caught my eye. What in the Crossings? I stepped forward to examine it more closely.

Oh.

A band of iron tightened around my chest, and I couldn't breathe. Amid a jumble of other trinkets rested a ring that resembled Ibbie's signet, the one she never took off, the one the Magistry had claimed was missing when they found her body.

With frigid fingers, I reached forward and plucked it from the vase. Around the band ran the scripted initials *IDM*.

It was Ibbie's ring.

The flicker of red and gold blurred before my eyes, and my heart thrummed in my ears.

Flee . . . I should flee.

But if I did, I might miss something important, might miss my only chance to bring about justice for Ibbie.

With shaking hands, I laid the ring upon the desktop. One by one, I lifted the other objects from the vase and set them across the polished surface.

Ten items.

Ten victims.

Bile burned the back of my mouth, and I pressed my fingers to my throat. I couldn't lose control, not now. I needed to restore the items to proper order, to return to the party and pretend nothing had happened.

But I could scarcely draw breath, let alone force my limbs into motion. Aunt Caris, Ada, and Ainslie were all here, all vulnerable. Never mind pretending nothing had happened, we had to leave—now.

Yet we also needed to depart without attracting attention. Could I plead a sudden headache? I certainly had one. Swiftly, I collected the items and restored them to the vase. Then Jade growled.

The gas lamps dimmed.

And he spoke. "Jessa. I've been waiting."

Time stopped. My limbs became leaden, as though I'd fallen into a nightmare from which I couldn't escape. Only this was no dream, and I could not wake to find relief.

Slowly, I turned to face the voice.

Mr. Upton stepped from the shadows. "It seems you've wandered astray. You're far too curious for your own good."

"I did—I do have questions."

"I rather thought you might. Indeed, I hoped it. I've dreamt of this moment since we first met."

When we'd first met, he'd said: *I wished to speak with you . . . before your blood ends up on my hands.* I'd thought it a warning, but it was a promise. Now I knew—the whole time I'd sought the killer, he'd stalked me, waiting to draw me into his snare.

How had I not considered Mr. Upton as the killer? How much influence had he exerted over me to prevent that line of inquiry? I couldn't restrain a shudder.

Jade stalked closer to Mr. Upton, her fur bristling.

Did he know that I'd seen the tokens he kept on his desk? How could he not? He may even have watched from the shadows as I'd removed them from the vase. And it seemed he thrilled in my discovery . . . in my *delicious fear.*

The tattoo of crimson that I'd sketched time and again seemed to fill my vision until it overlaid the entire room. Lines and patterns, marks and swirls destined for my body.

"I'm sorry to disappoint, but I'm afraid answers must wait." Somehow, I steadied my voice, taking refuge in conventions for once. "I've developed a headache and must retire for the evening."

"How unfortunate. I've found this gathering a welcome reprieve from the tedium of the past few days." His sharp winter-wind fragrance swirled between us. "I plan to hold another two evenings hence—gentlemen only, I'm afraid. Only a select few will receive an invitation."

As doubtless intended, his words chilled. I backed into the corner, hemmed in by Mr. Upton before me and the desk behind. Its curved edge dug into the small of my back. "I'm sure they'll be most pleased."

But it was a gathering that would never happen, not if it

remained in my power to prevent it—which I began to doubt. If only the sylph would fetch Riven.

But she hovered at my shoulder as always, no sign of change within her. Riven had warned me she couldn't perceive the killer, not while he remained in mortal guise. The desire to bid her to fetch Riven rose within me, but I choked back the words. I couldn't be sure she'd listen, and I dared not give away her presence. Or did Mr. Upton perceive her already?

He closed the distance between us. "I expect they will. But gentlemen don't possess the delightful range of emotion ladies do. Nor, of course, their beauty."

Jade didn't have the reservations of the sylph. She snarled and lunged at him, her muscles coiled, her teeth bared.

Swift as the strike of a snake, he snapped an ungloved hand around her neck.

And she collapsed.

I choked back a cry. Every sinew yearned to run to her, but Mr. Upton stood between us, blocking my way. Perhaps it was an illusion brought on by the flickering flames of the dimmed lamps, but it appeared as though small barbs protruded from his fingers.

Had he poisoned Jade?

I braced against the table, its solid form holding me upright. "What have you done to her?"

A smile twisted his features. "Given her cause to think twice before attacking her betters."

Jade moaned and strained to rise, to no avail. I had to get her away from him, to tend her before it was too late.

My cage of thorns frayed, the vines becoming translucent. In the distance, whispers gathered, pressing against my awareness, growing in strength. I pressed my fingertips to my throbbing temples.

Not now, please not now.

"Don't worry, Jessa." His smile grew. "She'll recover—unless you give me cause to dose her again. Then she'll die."

With that, he reached out and stroked my neck in the exact place where Ibbie had received her tattoo. His skin was smooth now, cold against my own.

Again bile rose.

But I held perfectly still, even as the whispers crept through thorned vines, and the room swayed about me. He craved my fear, but I'd not give him the satisfaction. I'd not struggle against him, nor give way to tears. Instead I would pretend ignorance. I would present the front of an offended young lady insulted by an over-familiar cad—rather than a potential victim terrified by a would-be-killer. It might not work, but it was worth a try. And I must act, before I lost control.

Before he made his mark.

His fingers caressed my throat.

I straightened and stepped away from the desk, which brought me closer to the one who had taken my beloved Ibbie and left so many families broken and bereaved. To the one who derived pleasure from my pain and that of countless others. To the monster.

Less than a handbreadth separated us. His frosty scent sharpened, sliced across my senses.

I met his gaze squarely.

And then I slapped him.

Oh, it felt *wonderful*. My fingers itched to repeat the strike, but instead I glared at him. "You, sir, are no gentleman. Unhand me at once!"

He allowed one finger to trace the line of my jaw, then he withdrew. "As you desire."

Fury fueled my feigned outrage. "I cannot fathom why you

imagined I'd accept such advances—to think nothing of the threat to my cat. I must insist you cease all such improprieties and step out of my way."

"Oh, Jessa. You're a delight." Slowly, his eyes transformed into pools of black, as though the pupil swallowed the white and the iris alike. "One day, you'll receive my attentions as you should. But clearly, more time is needed."

Wait . . . had it worked? One look into those black orbs, and I knew better. If he released me, it was because it fit into his schemes somehow.

"You'll wish to collect your family, no doubt. Since you've taken a headache."

He stepped aside, and I rushed to Jade. In an attempt to comfort, I stroked her fur. Her breathing came heavy and labored. Her tail twitched, ever so slightly—otherwise, she did not move.

A wave of heat coursed through my body. How dare he inflict such pain for his own perverted pleasure? He'd stolen so much already, and now he'd left Jade fighting for her life. Though I had no weapon, I was tempted to fly at him again.

For he gloried in her suffering, that much was clear. He stood towering over us, and then he inhaled long and slow, as if he drank in my distress.

I had to bring him down. But how?

Even had I a weapon at hand, I couldn't hope to fight Otherkind outright. Nor could I seize the evidence against him, with him hovering over us . . . but if I left, he'd only conceal it. Mr. Burke was present. If I cried out, would he hear?

Perhaps he would, but it would almost certainly provoke Mr. Upton to act. Better to survive to report to Riven. The Magistry required proof, but Riven would not. He could ascertain for himself the nature of Mr. Upton.

But if Mr. Upton knew about Riven, he must be aware of the risks of allowing me to report to him. So why would he release me? Was it part of his game? The thrill which he required?

Jade attempted a slight nuzzle of my hand, and my eyes stung. We needed to go, while we still could. Somehow, I hefted her limp form into my arms and conjured some semblance of calm. "Thank you for dinner, Mr. Upton. Now, if you'll excuse me—"

For a long moment, he did not move.

Was he reconsidering? Would he attack me here and now, with a house full of servants and guests?

Then he offered a slight bow. His teeth flashed white in the dim, like fangs. "Of course. Sweet dreams, Jessa."

CHAPTER 28

I stumbled over the threshold to my bedchamber, Jade an unwieldy burden in my arms, but one I'd willingly carry to the Fens and back. I'd no notion of how we'd gotten home, of what disjointed explanation I'd managed to stammer to Aunt Caris about Jade, indicating her limp form and the need to get her home. I'd wanted to shout to everyone: *run!*

But such an act would only have marked me a madwoman—and done nothing to protect the other guests. In fact, it might well have incited Mr. Upton to act.

My skin still prickled where he'd touched me, and I glanced in the looking glass to be sure. No tattoo marred my skin, not yet.

But I must talk to Riven at once.

Aunt Caris would never let me leave the house in the middle of the night—she'd taken to having Holden lock every door and window as soon as darkness descended. Nor did I want to abandon Jade. I draped her over the pillow on my bed. The scant rise and fall of her chest was the only indication she lived.

Perhaps Riven would come, perhaps he'd meet me in the

glasshouse as before. Would the sylph summon him, if I laced my words with sufficient flattery? "Oh most luminous and lovely sylph?"

To force the light compliment caused an almost physical pain. But her glow brightened.

"I have need of Riven. It's about the killer, and it's urgent. I believe he entrusted this matter to you—will you summon him? Ask him to meet me in the glasshouse?"

Her light pulsed thoughtfully.

"I have no one to rely on except you, brilliant one."

She brightened, and then in the blink of an eye, she vanished.

Cold to my core, I curled around Jade in the bed and drew a coverlet over us both. She did not stir, and the tightness in my chest nearly suffocated me. I'd dragged her into danger, and she suffered for it. What if Mr. Upton had lied? What if he wanted to raise my hopes, only to dash them cruelly with her death?

I didn't dare dose her with anything, not without knowing what ailed her. So I could only wait—and hope. I buried my face in her fur. How long would it take Riven to arrive? The sylph must find him and rouse him, and then he must traverse half the city. Surely I could linger with Jade a bit longer before I must go to the glasshouse.

I whispered prayers for her recovery as I held her close. I couldn't chase away the images of Mr. Upton reaching for her, his hand closing about her neck. He could have crushed her spine.

Yet he'd chosen to keep her alive, keep the game going. He'd toyed with her, as he did all mortals. Had he ensnared the true Mr. Upton as he had Lord Blackburn? Or had there never been a true Mr. Upton, only a form and identity invented by the shape-shifter, one he occupied when he didn't need another?

How he must have delighted in pretending to render aid to the Magistry, while leaving victims in his wake. What did he intend next?

He'd invited me to his home, clearly hoping I'd discover his identity. Did that mean he'd wanted to force a confrontation? If so, for what purpose? He'd made it clear he wasn't done with me and—

Strong hands closed about my shoulders and pulled me from the bed.

My pulse leapt. I gasped, unable to voice a cry in my terror.

But it was only Riven.

His light coiled around me, glorious and golden and altogether Other. This time, I did not fight against it, and the light bathed my body in warmth. For the first time, the chill of my encounter with Mr. Upton began to dissipate.

"You're not hurt." The tight lines of his body relaxed, and the light withdrew.

Perhaps it was only the influence of his glamour, but I could almost imagine he'd been concerned for my safety and was relieved to find me unharmed.

"You weren't in the glasshouse. I thought—you summoned me, using the sylph, no less. Why weren't you there?"

The sudden edge to his words cut deep across my raw emotions. "I'd no notion you'd arrive so soon, and I didn't want to leave Jade until I must."

I should have considered he had some Other means of transport, given how he seemed to appear at will—I should have done so many things differently. I dropped my gaze to the floor, following the even march of the boards as they vanished beneath the bed. Oh, I wished I could hide so from the world and its horrors, wished someone else would make everything right, wished that I could emerge to find all restored.

"What happened, Jessa?" This time, he spoke more gently.

"I'll tell you everything, but first . . . he's hurt Jade, and she may be dying. Will you help her?"

He didn't attempt to bargain, nor did he insist upon receiving my information first. He leaned over the bed and traced one finger along Jade's jaw, his touch surprisingly light.

She didn't move.

"My skills don't lie in the healing arts, but I'll do what I can. What injury did she receive?"

"I . . . I don't know. She tried to attack him. Then he gripped her neck, and she collapsed."

"She did not change?"

"Change? No, she fell at once. He moved with unnatural speed."

Riven shot me a sharp glance. "You don't know."

"Know what?"

"It's of no consequence." He turned to regard her once more, and I didn't press for answers. I didn't want to distract him from tending Jade, but later . . .

His brilliant light settled over her, a semitranslucent veil. The shift in its colors as it swirled about her body appeared to tell him something. When the light returned to him, he said, "It appears she's fallen victim to some sort of paralytic venom. Once it wears off, she should return to herself. She might be weak for several days, though."

I collapsed onto the edge of the bed. At once, I could breathe again. Think again. "So he told the truth."

"This venom could not have come from your world." He crossed his arms. "Who did this?"

"It was the killer."

"You found him?" A muscle in his jaw leapt. "The sylph said only that you had information."

"In a manner of speaking. I think he wanted me to find him and made it possible by inviting me to his home." With that, I spilled forth the tale, recounting my interactions with Mr. Upton from beginning to end in as much detail as I could manage.

As I spoke, any trace of the kindness I'd thought I'd glimpsed when he attended Jade vanished, leaving in its place something remote, detached, and distinctly fae. The prickling sense of Other gathered and strengthened.

"It was fortunate you denied your fears and defied him. I'm not certain he would have left you unmarked otherwise." Riven strode to the window and stared out into the black of night. "If I guess correctly, his purpose in tattooing his victims is to feast upon their fear as they wait in terror of death."

I curled closer to Jade, resting a hand on her motionless form. "He said that more time was needed before I . . . received his attentions as I should. What do you think he meant?"

"That you did not display enough fear or respect for his power. That he intends you to understand its extent before he makes his mark." Riven released a spark of light, and it skittered across the windowpane. "He may seek other, more susceptible victims in the meantime. His hunger grows."

I pulled my legs to my chest and stared at the bedquilt, its patterned flowers and vines blurring before my eyes. "Then what should I do?"

"Nothing. You're mortal, you have no means of defense. You amused him and escaped unscathed—this time. You may not be so fortunate in the future." He kept his attention fixed on the gardens below, his back toward me. "I'll go after him tonight. Now that he's revealed himself, there'll be no means of escape. It won't be long until this is behind you."

His words should have brought relief, yet they were flat and emotionless, and they left me unsettled. Why couldn't fae deign to display some sense of feeling?

I stroked Jade, keeping my touch whisper-soft. If she could somehow sense my nearness, I wanted to reassure her—and myself. "But won't he abandon his Upton guise now that I've seen him in it?"

"Possible, but unlikely. I think he's grown stronger as he's feasted in your world—and now he seeks a greater thrill."

"And you'll confront him alone?"

"I've faced far greater odds before."

Part of me wanted to argue, but what good could I do in an Otherworldly conflict? Still—I couldn't rest without some sort of reassurance that Riven had dealt with him. "Will you tell me once it's done?"

"If you stay away from Upton till then."

"Agreed."

The binding mark on my arm tingled and the warmth spread toward my shoulder. To distract from the disquieting sensation, I said, "One more thing—you never told me about Mr. Ludne. Do you think the killer approached him?"

"There was the faintest trace of *ilusne* around his home. It's possible the killer borrowed his form. He refused to admit to any gaps in his memory, but the cloud of deceit around him was so strong—it's difficult to say. Another explanation might be that the killer visited to see what information the authorities possessed on his actions. A sort of morbid entertainment."

At this juncture, it scarcely mattered whose form he'd borrowed in the past, if we could only stop him before he hurt someone else in the future. If Riven could remove the killer from Avons to face whatever justice the fae would mete out, my family—and all the other families within the city—would finally be safe.

At last Riven turned away from the window, and my breath caught slightly. I'd thought him remote before, but now he looked wholly detached, wholly Other. Light limned his features, the lines of his face were drawn sharp and distinct, and his eyes were a shade of darkest green that did not belong to our world. Only a small veil remained over the power charging beneath the surface. "I believe he wants open confrontation—but it is a guess, not a certainty. Be on your guard."

I couldn't speak, only nodded as the prickling sensation of Other became a raging storm around me. Before he left, I somehow gathered my courage sufficiently to whisper, "May the Infinite bless your steps."

A slight nod, and he was gone, the storm-charge of power with him.

CHAPTER 29

Not long now, not long...
    Time and again, I reminded myself of the reassurances Riven had offered. Not long, unless he was mistaken. Unless his considerable powers proved insufficient. Unless Mr. Upton had dealt him death, as he'd done the others—fae and mortal alike.

Somehow I'd slept, but my waking hours passed with agonizing slowness as one dire possibility after another presented themselves to me.

I crumbled a teacake into small pieces.

And still the minutes crept onward, the mantel clock endlessly ticking them away. I choked down a sip of tea, but it failed to calm my churning stomach.

Aunt Caris swept into the room and pressed a kiss to my head. "Are you still worried about Jade, my dear?"

I looked down at the bulky form ensconced in a basket at my feet. "I believe she'll recover, but it's difficult to see her so unwell."

And harder still to know I was the cause, but I couldn't think of it, not if I wished to retain my composure. "Shall I read from the poetry collection Ada bought?"

She beamed. "That would be lovely, my dear."

"My favorite is in the middle," Ada said. "Shall we start there?"

"Indeed." I did not much care, as long as I could attempt to distract myself.

But before I could begin, Holden appeared. "Mr. Burke has called, Miss Caldwell."

Aunt Caris sighed. "Does he wish to speak to Jessa again? One would think the Magistry could find a better course of action than harassing the innocent."

"No, Miss Caldwell. He's requested to see the ladies of the household together. Shall I show him in?"

She straightened her shawl. "I suppose you must."

"What in the Crossings can he want with us?" Ainslie asked.

Ada smoothed her skirts. "We'll find out soon enough. I very much doubt he intends to conceal his purpose."

When Mr. Burke strode in, a faint hint of soot and smoke wafted from his clothes, a harbinger of some disaster.

My throat tightened at the smell.

"Mr. Burke. Won't you take some tea?" Aunt Caris inclined her head.

"Thank you, but no." An unmistakable air of weariness hung over him. "I trust you'll forgive the intrusion, but I come bearing ill news. Late last night, Mr. Upton's home burned down."

Aunt Caris gasped, and it was echoed by Ada and Ainslie. The tightness moved from my throat to my chest, as restrictive as a band of iron.

"I trust he escaped unharmed," Aunt Caris said.

"I'm afraid not. His body was found amid the rubble." Mr. Burke straightened with visible effort. "We're speaking to everyone present at his dinner party last night to see if we can determine the cause. It may well have been an accident, but the fire was particularly virulent."

Ainslie paled. "How dreadful."

"And to think, only hours before, he hosted us all. Such a pleasant gentleman to suffer such a terrible fate." Aunt Caris shook her head.

I rubbed my chest, but the band refused to loosen. I could offer no condolences as the others had, not when I knew his true nature. Only . . . the killer was a master of illusion. I shifted uncomfortably. "Are you certain the body was his?"

Aunt Caris pressed her lacy handkerchief to her mouth. "My dear, I hardly think we need to know."

Mr. Burke ignored her, and his kestrel-gaze locked on me. "Who else might it be?"

"I only meant . . . a fire can cause a great deal of damage. Could there be a chance it was one of the servants or a guest who stayed late? Could he have survived—perhaps dazed by the fire or injured and in need of care? Has there been a search?"

"You're correct that the body was unrecognizable. Given the intensity of the fire, we're guessing at his identity. But the body bore his watch and signet, and it was male. So it seems a reasonable assumption—unless you have reason to believe otherwise?"

"I . . . I only wondered."

"I wonder too." His tone was grim. "Many things."

I ignored the implication, my mind spinning with possibilities. Was it fae justice to kill the murderer and destroy his body? But why then burn down the entire house? To conceal the true cause of death?

A virulent fire seemed altogether too careless and uncontrolled to fit what I'd observed of Riven. But what was the alternative? Had Mr. Upton somehow trapped Riven in the blaze?

Was it *his* body left in the rubble and decorated with Mr. Upton's belongings? My eyes slid shut.

Though I couldn't fathom Mr. Upton outmatching Riven, I knew nothing of his true form and nature, beyond his ability to shift. What was the extent of his power?

As from a distance, I heard Ainslie ask, "What about the servants?"

"Some escaped. Others were not so fortunate."

Then Riven *must* not have set the fire. I refused to consider that he might have carelessly dealt out mortal deaths. But then I remembered his face the night before, the wild faeness of his features. If the fire brought justice to the killer—as his king commanded—would he care about mortal casualties, however innocent? I sipped at my tea in a vain attempt to drown the lump in my throat.

Mr. Burke took the chair across from mine. "I must ask. Why did you depart so abruptly last night?"

I gestured toward Jade's motionless form. "My cat was taken ill. I wanted to return home to tend her. As you can see, she still suffers. I'm afraid that rather overshadowed the evening for me."

He was dissatisfied with my explanation; I read as much in the tight lines drawing his mouth into a frown. "You were away from the other guests for some time before your departure."

"Sometimes I weary of company. I sought refuge in the study."

"Mr. Upton was absent as well."

Aunt Caris shot upright. "Are you accusing my niece of some . . . impropriety?"

"Not impropriety, no."

"Then you'd do well to watch your words." Her color heightened till she appeared a rose in full bloom. "Simply because she doesn't delight in roomfuls of people doesn't mean she deserves to have her reputation tarnished."

"Perhaps not. But I must know: did Upton offer you some insult?"

How could I possibly answer that? I must be honest, else if he somehow uncovered the truth elsewhere, I'd be far more suspect. Heat swept up my cheeks. "He did come across me in the study, and he appeared to believe I'd . . . welcome his attentions. But when I made it clear I did not, he didn't attempt to detain me."

Something flickered in his eyes.

Aunt Caris half-reached for me. "My dear, why didn't you say something? To think we were so misled as to his character, that you endured such—"

"I didn't want to trouble you, not when I'd dealt with the situation. I felt we understood one another at the end. And I didn't want any scandal."

Mr. Burke gave a slight nod. "I regret that you suffered his unwanted attentions, and even more if my questions have caused you pain, but I could not overlook your absence, nor his."

"I understand." And I did—what kind of investigator wouldn't attempt to piece together a timeline of the evening, what confrontations and conflicts might have occurred?

"Were he living, he'd answer for his forward actions," he said.

Aunt Caris clutched her kerchief tighter. "He most certainly would."

Despite his sympathy, Mr. Burke wasn't fully satisfied. He still kept his kestrel-gaze fixed on me. "Yet it doesn't answer one thing. Trouble appears to follow you, Miss Jessa. Why is that?"

"What a dreadful thing to say!" Ainslie wrapped her arm around me and glared at Mr. Burke. "It's hardly her fault her cat fell ill, much less that Mr. Upton chose to press his attentions upon her."

Ada permitted herself to frown, a rarity for her gentle nature. "We shall make allowances for your weariness, but if you've nothing to do but cast careless accusations, then perhaps you'd best depart."

My sweet sisters and aunt—they defended me so readily, and yet Mr. Burke was right. I knew far more than I spoke, and I withheld the truth from him. But would he believe such a wild tale, if I dared speak?

"Forgive me." He gave a small bow. "If you should recall anything else, anything at all, please send for me."

When he departed, the words left unspoken rose up to choke me. After receiving a bounty of sympathy, I murmured an excuse and swept from the room, my fears rising to torment me.

What *had* happened last night? Had Riven succeeded in apprehending Mr. Upton—or was the killer still free, leaving us in more danger than ever?

CHAPTER 30

Night fell, and still Riven did not appear. I bent over my sketchbook, inking images of fire and smoke and devastation onto the page.

Did Riven's absence mean he still pursued the killer—or had he failed? Was he . . . dead? I pressed harder, and the nib of my pen scratched deep into the surface of the paper. I couldn't credit his death, not given his great strength. Yet he'd not returned, and the bargain binding us would compel him to come when he could.

I dipped my pen in the inkwell once more, forcing myself to maintain precision of line and form. How could I protect my family in Riven's absence, whatever its cause? In every way, the killer outmatched me—except perhaps my determination to stand against him.

I needed more information, a better plan, some means of defense . . . but what?

The sylph bobbed at my shoulder, offering the slightest flicker, as if to reassure me she remained at her post. Would she know what had befallen Riven? Could I persuade her to seek him?

I took the final sip of the chamomile tea that I'd brought to my bedchamber, but its grassy fragrance failed to bring calm. If I sent her away, assuming she would accept my request, and then the killer appeared . . . what recourse would remain? She might not be able to do a great deal, but her presence brought some degree of comfort.

A soft rap sounded at the door, and I jumped. "Come in."

Gaile, our housemaid, entered to fetch the tea tray. She collected the items with more than the usual clatter.

I closed my sketchbook and capped the inkwell. Though it was comparatively early, exhaustion tugged at me. I loosened my hair pins and rubbed my aching temples. Before I could consider retiring—and the blessed oblivion of sleep—I must determine what to do.

Gaile lingered, as though something weighed on her mind. "Do you need anything else, miss?"

"No, thank you."

"Shame about that Mr. Upton. Heard his whole house burnt down," she said.

It wasn't like Gaile to make small talk; she was quiet, dutiful, and intensely private. I lifted my gaze to meet hers in the mirror. "Indeed, it was quite a tragedy."

"But which was more a tragedy, miss? The house burning down—or the destruction of the evidence it contained?"

A chill burned down my back, icy-hot. I straightened. "Evidence of what?"

"Oh, you know, miss. The deaths. The ring belonging to Lady Dromley and the other articles."

My limbs prickled, grew numb. I closed my fingers around

my letter opener and drew it into the folds of my skirt. There was no time left to prepare; the confrontation was at hand.

Slowly, I turned to face her. "If you know something about such matters, you should speak to Mr. Burke at the Magistry."

"Now where's the fun in that?" Her eyes transformed into black pools.

The killer was here.

Riven was not.

Had the killer already taken his life? No, I refused to consider it. Perhaps Riven had been mistaken. Perhaps the killer hadn't wanted open conflict. Perhaps he'd fled long before Riven appeared.

The bitter taste of fear flooded my mouth, but I made one last attempt at normalcy. It had worked before—perhaps it would again. "I'm weary and wish to retire. If you'll take the tray, we can discuss this further in the morning."

"I don't think so," Gaile said. "Not and miss the entertainment. I've been waiting all day."

Cold sweat slicked my skin, made it difficult to grasp the letter opener. I didn't dare take my eyes from the killer for a moment, nor betray any sign of weakness. "What have you done with Gaile?"

"She's enjoying a nice rest in her bedchamber, just like your *kit-isne*." The killer gestured to Jade, still prone on the bed. "She won't remember a thing."

"Aren't you afraid someone will notice something's amiss?" Though I managed to keep my voice steady, it came out softer than usual.

"No one will notice. No one will hear." Her—his—lips twisted in a malicious smile. "This whole chamber is shrouded with *ilusne*. I have you all to myself—and I have the most delightful plans."

My heart drummed against my stays. Was this how he'd taken the others? Why no one besides the victims ever saw or heard the killer? I gripped the letter opener tighter, the scrollwork of its handle digging into my skin.

Somehow I must find a way out. Perhaps if Riven lived, if the sylph recognized the danger, if she fetched him in time . . .

If, if, if . . .

Beyond the window, the old oak rasped against the pane, its song resolute, even angry. It broke over my senses like a storm hurtling a wave across the sea.

I shuddered.

Not now, please not now. Was the killer provoking this? Did he seek to steal my wits to make me easier prey? I needed to stall him, to find a way out. "Tell me of this *ilusne*. Riven said only the most powerful of shifters can use it."

His dark orbs expanded into wide, hungry caverns, altogether unfitting for the face he wore. "He's right. But did he tell you that *ilusne* deceives fae as well? For all their powers of glamour, all the perception their affinities lend them, they're still vulnerable."

He strode forward, and I darted for the door that led to the corridor. If I could get out, if I could draw him away from my family . . .

A mocking edge crept into his voice. "Neither mortal nor fae wishes to admit that their own senses can be used against them. But even the fae feared us—else they would not have imprisoned my kin."

If fae feared his kind, what chance did I have? I clutched the knob, the brass ice-cold. A quick twist, and I stumbled into the dim corridor beyond. I couldn't let him mark me.

I sprinted down the long hallway toward the far stairs. Down would take me out, past my slumbering family. If the *ilusne* wasn't strong enough, if they woke and came to see what was the matter . . .

I must go up.

"Oh, Jessa." His voice, singsong now, echoed through the corridor, over the pounding of my pulse in my ears, before, behind, around me all at once. "Do you think you can escape?"

I dashed up the stairs, toward the attic. Stumbled, wrenching an ankle. The sharp pain burned up my leg.

"We always claim our prey, you know. I was one of the best hunters, so my clutch chose to preserve my life. They hoped I'd take vengeance on behalf of all my kind one day. Their venom sustained me through hundreds of years of slumber. In such state, no trace of my existence could be found—and the fae believed us all taken. I woke weak, but I have since remedied that condition."

How far was he? My chest tightened, my breath came in ragged gasps. Just a few more steps; I could make it. I slammed into the door atop the stairwell.

Locked.

I fumbled with the key in the latch. Twisted it hard. It gave way with a groan, and I stumbled into the attic, slammed the door behind me, and wrenched the key in the lock once more.

Safe, for a moment. But how long would the fragile barrier hold? If I could make it to the far window, the wide arms of the oak would receive me from below. I could lure the killer away from my home. If I did, would Riven ever find me?

No matter, I couldn't wait.

I must run.

I whirled around—and *he* was there, looming between me and the window.

How?

His teeth parted in a wild white grin; his dark-pool eyes widened with anticipation. "I told you, Jessa. There's no escape."

He blocked my path forward, and the way back would take me closer to my family. Every muscle tight, I edged closer to the door. What should I do?

He chuckled softly. One by one, the gas lamps along the wall flared to life with a faint hiss. "You don't seem to appreciate the nature of my work."

Bile burned the back of my throat. "Your work, as you call it, is to destroy lives."

"Those whose lives I took should count themselves honored: their emotions, their vitalities have sustained me, rebirthed my strength. Some part of them will live on forever." His sharp, frost-like scent intensified. "Yet they did not appear to appreciate my choice. They struggled; they suffered. Ibbie certainly did."

I recoiled as if he'd stabbed me through the heart. Perhaps that would have hurt less than the images spilling across my vision. Ibbie curled up with her knees to her chest, rocking back and forth, shrinking away as the killer approached . . .

Oh, Ibbie.

I should have been there.

"Jessa, you never disappoint." He licked his lips, as though savoring the taste of my pain. "Mortal emotions are so easily provoked—my time in your world has truly been a pleasure."

I fumbled with the lock behind me, my ragged pulse raging in my ears. "Why did you seek those connected to the Otherworld?"

"They have much to hide. They're conflicted within and without. Thus their emotions provide more potent strength." Shadows flickered about him, giving his features a spectral appearance.

I strained to see him as he was, to fight against whatever illusion he forced, but could bring about no change. Shadows danced about him like bodies writhing in torment. "Then why pursue me?"

"Don't pretend you're ignorant." One of his shadows flicked toward me and caressed my face, a cool, damp sensation. It took every ounce of will not to shrink from it. "Your emotions are stronger than those of all my previous victims. You bottle them inside, you try so hard to deny them. In the struggle, they gain power. And from the time we first met in the park, I knew there was something else—something more."

"When we talked in the garden, you planted the idea of Lord Blackburn, didn't you?" My voice quivered, despite my efforts to steady it.

"I injected you with the tiniest bit of venom. Just enough to make you more susceptible to my illusions." He rubbed his hands together, and his fingers lengthened. "Then I could speak to your mind in such a way that you would imagine my thoughts were your own. You assumed you'd stumbled upon a clue, and all the while, the one you sought stood before you. It was quite the pleasure to watch you follow up on the lead so assiduously, ignorant of my venom working within you."

His words twisted deep inside. When he'd clasped my hand in the garden, it'd caused pinpricks of pain. I'd thought it the tightness of his grip, when in fact, he'd chosen that moment to inject me. How could I have been so blind?

No matter, I couldn't let him make contact with me again, couldn't risk receiving more venom. Before I could force the lock, he closed the distance between us.

"Allow me." He reached past me, twisting the key with long, pale fingers. "It's time you returned to your bedchamber."

"Why should I cooperate with you?" A chill swept my body.

He was so close, the hands that murdered Ibbie only inches from my own. What did he intend?

"The choice is yours." Hunger sharpened his features. "Perhaps you'd rather I rouse your family after all?"

"No . . . I'll go." With the prickling awareness of his presence at my back, I stumbled down the stairs, clutching my arms to my chest to still their trembling. I needed to stop, needed to think. Ibbie had been killed in her bedchamber. So had Reynold. Did he mean to dispatch me now, without bothering to leave his mark?

He craved fear, perhaps even required it. As far as I could see, he had no other weakness, and I could not fathom how to turn this one against him. Eventually, he'd tire of his games, and he would strike—unless I could find a way out first. I slowed my steps. "Did you steal Mr. Upton's form as you did Lord Blackburn's?"

"The Upton family is real enough, but Mr. Upton was my own construct. How did you like him?"

Should I take the offensive? Could I? I still clutched the letter opener in my left hand. "I found him average at best."

A faint growl echoed behind me, and the shadows clustered thicker about my feet. He was angry—good. I wanted that anger to sear him from the inside out, to make him act in haste, to give me some advantage.

Yet he showed no such sign when we entered the bedchamber. Through the open window, moonlight poured its pale beams over the room as he latched the door. Then he approached. This time I would not run, would not show my fear.

Four steps away, three, two, and then he stood in arm's reach, his eyes glittering. "Your emotions are magnificent. A shame you're still not ready for me to take you. You fear, but not as the others did. You still dream you can resist. How can we change that?"

"You can't—not now, not ever." And with that, I sprang. I lashed out as hard as I could with the letter opener, but he moved, and it lodged in his shoulder, not in his heart as I'd intended.

His lips parted in a snarl. "You shouldn't have done that, Jessa. But you'll learn."

"You're wrong. I may be mortal, but it doesn't mean I won't fight." I scrabbled behind me for any sort of weapon and came up with a paperweight. "And unlike you, I don't hide behind the faces of others."

"You conceal a great deal, mortal. Perhaps not your face, but your nature." He laughed, a dry, creaking sound. "Still, I'm inclined to grant your wish. You shall see my true form."

The shadows deepened around him. They gathered into an amorphous tower, blotting him from sight.

When they parted, I couldn't restrain the gasp that escaped. I clutched the back of a chair to steady myself. Before me stood a monstrous spiderlike creature, its leathery hide of charcoal splotched with a large crimson tattoo. Many-jointed legs ending in hooked claws descended from a large, bulbous body. Enormous fangs parted its mouth, and dark eyes clustered above them.

I could not breathe. A stench like that of old blood hung heavy in the air, choking me. His clustered eyes locked onto mine, and an involuntary shudder racked my body. Every instinct shouted: *run*. Yet I'd tried, and he'd already caught me in his web, my family the cords he used to bind me. What now?

He stretched forth one of those dreadful legs and caught my wrist with a claw.

I flinched as he rasped it across tender skin.

"You find this form disturbing? I rather thought you might." He released me, yet his bulbous body remained far too close to my own.

My stomach lurched. I forced myself to straighten and don a calm facade—as if a powerful, intelligent spider-beast *wasn't* the stuff of my nightmares, as if my skin didn't crawl at the mere sight. "What are you?"

"Haven't you guessed? I am auvok. And you—you're one of the few privileged to perceive the true form of my kind."

Once again, the song of the oak drummed against my senses, deep and resonant. Calling me to stand firm, to reach out, to draw strength . . .

His lips stretched into a thin, fanged grimace. "Your kind knew our name once—and feared as we destroyed them by the thousands. So shall your world quail before me once more. I'll give them cause to tremble at the mere name of Uros."

"My world is stronger than you think. We will not bow in fear." Even as I spoke, my hold on the cage of thorns slipped further, and a flood of voices joined that of the oak. I trembled.

"Oh, mortal, you lie." His dry, rasping laugh befouled the air. "Don't you know? You can't hide your emotions from me. They're laid bare, even now. A delectable feast."

I shrank back, warmth rising in my face. In one moment, he'd stripped away my defenses, exposed all I longed to keep hidden. How much could he perceive? I couldn't dwell on it, or I'd become overwhelmed.

I must think.

He'd spoken of a feast. Was it literal? Did he feed on emotions as spiders fed on the blood of their prey? Did that mean if I could somehow stop feeling, he'd weaken?

In the end, it didn't matter, for it was impossible. I'd hidden them these many years, done my best to control and conceal them—but I could not purge them. And even if I did, he'd already grown strong, well-nourished by the terror he'd spread.

"You entertain me more than any of the others have, and it would be a shame to end you too soon." He drew his claws across the floor, and they left jagged scores in the wood. "Ibbie shared your determination, but in the end, she succumbed to fear. Will you do the same? Or perhaps you need additional inducement. Perhaps I should mark one of your relatives first."

No.

Please no.

His black-orb eyes glittered as he savored the tide of emotion I could not stem. "Perhaps I already have."

Fury coursed through my veins. I hurled the paperweight at Uros.

He dodged it, and his face twisted into a mocking grin. "Surely you can do better."

But I didn't have to . . . for a familiar surge of storm-charged energy snapped through the air.

Riven.

With a crackle of light, he appeared. He wasted no words, only tackled Uros with a fierce blast that knocked him off his feet.

Spindled legs clawed at the air. A hiss escaped Uros. Then he sprang up, and they locked in battle, leaving wreckage in their wake.

Riven moved with incredible grace, wielding weapons and light in tandem, while Uros lashed out with venom-dripping fangs and bared claws.

Then Uros became a tower of shadow once more. And when the gloom parted, he'd taken the form of a tremendous warrior, tall enough that his head nearly scraped the ceiling and tremendously broad of shoulder. Yet with spiderlike dexterity, he dodged every strike. He launched himself from the wall toward Riven, charcoal-dust shadows spiraling out like strands of web before him.

Bolts of light from Riven twined round them and forced them back. They clashed in a dizzying swirl of glamour.

Then Uros stretched a hand in my direction.

Coils of darkness reached toward me. Then fast as serpents, they struck. They wrapped round my neck, poured down my throat, burning as they went.

"Mind your mortal," Uros said, his voice harsh and rasping.

The shadows seared my lungs, tightened my chest. I braced myself against the mantel and brushed against the potted ivy that swayed down from it. Its tenacious strength thrummed through me.

I lost my grip on my cage of thorns. And the ivy surged forth from the pot, strong and lithe, twisting around Uros's legs. How?

He stumbled.

And Riven struck.

He slammed a light-edged dagger through Uros's heart, the force sufficient to drive the blade completely through his chest.

But Uros only laughed, the sound as grating as an axe against the heart of a tree.

I shuddered.

"You think me so easily killed?" He jerked free the blade, and the gaping, black-edged rent in his chest closed over. "Fool."

They stood poised, regarding one another.

"How long ago did you remove your heart?" Riven asked.

Removed his heart . . . was this anything like the ghouls? The implications sent ice through my veins.

"Does it matter? I've followed those of my kind who chose the path of greatness. This ability is our greatest strength. You can never kill me, never stop me. No matter the injuries you deal me, I will not suffer—for I can no longer feel." His teeth flashed white in his shadowed face. "I could fight you for an age and never weary. Fae may have great strength, but you have a fundamental weakness: you have a heart. Eventually it will give out, and then I'll claim you. As I did the others."

Pressure gathered in the air. And Riven gave a slow, grim smile. "You talk too much."

Light exploded around us, the brilliant flash searing my eyes. Uros formed a black blotch against the swirl of colors dancing across my vision. He stumbled, his massive body unbalanced.

Riven hurled another dagger into his chest.

It knocked Uros backward. He staggered into a pool of silvery-gold light on the floor behind him—and vanished.

Then the pool disappeared also, as if it had never been.

I blinked away the lingering spots before my eyes, and my legs quivered. I sank to the floor, the polished wood solid and smooth beneath me. "Where . . . where is he?"

Oh, how I wanted Riven to tell me he was gone forever, imprisoned like his impossible-to-kill kin—that the threat of such cruelty was removed from our lives.

Instead, he fetched his dagger. Little sparks licked the blade, burning the ichor from it. "He's near what you mortals call the Fens Crossing. Moonlight gives poor passage for those of my court."

"Then he's still within Byren." I clutched my legs to my chest. "He'll return."

"Likely. But he'll require time to recover. Being forced through the passing will have hurt him like no physical wound could. It will diminish his powers until he can gather strength once more." Moonlight spilled over Riven's expressionless face.

"Can't he be stopped?"

"Not unless we have his heart. Only then can he be killed. And it might be anywhere in the worlds."

"You weren't surprised he'd removed it."

Riven shoved the dagger back into its sheath. "No."

"But the others were imprisoned—"

"The most powerful in my world gave their lives to secure the prison. Such will not happen again." Darkness fell across his face, as if he'd quenched all the light he so readily wielded. "He's made his home here. Now the problem is for the mortal realm to manage."

"But you've said yourself we cannot." The words erupted from me, carried by pain and grief. "Even the fae cannot kill him. What do you suggest we do?"

"Flee—if you want to live."

I traced the claw marks Uros had left on the floor. I felt as though he'd gouged them into my flesh, for the sharp pain that burned through my body. "I thought you cared for justice, cared about catching the killer."

At times, I'd even thought he might care about protecting mortals. After all, he could have pressed for more advantageous bargains, could have refused to heal Jade, could have preyed upon those in his path while he was in our world—but he'd held to his purpose, even appeared to display kindness on occasion.

But perhaps that had been a glamour of its own, a deceit intended to ensure my cooperation.

"I have the answers I seek. We have his trace, we can seal him out of our court. My king knows this foe. He will be satisfied." Riven snapped his fingers with a flare of light, and the sun sylph hastened to his side.

Her absence left me cold and bereft. I rubbed my arms. "So you'll leave Avons to suffer Uros's wrath? I thought better of you."

"What are mortals to fae? No more than the insects that creep upon the earth, here today and gone tomorrow. Their lives are not those I must preserve." He spoke in frigid tones, and he angled away so I couldn't see his face. "My obligation lies in my own world. Not yours."

How could I possibly argue with that? How could I persuade him to ignore the demands of his own people and act on behalf of the mortals they despised? I stared at the gouges in the floor, and they blurred beneath my gaze.

"If you want to protect your family, gather them and go as far as you can from here. Perhaps flee Byren altogether. He may be more interested in finding easy prey as he regains his strength than attempting to track you."

"Perhaps—but perhaps not." I looked up at him. "You expect me to leave everything to chance?"

"What choice do you have?" His voice lowered. "Leave Avons. Don't return."

Then he vanished.

CHAPTER 31

Riven was gone.

Uros was not, not truly.

And he wanted me, wanted my pain, wanted my family.

Perhaps others might distract him from his aim, but could I cling to such a hope when it meant other families ripped apart and the deaths of those they loved, rather than my own? Sooner or later, that death left unchecked *would* come for us.

A vision of Avons, preyed upon by ceaseless terror, desiccated corpses with tattoos of crimson filling its graveyards, its people scattered and broken, clawed into my mind. The images simmered with their own peculiar venom, poisoning me into immobility, sapping hope.

I collapsed onto the floor, the cold planks beneath me offering no comfort. The marks that marred them would mar all Avons, in time.

And Riven had abandoned us to our fate. Perhaps if the fae chose, they could have stopped Uros, but he'd refused to consider it. I'd known fae were not to be trusted, but I'd allowed the fatal draw of my fae-touch to influence instinct and emotion, to overtake my reason and beguile me into extending some measure of trust.

Worse still, I'd taken countless risks, strengthening the fae-touch with each one, only to learn I faced an unstoppable foe . . .

Hours passed, cold and dark. And I did not stir, could not move, could not find a way forward.

The sky paled, turning gray at the edges. The faintest flush crept across the horizon, a reminder of the dawn of joy spoken of in the Script.

No night could last forever . . . could it?

A small scuffle sounded behind me. A moment later, Jade crept onto my chest, her movements unsteady. Her warmth spread through my body, her weight as comforting as an embrace.

And the tears I'd restrained spilled freely. They soaked the floor beneath me as Jade offered a rumble of sympathy.

I had lost Ibbie. I'd almost lost Jade.

This must stop. I refused to let those I loved be killed one by one; I would not accept any fate that allowed an Otherworldly monster to prey upon them. But what other choice remained?

Riven said he couldn't be killed—unless we had his heart. That was his weakness, and that was my way forward. But where would an ancient monster hide that which was most dear to him? How could I ever hope to find it?

Like the flash of lightning burning its afterimage across my eyes, the knowledge seared my soul. Uros was a creature of the Otherworld, and the taint of the Other within was my surest path to find him.

For all the danger it represented, I must admit it had also helped me in every dealing with the Otherworld, first with the sprites, then all the fae I'd encountered in Avons. It exacted its price, yet without the advantages it gave, I'd never have found Uros in the first place.

If the fae-touch hadn't allowed me to perceive Riven and to resist his glamour, I'd never have bargained with him nor learned all I had about the killer and the presence of the Otherworld in our midst. And if I'd never formed any sort of alliance with Riven, however temporary, Uros certainly would have claimed me tonight.

Were I to have any chance of success in finding his heart, I needed all my senses, including the fae-touch—whatever the outcome. When I'd chosen to allow a chink in my inner cage while dealing with the sprites, I'd imagined it easy to reconstruct. Now I knew otherwise.

Even so, *this* was how I'd protect my family—not by fleeing anything that might strengthen my fae-touch, but by allowing its influence in order to find Uros.

If I didn't, who would?

I staggered to my feet, Jade in my arms. She nudged my chin and gave a weak purr.

Once steady, I poured water into her bowl and placed her favorite dried fish alongside it. As she cautiously began to eat, I allowed my mind to run over all that had happened since I'd returned to Avons, from the first mention of the killer, to the tattoo upon Ibbie, to the marks I'd uncovered . . .

A golden glow filled the room as the sun peered over the tops of buildings, its shade reminiscent of the goldhearts I'd given Ibbie. And with the reminder, something nagged at the edge of my awareness.

The goldhearts, the spectre at Enderly, and—

A scream split the air, followed by the shattering of china.

I spun round.

Gaile—the true Gaile, alive and unharmed—stood in the doorway, the breakfast tray she'd brought upended on the floor at her feet.

Cries of *what's wrong?* resounded from the floor beneath mine, and in short order, my entire family assembled at my door, staring at the wreckage of my bedchamber: Aunt Caris pale as the last straggling birch leaf of autumn, Ada's eyes dark in her strained face, Ainslie flushed vibrant and fairly snapping with fury, and Father muttering curses under his breath.

Then they rushed forward as one.

Aunt Caris reached me first and clasped me fiercely to her chest. "Oh, my dear, are you hurt? Whatever happened?"

"I'm unharmed, but there was an . . . intruder."

"We heard nothing." Father surveyed the damage—the scored floor, the shattered vases and scattered blossoms, the upended furniture. "I'll summon the Magistry at once."

Aunt Caris released me long enough to survey every inch of me. "Thank the Infinite it wasn't the killer."

If she knew the truth . . . I sank onto the edge of the bed. "I don't think we need to send for the Magistry. He's gone—and I'm not injured."

Not in ways one could see, at any rate. But the Magistry could do nothing, and I didn't want to come under further scrutiny.

After exchanging a glance, Ada and Ainslie perched on either side of me, as though they intended to act as my guardians, both of them blessedly unmarked. Either I'd been wrong about Ainslie or Uros hadn't had time to brand her yet. I still had time to see her safe.

"You're certain you're well, Jessa?" Ada asked.

My eyes stung, and I blinked rapidly. "Only a bit shaken."

"Of course you are, my dear. What is Avons coming to—

with sneak thieves and bounders harassing innocent young women?" Though Aunt Caris tried to disguise her distress behind indignation, her voice quivered.

I lifted Jade to my lap and clutched her close. "Perhaps the presence of the killer has . . . unsettled Avons."

Father moved about the room, still muttering beneath his breath, and I struggled to gather my thoughts. If I failed in my undertaking to find the heart, then my one chance of keeping my family safe was to remove them as far from Avons as possible. And yet, they'd never leave and allow me to remain. How could I seek the heart while keeping them safe?

Ada plucked a bit of shattered glass from the coverlet. "Perhaps we should reconsider withdrawing for a time."

Ainslie frowned and gave a slight bounce, which jostled the three of us. "Don't tell me you're giving way too."

"Perhaps you're right." Father nodded slowly, as though struggling to clear the vestiges of suggestion planted by Uros. "Who could ascribe blame when there's been an attack in our own home? If we approach the matter with care, perhaps we can avoid stirring trouble. I'll consider it."

Ainslie folded her lips in a tight line and said nothing, while Ada wrapped her arm around my shoulders and rested her head against mine. "I cannot think how we slept through the destruction, but it's dreadful that you suffered all this alone. You shall move in with Ainslie and I tonight—for as long as you wish."

"Thank you, Ada." Never mind the impracticality of the three of us trundled into one bed, I soaked in the comfort of her closeness, her compassion.

But then I straightened. There was no time to waste. If I wanted to find out more about the auvok, and perhaps uncover some clue about what they did with their hearts once they'd removed them, I needed to return to the Cloister library—but first I'd have to persuade Father of the necessity.

Before I could speak, Holden charged into the room, his cravat slightly askew—a shocking sight, considering he always arrayed himself with precision. "Mr. Caldwell, your sister has sent one of her footmen. She demands you and Miss Caldwell come to her home at once."

"Melisina will have to wait." Father raked his fingers through his unruly auburn hair. "I've other matters to attend."

Holden straightened his cravat. "Her footman states she's in hysterics, and he dares not return without you."

Hysterics? Aunt Melisina? I stared at Holden. Surely he exaggerated—yet his unflappable nature meant he understated most things.

Something sharp as a blade twisted deep inside. Uros had tormented me with a threat to my family. What if he . . .?

Surely it was impossible.

But the knife-blade sensation pierced deeper.

Aunt Caris took a half step toward the threshold, then stopped. "Alden, what if something dreadful has happened?"

"If our home could be breached in the night unbeknownst to us all, I consider nothing impossible." Father pushed his spectacles farther up his nose. "We'd best go."

I sprang from the bed. "Father, may I come too?"

"Wouldn't you rather rest, my dear?" Aunt Caris interjected.

"I'd rather forget my troubles by offering aid to another." I summoned a smile. "You taught me that, Aunt Caris."

She couldn't deny it, not when she'd drummed the principle into us as children and had lived her own life accordingly.

"What do you say, Caris?" Father asked.

"I suppose she may." But lines of strain deepened around her mouth.

Jade was in no condition to trot alongside me, so I tucked her into the large basket I'd used for her transport when she'd first come to me. Aunt Melisina might hold her in contempt, but I refused to let her from my sight. Then we all bundled into the carriage, where Aunt Caris worried aloud, speculating about various woes that may have befallen. Yet she didn't mention the one that most consumed my thoughts: the tattoo of crimson.

When we arrived at the townhome, stratesmen bustled in and out, while some stood watch at the street corners. It didn't bode well. The knot expanded, constricting my breath.

Jade lifted her head enough to nudge my hand, and then we hurried from the carriage. The stratesman at the door must have been instructed to expect us, for he allowed us into the entry, where the butler took over, ushering us into the morning room.

Aunt Melisina lay prostrate on the couch, motionless. The sharp scent of hartshorn lingered in the air, and the lady's maid hovering behind her brandished the bottle vigorously.

"Sister!" Aunt Caris rushed forward, the differences and slights between them falling away in a moment. She knelt at her side, and Aunt Melisina clutched at her arm.

"It's Lovell." Aunt Melisina spoke in a rasping whisper, her voice nearly unrecognizable.

A cold silence fell.

Father stood rooted in place.

Aunt Caris pressed trembling fingers to her lips.

And Aunt Melisina wept, silent tears trickling down her cheeks.

My mouth went dry. I wanted to flee, to hide, to remain in ignorance—but I dared not.

"Is he . . . dead?" I whispered.

"Not dead, not yet." She swiped at her cheeks with a lace-edged handkerchief. "But marked. He woke this morning bearing the tattoo."

Even while Uros had taunted me, he must have already marked Lovell. After all my worries for Ainslie, he'd chosen another of my family. Did Lovell hide some connection to the Otherworld—or was I the link, as I'd feared?

Perhaps Uros had intended to reveal it in time, to revel in my pain, but Riven had arrived before he could. Still, Lovell was only marked. Hope remained, especially with Uros removed for a time. I had a chance to save him, as I could not save Ibbie.

Father moved forward. "Where's Milton? Has he left you here alone?"

"He's speaking with the stratesmen, demanding their best. But their best have failed every victim . . ." Her voice broke.

They'd failed because they didn't know the true nature of the murderer. They didn't know how he might be stopped. But I did, no matter how small and unlikely the chance. Riven had cast Uros from Avons and so bought us time—but how much?

I couldn't afford to waste a moment. And Aunt Melisina would receive comfort far better from Aunt Caris than she would from me.

I slipped into the hushed hallway. Servants clustered at the far end, brows drawn, speaking in whispers. When I emerged, they split up and hurried about their business. I stood still, irresolute. While I wanted to strike out immediately, could I justify keeping all this information to myself? If I failed in my attempts to find the heart, someone should know the truth about the threat that faced our world.

But who?

Mr. Burke had invited me to come to him. I'd take him at his word, trust his desire for justice would compel him to give me a hearing. It was a risk, but one required.

I might even find him here. He'd shown up at the scene of every murder; perhaps he was examining the bedchamber where Lovell received his mark. I made my way along the familiar corridors, now shrouded with the grief that hung over the household.

The bedchamber door hung at an angle, as though the inhabitant were undecided whether to welcome or deny visitors. I eased it open and found Lovell.

He stared out the window, his shoulders bent.

I moved toward him. "Lovell?"

He turned slowly, and sunlight fell on the tattoo, its stark, angry lines marring his flesh. I pressed my fingers to my lips to hold back a cry.

It was my fault.

If my tainted emotions hadn't drawn attention from Uros, would Lovell ever have been marked? I hugged the basket with Jade closer, its rough edges digging into my stomach. Somehow, I must make it right.

"Don't look like that, Jess." His jaw firmed. "It will be well, in the end. The Magistry will figure it out this time. They must."

But he spoke like one who attempted to convince himself, each word sharp-edged with fear.

"Oh, Lovell." I set down Jade and hastened to his side. I embraced him, feeling the shudder of his breath, the fear coiled inside tight muscles. "How can I help?"

"By getting out of Avons, you and everyone else in this family. I don't care what King Everill says, this place is cursed. And if the worst happens, I want to know you're safe. I've already told Mother and Father."

"What did they say?"

"Mother wants us all to leave the moment we can."

"But you won't go."

"I can't chance leading the killer to them, not if the mark somehow allows him to follow me." He touched the tattoo, then pulled his fingers away as though they'd been singed. "But the rest of you, you're not marked, not a target. If I could know you're safe . . ."

Flight was no longer an option for me, not with Lovell's life on the line, but I murmured my understanding nevertheless. He wanted what I did—to know those he cared about were safe from harm.

He shifted his weight from one foot to another. "There's something else, Jess, something I need to confess."

What in the Crossings? He appeared more sober than I'd ever seen him. A stone settled in my stomach. "What is it?"

"I'm P. Smith. Well, Ainslie and I are."

"You and . . . Ainslie?" I rocked back a half step.

"Perhaps I shouldn't have dragged her into it—after that threatening letter someone sent us through our publisher, I questioned it—but in truth, she dragged me into it as much as I did her."

After this, little could surprise me. Though upon reflection, the signs had been there—all the times Lovell and Ainslie had their heads together over the papers, the interest in political happenings Ainslie tried to conceal, and her shock at finding out I'd written to P. Smith.

"We both felt badly about deceiving you, about writing to you as if we didn't know who you were, about all your worries for Ibbie. Ainslie was for telling you, especially after you found her with the threatening letter and were so concerned, but I thought the more people knew, the greater the chances of something slipping somewhere, and everything coming to an end. It was selfish of me, and I wanted the account between us clear, in case . . . well, in case."

In case Uros claimed him.

I'd no intention of letting that happen. "There's no account to clear, though once this is all over, I'd like to hear how you and Ainslie happened into writing for the paper."

He scrubbed a hand over his face. "Good of you to take it so well."

How could I not, given my own secrets? I'd so many questions, but this was hardly the time. My shoulders tightened. "The only thing you need to consider is keeping yourself safe. Who's in charge here?"

"Dash it all, what's the fellow's name? Brooke? No. Burke, I believe."

At least I wouldn't have to find my way to the Magistry again. "I'd like to speak with him. Where is he?"

"He's set up in the library." Lovell half-turned back to the window, as though to conceal his emotions. "But he won't be able to tell you anything. If the Magistry knew the identity of the killer, they'd have taken him in long ago."

"I know, but I'll feel better after speaking with him." Or so I hoped. I clasped his hand, and the unfamiliar chill of it tugged at my heart. "Keep courage—this isn't over yet."

I needed to hear the reminder as much as give it.

He released me. "Go now. The sooner you're away from here, the better."

I didn't correct him; instead, I crept down the flight of stairs that would deposit me near the library, taking care not to jostle Jade in the process. My movements slowed as I drew closer, images of accusations and Institutions filling my mind.

I stumbled on the final stair and scarcely righted myself, burdened as I was. There could be no turning back, not with so much at stake. I'd find a way to confess to Mr. Burke without betraying my fae-touch. After all, merely finding oneself assaulted by Otherkind didn't mean one bore the taint, else those unfortunates who failed to keep proper watch in edgetowns would find themselves under constant accusation.

I halted outside the library. Mr. Burke sat within, his dark head bent over a report.

With a deep breath, I crossed the threshold. "Mr. Burke, may I have a word in private?"

CHAPTER 32

"**M**iss Jessa." Mr. Burke set aside the report and scrubbed a hand across his eyes. "Once again, you're in the heart of trouble. Why is that?"

"You may not be aware, but Lovell is my cousin. It's natural for family to band together in times of distress."

"Perhaps." He gestured to the nearest armchair. "If you wish to speak, then take a seat. But I can offer no more guarantee than before. We're doing everything in our power to apprehend the murderer—that much I promise."

"I'm not looking for assurances, not anymore." I settled into the chair, depositing Jade's basket onto the floor. "Yesterday, you told me if I recalled anything else, I should send for you."

"And have you?"

"Yes."

"Go on."

"When I was in Mr. Upton's house, I found some items in the study, ten tokens in a vase on the desk—including Ibbie's signet ring, the one that went missing when she died. I didn't want to say anything, because I knew it sounded absurd. But he knew I found them, and he paid me a visit last night—"

"Miss Jessa, let me stop you right there." A frown creased his forehead. "I don't know what you're after with this tale, but Mr. Upton has passed on. You know that. There's no way he can be the killer. Unless you mean to suggest he cooperated with the murderer in some way before his demise?"

"That's not what I'm suggesting." I stared down at my neat gloves, which concealed an ink stain on my forefinger. "The killer appeared in the guise of Mr. Upton, but it no longer suited him, so he burned down his home. In truth, he's an auvok, an Otherworldly creature who can shift form. And he's assuredly not dead."

He arched a brow. "Do you have any evidence to support this tale?"

"I saw him transform with my own eyes, Mr. Burke. I realize it sounds peculiar, but my family will bear out that my bedchamber was destroyed this morning."

"You expect me to believe this incredible story without any facts to back it up?" He steepled his fingers. "What, then? Did you confront the killer and put him to flight on your own?"

"Not on my own. There was a fae—" I was confessing far more than I wished, exposing too much . . . but what else could I do?

The lines on his brow creased deeper, but he waved his hand dismissively. "And I suppose he chased away the killer out of the goodness of his heart? This isn't a fae-tale to be told to children —this is a serious matter, one of life and death. And you are wasting my time."

"Mr. Burke, I'm in earnest. If the Magistry remains unaware of the true nature of this killer, how can you ever hope to fight him?" I leaned forward, willing him to listen. "You care about justice, about those suffering. I *know* you do. Please believe me that I share your concerns. I said nothing before because I know how odd it all sounds, because I don't have proof, at least not the kind you require. But after last night, I felt it my duty to speak."

Something flickered deep in his eyes. Would he believe me? Would he heed and act? He gave a sharp laugh, and my hope snuffed out.

"I give you credit for your creativity. We've had our share of attention-seekers crafting stories for us, enjoying their moment in the limelight. But your tale is by far the most inventive."

"It's not a tale, I—"

He held up a hand. "Spare me."

I collapsed back in the chair. Why wouldn't he consider my story? Granted, it did sound peculiar. But he'd known I was hiding something, and now, when I came out with the truth, he ignored it? Something didn't add up. "Why won't you listen?"

"Because I don't want to be forced to charge you with impeding this investigation or spreading mass hysteria through Avons. It would be unpleasant for us both," he said. "You will keep this tale to yourself. Don't mention it to anyone, least of all your family. Do I make myself clear?"

I'd feared possible accusation of fae-touch, but never had I dreamt I'd receive an accusation of being an attention-seeker who sought to deceive the populace. Weariness anchored me in place. No recourse remained.

If I found myself charged by the Magistry, I'd lose all chance of helping Lovell. My vision clouded, and I blinked hard. "Yes, Mr. Burke. You've been quite clear."

He picked up the report again. "I have my orders. These murders have nothing to do with the Otherworld—that statement comes from the highest authorities. I cannot let you claim otherwise. Do you understand?"

I nodded, no longer trusting my voice.

"I hope you'll receive this advice in the spirit it's intended, and you'll do what must be done." His gaze lingered on me, not sharp as usual, but almost pleading, as if he willed me to understand . . . something. "Now, if you're through, I must see to your cousin."

"Of course."

He strode from the room, and I burrowed deeper into the capacious armchair. Earlier, he'd invited me to come to him with concerns, yet now he dismissed them. Why? Had Uros influenced him in some way, or did he merely act on the Magistry's orders to squash any rumors of the Otherworld? Or did he truly believe what he'd said about me? Most likely, I'd never know. The bigger question was—what now? I'd done what I could to enlist aid. No choice remained but to make my best effort alone.

I walked over to the table, where gazettes from this morning were spread across the surface, each with sensational headlines proclaiming various so-called facts about the murder and the murderer.

I paged through the papers as I considered my next steps. A tiny article near the bottom of the page caught my eye. It referenced Enderly Park, and once again, something niggled at the back of my mind.

Oh.

Enderly had been the first place within Avons that I'd sensed Other. I'd thought the spectres accounted for it, but perhaps I'd not seen a spectre at all. Uros's true form, deepest charcoal with a splash of crimson, matched the coloration of whatever I'd seen in Enderly. And last night, he'd said *when I first saw you in the park.*

I'd thought at the time he'd meant garden, but what if he'd spoken of Enderly? What if our first encounter had been there? Had he known our lore and adopted the form of a spectre to his advantage? If he wished to frighten away spectators from Enderly, while also keeping the entire matter disconnected from the affair of the killer, this was an effective course.

But why would he want to keep mortals from Enderly? Was it possible he'd concealed his heart there? It was a stretch. Still, even if his heart were elsewhere, he must have had some reason to return to the park, given the frequent sightings of the spectre.

I folded the gazettes, their papers rustling in the stillness. Enderly was a place to start; it might at least provide a clue. If I went and uncovered nothing, I'd attempt to gain access to the Cloister library once more.

Yet searching Enderly would take considerable time. How could I conduct an investigation without raising suspicion? Already Father was considering a removal from Avons, and even if he decided otherwise, Aunt Caris would never allow me the freedom of movement to hunt for the heart, not after the attack within my bedchamber and Lovell receiving the mark. In order to effectively search, I'd have to remove myself from the family home.

Then I'd have liberty to search Enderly and beyond, even if it took days. Though I couldn't fathom trying to sleep out-of-doors. I stacked the gazettes neatly. With Riven gone from Avons, perhaps I could shelter within Wyncourt for a short time, swearing the servants to secrecy if necessary—or better yet, using the hidden hallways to gain access. While it might not be proper to establish myself within Wyncourt, if everyone believed I'd left Avons, it might work.

To succeed in the venture, I needed to find Father and persuade him that my departure was both reasonable and necessary. He'd not have lasted long with Aunt Melisina, and if he wasn't in the library, then most likely he'd taken refuge in Uncle Milton's study.

With Jade at my side, I hastened to the study, where I found Father in a state of evident melancholy. Though for once he did not have book or paper in hand, he took no notice of my arrival.

"Father?"

He gave no answer.

I took the chair across from him, leaned forward, and pitched my voice louder. "Father?"

"Jessa. You're still here. I thought perhaps you'd gone home."

"No, I went to speak with Lovell."

"None of them will see reason." Father stared into the distance. "Melisina and Milton won't leave Lovell in Avons, and it seems Lovell is angry with the both of them for staying. The place is a hotbed of emotion."

Which to him was a situation as abhorrent as being chased by the hounds of the wild hunt, or perhaps a recalcitrant dragon. He slumped into the depths of his winged chair and subsided into a state of abstraction once more.

"What of Aunt Caris? Does she intend to leave Avons?" I asked.

He remained locked in his inner world, so I repeated the question. This time, he roused enough to answer.

"Caris won't go, says she can't abandon Melisina in her hour of need. She intends to stay with her until the matter is—resolved." He shook his head. "Just yesterday she was convinced we all need to flee Avons, and now that I've come to share her point of view, she won't consider it."

It might bewilder Father, but I understood. Despite their disagreements, despite the slights Aunt Melisina delivered, they were still sisters. And Aunt Caris, with her warm, generous nature, would never dream of abandoning family.

Jade batted at my arm, and I stroked her head, the familiar motion a comfort I no longer took for granted. Despite my resolve, I struggled to propose my plan to Father. The moment I spoke, I would step far beyond any bounds of propriety and into the unknown.

I shifted forward, straightened the cushion behind me, and then settled back again. "I understand why Aunt Caris wishes to stay, but . . . I can't bear to see Lovell with the mark, after what happened to Ibbie."

Father didn't reply; he only retreated further into himself. Perhaps he hoped I'd give up and leave if he didn't speak.

"I need to get out of Avons. I'm making arrangements to go on a botanical expedition." I winced at the fae-like nature of my words—a technical truth, designed to mislead.

"Mm." He stared into the distance.

"If I have your permission, I'd like to depart at once."

"Whatever you need. Best to leave, in my mind. We have just cause to go, after what's happened." He picked up a book and leafed through the pages. "But no one's listening."

Aunt Caris would have asked a thousand and one questions about the traveling arrangements, the names of every companion and chaperone, our intended destination, and the like. She would have pointed out all the possible improprieties and demanded satisfaction as to the convention of the arrangements, as Father should have. If he wished to safeguard my reputation, he should have inquired if this were a collection of young ladies sketching flowers under the supervision of their devoted mothers, if we intended to tour only the more civilized areas, and who would see to my well-being in the absence of my own mother.

But Father asked no questions. Perhaps none of the possible improprieties occurred to him—he often remained oblivious to the usual expectations for young ladies—or perhaps he simply did not wish to prolong our interview in light of the emotion that had seeped into my voice.

Often, his distance stung. This time, it worked in my favor, clearing the way for me to act. "You'll tell the others for me?"

"Yes, yes," he murmured, then he rose and crossed the room to select a book from the shelves.

I sat for a moment, listening to the quiet tick of the clock, the familiar clatter of carriages in the street outside, the soft rustle of paper as Father turned the pages of his book.

It was past time to go, particularly if I intended to make the necessary preparations to ensure success. I shook off my fears and hurried from the townhome. From the corner of my eye, I caught Mr. Burke addressing one of his men at the edge of the walk. Instinctively, I rounded the corner before flagging a hack. I didn't want to draw any more of his attention than necessary, not when he already thought I invented tales for my own amusement.

Once sequestered away from prying eyes, I drew a long breath, attempting to calm myself. Then I stepped into the carriage—and toward the unknown.

CHAPTER 33

Whatever the urgency of the situation, I couldn't search Enderly without proper preparations. I must give myself the best possible chance to find and destroy the heart, for if I failed, the consequences were unthinkable.

With that in mind, I requested the driver stop at the market, where I procured a dagger, water flasks, and the most lightweight of preserved foods. If I did not wish to draw attention to my presence within Wyncourt, I'd need to fend for myself while there. And though I didn't imagine I could fend off Uros with a dagger, any weapon was better than none.

Once home, I packed the supplies I'd gathered into a small rucksack that I could carry on my back, then I coaxed Jade to take some food and water. After some consideration, I changed into a dark blue riding habit. Of all my wardrobe, it would offer the most freedom of motion—not to mention far greater durability than a gauzy gown of muslin.

I stopped before my dressing table to add a few pins to the unruly curls that spooled about my face, and then I considered the small chest that contained the few pieces of jewelry I owned. I lifted the lid and then picked up my ward-pendant. I'd stored it here since Riven had told me it was useless. Had he told the truth?

He'd certainly appeared unaffected by it. Which left only one option. Reluctantly, I opened the small leather pouch I'd tucked within the chest. It contained the pendant Mr. Heard had given me.

I'd hidden it there due to the discomfiting sensations it roused, an alluring hint of Other I could not deny. I lifted the silver chain, and the teardrop-shaped jewel at the end of it shimmered. Its depths sparkled with a vibrant array of colors, shifting from the deepest of sapphires to the most vibrant of violets and back again. It was magnificent, a gift fit for royalty.

Mr. Heard had refused to offer any explanation for his generosity or for the gift itself, saying only that I'd know its purpose when the time was right. As brusque as he could be, I couldn't imagine he'd give me something that would cause harm.

Perhaps, just perhaps, it would even help. I clasped it around my neck and tucked it into my bodice, where it rested warm against my skin.

Jade finished her meal, and then she twined around my ankles, evincing no signs of her poisoning, and I whispered a prayer of thanks for her recovery. She batted at a residual strand of cobweb, one missed by the maids when they'd cleaned the wreckage this morning. It twined around her paw, and then she licked it clean.

Her lively state provided a stark contrast to her unmoving form of the day before. If she'd not recovered . . . it didn't bear thinking about.

Could I justify taking her into danger again? It wasn't as if she could give her consent. No, it was far better that she stay.

I summoned Gaile. "I'm going on a short trip. You're to see that Jade is cared for in my absence. Lianne will assist you, if needed."

Jade whirled round to face me, bristling all over. Her eyes glowed like stars in a midnight sky, their green light uncanny. She bared her long white fangs at Gaile and growled.

She paled. "Begging your pardon, miss, but I'm not certain she'll let me."

Then Jade climbed onto the chest of drawers and launched herself at me, nearly knocking me over. I staggered under her weight and only just managed to brace myself against the bedframe before we both toppled to the floor.

Could I leave her here, if she refused care and terrorized the household? Yet surely her distress was better than her death. As if she could perceive my thoughts, she deliberately dug a claw into my neck.

I flinched. "You cannot come."

She began her banshee-like yowl, and Gaile placed her hands over her ears. If I left Jade, and she caused trouble for the household, Father might well put her out, and then what would become of her? The streets were not kind to strays.

"Please, Jade. I'll return as soon as I can."

But she persisted, determined not to be ignored. At last, I pitched my voice loud enough to be heard above her wails. "Never mind, Gaile. I'll bring Jade along."

At once, the eerie caterwauling ceased. A rumbling purr of approval emanated from her.

"You ridiculous creature. I was only trying to look after you."

She nudged my chin, and I let out a breath. She'd helped me time and again, and though I'd wanted to protect her, her choice imparted fresh courage, for I'd no longer have to go alone.

With Jade at my side and the rucksack over my shoulder, I slipped from the house and summoned another hack.

～

W‍HEN I REQUESTED the driver wait at Enderly, he squinted dubiously at me. "Suppose you know your own business. But it'll cost you double."

I paid him and descended from the carriage. Patches of sunlight and shade dappled the lush meadows bordering the narrow dirt path. I crested a hill as the hack and its driver vanished, and the Other within Enderly surged into my senses, the pinprick sensation now as familiar as the beat of my heart. Jade roused herself and nudged me with her nose, her paws pressed to the edge of the basket.

When I set it down, she climbed out and wound herself around my shoulders—her favorite perch. I left my basket to fetch on the way back, and together we ventured into the unknown.

If I wished to hide something of value, it wouldn't be out in the open for anyone to find . . . unless I possessed *ilusne* and could hide things wherever I pleased. I hesitated.

In any case, I'd seen the spectral form in the forest near the goldhearts, so I'd try that area first. As we drew near to the tree line, the cheery song of the goldhearts swirled the air, imparting courage.

With their melody fortifying me, I pressed into the woods. Despite the brilliant morning sunlight, the trees formed a world of shifting shadows that played among the bracken of the forest floor. A twig snapped in the distance, and I whirled round, but could find nothing. Doubtless it was some small creature scampering through the brush, but my mind conjured vivid images of Uros stalking me from the shadows, his spindled legs scrabbling along the leaves and detritus of the forest floor.

I kept motionless for several long moments, but no sound followed except the high reedy call of a bird, so I forged onward, trying to ignore the creeping sensation of watchful eyes.

After a while, I discovered what appeared to be a path of sorts, a thready way woven through the trees and brush. Clearly man or beast had passed this way before, so it was worth exploration.

As I followed the circuitous weave of the trail, the forest pressed against my senses with increasing strength. The trees whispered around me, a near-continual susurration in the background that no effort could drown out. On every side, life surrounded me, and it threatened to unravel my cage of thorns entirely.

I halted in front of an enormous elm, its canopy stretching out over a host of smaller trees and shrubs. If I touched it, might I gain insight into what I sought? Perhaps, but it could have equally devastating effect. I might find myself attempting a connection time and again to discover nothing of value—assuming I could replicate what had befallen me in Milburn.

I did not know how often I could sink into the fae-touch before it took control completely, and if I fell insensate here with none to rouse me, who would act on Lovell's behalf? I settled upon a fallen log and stretched my aching muscles.

Weariness pressed in upon me, and I allowed my eyes to slide shut, allowed my senses to open, ever so slightly . . .

In the stillness, a slow, resonant song seeped through the weave of my inner cage and into my awareness. It pulsed with a sense of Other, sparked swirling images of cool shadows and air heavy with damp, of stagnant waters and deep networks of roots.

Longing laced every note, an ache for what was not but should be.

And it was somehow familiar. Why?

I smoothed the tattered bark of the trunk on which I sat, dead wood with no pulse of life remaining. However much I wanted to ignore the whispered melody borne on the wind, such a strong trace of Other might well lead to the source of the peculiarities within Enderly—and perhaps whatever Uros had concealed.

If he'd concealed anything at all.

Jade nudged my shoulder, as if urging me to my feet. It was time. So I followed the song, and it drew me to a stand of ancient chestnuts, their gnarled trunks twining one with the other.

Far above my head, dark weblike strands wove tight through their branches, forming an octagonal structure. My heart leapt. Uros had crafted this, I had little doubt. But what did it hold? Had he woven *ilusne* within the structure? Did traps await?

I'd have to take care.

As a girl, I'd delighted in climbing trees, but once I'd left childhood behind, my aunts forbade the activity. Still, it wasn't something one forgot.

I lifted Jade from my shoulders and set her on a nest of moss and fern. "I can't climb while carrying you, so you'll need to rest here."

Contrary to my words, she immediately started to rise.

She seemed to respond best when I spoke to her as if she could understand, so I chose that approach. "Jade, please. You might not have the strength to climb, not yet. Uros won't be here, so will you wait for me?"

She chuffed and ascended the tree with feline grace, then sat watching and waiting from her perch above. Clearly, I'd underestimated her recovery, and she'd made sure I knew it.

I tucked my gloves within my reticule and placed my hand against the trunk of the nearest chestnut. It sparked with life beneath my touch, a sense of long growth and patient absorption of nutrients from soil and sun, and something else—a slow, thrumming anger, a protest at the structure it was forced to uplift. Yet it also invited me upward.

As I climbed, it seemed the branches bent and swept around me, aiding me along the way. Always, when I needed it, I found a hold for my hands and feet. And always, the deep, slow song pulsed through the air about me. At last, I clambered onto a wide, straight branch that led to the lair I'd spotted from below.

I passed through a wispy net of strands that served as a sort of doorway and into the gray-shadowed interior. It was a dwelling of sorts, the walls made up of a weblike substance, and the spongy floor holding furnishings constructed from the same, though these were hardened with some sort of inflexible surface coating.

Against one of the walls rested a table, and it held the vase of evidence that had caught my eye in Upton's townhome. Uros must have brought these items here before he burnt it down. There were other oddities too: an enormous collection of hats hung from protrusions on the wall, a large assortment of canes, and—oh.

My stomach lurched.

The farthest wall was set with small bones in an elaborate pattern, a sort of macabre wallpaper. Why would he do such a thing? I swayed, steadying myself on the wall, and the threads of it stuck to my skin. I scrubbed my hands against my skirts once more, wanting nothing more than to escape this place.

But I had to find the heart.

I forced myself to closely examine every inch of the gruesome structure. Yet there were no hiding places, at least none visible to the mortal eye.

Did that mean Uros concealed the heart with *ilusne*? If so, finding it would be an impossible task. Or was it not here at all?

I rested my back against the trunk of the tree, allowing its steady pulse to slow my own. And I considered the sense of Other that had drawn me here. Certainly, it was nothing within the dwelling, so what then? I resigned myself to ascending farther and pulled myself upright, the chestnut bark digging into my skin.

The song strengthened as I climbed, and a moment later, I reached its source: a small, spreading plant with almost luminescent greenish-white fronds. It nested in a crook between branch and trunk, where soil-like detritus provided material for growth. Small pearl-pink buds nested amid the fronds, but the plant struggled, calling out for moisture and warmth and something else, something not found in our world, something essential for its life.

The unusual feathery leaves resembled that of the dried scrap I'd found in Reynold's bedchamber. Had this been their source?

I brushed my fingers across its velvet-soft surface, and an image flashed through my mind of a swamp, teeming with life, of seeds clinging to a spindle-jointed auvok leg, then dropping here in the cleft of the tree, which held just enough moisture to allow them to survive—survive and yearn for the home they'd left, where they might thrive.

I recoiled. To theorize I might experience something of this sort again was one thing, but to embrace it was another. This time, there was no edgetown to blame, nothing but my own choices.

And I'd make those choices again, for the sake of those I

loved. So I reached for the plant once more, holding the image of the auvok leg in my mind and pressing it further. The image expanded and sound layered over it—

Uros's voice, speaking some sort of dread liturgy.

Then he loosed a deep cry of pain.

Droplets of dark blood scattered over moss and mud, spattered the mother plant from whence the seeds sprang. He dropped to the ground, clasping a large, gray-mottled organ.

His heart.

Then he staggered upright.

But how much memory did a seed retain? How much could it show me? From its low vantage, little could be seen.

Uros crossed back and forth over the clearing several times, his movements unsteady, collecting the seeds as he brushed against the mother plant.

Then another anguished cry rent the air—ancient, green, strong.

Not Uros. Then who? Or what?

Still slightly unsteady, Uros strode away, splashing into muckwater, which submerged the seeds, obscuring all from sight. In the warm wet, they clung to Uros, for such was their nature, persistent burrs that resisted all attempts to dislodge.

And so they passed to our world with him, at last brushed off by the rough bark of the chestnut to land in an inhospitable home.

My hands trembling, I released the plant. The world tilted and spun around me. I clutched at the tree trunk, clinging to it as though it were an anchor to keep me from drifting into a storm-tossed sea. Slowly, my senses righted.

His heart wasn't here.

He'd concealed it in the Otherworld.

Every bit of remaining strength drained from my body, and I slumped into the cradle of the branches. What now? I couldn't leave the plant here to perish, so I removed my handkerchief, filled it with some of the dirt from the cleft, then gently dislodged the blossoms. I wrapped them in the soil-filled kerchief, and then nested the whole bundle in my reticule. With the plant secured, I sank into the cleft of the tree, Jade spilling across my lap, and reflected upon what I knew of Uros.

While arrogant and driven by his cravings, he'd never taken erratic action. So if he hadn't chosen to hide his heart here, then why bother crafting this peculiar dwelling and haunting Enderly in spectral form?

Could a creature who claimed to lack feeling have acted from sentiment, wanting a place in which he could adopt his true form? A home perhaps, reminiscent of his kind? Or did he have another purpose, something else he'd hidden here?

I leaned back, careful not to lose balance, and peered upward. High and to the right, a gleaming rainbow of light played across the leaves and branches of the chestnut.

So I ascended once more, clambering into a nook formed by entwined branches. Across from me, sunlight poured into a gap in the tree limbs and through a tremendous prism, casting multihued light into the shape of a door.

My breath caught.

What had Riven said? Uros had stolen something called a *passing prism*. What else could this be? It beckoned, warm and welcoming, even as it remained wholly Other. If the prism allowed Uros to pass between worlds without using a Crossing, would it also permit my passage? Could I follow traces of the swamp blossoms to their source and so find his heart? I would have to rely on whatever sense I could gain of the terrain and hope that my fae-touch would guide me to the plants where Uros left his heart.

What would such an act cost me? My chest constricted. Already my fae-touch spread like the roots of a quaking aspen, sending up new shoots in surprising ways and at unfavorable times. Venturing into the Otherworld would create the perfect environment for those roots to lengthen and strengthen, for the trees to shoot upright where they might no longer be concealed. And where I may well be consumed in their growth.

I brushed at a long streak of grime down the front of my gown and only succeeded in spreading the debris further. Apart from the fae-touch, I'd face an array of dangers for which I was ill-equipped. If I didn't manage to stay out of the path of hostile fae, I could find myself trapped forever.

But what other options remained? Riven had abandoned Avons, leaving it for Uros to ravage. Even if he would consider this new information, I'd no way to convey it to him—and he'd made it clear he cared nothing for our plight. Mr. Burke and the Magistry had refused to consider my claims. And if I did nothing, Uros *would* return.

He'd come for Lovell first.

Perhaps then he'd claim others.

And when he'd deemed I'd suffered enough, feared enough, he'd come for me. I drew an unsteady breath. I refused to allow myself to succumb to emotion, for if I did, I'd never regain control.

Instead, I fixed my gaze on the eddies of light rippling across the gnarled tree limbs. It lapped against them almost like waves upon the shore, inviting me to come and play, to forget that venturing into the Otherworld was death to mortals—in one form or another.

No matter what awaited or what it might cost me, I must cross. For within lay my one hope of stopping Uros.

CHAPTER 34

Before my resolve could waver, I lifted Jade and clutched her close, and then we stepped into the pool of light.

My stomach dropped as though I'd fallen off a steep cliff. Light and color swirled about me, and I reached for the tree but found nothing—no sturdy limb or thick trunk to anchor me.

My ears popped as the pressure around me changed, and my whole body chilled, my skin pebbling. Jade purred deep and low, a soothing sound. I closed my eyes and stopped fighting the uncanny sensations.

Then branch and bark solidified beneath me once more. Had I failed?

No.

A tree cradled me once more, but this one decidedly not of our world. A flood of sensation swept over me. It was as if the light of sun and star and the force of wind and water mingled and poured themselves into me, a power that seared my very soul. The potency of Other sent me to my knees as every leaf, every blade of grass, and every blossom surged into my awareness with unstoppable force.

My head throbbed as thousands of melodies layered one over the other, and I fought to wrestle the sensations back into my cage of thorns. But in the span of a single breath, the vines within my mind had unraveled. No longer could I hold them to rigid form—they became instead boughs and blossoms that swayed in response to the living songs.

Though I fought, no amount of urging would shift the graceful branches within back to thorned vines. The essence of the Otherworld, all its wild melodies and sensations, wove in and through the blossomed boughs. The fae-touch celebrated its freedom.

And it was too much, far too much.

My vision clouded. I could no longer see, could only feel endless Other pouring into my mortal frame—warm and wild as a summer tempest—and just as sure to shatter me with its force.

My heart drummed faster, more furious. My awareness of my arms, legs, body began to fade. Then something warm and damp nudged my nose.

Jade.

Though my lids felt weighted, I forced my eyes open. Her brilliant green gaze met mine, her face less than a handbreadth from my own, her front paws resting on my shoulders.

She nudged me again, her sweet-grass fragrance thickening about me, drowning out the wilder scents of the Otherworld. And for a moment, my mind cleared.

I'd spent my life exercising control, though never in such circumstances. Surely I could bend these sensations to my will again. My cage of thorns may have vanished, but I wouldn't surrender—not yet.

I must stave off the madness of fae-touch if I were to help

Lovell. I conjured his face in my mind, and that single focal point cleared my thoughts further.

If I no longer had a cage to constrain these sensations, what then? They would not be denied, so I must work *with* them somehow—perish the thought.

Jade still held my gaze, her own steady and confident, and my breathing evened. Rather than command, I coaxed the boughs within to grow closer, to weave their branches and blossoms together once more. This they did willingly. It wasn't the tight, faultless cage of the thorned vines, it didn't block out songs and scents and essence of Other, but somehow the luxuriant hedge within my mind reduced the intensity of the onslaught.

I lowered my head to Jade and whispered my thanks. If I'd not allowed her to come, I'd have lost myself already. Perhaps on some level, she'd sensed the danger and thus insisted on accompanying me.

Now that my fear had subsided, a glorious sense of life pervaded every limb, a sense of strength and energy so strong it seemed as if I could leap from the tree in a single bound. I wasn't foolish enough to try, however.

Instead, I shifted my attention to the swamp blossoms resting in my reticule. Their song had become triumphant, and they filled my mind with an image of the companions they sought . . . a vast carpet of pale fronds and pink flowers spreading over dark, boggy muck.

I crept along the limb, intending to seek a path down from the tree, but as I descended, the rough bark smoothed and warmed. The now-limber branch coiled around me, gently lifting me and depositing me into the grassy meadow below.

A shivering sensation swept my skin, and I stumbled away the moment it released me. How—

Never mind. If I contemplated all the possibilities, I'd never make progress. But oh, I could examine the wonders before me for several lifetimes. If only I had my sketchbook . . .

This tree stood not in a forest, but atop a knoll, carpeted in impossibly green grass and dotted with a riot of blossoms in every imaginable hue. It joined its fellow foothills, tumbling downward toward a silvery-gray river bordered by dark, purplish shrubbery. Altogether, the colors formed a vibrant, harmonious whole.

Rich golden sunlight bathed the whole landscape, drawing out sharp grassy scents and redolent fragrances from every flower. And above it all, something wild and sweet and altogether unfamiliar laced the air.

A piercing cry came from some sort of bird as it swooped and snatched its prey from the river. It was untamed; it was glorious. And I wanted to dance to the melodies that thrummed through my veins . . .

No.

I was here for Lovell, so I must not lose myself, must focus on my aims. If I followed the river, would it lead me to the lowlands and the swamp I sought?

There was perhaps a way to test the theory. I walked away from the river, toward a towering array of mountains in the distance.

The swamp blossoms quieted; the pictures they drew vanished. I turned back toward the river, and the images of black waters drawn sharp against vibrant greenery returned. Very well then, my course was set. Never mind the peculiarity of taking directions from a plant, what better option did I possess?

I hastened toward the river, yet Jade was faster, and she always kept a pace or two ahead. She appeared delighted, and no signs of her weakness remained. Perhaps I hadn't been selfish to bring her after all.

Or was this further evidence that some sort of fae-touch plagued her as well? Was she pleased because it satisfied the desire of those so afflicted to immerse themselves in Other? I resisted the urge to reach out and snatch her close.

If I was right, if an animal *could* be fae-touched, what would become of her? Would she too be driven to madness? Was that what happened when an otherwise ordinary, well-behaved cat or dog suddenly snapped and started lashing out at its owner or attacking innocent bystanders?

If so, perhaps I'd done the worst possible thing to bring her. I couldn't endure the thought of causing her harm . . . but it was done, no turning back. If we survived this, I'd find a way to get her help, should she need it.

For now, I must attend to finding the heart—and surviving the Otherworld. At least no fae had materialized and no Otherworldly predators stalked us. Not yet, at any rate. But sometimes, what was hidden was far more dangerous than what one perceived.

In the growing dusk, I followed the course of the river, keeping some distance from its banks. I'd no wish to be lured into the depths by rusalka or seized by a shellycoat or some other predatory creature.

Whenever the sensations threatened to overwhelm me, Jade hovered close, her presence a steadying force. So we forged on, until the brush became so thick that I must either abandon the river completely or descend to its very edge. When I turned away, the swamp blossoms fell silent once more.

If I left the river, would I soon lose my path altogether? It wasn't as though the forest offered greater assurance of safety. So

I turned back, and the swamp blossoms swayed slightly, evidently pleased with my decision.

The river here was placid, the bank soft and unstable beneath my feet. Soon a disquieting murmur met my ears, distinct from the voices of the plants and the gentle rush of waters.

My skin prickled; the fur on Jade's neck rose. The sound became more distinct: it was a low grumble of sorts, altogether too sentient for my liking.

I whirled about and found nothing. Yet even as I resumed my course, I could not shake the unnerving sensation of eyes on my back.

Then a squelching, muck-marching sound broke the stillness. I spun around once more, to find a small horde of malevolent fae clustered on the bank, their bright, lidless eyes locked upon me. Their long arms far surpassed their short bodies, brushing the ground alongside them, and their claw-tipped fingers swayed like seagrasses.

Grindies.

Mother had told tales of these faefolk, of their unnatural strength, of their bent toward destruction. Their scaly green skin suited itself to camouflage within the river, but unlike sprites, who cast illusion and so lured their prey to its doom, grindies seized upon one with brute force—and they never let go. Chuckling and chortling among themselves, they approached.

Jade coiled her body tight, as though she intended to strike.

I reached for my dagger, but the pendant on my chest warmed so that it nearly scorched my skin. I withdrew it from my bodice, and the shimmering blue strengthened. It flared with an inner light, which surged forth to spread in a circle around me and Jade.

The grindies stepped back—all save one. It hurled itself at

me, only to shriek when the light touched it. It lurched away as though injured. The other grindies muttered angrily.

Would they understand my speech? The sprites had, so it was worth an attempt. I backed away, one step, and then two. "I've not come to cause trouble. Only let me pass, and I'll leave you in peace."

"Care not for your peace." One of the grindies spat a grayish substance on the ground, and a stench rose from it. "Know what we do to your kind?"

Another cackled. "Take you to decorate our dwellings, we do."

The first grindie stepped forward, his thick knuckles bulging as his hands fisted. "Crossed our territory, you did. Belong to us by right."

"I belong to no one. And I shall leave your territory promptly, if you give me no cause for delay."

They eyed the pendant at my neck and muttered once more amongst themselves. Slowly, slowly, they retreated into the waters, submerging themselves until only their gray-green eyes regarded me from the depths.

I backed away pace by pace until I rounded a bend, and they vanished from sight. Then I clasped trembling arms around my chest.

The pendant still pulsed a reassuring light. Whatever it was, it had saved my life. I owed Mr. Heard a greater debt than I ever imagined—and if I somehow managed to return with body and mind intact, I had many questions for him.

Vigilant for any other fae that might lurk nearby, I trudged along. Whether there were none or the pendant held them at bay, I passed unmolested as dusk deepened to full dark.

Though stars bejeweled the sky, none of the constellations were familiar. They hung closer and brighter than those of my own world, their colors more brilliant. Yet I would have exchanged them in a moment for the constellations Father had taught me when I was a girl, for the comfort of those moments sitting between him and Mother and watching the night sky.

I blinked up at them. Father had spoken of altered constellations . . . could it relate to the Otherworld encroaching into our own? Blight and rot, I hoped not.

I stumbled over a fallen log. A half-moon stared down coldly upon us, and between it and the light of my pendant, I had enough illumination to continue—provided I kept my eyes on the ground, rather than the firmament above.

But I did not possess the strength. Exhaustion left me unsteady. No matter the urgency that compelled me onward, sooner or later, I must sleep—or I might make a fatal error. But I could not bring myself to rest exposed along the riverbank. On my left, the thick brush had given way to a dense forest, and I peered into its depths.

From within drifted a gentle whisper of peace and strength. I strained to look deeper into the shadows, and the sensation intensified. I followed the reassuring sound until I reached a mighty oak. Its tremendous trunk had split into four smaller ones a few ells off the ground, an ideal situation in which to pass the night.

With the last of my strength, I clambered within the proffered nest. Jade settled into my lap, warm and heavy, and the warm blue light bathed us both. With the melody of the oak thrumming in my ears, I drifted to sleep.

CHAPTER 35

After a blessedly uneventful night, I woke restored. Jade and I ate a simple meal, then we followed the prompts of the swamp blossoms and took one of the smaller tributaries that branched off the primary river. As the sun crept higher in the sky, the land grew flatter, softer, and more fen-like. Reeds and bulrushes soon overtook grass, and finally, when we faced the swamp proper, no solid ground remained except for where we stood.

The scent of stagnant water and decay wafted out with choking intensity. Despite the unpleasant odor, from the muck rose abundant life, cypresses with thick-bottomed trunks and lush green canopies, mosses of every variety, floating water plants I'd never seen before, and the chirring and chittering of a variety of insects and birds.

If I intended to continue into the swamp, I'd have to pick my way from root to root, crafting a tortuous path through the murky water—which meant close, constant contact with the plants that already pressed against my senses with near-overwhelming force. Could I manage?

Only the inner hedge of blossom and bough kept the impingement of Other from consuming me. How long would it last? I brushed a renegade curl from my face. Never mind—I'd come too far to shrink back now.

With Jade alongside, I plunged beneath the canopy of whorled, moss-laden trees. Warm, humid air enveloped me, tightening the ringlets that fell down the back of my neck and causing my gown to stick unpleasantly to my skin. The overpowering stench nearly choked me, and far worse, an unmistakable sense of fae-presence pervaded the air.

When Riven had appeared, he'd brought with him a sense of potent energy, powerful as lightning. But this was different, just as distinct but heavier, more oppressive somehow. It was as stagnant and still as the placid waters of the swamp, yet tinged with a sort of erosive force.

How close must this fae be to exert such influence? I hoped I'd not have cause to find out.

As we moved deeper into the swamp, the ground vanished into channels of dark water, and I was forced to pick my way from one knobbed root to the other to avoid its depths.

Jade halted abruptly and bared her teeth in distaste at the muck staining her paws. I lifted her and she attempted to scramble onto my shoulders, nearly upending us both into the murk below. At last, she settled for climbing into the low-hanging branches above and keeping pace from the higher—and drier—vantage.

The colors of branch and root, vine and blossom were vivid—brilliant greens and luminous whites contrasting with the dark pools of water below, their beauty eerie. Grayish-green mosses draped over the trees like some sort of ancient shroud, and the low, mournful cry of some forlorn creature echoed in the distance. If I held my breath to avoid inhaling the reek of the mire below, I could appreciate the loveliness far more.

A soft chirrup drifted from the treetops above, and then a magnificent bird of dove-gray plumage fluttered down to inspect me. Its downy fluff invited touch, and its bright eyes sparkled with interest as it approached.

And then its beak opened wide, revealing razor-sharp teeth in an impossibly enormous mouth. It dove toward me, and I staggered back, nearly losing my balance.

I fumbled for my dagger, but before I could withdraw it, Jade pounced on its back, sinking in her claws and teeth alike. With a single swift motion, she ripped off its head, which she deposited at my feet.

Blight and rot.

If I'd left her at home, the outcome of this encounter might have been far different. I clutched the rough trunk of the cypress to steady myself. "Thank you."

She licked her lips, her satisfaction evident. Then she leapt back to the branches above, and we traveled deeper into the swamp. Mists began to swirl through the branches and over the waters. They gathered around me, strengthening until they concealed all but a step or two before and behind. Of course a fae swamp *would* possess dense, unnerving fog.

I clutched at the pendant, its warmth some small reassurance —yet it was not sufficient to prevent the encroachment of the deep, stagnant fae-sensation. It pressed against me, a weight against my chest that made it difficult to draw breath. The mists thickened, and the air became denser, as though something within it *lived*.

The slightest of sounds whispered behind me. I jumped, then slipped on a slick root. I snatched the nearest vine to balance myself, and it curled around my fingers, pulsing with a quick, evergreen life as I peered into the fog. What was lurking beyond sight?

In the distance, diffused lights appeared, some palest gold, others lavender, still others the softest of greens. Some sort of sylph, perhaps? If there were sun sylphs, could there be swamp sylphs? Or was it a more malevolent creature—a will-o'-the-wisp or some unknown Otherkind ready to lead me astray or draw me into captivity?

Green eyes alight, Jade began to descend from her perch. The fur at her ruff rose.

My skin prickled, and the light shimmering from my pendant brightened. Was it safer to stay and face whatever came or to flee deeper into the swamp? Could I find some place of concealment? Perhaps if I climbed the nearest tree . . .

The water rippled, then surged up and over me.

Jade snarled as a tremendous hand grasped my ankle and pulled me into the depths below.

∾

Thick arms coiled around me, bruising with their force, pinioning my own. Though I thrashed against its grip, the creature did not loosen its hold. Whatever protection the pendant had offered before, its light could not pierce these murky waters.

Nor could I long survive here.

I must get free. I strained against the bulk that held me, bracing my legs against an enormous torso. I might as well have pressed against a boulder. The Otherkind did not yield, but dragged me at a tremendous rate through the unnatural depths of the swamp.

And my lungs burned, already starved for air. I kicked at

unyielding flesh to no avail. Black spots danced before my eyes, and every sinew cried out: *breathe!*

Just before my body overruled my mind and forced inhalation of the fetid waters, the creature surfaced. It climbed up onto a hill that did not belong within the low, flat features of the swamp.

I gasped for air, and when my vision cleared, I looked into the face of a massive creature who appeared crafted from swamp matter. Its dark gray-green skin rippled over enormous muscles—arms as thick as cypress trunks, and legs resembling their thick knobbed roots. The hair on its head was as coarse and wild as the mosses that hung from the branches above.

A chill pebbled my skin. I'd no defense against it except the dagger strapped to my side, now inaccessible. When it had seized me, it had dislodged all my belongings—the rucksack and, even worse, the reticule with the swamp blossoms that had been my guide. They remained somewhere in the depths of the swamp.

And Jade. What had become of her? Had she escaped? Was there another such creature who'd claimed her?

I must try to gain my freedom, must try to find her. With all my strength, I pushed against the creature. Yet it paid no more heed to my struggles than if I'd been the lowliest of worms. Muck and detritus dripped away from my pendant at last, and its light burst over him.

He shuddered and gave a low, pained moan. Yet he carried me onward, keening as he went. What compelled him to hold me captive, when it caused him such pain?

He staggered up the hill toward a fortress of dark stone that shared the eerie allure of the swamp. It dominated the landscape, yet its stark beauty failed to charm, given the dangers that must lurk within.

As we approached, the creeping sense of fae-presence strengthened, the stagnant stillness tinged with the power of decay now many times more potent.

My captor lurched toward double doors crafted of dark wood and strap-hinged with a pale, silvery metal. They led into a massive entrance hall. At the end, a wide hearth blazed with white flame, and in front of the fire, a tall fae lord stood waiting.

My captor dropped me before the lord and then himself collapsed, cringing away from the light of the pendant.

Given the sensation provoked by the fae's power, I expected to find some sort of creature like the one who'd taken me captive—not this magnificent, stately man. His eyes and hair were the richest of browns, his pale skin as flawless as polished ivory, and his features drawn as if by a master artist. He was beautiful. And no doubt as cruel as the rest of his kind.

What now? Even if I escaped him, I'd no hope of finding the location of the heart without the swamp blossoms. And I'd lost Jade, a fact more unbearable than all the rest.

My eyes burned, and my gaze dropped to the floor. Muddy water dripped from my gown, splotching the silvery stones with dark drops like blood.

The fae lord stepped forward, his leather boots clicking against the polished stone. "What have you done to my servant?"

I lifted my chin. I must show no weakness. "What have *I* done? He abducted me. I'm the innocent party in this situation."

"And you are bold, for a mortal." He rubbed his hands, his elegant silver rings glinting in the light of the fire. "This should prove entertaining."

He stepped closer still, into the light of my pendant—and it appeared to do him no harm. Perhaps it did not have the power to influence high fae, only low.

He jabbed an imperious finger toward the blue jewel. "From whence did you steal that, mortal?"

"It was a gift." I straightened to my full height. "Why have you brought me here?"

"You chose to enter my domain. Did you imagine I would not notice?"

"I gave no consideration to it, one way or another." If I revealed my fear, I'd appear more like prey. So I held his gaze. "I'd no notion the swamp belonged to you, nor would I have come unless it was necessary."

His lips tilted in a cold smile. Had I amused him? "What business would bring a mortal to the Ecvan?"

"It's a long story."

"Divert me with it—and perhaps I will let you live."

"I'm afraid it's no great tale." Yet a little spark of hope began to burn inside. "Perhaps you already know its beginning. Perhaps you may influence its end."

He leaned forward. "You intrigue me. Go on."

"First, I must know—what sort of fae are you? Do you perceive all that happens within the swamp? Could a powerful being enter the Ecvan without your knowledge?"

He lifted a brow. "You seem under a misapprehension, mortal. I owe you no answers."

"I only thought . . . but I should have known even fae would not possess such powers." I shrugged, as if everything did not hinge on this small chance.

"You seek to provoke me into a declaration of how far my power extends. Perhaps such tricks work in the mortal world, but not here." The floor beneath us rippled, as though its silvery surface were no longer stone but water. Water that could drown, destroy, erode . . . in time, decay all.

I swallowed hard, but did not move.

"Yet it has been long since a mortal ventured into the Ecvan, longer still one that was not a frightened mouse. I will grant you this much: not a creature moves in the swamp without my knowledge. What will you do with possession of this fact?"

"I'll give you information in exchange. Are you aware a killer moved within your world some months ago?"

He reached forward and tilted up my chin, studying my face. My skin crawled, and I wanted to pull away—but I couldn't afford to give offense, so I stood rooted in place.

"I am aware." He brushed a bedraggled curl from my cheek. "But how did you come by this knowledge?"

"The killer came to my world, to my city. He killed many before revealing his identity. He's auvok, and I mean to find his heart and put an end to him."

"My, you are bold. Misguided and foolish, but bold." He released me and rocked back. "How did this bring you to the Ecvan?"

"Evidence suggests he came here before he entered my world—and I believe he left his heart behind."

"Ah, the beginning of your tale." He stroked his chin. "As it happens, one such as you describe entered the Ecvan several passings of the moon ago. He spent a great deal of his life force within the swamp. If he left his heart, as you say, it would explain the matter."

"You allowed him to cross through your domain without challenge?"

He shrugged. "I judged it would prove to my advantage, if I exercised patience. It appears I'm about to receive my reward."

Did that mean he was willing to help? I ventured a suggestion. "I imagine you could get a great deal of credit if you stopped him, given the murders he committed in your world."

A slight smile tilted his mouth. "Perhaps."

I may have lost the blossoms, but if this fae knew the places Uros had visited, he could take me there himself—abhorrent as I found the notion of partnership with him. "Then you'll help me end the auvok?"

"Do you think fae services are so readily procured?" He laughed softly. "If you want my aid, we must bargain."

Despite the heat of the blaze, I shivered. Fae and their bargains. I'd escaped twice before, but could I hope to emerge unscathed a third time? I was in the domain of this strange fae; he held every advantage. If he offered a bargain, it could only be one weighed in his favor—yet I was also at his mercy. What choice did I have?

I folded my arms across my still-damp bodice. "What do you want?"

"Your service."

"I . . . I don't understand."

"If I give you the location of the auvok's heart, I require your service. For five years, all your labor and the fruit of it will belong to me."

"Five years?" My mind spun. "Perhaps you've forgotten how short mortal lives are. I cannot possibly agree."

"Fine. Two years should be sufficient, if all they say is true."

Sufficient for what? Clearly he had some purpose in mind. With the way my fae-touch strengthened, two years might as well be an eternity, not to mention the incredible pain it would cause my family. With two years' absence, they'd believe me dead. Not that this fae would care about their suffering. "Surely you're aware of how your world influences mortal senses. It would be akin to death for me to remain even a fortnight."

The floor rippled once more, and cool water lapped my ankles. I refused to look down.

"There are protections I can set on those within my domain."

"Then that must be part of our bargain. You keep the influence of the Otherworld at bay and ensure I retain my full faculties while I'm in your service—and until I am safely returned to my own world."

"It shall be."

Why was he so agreeable about this? I plucked a decaying leaf from my skirt. "Why do you want my service? A fae with your power must have his share of servants."

He shrugged. "Mortals are highly valued in my world for the novelty they provide. You might say your presence here will enhance my power."

At least that was slightly more believable than that he required one more drudge. If fae viewed mortal slaves as a sign of status, then perhaps it was worth it to him to bargain for my service—especially when all he had to offer in exchange was a small piece of information. And yet . . . surely even fae wouldn't act without conscience. Uros had killed his kind too. "What if I decline your bargain? Would you allow Uros to continue taking lives?"

"He's in your world now. What concern is it of mine?" The fae straightened his green-and-brown-vined jacket. "You must make a choice: agree to my terms or see him go free."

I pressed my palm flat against my stomach, but failed to still the churning within. What was he concealing within this bargain? I'd no notion, and I was running out of stalling tactics. I edged backward. "I cannot possibly agree without knowing your name."

"You may call me Lord Mocvar," he said. "And what of you, little one? What is your name?"

"I'm Jessa."

"Jessa." The name rolled off his tongue as though he savored it. Then his eyes narrowed. "Most mortals are not wise enough to withhold their true name. How very interesting."

My true name? What game did he play? My legs trembled, and I wanted to sink to the floor, which finally appeared like stone once more. But my weakness would only give him greater pleasure. "If I agree to your terms, I want my cat back—and I want your word she'll come to no harm, and receive her release when I do."

"You speak of your *kit-isne?* That will be a problem."

"If you've hurt her . . ." Sudden strength surged through my limbs.

"She's unharmed." He crossed to a table carved in the shape of a leaf and there poured amber liquid into a goblet. "But I refuse to accept *kit-isne* within my demesne."

Would she survive the swamp? She'd shown herself as canny in this world as in my own, and I could do no more for her, though the thought of her wandering alone tugged at my heart. What if she became injured, as she'd been when we'd met? What if Mocvar hurt her himself, once he secured our bargain? I straightened. "Then you will swear—within our bargain—that you'll not harm her, nor command or suggest that any other hurt her."

"I'll grant that much." He sipped from the thick-cut glass. "Now, mortal, I've been more than generous. Do you consent?"

"I have one more requirement."

"I weary of your demands." His features sharpened. "Why should I offer further concessions when I could end your life here and now with the snap of my fingers?"

"Because clearly I have something you want, something you can only gain by bargaining—else you would have already taken it by force."

Something flickered in his eyes, a hint of—anger?—that confirmed my assessment.

I ignored it and forged on. "For the information to have value, I must be able to act on it. I must have time to find the heart and see the auvok ended before I enter your service—and you must swear to tell me the true location of his heart."

"You've bargained with fae before." The light caught on the few strands of silver in his dark hair. He set down the goblet. "I'll grant your requests—a matter of a few weeks makes no difference to me. I'll give you a fortnight to deal with this auvok, if you are able, and then you'll return to complete your service. Are we agreed?"

I'd run out of ways to stall him and stipulations to add to our agreement, but every fiber of my being protested this bargain. How could I condemn my family to suffer so? Not to mention whatever Mocvar held in store for me. Yet I saw no way out. "I—"

A brilliant light seared the air, sending a flash of heat across my skin, snatching the words from my mouth. When the radiance faded, Riven stood in the center of the room, Nikol at his side. Another form stumbled out from behind them, blinking and bleary.

Mr. Burke?

How was it possible? How had he . . . how had any of them come?

Riven strode forward, not Lord Riven of Elmsford, his fae form glamoured into human guise, but the full-fae Lord Riven —the contoured planes of his face set in grim lines, his green eyes hard and glittering as emeralds. "She'll enter no bargain with you. Stand down, Mocvar."

CHAPTER 36

The pressure in the air became nearly unbearable. It tingled along my skin and tightened my chest, driving my questions about their appearance from my mind. What kind of power did Riven hold? And what would happen if he freed it? Would either of us mortals survive? According to his own words, it would not matter to him.

Mocvar faltered, his eyes fixed on Riven. His face took on the pallor of sapwood. "Arbiter. To what do I owe this pleasure?"

"The presence of the mortal with whom you attempt to bargain." Riven evinced no emotion; his features were impossible to read. "Do you attempt to interfere with my affairs? She's already bound to me."

The gold binding mark flared with brilliant light, stinging my arm.

"I assure you, I was not aware." He rubbed his hands together. "You sent her after the heart?"

"Why not? Mortals can be useful, at times." The sharp scent of an impending storm swept the grand hall. Riven closed the gap between them. "What do you know of the auvok heart? And how long have you known it?"

Beads of sweat formed on Mocvar's forehead, then words wrenched from him. "Some months ago, a shifter entered the Ecvan. He offered a favorable bargain for the ruined demesne of the former lord of this land, and he spent considerable power there. But I did not know he was auvok."

The storm-scent swirled round me, and I shivered. I'd no doubt Riven was compelling Mocvar to speak, and moreover, to speak truth, for he'd unfolded far more detail to Riven than he had to me.

Mr. Burke edged between me and the fae, though what he intended to do if the situation deteriorated, I had no notion. Still, I appreciated the intent.

"You did not know? Or you chose not to consider?" The storm-charged scent strengthened, laced with something new, something sharp and bitter and biting—something that tasted of death. "I spread word that a shifter had caused the deaths in our court. Yet you did not bring this information before the king."

Mocvar eyed Riven as though he were a dragon about to strike, perhaps devour him alive. What did that say about Riven? I wrapped my fingers around my pendant, and through the muslin of my gown, it pulsed as rapidly as my heart.

Though Mocvar looked as if he'd rather cut out his own tongue than reply, he said, "The shifter offered a compelling price for my silence."

"You know how the king will deal with you."

Mocvar paled further. "I shall make the amends he requires."

"You'll be fortunate if it's not your life he requires." Riven inclined his head slightly. "Cooperate, and when I bring your case before the king, I will suggest leniency. You'll give me the location of the old demesne and allow us unhindered passage through the Ecvan until the matter of the auvok is resolved. Further, you'll allow the mortal to depart with us, unmolested."

His eyes hardened. "By right, she—"

"By right, you should have reported the presence of an unnatural creature within the Ecvan at once, since you were well aware of the murders." His voice snapped like a whip. "Your only chance of leniency is if you render the aid now you should have then."

Mocvar bowed his head. "I am his humble servant."

A soft scoffing sound escaped Nikol, yet Mocvar didn't spare him a glance—he was still fixed on Riven. Then Mocvar sketched a brief account of his dealings with Uros and the small portion of the Ecvan he'd sold as part of a bargain between them. After Riven pressed, he added how Uros had inquired in particular about the presence of an ancient well upon the knoll.

Would Uros have chosen to conceal his heart within it? It would offer natural shelter from those who might stumble upon it by chance. Could it have some other power?

A faint smile played about Nikol's lips as he watched Mocvar confess, and I shuddered.

Mr. Burke, on the other hand, appeared shaken, his shoulders stooped and his body motionless. His entire posture lacked its usual purposeful energy. If he'd been pulled into the Otherworld, possibly against his will, and then dragged into this interrogation . . . he must be fearing for his fate—and mine as well, unless I misjudged his nature.

How *had* they come?

At last, Riven said, "That is sufficient."

Then he spun and walked away, with a gesture toward us to follow. I dared not ignore it. I hurried after him through the fortress doors, Mr. Burke at my side.

Just over the threshold, I glanced back. Dark waters churned on the floor about Mocvar. He may have had no choice but to surrender to Riven's demands, but his anger surged through the swamp, thickening the air and agitating the waters.

Would he yet do us harm?

Before I could consider further, Riven opened a gleaming pool of light in front of us. It tugged me into its depths, with a jumble of sensation reminiscent of the passing prism—only this swirl of light and color was far more focused and controlled.

Still, my stomach twisted, and I struggled to regain my footing after the door of light deposited us in a copse of cypress trees, their netlike lattice of roots keeping us above the muck. Across an open expanse of swamp stood the knoll Mocvar had described. The fading light revealed only the vaguest of jagged outlines looming above the waters—an unnatural sort of growth, like the one on which Mocvar had constructed his demesne.

I strained to perceive the ruins it must house, but then a shimmering haze obscured my vision. It spread from Riven to envelop the four of us, blocking out sights and sounds of the swamp behind—ensuring no trace of our presence escaped?

He stalked across the roots of cypress toward me, lithe as a cat, a furious sort of energy crackling around him. "What are you doing in the Ecvan?"

The edge to his words cut deep, laid bare my mortality. I was disheveled, weary, and so very weak compared to even the most insignificant of Otherkind—let alone two high fae. Riven may have delivered me from Mocvar, but who would preserve me from him? Whatever he intended, I refused to shrink back. "I was trying to find Uros's heart, since you would not."

He muttered a curse under his breath. "I told you to flee to safety. Not enter the Otherworld."

He dared to accuse, after abandoning our world to death and destruction? My pulse quickened as I wrestled to hold myself in check. After all, ladies don't reveal their anger. They measure and modulate their words; they're gentle, kind, and gracious at all times.

But I was in the middle of an Otherworldly swamp. I'd been dragged through its waters by a grelum and forcibly detained in the demesne of a fae lord, all the while enduring the constant encroachment of my fae-touch. I'd been left bruised and aching from head to toe, and the restraints holding in my emotions wore perilously thin. If there were only fae present, I'd not have bothered to try—but Mr. Burke stood here, a representative of the world of propriety I'd left behind.

"What did you imagine you'd accomplish?" Riven demanded.

When he hurled the question at me, my fragile control shattered, despite my efforts. "You have no right to ask. Did you expect me to cower in the dark and wait for death, just because an almighty fae commanded it so?"

Nikol gave an abrupt laugh, and Riven shot him a glare that would have wilted even the hardiest of plants, before advancing once more toward me. "I expected you to exercise a modicum of common sense, not blunder from one danger into another."

"I say." Evidently, Mr. Burke had regained his equilibrium, for he edged between us. "There's no need to—"

Riven coiled a strand of solid light around him and bound him to the nearest cypress. "Stay out of this."

"I didn't blunder into the Otherworld, whatever you believe of mortals." My shoulders tightened. "I considered the cost, and I came by choice."

"Do you mean to say emotion didn't drive you? That you thought nothing of your fears—or your desire to protect your family?"

"Of course my feelings for them influenced my decision.

Would you abandon those you love to death? Wait—don't answer that." I drew a shuddering breath, a vain attempt to stem the tide of emotion flowing from me—which only proved his point.

His voice deepened, and the haze thickened. "What did you dream you would do? Search the length and breadth of the Otherworld till somehow you stumbled upon his heart?"

"That's not what I—"

"Have you forgotten the entire history of your kind? When has passing through worlds ended well for mortals?"

I blew out in frustration. He wasn't listening. Did he imagine I'd accidentally ended up in the same swamp that contained the heart? Possibly, for to do otherwise would be to give mortals some credit. I shoved my hair from my face and countered with a question of my own. "Did you come all this way just to chastise me? How did you even know I was here?"

"I investigated the lair in Enderly, and Burke arrived, seeking you. He'd assigned men to watch you—"

I spun to face Mr. Burke, who stood at the edge of the cypress bank, unbound now, but eyeing Riven warily.

"You set men to watch me?"

"Not watch you—watch over you. They were meant to protect you." Mr. Burke shook his head. "If you knew about the Otherworldly monster, you were in danger."

"You . . . you knew? But you wouldn't listen—you forbade me to speak!"

"Apologies, Miss Jessa." Regret tinged his voice. "The Vigil mandated it so, and I never dreamt you'd take such extreme action."

I steadied myself against the nearest cypress. "Then they knew, all along?"

"Not all along, but by the fourth victim." His jaw tightened.

"Orders came from the king and Magister alike: the Vigil was to take charge of the investigation behind the scenes. It must appear that the Magistry was in control, else rumors would spread of Otherworldly involvement and create the sort of panic that would devastate Avons."

"They thought it better to deceive the entire populace while an Otherworldly predator killed them off one by one?"

"Don't take off my head." He held up his hands. "I agree, it should never have been kept hidden. But the choice was not mine to make."

"And your men told you I entered the Otherworld?"

"They weren't sure what happened. They watched you ascend and reported that you never came down, nor could they find you thereafter. When I went to investigate, I encountered Riven. At the time, I thought him connected with the Magistry."

Thanks to Riven's glamour, no doubt.

"He—ah, demanded to know my purpose there. When I told him, he said he'd handle the situation, but I wasn't inclined to let a stranger take over my case."

And Riven had not forced the matter?

"To glamour without shattering the mind is a delicate task when the knowledge runs as deep as his, and we'd no time to waste." Riven gritted out the words. "So I brought him."

He spoke as if his actions were the logical choice, but I'd little doubt another fae would have rent the knowledge from Mr. Burke and left his mind broken without a second thought. Perhaps I'd not been altogether wrong about Riven. I hesitated. "Wait, you said you investigated the lair. How long had you known about it?"

"Not long. Uros spent considerable time crafting false trails for me to follow. Each one required investigation and elimination."

Which meant, after all he'd said, Riven *had* still tracked Uros. Would he have found the heart in the end, without all the risks on my part? I wove my arms across my chest, attempting to hold in my fraying emotions. I'd surrendered to them far too much already.

"Which brings me to another question." The flicker in Riven's eyes became green flame, kindled bright in the growing dark. "I find it difficult to believe you stumbled into the same swamp that housed the heart by chance. How did you know it was here?"

What could I say? Anything less than the truth wouldn't make sense, yet to confess before them all . . . my throat tightened. "I found evidence at the lair."

Riven shook his head, stepped closer.

And then a dark, bulky form dropped from the cypress above, and a familiar sweet-grass scent filled the air around me.

Jade.

I forgot everything but her presence. I scooped her up and held her close, burying my face in her fur. Though her ears pricked, she did not protest. When I released her, she sniffed my face, my hair, my gown, and at last purred her satisfaction.

How had she found me? I turned to Riven. "Did you bring her here?"

"I left signals for her to follow."

Then I'd been right, and something had altered Jade's senses, otherwise how could she have perceived whatever trail Riven formed for her and made her way through the barrier, which presumably he'd left open for her passage?

Mr. Burke cleared his throat, taking advantage of the break in conversation to interject. "Perhaps it was unwise of her to enter the Otherworld, but since she has located the heart, surely she deserves some credit."

"Locating the heart would have accomplished nothing. Mocvar would have ensured she never got near it. He'd never endanger his prey." Riven raked a hand through his hair. "Tell me, what were his conditions?"

"He would give me the location of Uros's heart and a fortnight to retrieve it and put an end to Uros, if I could—and in exchange, I would serve him for two years."

"What were the precise terms concerning your end of the bargain?"

"For two years, all my labor and the fruit of it would belong to him."

All trace of emotion vanished from Riven. He might as well have been formed from stone. "Are you aware of what he meant?"

"I thought he concealed his true desires." Some part of me needed to understand. "What was his purpose?"

Riven snapped his fingers, and fae-lights kindled, driving back the dark of gathering night. "To gain an heir. He intended to bed you, get a child on you, and keep it once your term of service was done."

"He . . . impossible." But it was not, and I knew it. The fae-lights wavered before my eyes, and the world became a swirl of black and gold.

Your labor, and the fruits of it.

Jade chirred low and nudged me, but a peculiar numbness seized my limbs, and I could not will them to respond. I had come so close to binding myself to an unthinkable fate. The murmurs of the mosses above roared in my ears, and the song of the cypress surged over my senses. I swayed.

Mr. Burke stepped forward and wrapped a steadying arm around my shoulders. He smelled of bergamot and clove. Comforting, human scents, reminders of a world that would never consider such a dark and twisted bargain. For just a moment, I leaned into him, hiding from the horror that had nearly taken me captive. Then I forced myself away from the shelter he offered. "Why wouldn't he just wed?"

"He likely will, when he finds an advantageous partnership. But fae have trouble bearing young. Mortals are fertile, and their joint offspring will be full-blood fae, if they so choose." Riven spoke in clipped tones. "You would have served his desires and gained nothing but torment. What possessed you to—"

"Leave off," Mr. Burke snapped. "Can't you see she's frightened enough already?"

"If only she'd been frightened into wisdom earlier." Riven folded his arms across his chest. "Perhaps you'd prefer I take the mortal course and lie to reassure her? Allow her to remain blind to the fate that awaits mortals in my world?"

"Of course not—I want you to remove her from the danger altogether."

"An impossible task." The fae-lights brightened. "In your world, Uros may await. His whereabouts remain unknown. If he tires of the trouble she's caused, he will claim her life—and she could not hope to stop him."

Mr. Burke's lips drew into a tight line. "Then she's to remain at risk?"

"Please don't talk about me as if I'm not here." I struggled to keep my tone even. "I appreciate your attempts to look after my safety, Mr. Burke. Perhaps I should not have come to the Otherworld on my own, but there's no sense in discussing it further. I'm here now, and I will see this through."

Because how could I trust the fate of the mortal world to Riven? What if something went wrong, and he chose a path that protected the fae but left Lovell and my family vulnerable? I wanted to trust him. After all, he could have abandoned me to

Mocvar and gone after the heart himself. But if I was wrong . . . the cost would be staggering.

"And then there's Mocvar to consider. He was none too pleased at having his toy snatched away." Nikol's light tone belied the serious nature of his words. "If you sent the mortals to safety, it might raise unwanted questions. Doubtless he's made assumptions about the nature of your bargain with Jessa. He likely expects the mortals will serve as bait for any predators we may encounter. After all, why not let them set off any traps Uros may have left—clear a path for us?"

Jade bristled, and Mr. Burke's hand went to the blade at his side.

Riven wouldn't consider such a course . . . would he? I pulled Jade closer still. Was Nikol even suggesting it, or was he merely speculating on Mocvar's views? He'd left it unclear, perhaps intending to stir trouble.

But Riven offered little reaction, merely raising a brow. "That's not part of the plan, whatever Mocvar imagines. If you still intend to assist in this matter, fetch the *ishtar*. It should be ready by now."

"It will delay us till morning. You know how Sylvi is."

"So much the better. The daylight will give us a small advantage against the *ilusne*, one which we require." As Riven spoke, the barrier he'd formed about us thinned, and the vivid sights and sounds of the swamp returned. "Or have you already forgotten the snares he managed in the mortal world?"

Nikol gave a slow nod. "I'll return as swiftly as I can."

I took little comfort in the notion. What might befall us in the meantime?

In short order, silence fell over the stand of cypress. Nikol had departed at once, and Riven suggested we sleep while we could. If his even breathing were any indication, Mr. Burke had fallen into slumber right away. But I remained wakeful, despite my exhaustion.

If I had stayed home, I would have been tucked between Ada and Ainslie in their large bed, surrounded by soft coverlets, downy warmth, and sisterly love. Instead, I rested with Jade in a knobby nest of roots, with only the unfamiliar constellations above me. Their unnatural brightness and unusual colors soon blurred like a watercolor painting given one wash too many.

I wanted to stay, would have fought to stay if Riven had attempted to send me home. I'd come too far to turn back without ensuring Uros was defeated . . . or I met my end at his hands. But what horrors might await us?

He'd stored his most precious possession in these ruins, and I couldn't imagine he'd left it undefended. Already I'd nearly fallen into the trap crafted by Mocvar. Nearly found myself forced to endure violation and abandon a child, *my* child, if Mocvar had his way . . . And Uros was a far more powerful foe.

With Mocvar, it had suited Riven to intervene—but if it did not in the affair with Uros, if he deemed mortals a suitable sacrifice to secure the safety of his people, how could I hope to survive? And my presence here had dragged Mr. Burke into the Otherworld. Would I become his downfall also?

Then there was Ainslie. Mocvar's intent with our bargain opened a world of dreadful possibilities with hers. Only, why had no one claimed it? Could it be part of some larger plan that awaited an appointed time? I shoved upright, unable to remain still any longer.

"Jessa?" Riven spoke so softly, I almost didn't hear. The edge in his voice was gone, so also were the coldness and the anger. "Will you join me?"

Anything was better than lying here tormented by my imagination. I swiped the traces of damp from my face—grateful for the shadows that offered some concealment—and then crossed the uneven expanse of roots. He kept watch from a broad, flat stone at the edge of the copse, and I joined him there, perching at the farthest corner. We sat in silence.

Riven broke it first.

"I was . . . unjust to speak to you as I did." The lone fae-light he'd kept lit softened his features.

Whatever I'd expected, it was not a concession of wrongdoing from a fae—and it dismantled my defenses.

Jade perched between us and glared at Riven. She did not appear as ready to listen as I. Her tail twitched against the stone.

Could I trust him? That question drowned out all others. He could have taken advantage of me, as Mocvar had. He could have ripped away Mr. Burke's memories and left him senseless. He could have abandoned me to navigate the Otherworld alone. Yet he had not. I knew what Mr. Heard would say, what all our lore concluded: *never* trust a fae. But if we were to face whatever Uros prepared together, I must know. Did he share the cruelty of his kin? Or did he choose his own path?

Tucked in the shelter of the cypress, with the black of night only scarcely pressed back by the Otherworldly light he'd kindled, all the niceties were stripped away, and I found courage to ask. "Why were you angry? Why did you come for me?"

Just when I thought he'd not heard—or would refuse to answer—he turned toward me. "You want the truth? I've seen mortals suffer. Too often. And it gives me no pleasure."

He spoke as one confessing a grave fault, a weakness to be condemned. Perhaps among his kind, it was.

A soft buzzing of wings sounded to my right. Without bothering to look in its direction, Riven sent out a gleaming net of light and snared a dread-aught. I edged a bit closer to him. What other foul creatures lurked just beyond sight? "I didn't think fae cared about the plight of mortals."

"To care about the plight of anyone—mortal or fae—is to become weak."

"I cannot think it so." Yet clearly he did. Nikol had spoken of entanglement with mortals, nearly taunted him with it. What lay in his past? I twined my fingers in Jade's fur. "Yet you made me believe you did not concern yourself with the fate of my world."

The slightest of laughs escaped him. "Evidently I missed the mark. I expected you to behave like the rest of your kind—and flee danger."

"Then you don't understand us as well as you think."

"Perhaps not." He shifted, and the sensation of pressure in the air increased. "Now—you owe me an answer. Why didn't you seek safety, as I advised you? You could have avoided all this."

"Because doing so would have condemned Avons, with many I loved trapped inside it. And Uros didn't intend to stop there." The cold of the stone seeped through my clothing, and I shivered. "You said you didn't care about our world, and I believed you. Someone had to care . . . and act."

"Why you?"

"I thought no one else knew. I tried to tell Mr. Burke and involve the Magistry, but you know the conclusion of that endeavor." I reached for Jade, and she nestled alongside me. "And there's more. Lovell received the mark—Uros tattooed him before he came to me."

A damp breeze swirled through the cool night air, and I

rubbed my arms to warm myself. Riven sparked another faelight, this one burnt umber. While far dimmer than the others, it gave off tremendous warmth.

Jade gave a soft *mrow* of approval and regarded Riven with less distaste.

"You care so much for your cousin?"

I should have known Riven would have familiarized himself with my family. He was nothing if not thorough. "He's more like a brother to me."

"I see. And do you regret your choice?"

"If I'd chosen to seek my own safety first, I could never have made peace with myself. I would have felt the weight of every death thereafter, since I had the knowledge to stop the killer and shrank back." I tucked my knees to my chest and rested my head on them. "And I cannot pretend it was entirely disinterested. Uros wanted my life as well."

"To seek the end of a foe who desires your life is logical—but only if you have a chance of accomplishing that end." He turned toward me, and the scent of sun and storm washed over me. "I'll ask again. What gave you that confidence? What made you believe his heart was concealed here?"

Had he called me over just to attempt to pry my secrets from me? To trick me into trusting him and spilling my soul? Certainly, keen interest blazed in his eyes.

Yet I wouldn't willingly confess. It would expose far more than I could bear. If he was determined to confirm his suspicions, he could force the truth from me—and in so doing, he'd reveal the truth about himself.

I drew my legs closer, shielding myself from the encroachment on my defenses. "I had my reasons. But I . . . I don't want to talk about it. It's over and done."

Riven twisted the green-and-gold ring on his right hand. "Very well."

That was all. No pressure followed, no compulsion to speak the truth. The tension in my shoulders eased, and I released the grip on my legs. He'd asked a great deal—now it was my turn. "Why did you try to make me believe you'd abandoned us to Uros?"

"I intended to provoke him further. To try to draw him out. If you remained involved, he would have killed you. He'd already killed fae. You didn't stand a chance." He rubbed a hand across his jaw. "I meant to distract him from you and your world altogether—he's not the sort to shrink from a challenge."

"Why didn't you tell me? I would have listened."

"Would you? Does your trust in fae extend so far?" The faelights brightened, casting sharp, jagged shadows from the cypress branches and roots. "Would you ever have believed that I acted in the interests of your world as well as mine?"

He saw too much. Even now, I wrestled with how much I could trust him—or any fae. I shrank back, and he pressed his advantage.

"Information is power. The power to betray, the power to act, the power to destroy. It should not be given freely." He gave me a sharp look. "Can you claim you don't understand this?"

"No," I whispered.

If I condemned him for withholding the truth, I condemned myself. He'd acted as he'd thought best, concealing information, hiding his true purpose, twisting the truth to his own ends—as I'd done myself, time and again. Had my concealment hurt my family, altering their choices as his had mine? I stared into the blackness of the swamp toward the knoll. An ache formed beneath my breastbone, deep and throbbing.

"If it brings you any comfort, you've bought time that may well spare your cousin—if we succeed." Riven weighed his words. "When Uros revealed his auvok form to you, he exposed his true essence for the first time. That he did so in my presence would have allowed me to locate his heart, in the end—once I sorted through all the false leads and snares he'd left for me and any other fae that might seek to move against him. He did not think to protect himself against a mortal. And it may yet prove his undoing."

I let out a breath, the pain in my chest easing. If I could spare Lovell, it was worth it after all. "Thank you for telling me. For coming after me. For intervening with Mocvar."

Starlight and fae-light played across his features, etching shadows across the planes of his face. "Have you learned nothing from your time here? You should not offer thanks so freely, lest you find yourself indebted once more."

I lifted my chin. "I'll not forgo offering gratitude when it's due."

"You may come to regret that choice."

"Well, it's not as if I intend to make incursions into the Otherworld a regular occurrence." If I had any say in the matter, this would be my first and only time.

His lips parted slightly, then he shook his head. "You may not have the luxury of choice. You're still in danger. I can promise no protection."

"I don't expect it, only that you'll do what you can to end Uros."

"You have my word."

But would it be enough?

CHAPTER 37

The morning sun kindled the swamp waters with golden fire, but the knoll with the heart remained shrouded in impenetrable gloom, strong enough that we could not discern its true form.

The first light also brought Nikol. When he appeared at the edge of the copse and began to speak with Riven in the fae tongue, Mr. Burke took the opportunity to approach me. "Miss Jessa, I wish I could remove you from this situation, but since I cannot, I'd be remiss if I didn't offer you what little protection I possess."

His hand went to a silver chain around his neck. "When it became apparent we dealt with an Otherworldly predator, the Vigil saw that the statesmen assigned to the case were given wards as a safeguard."

"Thank you, but I've learned our ward-pendants are of little use against fae. Neither of us should rely on them."

"These aren't the ward-pendants peddled about to the general populace—they're what the alchemists give Collectors to keep their minds intact. And my cloak also offers protection, not specifically from fae, but against physical attack. I'd feel better if you took them."

So the Magistry had provided elsingers to a select few alongside their wards. That indicated far more worry than they'd admitted to the public. "You're very gracious, but I can't accept."

He drummed his fingers against his leg. "Why not?"

"You only came into the Otherworld because of me. I won't be the cause of your downfall." Not to mention that fae-touch already plagued me. If he bore the wards Collectors used to protect themselves, then perhaps he'd emerge from the Otherworld unscathed. "The ward was issued to you because of the risks you undertook on this case. It's only right that you keep it."

"Miss Jessa, you can't possibly expect—"

"Please, Mr. Burke." I rested my hand on his arm. "Trust me in this?"

He inclined his head ever so slightly. "I suppose I owe you that much."

But the admission appeared to pain him. How many deaths had he seen as a stratesman? Was the thought of witnessing another worse to him than the possibility of his own? That much I could understand.

"If you'll accept it, I'd offer one more caution." He lowered his voice further. "Riven forced one of his own kind to confess his misdeeds. I don't know what sort of power that requires, but if fae fear him, we should all the more. He may have chosen to spare you from Mocvar for reasons of his own, but don't mistake that choice for kindness. Fae have none, and I would not see you taken in."

Yet he'd not heard the exchange I'd had with Riven last night. Would it have changed his views?

It was too late to discuss the matter further, since Riven crossed the copse to stand before us. "It's time."

Mr. Burke frowned at the distant knoll. "Before we go—there's one thing troubling me."

"Just one?" Nikol withdrew a gleaming silver dagger and polished it on his sleeve. "How remarkable."

Mr. Burke ignored him. "This Uros fellow. Why would he leave his heart here? Why not in the bottom of the ocean or atop an impassable gorge or some such?"

I looked to Riven, as curious as Mr. Burke.

"Our land isn't like yours. The depths of the oceans belong to the merrows and other seafolk, the heights to sylphs and wind sprites and the like. Such places offer no haven." A gust of wind burst through the canopy, stirring the leaves around us, but Riven remained unnaturally still. "Uros chose well. Mocvar is powerful and fiercely protective of his territory, yet he's far removed from the king's seat in Caslon. Few have cause to pass through this region, yet not so few that his appearance would raise undue questions. And he will have left it well protected."

Nikol shook his head. Evidently, he preferred to keep us mortals in the dark—and Riven had been remarkably forthright. What prompted such generosity? I only hoped it wasn't the possibility of our demise. My pulse picked up, and the pendant warmed against my skin, as if preparing to ward off potential threats.

"What sort of snares do you expect he's laid?" Mr. Burke wore the expression of a soldier preparing for battle—grim and determined. "Will he seek to control us with glamour?"

"He doesn't use glamour. But he can force you to perceive what he desires." Riven's tone was clipped. "Don't trust anything you see on the island."

"Uros told me *ilusne* can deceive even the fae," I said.

"He would. Arrogant *ashna*." Nikol sheathed the dagger. "I

assume he did not tell you how the fae warriors of old battled auvok?"

I shook my head.

"When they realized auvok could deceive them into turning on their own, they used blindfolds to protect their eyes and keep them from falling prey to deception. They'd go in teams of a dozen, guided by their affinities alone. The auvok fell before them in the end—at least those unwilling to hide their hearts."

Mr. Burke straightened his cloak. "You took a dozen warriors to tackle one auvok then, and now we go alone? What of summoning allies?"

Most mortals lived in fear of fae, but Mr. Burke didn't hesitate to question them, despite the risks. Why? Did he expect them to act as mortals and spare us because we temporarily fought a common foe?

"We don't seek open battle. To bring more fae into the matter would gain us nothing—it would only add to the confusion," Riven said. "We cannot defeat Uros, no matter our numbers, unless we locate his heart."

"But if we cannot rely on what we see, then how are we to find anything, let alone an object he'll protect with all of his power?"

"Mortals." Nikol smirked. "You have so few senses."

"And yet we manage quite well. I've solved countless crimes without the resources and abilities you take for granted," Mr. Burke snapped. "And somehow Miss Jessa located the heart before you."

Yet it was the taint of the fae that had allowed me to do so, though I could never confess it to Mr. Burke.

Nikol stalked toward Mr. Burke, his silver-gray eyes gleaming. "In your world, you manage. Here you're nothing but a liability—or entertainment, depending on the fae you encounter."

Mr. Burke paled slightly, but stood firm. "Then why bother to bring us?"

"Were it up to me—"

"Enough." Riven sliced his hand downward, cutting off further conversation. "Burke, you and Jessa will stay where I can see you. Keep close, and you'll have the best chance of safety."

"And if Uros appears as one of you?"

"Judge by words and deeds. He cannot steal your reason, however powerful his illusions. The fact that you know he'll cast them gives some small advantage." Riven turned to the knoll, his jaw tightening. "You should know, we may face more than whatever traps he's left behind. Uros may be present himself. It would have been natural for him to withdraw to the location of his heart when injured."

Mr. Burke's kestrel-gaze sharpened. "Then we shall do whatever is required to end him."

"You'll keep clear of Uros—you understand?" Riven held his gaze. "Mortals are far more vulnerable than fae. Don't let him get close."

"He's taken more victims in our world than yours," Mr. Burke shot back. "If there's a chance—"

"The matter is not up for debate." The storm-pressure sensation increased, charging the air around us. Riven had clearly reached the end of his patience, which extended much further than I'd expected.

Mr. Burke subsided, and Riven continued.

"Uros believes mortals are useless—we'll take advantage of that view. Nikol and I will distract him while the two of you go to the well and destroy the heart."

The mist-shrouded knoll loomed ominous against the dark waters of the swamp. I turned away. "And if it's not there?"

"Then we must attempt to escape. Because no matter how many times we slay him, he'll revive. And when our strength fails at last, he'll kill us all." Riven displayed no emotion at the prospect. He might have been speaking of a planned pleasure expedition rather than a battle to the death.

"Wonderful," Mr. Burke muttered.

Riven's eyes darkened a shade. "Uros doesn't seek you as he does Jessa, nor has Mocvar taken note of you. I can send you back to your world if you choose—but this is your final chance."

"I've sworn to protect my city and everyone in it. That includes Miss Jessa. If she remains, then I'm not leaving."

"Very well." Riven shrugged. "I take no responsibility. Whatever harm comes to you, it's on your own head."

Mr. Burke's hands tightened. "I did not expect otherwise."

"Then we've delayed long enough." Without waiting to see if we followed, Riven stalked to the edge of the copse.

Did he expect us to swim across the open expanse between us and the ruins? I hesitated. The humid air gathered thick around us, and my palms dampened with sweat. No matter how unpleasant the process, we must cross. I lifted Jade, and she scrambled onto my shoulders. She'd kept close to my side all morning and even now remained unusually quiet. What did she sense?

Riven stepped onto the water, and where his feet touched the surface, the water glinted and became solid—or perhaps not the water. Perhaps he drew something underneath it to fashion a path of sorts.

How fascinating. I tilted my head to better inspect his work. It appeared we'd not plunge into the muck after all.

Nikol stepped back with a flourish. "After you."

Mr. Burke and I hesitantly followed in Riven's footsteps, and whatever lay beneath the surface of the waters supported our weight. Nikol hemmed us in from behind, and despite my uncertainty regarding his intentions, I took some comfort in having a rear guard.

We all halted on the soggy ground at the edge of the island. The huge, jagged knoll stretched high above the water, allowing for a greater variety of trees and foliage. Pale moss draped every branch, like ancient cobwebs drifting on the breeze, and darker threads of charcoal wove together with the silvery strands.

Uros.

I clutched at my pendant, but even its steady warmth failed to soothe. Jade's muscles bunched tight, as though she prepared to spring from my shoulders and enter battle at any moment. But battle with what?

How did one fight illusory foes?

Mr. Burke offered me his arm. "If we cannot trust what we see, perhaps we should remain in contact."

Riven gave a curt nod of approval, and I accepted, welcoming the familiar ritual in this foreign world. Together, we stepped into the dense canopy of trees, and the mists closed around us.

The wispy tendrils brushed my skin, leaving chill pinpricks in their wake. And then they closed in, thick and blinding as a shroud. Sounds muffled, garments dampened, and the sense of pressure suffocated. The gnarled shapes of the underbrush loomed dark and threatening, amorphous in the mist.

My fingers numbed, but I kept my grip on Mr. Burke's arm. Jade gave a soft *mrow* in my ear, the commonplace sound an anchor. I wasn't lost, nor forsaken in this ghastly fog. As long as I held to my companions, all would be well.

Riven kindled fae-lights, but they appeared dull in the

oppressive gloom. And then one by one, they winked out. My skin pebbled.

Uros had done such with the gas lamps in my bedchamber. Was he here, even now? Did he creep up from behind, concealed by the mists, ready to inject his venom . . .

I pulled in a ragged breath.

It was illusion; it must be. Uros could control appearances, but nothing suggested he could control the power of another. If Riven lit those fae-lights, I had to believe they still burned. However it appeared, we were not stumbling in the dark.

As though my recognition restored them, the fae-lights gleamed once more. But what they revealed . . .

I staggered to a stop, nearly losing hold of Mr. Burke. Mother?

Her dark curls tumbled down her back, her vibrant beauty untouched by the grief that had marred her final days.

"How?" She stood rooted in place, her lips parted in shock. "All these years, and you came. How did you know, my golden one?"

She'd always called us that, her daughters . . . her brilliant girls, her golden ones. We lit up her life, so she said—but not enough to keep the darkness at bay, not in the end.

It was *ilusne*, surely. But she'd called me *golden one*. How could Uros know? Remnants from my nightmare stirred, images of Mother dragged away into the darkness, reaching for me, whispering my name.

I couldn't help her, not then. But now, if there was the slightest chance she lived . . . Longing burned through my veins, driving back the chill mists, drawing me toward her.

"We don't have much time." She drew closer, close enough to reveal the flecks of silver in her bright blue eyes. "I must tell you—"

A strong hand grasped my elbow, a voice spoke low in my ear. "Keep to the path."

It was Riven—and when he spoke, Mother vanished. At my other side, Mr. Burke remained motionless. He strained into the gloom as I had done. What did he see?

His brow furrowed as if he were snared in some private pain, and he whispered something low and edged with sorrow, the words indistinguishable. I clutched his arm tighter. "We cannot stay here."

We shuffled forward, one step, two, three. Then Nikol shot a sharp-edged shadow in front of us. It quivered for a moment on the smooth path, then sank into a chasm. Whatever power Nikol had laced into the shadow must have burned through the *ilusne*, revealing the enormous pit that would have engulfed us had we taken one more step.

Mr. Burke muttered a choice word as a swarm of spiderlings scurried out of the chasm. We stumbled back, and Riven and Nikol sent streams of light and shadow sizzling across them.

As though exhaled by the spiderlings, thick fog engulfed us. It blotted out the world around us, erased every trace of Riven and Nikol and the creatures they battled. We careened through in a world of white, one which could conceal monsters, another yawning abyss, or something worse—Uros himself.

Riven and Nikol might rely on their Other senses to navigate the *ilusne*, but we had no such aid. Unless . . .

Unless the fae-touch warped my own enough that I might do the same.

Would I betray myself to Mr. Burke by such an act? Unlikely, with how little we could perceive. I closed my eyes, excising the choking fear that swathed me along with the mists. This time I neither sought to stifle the whispers nor lower my guard to them. Instead, I sought one particular song, as one might peer through a crowd for a familiar face. I strained for a trace of the swamp blossoms, of their sweet melody that celebrated life-from-death, beauty snatched from decay.

And it surged to greet me, swirling soft, cool, and refreshing across my senses. I clung tighter to Mr. Burke, and with my eyes firmly shut, I followed the song.

Jade purred softly, her pleasure mingling with theirs. Then light flared red against my closed lids, and involuntarily they opened. We'd stumbled into a clearing, almost colliding with Riven and Nikol.

Riven shot me an assessing glance. His eyes kindled bright as burnished gold; only the faintest trace of green remained. When he turned to the clearing, sunlight poured into it, burning away the fog and revealing a vast ruin.

Along the edges of the tumbled stones, the swamp blossoms swayed, their fronds absorbing the light. At another time, the beauty of the scene would have stopped my breath.

But not now.

For we'd found the well—and Uros.

He'd woven an enormous web around the ancient well, an impossible boundary that stretched to surround it. And in the center, far above the well, he perched in auvok form. Only now, he was much larger than he'd appeared in my bedchamber. His tremendous frame rivaled that of an ancient dragon.

Jade bristled. A low rumble issued from her chest as Uros lowered himself down on strong, spindled legs until he dangled just above the well. Like the spiders he resembled, he held himself by a cord of his own making—and like those spiders, he would drain us dry if he snared us.

"You think to stand against me?" He bared dark fangs. "This puts me in mind of the time I destroyed the four fae lords of Athar. Though in this case, there are only two of consequence."

Riven had said Uros would be weakened, yet he appeared stronger than ever and utterly unshaken. Was it an illusion? Or had his return to the haven he'd crafted for his heart restored his strength? A swamp-scented wind brushed over the heavy web, failing utterly to sway it.

The back of my neck prickled as if Uros's spider legs crept across it. If I'd have arrived here alone, he surely would have ended my life—or worse, tormented me before turning me back over to Mocvar. At least together we had a chance . . . I hoped.

"It was generous of you to seek me on my own grounds—generous and foolish." His clustered eyes swept over us, hunger glinting in their depths. "Did you think that Mocvar would fail to inform me you encroached on my domain? Our bargain bound him to keep watch."

Small wonder Mocvar had looked so pale, caught between the wrath of Riven and his bargain with Uros.

"It appears you've claimed his fancy, Jessa. He went so far as to request a new bargain with the condition that I leave you alive until he's through with you. One dose of venom should make you pliable enough to suit his purpose." Uros's dry, creaking laugh fouled the air. "Of course, he gave me leave to visit and feast on your fears from time to time, which may well have stacked the deal in my favor. By then, you will respect me as you ought."

Mr. Burke tensed beneath my hand but kept still. Riven made no advance, but he restrained the mists. They wisped angrily at the edges of the clearing, their strands lashing against the light, but they could not advance.

If this troubled Uros, he gave no indication. He lifted one claw-tipped leg. "Certainly, I can make no complaint about how the situation has unfolded. I hunger, and you shall sate me. For a time."

"I see you've learned nothing." Riven's eyes brightened, green and gold swirling in their depths. And he sent a spear of light hurtling toward Uros.

Uros shifted into some sort of mottled black-and-gray flying beast. He soared into the air, narrowly evading the spear of light. A gout of black flame escaped his maw, clouded as though laced with venom.

Riven burnt it with a flash of light before it scattered over us, and Nikol cast a net of shadow toward Uros. He charged toward them, and they withdrew, pulling Uros away from us.

They vanished into the mists. Riven and Nikol were buying us time, at an unknown cost. I'd not allow their efforts to go to waste. Mr. Burke and I hastened toward the well and the vast web stretching over it.

A shiver snaked down my spine. I couldn't bear to touch this gossamer structure, so I snatched a large stick from the ground and pressed it against filaments. But they did not yield. I cast aside the stick and pressed my dagger against the strands, to no avail. They may as well have been crafted of diamond. At my side, Mr. Burke hacked at the web with his blade, his strength far greater than mine.

Still, not a single strand shifted.

I stepped closer, pressed harder.

And one segment of the web uncoiled from its companions. It snapped against my arm, a sharp stinging pain surging in its wake.

It drew back, then coiled again, as if seeking to land another blow.

Jade snarled and leapt from my shoulders. She hurled her full weight against me, knocking me down just in time to avoid the next strike.

Mr. Burke snatched me to my feet and pulled me to the far

side of the clearing, beyond the reach of the lashing filament. The web blurred before my eyes, its strands multiplying.

Mr. Burke spoke, his voice distant and indistinct.

My arm throbbed, and a deep ache crept toward my shoulder. If I couldn't break through one strand of the enormous web, how could I ever reach the well? I'd had one task—only one. Riven and Nikol took the brunt of Uros's wrath. All I had to do was find the heart.

And I'd failed.

Perhaps Riven was right. Like all mortals, I was useless in the Otherworld—nothing but a liability. Uros was ancient and cunning, with abilities I'd no notion how to combat. I was far out of my depth, like a child playing at war.

And what of Riven and Nikol? If the fae hadn't fought auvok in ages, could they truly know the extent of his power? Could they hope to resist?

With each pulse of my heart, pain spread up my arm and toward my chest, tightening muscles and searing nerves.

A gentle hand stroked my tangled hair. Mr. Burke? Surely not. He'd never approach me in such a way. And this hand was small and soft; this presence carried the scent of summer rose. *Mother.* "Rest, my golden one. I know how you've suffered—what you've feared."

How I'd longed for those sweet words of understanding. They sank into my soul like rain into dry soil.

Mother's hand trailed down my arm. "Let me keep you safe. Your world condemns you, but I never will. You belong with me. There's no need to fight any longer."

I sank to my knees, indescribably weary. I'd fought so long and so hard . . . and for what? For all my effort, my very nature would bring shame and suffering to those I loved as I descended into madness. Why not surrender? All that awaited me in my world was the loss of my family, my freedom, my very self.

"I will protect you; I will keep your mind sound." The tender voice wove round me. "Only rest, my Jessa."

My eyes slid shut, and I leaned into her embrace. I would rest, just for a moment . . .

Something warm branded my forehead, a low rumble resounded in my ears. I struggled to open my eyes and found Jade perched in my lap, her nose pressed against my face, her breath hanging sweet in the air.

Mr. Burke knelt before me, his hands gripping my shoulders. He was shaking me hard—how long had he been doing that?

"Your arm!"

I struggled to make sense of the simple statement. Then I looked down. A series of pinprick marks revealed the path left by the strike of the web. From them, dark streaks stretched like roots, spreading up my arm.

Venom.

It explained the grayish fog clouding my vision, the deep despair shrouding my thoughts. Was this how Uros induced his victims to slumber, by poisoning them into a melancholic stupor?

I twined my fingers into the mosses at my feet, seeking strength. Their evergreen persistence thrummed through my veins. Then they yellowed, as though they were siphoning the venom from my body into their spiked leaves and seta, only to brighten again as they purged it into the soil beneath.

Jade churred low, her face still less than a handbreadth from my own. Her eyes glowed like lamps, and the brilliant white starflower patch on her chest shone like a beacon of hope.

My thoughts cleared.

Perhaps the fears drawn to the surface by the venom held

truth. But I had more to fight for than myself—and while I drew breath, I refused to give up hope. I might face a thousand unthinkable horrors in the future, but I'd never surrender.

Not when I might still protect those I loved.

If Mother *had* truly been here, she would have told me the same. There was always a way, if one was willing to pay the price. That's what she believed.

But was I willing? Could I embrace the fae-touch—and everything it might cost me? If I did, would it become the weapon I needed for this battle? My altered senses hadn't fallen under the influence of *ilusne*—it was the one advantage we possessed that Uros wouldn't expect.

I staggered to my feet, accepting the steadying arm Mr. Burke offered. It was time to fulfill my purpose here and find the heart—time to embrace the fae-touch, and if possible, use it for good. Never mind that Mr. Burke would witness my actions, never mind that the fae-touch could consume me.

I was done hiding the truth.

CHAPTER 38

Other sparked and swirled around me as though anticipating our connection. Though my heart pulsed an unsteady rhythm in my ears, my resolve held. We couldn't approach the well without risking the venom, but now we didn't need to.

Reddish vines swirled over the mouth of the well and spilled into its depths; they also spiraled out beyond the expanse of the web.

I pulled free of Mr. Burke.

"Jessa, wait," he said.

But I ignored him. If I explained my purpose, he'd think I'd taken leave of my senses. I crossed the clearing, approaching the vines.

Uros was a creature of trickery and deception. What if he'd already removed the heart and intended to pin us here, battling for control of an empty cistern until he ended us all? It was time to discover the truth—and not on his terms.

Mr. Burke charged up behind me, only to stumble to a stop when I stooped down. I stroked the broad leaves of the vines and opened my senses to their song. Their resonant voices echoed within the well as they absorbed water and strength. A jumble of images swept over me, simple impressions of dappled sun and shade coupled with the scents of damp and mud. There was no hint of blood or pain or auvok.

Uros had never placed the heart within. Such an act of violence would have impressed itself upon the inhabitants of the well. The well was a decoy.

If not in the cistern, then where? I straightened.

Deep lines furrowed Mr. Burke's brow. "I'm going to make another attempt—stay here. Don't touch anything."

"Don't go." I straightened. "His heart isn't in the well."

"How do you know?" He lifted my arm and inspected it as though he sought some trace of venom. "Riven said our senses would be subject to deception."

"And Nikol said other senses could be used."

"Not by mortals."

Not unless they were fae-touched. But I choked down the confession and turned from him, untwining the boughs within. At my coaxing, they unfurled their limbs, until they no longer resembled a hedge but a vibrant grove. Through the gaps, an unstoppable deluge of sound and scent and strength flooded. Like a shock of cold water on a summer day, it sent tingles rushing through my limbs, down even to my toes.

Every botanical thing limned with new color, shades that separated themselves from the strands of *ilusne*. The trees loathed the touch of Uros's web, the clinging illusions and lies hiding them from the clean touch of sun and wind. A litany of grievances surged into my ears. But one song pierced my heart, a keening cry of grief and pain. The bitterness of mourning stung my eyes and tightened my chest.

I knew that voice.

The cry filled my senses; my surroundings faded. As one caught in a dream, I moved across the knoll to a gnarled swamp oak, its strong limbs draped with hanging mosses. In the distance, Mr. Burke spoke, but the song of the oak consumed me, drowning out his words. I placed my hand against its trunk, seeking the source of the pain.

Uros.

His claws split the oak.

His spindled limbs wrenched out its heartwood.

A great cry of anguish ripped the air, but Uros paid it no heed. He cast the magnificent heartwood onto the ground, abandoned it to rot and ruin and slow, lingering death. Then he placed his own heart within the wound and webbed the opening closed, cloaking it with ilusne *to appear like bark. The oak shuddered in agony, its leaves quivering.*

My lips trembled. *I'm sorry, so sorry.*

I withdrew from the unbearable pain, and the mists closed around me, obscuring my vision. Then came a slow, shuffling footfall from somewhere nearby—the unmistakable lurching steps of a ghoul. A tingle skittered down my spine. *Cold hands, closing about my throat, dead eyes, claw-tipped fingers . . .*

No!

I would not succumb to terrors planted to haunt me. I closed my eyes, blocking out the oppressive *ilusne*. And I placed my hands on either side of the wound Uros had left in the oak.

The *ilusne* might deceive my mortal senses, but when I allowed my fae-touch sway, its influence failed. Now only the slow, steady murmur of the oak filled my ears. Uros had ripped out its heart and abandoned it to a slow death, but it had not surrendered. Some spark of life remained.

Please, won't you open for me?

With a creak and a groan, the swamp oak tore open its trunk, exposing the gaping wound within.

A shout of rage echoed through the clearing.

Could Uros sense the danger to his heart? Jade growled impossibly deep, her presence stalwart at my back. But she could not fend off Uros, if he came.

Hurry.

I plunged my hands into the wound. Heartwood should have sent life pulsing through trunk, branch, and root. Instead, my fingers brushed something cold and slick. I lifted it.

Uros's heart thumped in my hands.

It beat slow and steady, a march like that of an ancient drum. A shout from Mr. Burke split the air, drowning out the disconcerting rhythm. Fainter and farther off, the sounds of battle drifted in the wind. Riven and Nikol standing against Uros? Or some other foe he'd brought against them?

I needed to end this . . . but I was too late.

A spindle-legged spider dangled from the nearest cypress. Uros. He showed no trace of fear; his lips parted in a mocking smile. "What do you think you're doing, mortal?"

"What must be done." I swallowed against the bitterness in my throat. "Stay back."

"Or what? You'll kill me?" He jabbed a claw in my direction. "Why not say it? You intend to take my life. To become a killer, like me."

My hands dampened. "I'm not . . ."

Shadows gathered round him and dripped like poison from his fangs. "Not what? Not a killer? Then drop the heart. You already bear one taint—are you so ready to add another?"

The ruins faded. I stood before the Vigil, my fae-touch laid bare. *She's mad. A murderer. Other consumed her; she'll never recover.* Cold iron bit my skin as they dragged me away . . .

I closed my eyes, and the scene vanished. The heart throbbed in my hands, its repulsive weight heavier with each pulse. "I'm nothing like you. You prey on others—I'm trying to protect them. And you've left me no choice."

"There's always a choice." Did he wield Mother's words against me on purpose? He dropped lower. "Consider a bargain. Return my heart, and I'll spare your family, and your world. I'll limit myself to this one."

"You think I'd condemn the Otherworld to death and torment to preserve my own?"

"Why not? They would, if given the chance." His dark eyes took on an uncanny sheen, their iridescent surface reflecting back my fear. "Other encroaches on your world. Why not let me stand between your kind and the coming destruction? Then you'd truly be protecting your people."

The cold from the heart crept up my arms. If he spoke truth . . .

No. He was a creature of lies. If given opportunity, he'd destroy everything within his grasp—and his pride would allow no limitation. Any bargain he offered would be corrupt.

Perhaps if I took a life, it would taint me more deeply. Perhaps Mr. Burke would report my fae-touch, what I'd done here, and I'd find myself condemned. But I'd made my choice. I snatched up my dagger.

And I plunged it deep into the heart.

Dark ichor spilled over my hands, splashed onto the roots, seeped into the ground. Then the heart turned to ash and spilled upon the earth below.

Uros crashed to the ground, not before me—but a few ells *behind* me. I'd spoken to an illusion. He'd pretended to offer a bargain while he crept up on me, seeking my life.

Shadows swirled round his frame. His limbs twitched, then

curled up against his abdomen. And his body dissolved into dust, soon snatched by the wind and carried away.

The *ilusne*-birthed mists lifted. Sunlight spilled over trees and brush alike, and the strands of webbing woven through them vanished like smoke. My family was safe and justice for Ibbie achieved.

Other poured into me, a relentless force that pulled me from the jubilant murmur of the mosses to the celebratory chatter of the swamp grasses to the stately songs of the swamp oaks and cypress and whitespire. These and countless others sang their triumph. The scents and sounds and songs flooded in with such intensity that my vision dimmed.

I stared at my hands, but could scarcely discern the dark splotches that lingered—the stains of death. Uros was right about one thing; I'd become a killer. I'd taken a life by choice. Now it seemed the fae-touch would consume mine.

I sank to the ground, and the world went black.

CHAPTER 39

When my vision cleared, Riven was bent over me, light coiling from him and pouring over my body. Something restrained the flood of Other; it no longer overwhelmed, only gently brushed the edges of my awareness. Had Riven driven back the influence of the fae-touch?

I wanted to ask, but I felt as though the world spun around me. A deep, lingering ache pervaded every muscle and held me immobile—but somehow, I lived. Somehow, I reasoned. The fae-touch hadn't stolen my senses, not yet.

As awareness seeped back in, I discovered Jade curled up in my lap, her body rigid. When I stroked her head, her tension subsided. She began to purr as vociferously as a steam engine.

I struggled to untangle the scene before me. Someone—Riven, perhaps—had propped me amid the knee-knobbed roots of a cypress, and its steady strength poured into me.

"Are you well?" he asked.

Well? I scarcely held together the tattered edges of my emotions.

My chest burned with the effort of constraining them. I didn't know what had happened or what might happen next—what had brought this relief and what might end it. Choosing to embrace my fae-touch was one thing, living the consequences was another altogether.

At last, I managed a nod.

"I regret that we allowed Uros so close." Every line of his body tensed. "When all else failed, he brought low fae enthralled by *ilusne*, bent on our slaughter. If we'd put them all to death, we could have come sooner, but—"

"I'm glad you didn't." The thought of Uros forcing Riven to slaughter innocents of his own kind twisted like a knife inside my chest. "What about Nikol and Mr. Burke? Were they injured?"

"Nikol took a claw to the chest, but the *ishtar* spared him the venom—and fae heal quickly. Burke is fine, but I thought you'd rather not have him here while you recovered. I told them to scout the island." Riven lifted a brow. "He thinks you were overcome by slaying Uros. He says in your world ladies don't kill monsters."

"That part is true." I rubbed my throbbing temples. "I believe I've fully failed in that regard."

"Does that concern you?"

"Not as much as . . ." My throat closed around the word —*madness*.

"As what?"

His light dimmed, and as it faded, all the murmurs and songs and shouts of the rich green-and-gold voices clamored for attention. Currents of life swirled from them to touch me, pressing around me once more with joyful intensity, welcoming and overwhelming. My vision blurred at the edges once more. "I can't, it's too much."

"Will you tell me?" His voice rumbled like distant thunder. "How did you find the heart?"

"The swamp oak sang its loss to me." The confession wrenched from me as the world faded into a blur of color once more. "Now I feel them all—and it's too much, too strong."

Jade nudged my chin. Then she faced Riven and gave him a soft, expectant *mrow*.

Riven touched his fingertips to my temples, and liquid light poured into me, warm, golden, and indescribably rich. The pain ebbed, and the overwhelming sensation of Other subsided. Then he drew back. "You must learn to exercise control yourself, but I can grant a small reprieve."

"But I can't, not anymore." The words spilled out, tinged with the grief I could no longer hide. "I've tried for so long—and now that I've come to the Otherworld, I've surrendered any ability to constrain it."

"Who told you that?" He looked at me as though he could see to my very soul.

Oh, how I wanted to hide. But there was nowhere to go, no remnant of dignity to wrap about myself. Whatever his Other senses allowed him to perceive, it exposed all my weakness—my emotions, my fears, my taint. My gaze fell to the ferns and mosses springing from dark, rich soil below.

Then Riven gently lifted my chin. "What is it you fear, Jessa?"

"I fear that this fae-touch will take my reason and leave me mad. That it will condemn me, and my family also." Tears stung my eyes, but I refused to allow them release. "When mortals succumb to fae-touch, it never ends well."

"I'm familiar with what you mortals call fae-touch. I'll grant that it alters the senses and often leads to madness." His brows drew together. "But it hardly applies to you. You're not fae-touched."

"That—it's impossible." I rocked back. "Don't lie to me, not about this. I can't—"

"Fae can't lie. And I wouldn't make light of this." His voice dropped low. "I didn't realize that's what you believed, but fae-touch cannot possibly give mortals the abilities you've exercised."

For a moment, I couldn't breathe. His words upended my world . . . but could I believe them? *Never trust a fae.* And yet, I did trust him. He could have pressed his advantage time and again, and yet he'd refrained. Even now, if he acted after the pattern of his kind, he could withhold this information or require a bargain in exchange for it.

A gentle breeze tugged at my hair and played in the branches above. It carried the sweet aroma of the swamp blossoms mingled with the sharp scent of decay. I wrapped shaky arms around Jade and rested my head on hers. "If not fae-touch, then what? Something is wrong with me."

"I can't answer that, not now." His eyes darkened until their shade resembled a forest of fir. "You're not in danger of madness either, unless you continue to stifle your abilities. Fighting against them is like waging war upon yourself—there can be no winner."

I ran a finger over the chain of my pendant. "You're asking me to take a great deal on your word alone."

"Yes."

Even if I was *not* fae-touched as the folk of Byren understood it, I'd still fallen afoul of some Otherworldly influence—and this as-yet-unnamed malady threatened to consume me. Riven represented my best hope of answers, but before I could form another question, Mr. Burke appeared in the clearing, Nikol on his heels.

"Miss Jessa, are you recovered?" Mr. Burke asked.

My opportunity to gain answers vanished. Riven stood, placing greater distance between us. Even if he had been willing to continue the conversation, I wasn't about to draw Mr. Burke's attention to my condition. Perhaps he hadn't taken note of my actions in the confusion before the discovery of the heart, but if he knew, if he chose to report me . . . what could I do? All I could offer in my defense was: *I know I'm not fae-touched because a fae lord told me so when I visited the Otherworld.* That was the surest path to a permanent place within an Institution.

Only time would tell what Mr. Burke had seen—and what he intended to do about it. So I swallowed my questions and fears alike and drew a shaky breath. "I believe so."

"There's no lingering venom or other . . . abnormalities?" His gaze drifted back to my arm.

"No trace of his venom remains in Jessa," Riven said. "You may set your mind at ease."

Mr. Burke scrubbed a hand across his face. "After seeing so many succumb to that monster—my optimism had worn a bit thin."

Nikol drew his leather-clad foot across the ground where Uros had fallen. "He'll never claim another life."

"And what of Mocvar's betrayal?" Mr. Burke frowned. "Will he attempt further harm?"

It appeared Mr. Burke couldn't tolerate the notion of any sort of evildoer escaping justice, even if it were far outside his jurisdiction. And I must confess, I felt the same.

A grim stillness settled over Riven. "He will be dealt with—after the two of you return home."

Inky shadows gathered around Nikol. "As much as I'd like to see that show, it's time for me to return to my queen. But I must say, I wouldn't have missed this for the world."

Then Nikol vanished into the dark pool.

Riven turned toward me and Mr. Burke. "Are you ready?"

At our nods, he drew us back to our world with an impossibly brilliant swirl of light. When it faded, the familiar environs of Enderly Park surrounded us. Riven had brought us back beneath the tree that contained Uros's lair.

Our effortless passage between worlds brought countless questions. Could all fae enter our world when and where they pleased? The Vigil maintained they could only come through Crossings—and the prevalence of Otherworldly influence at those junctures supported their claims. If they could cross anywhere they pleased, why had they not invaded in force?

How much of this had mortals once known and now forgotten? And why? Did it have anything to do with the Dark Era and the war with the Otherworld I'd found mention of? If in fact those events had happened, how could they have left our collective memory? Unless someone had tried to conceal or purge them . . .

Before I could begin to work out the answers, exhaustion swept over me, jumbling my thoughts. And for a moment, my own world felt like a strange land. It was devoid of the powerful essence that had coursed through my veins in the Otherworld. It felt almost . . . dead.

Instinctively, I reached for the nearest tree and the green pulse of life within offered reassurance. It wasn't dead; it was simply different.

As was I.

Cautiously, I sought the cage of thorns. Could I restore it in my own world? Did I want to? It didn't matter, for it had vanished utterly. In its place, blossoms and boughs rejoiced, more a garden now than a hedge. A band of light wove between them. Was that Riven's work? How long would it last?

Before he vanished into the Otherworld, I must have

answers—yet from a fae perspective, I already owed him. Would he require another bargain between us? The idea of binding myself to another fae—even if it were Riven—sent a shiver down my spine.

And then there was Mr. Burke. What did he plan? Would he go to the Vigil with all he'd witnessed?

"Burke, a word." Riven started walking off, without checking to see if Mr. Burke followed.

Unease flared within. I didn't want Mr. Burke to speak to the Vigil, but nor did I want Riven to purge his memory. After all he'd witnessed, the strength of the glamour required to purge it might well shatter his mind. "Riven, I—"

"This isn't your affair," he said.

Mr. Burke straightened. "He's right."

And with that, he marched after Riven to the edge of the clearing. It appeared both fae and mortal men could be equally intractable when the mood fell upon them.

Though the wait felt interminable, I forced myself to remain in place. Even if I ignored their wishes and joined the conversation, it wasn't as though I could prevent Riven from acting as he chose.

I leaned against the tree, and though its whispers were weak compared to those I'd experienced in the Otherworld, they refused to be vanquished.

Why? If I hadn't been experiencing fae-touch, then what had befallen me? My utter lack of knowledge left me unnerved. I couldn't come up with a single theory. I'd have to seek answers once more—if Mr. Burke did not turn me over to the Vigil in the meantime.

My shoulders slumped, and I twined my fingers through Jade's fur. After a time, Mr. Burke rejoined us, wearing a contemplative expression, while Riven climbed the tree toward Uros's lair with the lithe grace characteristic of the fae.

I tilted my head to watch his progress. "What did he say to you?"

"Let us say I received a very... detailed warning about what will happen if I speak to anyone of what I've seen." Mr. Burke scrubbed at his stubble. "I'm to tell a story about what occurred that will satisfy the authorities... and leave you out of the affair altogether."

"He left you your memories?"

Mr. Burke nodded. "I didn't expect it, not given what I've heard of fae—but I think it suits his purposes to have a mortal passing on the information he desires the Magistry to receive."

"I'm glad to hear it." For more reasons than one. "Does Riven mean to come with us?"

"No." Riven leapt from the tree, the passing prism in his grasp. "You'll report that fae absconded with the passing prism."

Mr. Burke nodded.

"What do you mean to do?" I asked Riven.

"Return to the Otherworld and the responsibilities that await."

"I see." My unanswered questions burned within, yet I dared not speak freely in front of Mr. Burke. "Would you be willing to pay me a call before you leave?"

Would he understand what I meant? That I spoke of his surreptitious visits to the glasshouse that would surely scandalize society if they became known?

"Yes." With that, he disappeared in a swirl of light.

Mr. Burke sucked in a breath. "I'll never grow accustomed to that."

Nor would I. But it was not required now that I was within my own world once more. A sudden surge of longing to see my family and assure myself they fared well swept over me. "Shall we go?"

"We're in for quite a walk before we can expect to find a hack. May as well get started."

"As long as we're not trudging through an Otherworldly swamp in pursuit of a heartless monster, I don't care how many miles we must journey."

Jade strolled down the path before us, entirely at ease. I inhaled the delicious scent of wild roses that rambled along the path, and their winsome song filtered faintly through the hedge of entwined bough and light within. Instinct told me to drown it out, yet I resisted. I no longer possessed the means, and if Riven was right, I must somehow work with these new senses, rather than fight against them.

Assuming I had the opportunity. I glanced at Mr. Burke. "What do you plan to say to the Magistry . . . and the Vigil?"

"Do you want to discuss this now?" Mr. Burke studied my face as though searching for the truth I concealed. "You've been through a great deal."

"I'm well, only weary." I brushed a fragment of moss from my skirt. "And wondering what comes next."

"You'll be left out of it. I owe you that much, even if Riven hadn't insisted. I'll report that I found the lair, crossed into the Otherworld through the prism, and watched a fae battle the murderer before his demise."

It was very fae wording—all technically true, but wholly misleading. Had Riven suggested it? "Won't they ask how you knew it was the killer?"

"I'll elaborate on the evidence found in the lair—and tell of a conversation overheard between the fae and the killer where he confessed to his crimes."

"And you think they'll believe you?"

"In the end, yes. I expect they'll press, but the details I provide will confirm the veracity of my tale. And when the murders stop, it will lend it further credence." He showed no signs of impatience with my questions, as a lesser man might. "It will be true, as far as it goes. And the Vigil will have reason to support my story. If they want the Magistry—and the king—to place trust in their devices, they'll have little room for accusation of fae-touch altering my account."

It was logical. If Mr. Burke presented himself in a fully rational fashion, with an airtight story and the claim that their wards had shielded him in the Otherworld, he'd likely be safe. Particularly when the murders ceased.

"But what of the men you had following me? Won't they come forward and report on my involvement? And my subsequent disappearance."

"Riven says he'll handle that." His steel-gray eyes held mine for a moment.

And I looked away first. I knew what he meant. Riven would glamour them into forgetting. It was a small detail and should do them no harm, but still, it shamed me that I wanted him to do so, despite my general objection to the practice.

Was it wrong that I longed for the protection his glamour offered? That I did not protest the story Mr. Burke would advance, which contained the substance of truth but not its entirety?

"Do you object to the plan?" he asked.

"I wish it were not necessary to withhold so much." Because the pressure of keeping so much within began to feel unbearable. I pushed an unruly curl from my face.

"As do I." Mr. Burke hesitated. "But there are those who would use the full tale as a weapon against us—or as a means to advance their own agendas."

I considered Mr. Burke. What did he know that I did not? What had he seen as he'd taken his orders from the Magistry—and then the Vigil? I stopped at the edge of the forest. "You've witnessed this?"

"There are things of which I cannot speak. But apart from the injunction Riven laid upon me, I'm confident this is the best course. Certain individuals would use the knowledge gained for—undesirable purposes." Mr. Burke surveyed the broad field. "I have no authority to order this, but I strongly suggest you speak of your incursion into the Otherworld to no one. It only takes one chance mention to endanger everything."

And I could think of countless ways that might occur, with no malice aforethought. I'd believed I was through with hiding, but now I must not only avoid burdening my family with my unknown malady, lest it entangle them with the Vigil, I must also accept that they could never know all I'd experienced with Uros and the Otherworld. If word leaked out and the Vigil found out Mr. Burke had misled them . . .

A band tightened around my chest. "I understand."

"I hope you will take time to recover from this ordeal." His concern appeared genuine, not patronizing. Doubtless it was brought on by my peculiar behavior when I'd sought the heart—which I hoped he attributed to exposure to the venom and *ilusne*.

"I'll take the time I can." All the worries I'd left behind flooded back, not only my family and what they must think, but also my impending appearance before the Magister. "I must appear in court soon."

"What?" His voice sharpened.

"A relation of Lady Dromley seeks to contest my inheritance."

"Have you no representation?"

"My trustees did not deem it necessary."

"Therefore you have determined to appear yourself." He did not seem surprised at the irregularity. "I see."

In silence, we forged on, then by agreement we separated at the outskirts of Enderly. If I appeared in the company of a gentleman after an absence of several days, even the fact he was a stratesman would not protect my reputation.

I righted my appearance the best I could manage and then hired a hack not far from Enderly. When the driver looked askance at me, I murmured a story about fleeing the spectres, which was true enough. This particular spectre—and the cost of battling it—would haunt me for some time to come.

CHAPTER 40

My legs throbbed as I climbed the steps to our townhome, but Jade trotted beside me as though weariness were a foreign concept. She perched on the doorstep while I knocked.

When Holden answered, relief swept his features. "Miss Jessa, I am glad to find you home. Mr. Caldwell could not say when you'd return or much at all about your travels, and Miss Caldwell has been much in dismay, as have your sisters. They'll be thankful to see you."

Would they? Or would they reprimand me for deeds they could not possibly understand—for the heartache and worry I'd never wanted to cause? I crossed the threshold. "I'll go to them at once."

Holden peered at the hack. "Shall I send Ives to fetch your things?"

"I'm afraid there were several difficulties along the way, and my belongings were destroyed."

By a grelum, no less. I tucked the truth inside and offered him a smile.

"I'm most sorry to hear it." He gave a slight bow. "You'll find your aunt in the drawing room with your sisters."

I offered my thanks and then trudged along the familiar corridor. Ainslie's animated tones swept out to meet me, while Aunt Caris and Ada murmured softer replies.

I stood quietly in the doorway. Their heads—two dark and one copper—bent together over the needlework in Aunt Caris's lap as they debated the merits of silk thread versus wool. They belonged in this world, belonged together.

I did not.

Yet I forced myself onward. "Aunt Caris, I'm home."

"My dear!" Aunt Caris tossed aside her embroidery and leapt to her feet. She wrapped me in a tight embrace, her soft lavender and violet fragrance an indescribable comfort.

Just as I relaxed in her arms, she shoved me away, all the while maintaining her grip on my shoulders. "What were you thinking to leave at such a time? And on such an absurd trip? Your father could tell almost nothing about the expedition, not even who made up the company and how long you'd be gone, let alone if there were proper chaperones overseeing the excursion. I never dreamt you'd be so thoughtless."

Her rebuke cut deep, and the tears shimmering in her eyes poured salt in the wound. I'd hurt her, and I could offer no justification.

"I'm so sorry, Aunt Caris. It's just—it was impossible for me to stay. After Lovell received the mark, I had to do something . . ."

"Did you imagine we'd fail to understand your pain?" Ada wrapped an arm around my shoulders. "If you'd only waited long enough to say goodbye, to let us know you were safe and in good hands."

But I could have offered them no such assurance. To confess

my plans would have inspired fear far greater than the worries that plagued them in my absence.

Perhaps Aunt Caris read something of this in my face. Her gaze swept from my disheveled curls to my bare hands to my decidedly rumpled riding habit. "My dear, what happened? Are you injured?"

"No, but I encountered several mishaps along the way." I resisted the desire to straighten my habit. "And I decided it was time to come home."

Ainslie narrowed her eyes, but before she could speak, Aunt Melisina burst into the room. Her hat and gloves were missing, but her whole face was alight. "Oh, Caris! Caris! It's gone."

Aunt Caris looked fairly staggered. "What's gone? What's happened?"

For the first time I could recall, a genuine smile lilted across Aunt Melisina's face and sparkled in her eyes. "It's Lovell! The tattoo has vanished, he's safe."

Incoherent exclamations of joy erupted, and I sank into the nearest chair. This time, I hadn't been too late—Lovell would live. Even the sunbeams pouring through the open windows seemed to celebrate with us as they danced through the prisms of the chandelier and scattered small rainbows about the room.

Then Ainslie pitched her voice above the rest. "But how was he spared? The tattoos have never vanished before. What can it mean?"

Ada spoke slowly. "Perhaps they only last a limited time, but the killer usually slays his victims first? Perhaps it means the Magistry has apprehended him before he could act?"

"What does it matter, as long as Lovell is safe?" Aunt Melisina declared. "We've been closeted with the Magistry all morning, else I would have come sooner."

"Indeed, such news deserves to be shouted from the

rooftops." Aunt Caris beamed and enveloped Aunt Melisina in an embrace—and for once, she did not pull away.

But when excited chatter swept the room once more, Aunt Caris's gaze returned to me, a furrow creasing her creamy brow. Though her concerns may have been subsumed by joy, they'd not vanished. And unless I was much mistaken, there would be consequences to come.

∽

AFTER A CELEBRATORY DINNER that included Lovell, Uncle Milton, and Aunt Melisina, we all retired to the drawing room. As befitting a man who had cheated death, Lovell was the life of the party—his energy and enthusiasm fueling the lively banter that swept the room. All my questions for him and Ainslie about their P. Smith persona, all my curiosity about what they planned for the future could wait, as could my worries about Ainslie's binding. I wanted to savor my family all gathered together and safe—from Uros at least.

Aunt Melisina proclaimed her intent to hold a grand celebration, and she emphasized her plans to include Lord Bradford and see that we had yet another cause to celebrate. Ada did not gainsay her, but her face remained shadowed for the rest of the evening. I'd have to find a way to lend Ada support, lest Aunt Melisina wear away her resolve—or sway Father to pressure her toward the match.

Despite my concerns for my sisters, I could scarcely keep my eyes open. I managed to engage in conversation until everyone departed, Aunt Melisina and her family to their townhome and the others to bed. I wanted to sink into my own, but instead I moved toward the glasshouse.

Would Riven come? He hadn't bound himself, only

expressed his willingness. He could easily decide it wasn't worth the trouble . . .

But for some reason, he had not. He awaited within, lounging on the bench and toying with a spark of light.

"I'm sorry I kept you waiting."

"I haven't been here long." He lifted a shoulder. "I had some loose ends to tie up before my departure."

Some of which included glamouring stratesmen, if I understood aright. A tangle of emotions rose, but I pressed them down to sort later.

He extinguished the spark, leaving only moonlight to illumine the glasshouse. "You have questions."

"More than I can count." I studied his face, wondering how much he would divulge . . . and how much more he would conceal. He'd said before he *couldn't* tell me what was wrong with me, not that he didn't know. "Do you know why I have these abilities?"

"No."

He'd left no room for dissembling in that reply, and yet . . . "You have suspicions?"

"There are possibilities."

All of them concerning, if his expression were any indication. Jade prowled between us, stalking a moonbeam, and I fought the urge to clasp her in my arms. After all she'd endured, she deserved her liberty. "Will you speak of them?"

Riven shook his head. "I don't have sufficient information to speculate—and I won't mislead you."

"Then will you at least tell me how I might manage this . . . condition?"

"First tell me this." He leaned forward. "Do you want to be rid of it?"

Did I? Before, I'd imagined these sensations a taint, poisoning my mind, endangering those around me. But without them, I would have never survived the Otherworld, never defeated Uros, never protected my family. If Riven was right, my abilities might *not* lead to madness . . . but where would they take me? Did I dare venture into the unknown? I traced the spike-stiff leaves of the lavender, and its promise of peace soothed my soul. "I don't know."

"Then what is it you want?"

"To learn how to manage these . . . abilities and keep them hidden, so they don't endanger me or my family." I breathed deeply of the lavender. "But ultimately, I want answers. There must be a reason for my condition."

"Answers are always available—for a price. I suggest you consider what they might cost you."

Already I'd plunged into dangers beyond what I'd ever dreamed. How much greater a price would this quest for understanding demand?

Riven tented his fingers. "As for managing your abilities, do you think about managing your sight or your hearing? Or do you simply use them to engage with the world around you?"

"It's hardly the same. Those senses are natural to mortals—these are not."

"You have no notion how you came by these abilities. Who is to say what is natural and what is not?" he asked. "You want my advice? Stop fearing them. Stop fighting them. Assume they will work with you and for you."

"And what if they don't?" I whispered. "What if they consume me?"

"I can make no promise, only tell you what I believe true." He kindled a fae-light and inspected me by its glow. "How long have you had these experiences? And how did you restrain these sensations before?"

I hesitated. I'd kept all this locked inside so long. Even now I must keep it from those I loved most—and the weight was almost unbearable. Unlike my family, Riven wasn't bound by mortal law to report me. Knowledge of it would not endanger him, nor render him vulnerable to censure. So hesitantly, I confessed the whole: my battle from childhood, the strengthening of the sensations, my cage of thorns and the gentle hedge that had replaced it. Through it all, he remained quiet—intent but undisturbed—and when I finished, I felt as though I'd taken a millstone from my chest and cast it into the sea.

The fae-light strengthened. "You can still find this hedge?"

I nodded.

"Good. If you feel overwhelmed, convince those trees to grow. But when you feel more confident, allow gaps to form between them and let the sensation expand. Now that you've stopped fighting against them, you should learn to integrate these abilities alongside your so-called natural senses. But it will take time and practice."

Which meant opening myself, becoming vulnerable. Risking oh so much. "But isn't this hedge just a figment of my imagination?"

"It's a construct of your mind, yes." Something shifted in his expression, as if he wanted to say more and changed course. "But it serves a purpose. Our minds govern our actions, filter our perceptions. Take advantage of that."

I plucked a yellowing leaf from the sweet orange, then brushed my fingers across the blossoms, and their fresh, bright fragrance drove back my weariness for the moment. For every answer he gave, I found a dozen more questions. Yet his generosity placed me dangerously in his debt, by fae accounting.

Dared I inquire further? My gaze fell upon Jade, sprawled beneath the sweet orange. If I was never to see Riven again, I must know if some element of the Otherworld touched her—if she required help. For her, I'd take the risk. "When Uros attacked Jade, it seemed as if you knew something more about her nature. Does she bear some influence of your world?"

"She's your *kit-isne*. The answer to that lies between you."

Before I could press further, a sun sylph flickered into appearance, pulsing with a rapid sequence of light.

Riven stood. "My king waits. I can stay no longer."

His king. Nikol had suggested his king would be displeased with any clemency shown in the situation with Uros. Would my involvement in the affair with Uros or Mocvar somehow cause Riven trouble? I knew little of how the fae courts worked, but a king was a king. Surely he couldn't hope to keep his position among the fae unless his power was unparalleled.

"I release Wyncourt back to you." The fae-light winked out. "No bargain binds us."

The golden binding uncoiled from my arm, and the shimmering strands returned to Riven. Sudden relief swept over me. "Riven, I . . . thank you for everything."

This time he didn't admonish me for offering thanks. Perhaps he'd given up on it, a lost cause with a foolish mortal. In the absence of the fae-light, the dark pressed in. Would he ever come back? I couldn't conjure a reason to request he stay, aside from my pressing need for answers, so I checked an illogical appeal that he return one day.

He hesitated a moment on the threshold between glasshouse and garden. "I'll leave the sylph with you for now. Her name is Asrina. If you have need, tell her to fetch me."

She flitted over to settle on my shoulder, her presence a comfort. Yet I must know.

"Why are you helping me?" This time, I closed the distance between us. "Why leave Asrina? We no longer have a bargain."

"I require answers about your abilities—and I'd prefer you stay alive until I have them." With that, he vanished.

CHAPTER 41

Slowly, I ascended the stairs with Jade keeping stride. *I prefer you alive.* Did Riven believe someone or something still threatened my life? Had he intended his parting words to put me on guard? He would not have left Asrina unless he believed there was cause.

I collapsed into bed, fully clothed, unable to remain upright a moment longer. My mind rebelled against such questions, and despite my best efforts, slumber soon claimed me. I didn't wake until nearly noon the following day, and only then because I could not draw a full breath.

Jade perched on my chest, her weight driving the air from my lungs. Evidently, she believed I'd slumbered long enough. Her green eyes sparked with satisfaction when I pressed myself upright.

Asrina glimmered on the bedside table, her companionship welcome, and the link she represented to Riven and to answers even more so.

Gaile had left a breakfast tray and several gazettes on the

table beside my bed. Jade eyed the food with an expectant *mrow*, and I fetched her a sausage while I surveyed one of the papers.

I couldn't restrain a smile when I read the first headline: *Crimson Tattoo Killer Meets His Demise!* The article contained an abundance of speculation, punctuated with frequent celebratory remarks, but it held little detail—nor did Mr. Burke receive a mention, which was perhaps for the best.

When I set it aside, the date at the top caught my eye. Only two days more, and I must appear before the Magister. I'd given no further thought to how to approach my defense, so caught up was I in the conflict with Uros.

And yet it was no small matter. This had meant everything to Ibbie—it was her legacy. And her secrets were the ones at stake. She could no longer defend them; she only had me to act on her behalf. After what I'd learned about Wyncourt and about the Otherworld, I couldn't afford to let the estates fall into Mr. Broward's hands. He could cause untold harm if he stumbled into her secrets and loosed Otherworldly forces into a battered Avons.

I'd little time left to investigate or prepare a defense. Would it be as simple a matter as my trustees had assured me? I'd certainly defend myself the best I could, but if something Other were involved . . .

I descended to my compounding room, where I attempted to distract myself from the looming threat by working on a new tincture. Yet it did little to relieve my worries. Perhaps I should turn my attentions back to my herbalism guide. It had always soothed me in the past, but now the mere notion sparked pain, since Ibbie no longer remained to champion my efforts. Still, what better way to honor her than to find a way to succeed as she'd desired?

Holden appeared, and I greeted him with more than the

usual warmth, welcoming the interruption from painful reflection.

He gave a slight bow in return. "Mr. Burke is here to see you, Miss Jessa."

I hastened toward the drawing room, calling my thanks as I went. I found Mr. Burke ensconced with Aunt Caris and my sisters. With his best statesman demeanor, he deflected Ainslie's attempts to gain information on the identity and death of the killer. By mortal standards, she might be a force to reckon with, but compared to Riven . . . she'd lose out every time. Mr. Burke would hold his silence, and she'd be none the wiser.

But oh, how I wished it might be otherwise.

When I entered, Mr. Burke stood. "Might I take you on a stroll, Miss Jessa?"

"I would enjoy that, if my aunt will agree."

Aunt Caris gave a slight nod. "Only don't be long, Jessa. Lianne will accompany you."

I couldn't object without drawing attention to the fact that I desired a private word with Mr. Burke, so I murmured my acceptance. Evidently, any tolerance for my flouting of convention had come to an end.

When Lianne joined us, Jade glared at her, growling when she attempted to draw closer. So she settled for trailing us at a slight distance, a nod to propriety that still afforded us opportunity to speak.

I set my gaze on the bustling street and pitched my voice low. "Has something gone wrong?"

"Indeed not. In my view, something has gone quite right, and I hope you'll agree." He appeared every inch the well-born statesman once more, his stubble vanished, his coat and cravat immaculate. "Since our return, I've spent nearly all my waking hours with the Magistry or the Vigil, answering questions.

While closeted away, I happened to notice your upcoming case in the articles of the Magister. There's a barrister who owes me a favor, and I took the liberty of engaging him on your behalf. If you'd rather not have him, you're free to decline his services, of course."

"I . . . I don't know what to say." At once, I stepped more lightly. "I cannot thank you enough, but I'm sorry to have put you to such trouble."

"It's no trouble." Mr. Burke glanced back toward Lianne and selected his words with care. "Even if it were, I believe there's a debt owed. You could consider this a small step toward settling the score."

"There's no score to be settled, but I confess I'm glad of the help." The rich scent of wisteria drifted from a nearby bower, impressing upon my senses its determination and energy as its roots sunk deep into the stone arch. I rubbed my chest, fighting the urge to stifle the sensations. I must attempt to live with them, difficult as it may prove.

Mr. Burke continued. "Barrister Starne informed me that he didn't have time to explore the matter as thoroughly as he'd like, but his investigator did uncover tremendous debts Broward has amassed."

We left the wisteria behind, and I turned my attention more fully to Mr. Burke. "And he believes that's why Mr. Broward wants the property?"

Mr. Burke inclined his head. "It's the most logical reason for his odd behavior. It's one thing to resent the terms of a will, quite another to take it this far. But it seems Broward had lined up a buyer for the nonfamilial properties, on the assumption that he'd inherit them as well."

"And he won't relinquish what he views as his." It was plausible enough, though it did not fully explain the behavior of my trustees. And if he were in such dire straits, where had he found the funds to engage a barrister of his own?

Whatever the means or reasons of Mr. Broward, the involvement of Barrister Starne gave me a far greater chance of success. Nevertheless, I would attend to ensure he represented Ibbie's interests as he should.

My presence in court might still create a scandal, but if I could secure victory for Ibbie, I'd count it worth the cost. After all, I'd learned one couldn't hide forever. I would appear before the Magister and claim my inheritance, and then I'd attempt to uncover the truth of the Other within Wyncourt—and myself.

***

When I descended the stairs the following morning, I found Aunt Caris waiting for me on the landing. "Do you still mean to go to court?"

"Yes, aunt."

"I'll make no secret of my view." She donned her own hat and gloves. "Your father should have forbidden this. Yet since he did not, I intend to come. If I'm at your side, it will lessen any gossip."

I pressed a kiss to her cheek. "Thank you."

She patted mine in return. "It's not too late to reconsider, my dear."

"I know. But I can't let Ibbie down."

"I don't think Lady Dromley ever anticipated this turn of events, nor would she fault you for allowing things to take their course."

"You didn't know her." Nor did she know what Wyncourt concealed.

"I'll grant that." She sighed. "But perhaps after this, you can put her to rest and think less of her wishes and more of the concerns of your family."

However gently spoken, the rebuke stung. I trailed her from the study, and Jade stalked between us, as though she herself had been slighted. The carriage ride stretched long, as did the silence between us. When we arrived before the Magister's chambers, I emerged into the bright morning with relief.

Mr. Burke awaited within to perform the introductions to Barrister Starne, and then we went to our seats, hard wooden affairs that did not invite one to linger.

A pungent aroma of dried herbs pervaded the air, verbena and Saint-John's-wort among them, and prominent ward-signs were set onto the surface of the Magister's stand. The Magister himself wore a thick pendant on a heavy chain—different from any ward-pendant I'd ever seen, but clearly an alchemical device.

My skin prickled. "Has the Magister always been warded so heavily against fae influence?"

"Indeed not. Our mutual friend Mr. Burke suggested it after the apprehension of the killer, just as a precaution." Barrister Starne's mouth firmed. "The Vigil seconded, though they took some offense at the source of the suggestion."

Mr. Burke wanted the Magister warded. I fought the desire to turn and look for him in the back of the chamber. Perhaps the peculiarities of this case stood out to him also—or perhaps our time in the Otherworld merely moved him to take the threat it represented more seriously. Either way, the presence of the wards pricked at me like a thorn, stubborn and persistent.

Across the chamber, Mr. Broward practically bristled with offense, his heavy features set in lines of anger, though no verdict had yet been issued nor arguments heard. By his side sat a gentleman in every way his foil, tall and slim with fine-sculpted features, his dark hair cropped and perfectly styled. Yet despite his attractive appearance, something about him discomfited me far more than Mr. Broward did.

I leaned toward Barrister Starne. "Who is the man seated beside Mr. Broward?"

"Lord West, so I'm told. He's not from this region." Barrister Starne kept his voice hushed so as not to break the relative stillness of the chamber. "My investigator informed me this morning that he's funded the opposing barrister. He seems to have an interest in the whole affair, but I can't imagine why. Unless Broward owes him the properties for repayment of a debt or some such. That still begs the question of why he would pour further funding into the matter."

It did indeed.

The gentleman in question turned to survey me. A faint smile played about the corners of his mouth, and then he tipped his hat in my direction. I averted my gaze, lacing my gloved hands in my lap and waiting for the proceedings to begin.

Barrister Starne presented the facts on my behalf in a succinct, effective fashion. He chose to portray me as a prosecuted innocent, and to proclaim that Mr. Broward sought to intimidate me and take advantage of my inexperience and my gender. "Had she not retained me, it is possible Mr. Broward would have succeeded in frightening a young lady—not even full come into society—into giving up her inheritance, against the express wishes of Lady Dromley. We hold the desires of those who have passed on to be sacrosanct, not something to be violated on a whim."

Mr. Broward's features twisted, as though he struggled to keep himself from flying at Barrister Starne. He muttered something under his breath, and the Magister shot him a sharp look.

Then the opposing barrister presented his argument, which was feeble enough that I wondered at his aims. Had he intended to use some alchemical or Otherworldly influence to sway the Magister, only to be thwarted by the new wards? Could wards provide an effective defense against such stratagems? So much of the Otherworld I still failed to understand.

My gaze kept drifting back to Lord West. With subtle motion of his fingers, he signaled to the barrister. So he *was* the one in control. Why? What did he want?

Abruptly, the opposing barrister wound down his arguments.

When he concluded, the Magister steepled his fingers. "While I appreciate the argument for the importance of bloodlines and the suggestion that one's faculties may diminish in age, there's nothing to indicate that Lady Dromley was not in full possession of her wits when she left a portion of her property to Miss Jessa, nor that Miss Jessa leveraged anything against her to force this. All evidence supports clarity of mind in Lady Dromley and a close relationship between the two ladies. I find in favor of Miss Jessa."

The tightness in my chest released. Now I could carry out Ibbie's wishes—and find the answers I craved.

Mr. Broward looked as though he might leap up and shout a protest, but Lord West whispered something to him, and he subsided. Without another glance in my direction, Mr. Broward stalked from the chamber.

Then the barrister and Lord West strolled toward us. Something about the grace in Lord West's movements left me unsettled. When he stopped before me, the air held the tang of ancient, long-buried stone—and unmistakable power.

Oh no.

I angled my body forward, shielding Aunt Caris from whatever glamour he wielded. It must be a strong one, to hide his true nature so effectively. At once, the illogical reactions of my trustees to my request for a legal defense made sense. No doubt Lord West had reached them before I had . . . which meant the only surprise was that the Magister had ruled in my favor. Perhaps I owed that to Mr. Burke as well.

The opposing barrister addressed mine. "Allow me to introduce a friend of my client, Lord West. He would like an introduction to Miss Jessa. He has interest in Kilmere, if she will sell."

Barrister Starne raised a brow, but performed the introductions to me and Aunt Caris. I offered a small nod to Lord West, the least cordial greeting I could extend without giving rise to questions.

"Good day, Miss Jessa." Lord West offered the smile of a wolf, his teeth sharp and gleaming. "I'm pleased to make your acquaintance."

I murmured some inane reply.

"If Mr. Broward carried the day, I'd hoped to purchase Kilmere from him, but it appears you retain ownership." He drew closer, and the scent of ancient stone strengthened. "Shall we discuss terms?"

A thread of power laced his words, carrying with it a suggestion: to sell was the only wise course of action. The notion settled deep. To sell would bring wealth to my family and rid me of an unnecessary burden.

Blight and rot. I'd experienced this sense of coercion before, when I'd ascended the hidden stairs of Wyncourt. Then Riven had broken the compulsion by provoking me, but now I must act.

The hedge of blossom and bough still flourished within, and I coaxed the graceful trees to form gaps in their open weave. When I did, the songs of the twin oaks that stood sentinel outside the Magister's chambers surged into my awareness— steady and strong and unshakable.

The compulsion dispersed like so much smoke. "Thank you, but I've no intention of selling."

Then his gaze drifted to my shoulder, where Asrina fluttered, and his eyes hardened till they resembled shards of granite. "You've had a harrowing day, no doubt. I should have waited to address you. Perhaps we might speak again on the morrow? With your permission of course, Miss Caldwell."

Aunt Caris blinked. "Of course, we'd be delighted to receive you."

"Excellent." Then he spun on his heel and strolled from the room with the confident air of a gentleman who has achieved his aims.

Only Lord West was no gentleman. He was fae, and he wanted Kilmere. But why?

And what would he do to claim it?

AFTERWORD

There's more mystery afoot! When Allston Burke is summoned to appear before the Vigil, he has a difficult choice to make. **Read from his perspective in the bonus scene.**

https://go.sarahchislon.com/toc-bonus

Jessa's adventures continue in *Ruins of Bone*, which will release October 2023. **Pre-order today so you don't miss a thing.**

https://go.sarahchislon.com/rob

ACKNOWLEDGMENTS

Tattoo of Crimson has simmered in the back of my mind for years, and it's a joy to see the story in its final form at last. I couldn't have done it without those who have offered support on this journey of writing and publishing. As ever, my wonderful husband has been my biggest champion. He's my first reader and my technical support on the business side of writing—and he's tireless in his enthusiasm and support for my stories. CJ, I love you!

I'm also appreciative of my beta and ARC readers. Thanks to all of you for your insights and thoughtful reviews.

In addition, I'm fortunate enough to have stellar editors—Lauren Donovan and Kara Aisenbrey—for whom I'm deeply thankful. I truly could not have asked for better editors.

Lauren, you understand my stories in a way that means the world to me, and your insights make them so much stronger. I appreciate your thoughtful, well-organized feedback, your knowledge of and enthusiasm for discussing all things story, and the encouragement you always offer.

Kara, you understand my writing voice, and we share a delight for polishing prose and savoring the beauty of words and language. I'm thankful for your knowledge of the fine points of grammar (and your willingness to dialogue about the nuances of it with me) along with your keen eye for detail. Your love for

Jessa from the very beginning has been a tremendous encouragement.

Thanks also to excellent proofreader Deborah O'Carroll for the final review of *Tattoo of Crimson*. Deborah, I appreciate your attention to detail in proofing—and also your enthusiasm for this story! Your comments were a delight.

To my darling daughters—you bring joy to my life every day, and you're one of God's greatest gifts to me. I love that we share a love for words and stories, and I love you!

To my family and friends who have offered encouragement and support in this journey of publishing—thank you! I'm grateful for you all.

And to God, first, last, and always. Soli deo gloria.

ABOUT THE AUTHOR

Sarah Chislon lives in Virginia with her husband and three daughters. When she's not writing, she's homeschooling her children and running a web development business with her husband. As an avid reader and a lifelong story-weaver, she delights in creating fantastic worlds and exploring them alongside her characters.

For more information on her books, visit her website sarahchislon.com—or sign up for her newsletter to receive updates and free bonus content.

- facebook.com/sarahchislon
- instagram.com/sarahchislon
- bookbub.com/profile/sarah-chislon

Printed in Great Britain
by Amazon